Hans

ALLIANCE BOOK FOUR

S. J. TILLY

HANS
Alliance Series Book FOUR
Copyright © S.J. Tilly LLC 2023
All rights reserved.
First published in 2023
ISBN 9781962096034
No part of this book may be reproduced, stored in a retrieval system, or
transmitted in any form or by any means, without the prior permission in writing
of the publisher, nor be otherwise circulated in any form of binding or cover other
than that in which it is published and without a similar condition, including this
condition, being imposed on the subsequent purchaser. All characters in this
publication other than those clearly in the public domain are fictitious, and any
resemblance to real persons, living or dead, is purely coincidental.
Cover: Lori Jackson Design
Model Image: Wander Aguiar Photography
Editors: Jeanine Harrell, Indie Edits with Jeanine
& Beth Lawton, VB Edits

This book is dedicated to Nero, the beautiful bastard who started it all. I love your unhinged ass.

-

This battle belongs to all of us. Because we're all human. And that makes it ours.

Content Warning

This is a dark vigilante romance.

It contains a lot of graphic violence and death. There is stalking, breaking and entering, and surveillance.

This book deals with human trafficking. There are no first-person POVs of any trafficking victims, but you will see firsthand the trauma it leaves behind.

This book also contains death of parents, death of a sibling, and the torment of wishing you'd done more.

Since Hans only lives between these pages, if you, or someone you know is a victim of human trafficking, please call 1-888-373-7888. If you are outside of the United States, visit this site for further help https://bit.ly/InternationalTraffickingHotlines There are people who care about you, and they will help you.

Please proceed well informed and with caution.

CHAPTER 1
Hans

THE SOFT SCRAPING SOUND OF MY BLADE GLIDING OVER the whetstone fills me with a sense of calm.

It's familiar.

My dearest friend.

Instinctually, my wrist twists to hold the metal against the stone at a fifteen-degree angle, five degrees shallower than most brand standards. A little sharper. A little more dangerous.

A little more my style.

Ahead of me, a yellow light blinks in the corner of one of my monitors.

I move my eyes up from my knife to the signaling screen and watch Cassandra, my neighbor, the bane of my existence, hop across the street from her driveway to mine.

Okay, so she's not hopping. But in that strappy little tank top and shorts, she might as well be for how much every inch of her is fucking jiggling.

The work surface in front of me creaks as I lean forward, my fist gripping the knife handle, pressing the butt of it against the old wood.

Does she not realize what a fucking temptation she is?

Does she have no sense at all?

1

Her big tits bounce as she takes her next step, her flimsy flip-flops doing nothing to protect her feet from the cracked blacktop.

A girl like her should wear...

Nothing.

A girl like her should wear absolutely nothing, and she should spend her nights on her back with her thighs spread, her hands pinned, and her body heaving... underneath mine—where no one else can ever lay eyes on her.

I grind my teeth.

This world isn't made for delicate creatures like her.

On the screen, Cassandra brushes one hand down the front of her purple top as she turns off my driveway and down the little brick pathway that leads to my front door.

My front door, which is one level up from my current spot in my basement.

My front door that I never answer.

Because I can't talk to her.

I can't let myself get that close to her.

The doorbell is inaudible through the reinforced walls of my hidden safe room, but I hear it clearly through my speakers.

Another screen shows a different view, and this one might be my favorite.

The camera is in the peephole, so it's a perfect angle of her perfect face.

She bites her lip.

She shifts the glass container of badly made baked goods in her hands.

She reaches up and brushes her curly black hair away from her face.

I shove the air out of my lungs.

It's almost time for her next haircut. Her bangs are a little long, hanging into her eyes, the curls even more apparent in the short strands, making her look just the right amount of unkempt.

I love them.

But I hate when they block my view of her soft brown irises, even if it's only for a second.

Her tongue darts out, swiping across her plump bottom lip.

And I look to the ceiling.

The doorbell sounds again.

Maybe if I focus, I can slam my head forward, impaling my eye socket onto my blade, and put myself out of this fucking blue-ball misery.

"I thought you were home, Hans." Her soft voice slides through my speakers, and I snap my eyes back up to the screen.

She almost always mutters something to herself when she stands at my door. But she never says my name.

My dick reacts, knowing exactly how her lips would've parted while she breathed out my name.

I'll play the recording back when she's gone. Watch the shape of those perfect pink lips as they open and close.

"Dammit, Butterfly." I press my palm down over my growing erection.

Her exposed cleavage rises as she takes a big breath, then she dips down, setting the container on the worn welcome mat in front of my door.

It doesn't actually say *welcome*. But it does have a sheet of carefully crafted explosives woven into the inner layer of the mat, so there's that.

I keep pressing down on my dick as she straightens.

And I press harder when I watch her glance at my front window.

The curtains are closed, so there's nothing for her to see, but I love that she tried.

Then I keep watching as she turns away from the tiny camera and hops back down the steps, the sunset causing her form to glow.

She's so fucking thick. And soft. And beautiful. And the spark behind her eyes is so trusting and healthy and...

I let my fingers grip my length, squeezing until she's crossed the dead-end street, skirted past her car—that she always leaves parked in the driveway—and closed her front door behind her.

I slouch back in my chair.

The only other time I've heard her say my name was the day we met.

I'd been out of town—out of the country. I was busy killing terrible men, so I hadn't known my original across-the-street neighbor had died. She was a nice old lady who couldn't hear for shit, couldn't see past her front yard, and had an online poker habit that kept her away from the windows. She was perfect. But then she up and died, and her sister had a friend who had a daughter who was looking for a place, and by the time I got home, I had a new fucking neighbor.

Cassandra.

That was last summer. One year, one month, and two weeks ago.

I had just climbed out of my truck, and she had hurried across the street, already at my tailgate by the time I shut my door, and she thrust her hand out toward me.

Before I could stop myself, I placed my calloused palm in her smooth one while she said *I'm Cassie, your new neighbor.* And since my brain could come up with nothing better to say, I replied with *Hans.*

Just that. Just my name.

And then she repeated it back. Just as simple. Just once. *Hans.*

And I haven't fucked anyone since.

If I don't push her out of my brain soon, I'm going to lose it.

I reach out and tap the button to switch on more monitors.

Four across and two high, all eight screens flicker to life, their displays divided into four quadrants, giving me views of the whole cul-de-sac.

The house at the end is abandoned. And since *some corporation* bought the property for tax reasons, it'll probably sit abandoned for the next twenty years. And if Cassandra hadn't swooped in on 1304 Holly Court, I would've—I mean, *that same corporation* would have—bought that house too. And then they probably would've rented it out to Karmine, letting her use it as a sort of forward operating base for her self-built army.

But that didn't happen, and I don't have complete control of my little street because of Cassandra.

The curvy little vixen who just turned thirty, twelve days ago —making her nine years my junior and too young for me—and has been doing her best to kill me with food poisoning through her little deliveries.

Maybe it's actually been working. Maybe she's been micro-dosing me with some sort of secret government toxin. Maybe that's why I can't get her off my mind.

From the camera positioned on the top point of my garage, I watch her shadow move behind her thin living room drapes as she turns the lights off on her main floor.

Her form disappears, but then the windows on her upper floor light up, and I know she's going to bed.

CHAPTER 2

Cassie

I TUG BACK THE PAISLEY SHOWER CURTAIN AND GRAB my facewash off the tub's ledge, squeezing a careful amount into my palm.

The citrus scent is usually enough to lift my mood, but not tonight.

Sighing, I turn back to my sink, the running water finally turning warm, and lather my hands together.

"You gotta give up one of these days," I reprimand myself before tipping my face down and scrubbing the bubbles into my skin.

Every couple of weeks, ever since I moved in, I deliver cookies or breads or desserts to the incredibly hot man across the street. *Hans.*

He's... I don't know how to explain it. He's just different. And I shouldn't even have an opinion on him because I've only seen him up close that one time. That first time I saw him.

And if his track record since is any indication, I only got that close because I caught him off guard. Because he hadn't known I'd moved in.

I had begun to wonder if I even had an across-the-street neighbor, but the realtor promised the single-story home was occupied. And I asked no less than three times because I was a little creeped out by the empty house at the end of the street. So I kept an eye out for my supposed neighbor.

Even though the lots here—on the edge of this little town—are large, our driveways are perfectly lined up. It made me feel a weird sort of companionship with the neighbor I hadn't met yet. Like we were in this together, with the other houses in our neighborhood out of sight around the corner, feeling a world away.

It was three weeks and four days after I spent the first night in my first home that a plain white pickup truck pulled into the driveway across from mine.

I was so excited that I didn't even check what I was wearing, didn't take even a moment to dust on some bronzer. I just leaped off my couch and walked as fast as my legs were willing to go out my front door, down my cracked driveway, and up his. I was already at the back bumper of his truck when he climbed out.

And then my breath caught. Because he was... handsome. Like *so* handsome, but also intimidating. And strong. He looked so freaking strong.

My neglected libido tumbled out of hibernation like a hungry bear rolling out of her cave, dried leaves shaking off with each roll, until she splashed headfirst into a lake that smelled of *man*.

I snort at myself, causing water to splash over the edge of the sink, as I remember the way I acted that day.

My palm was probably sweaty when I stuck it out between us.

His long dark blond hair was pulled back into a bun, with a few pieces escaping and falling across his eyes. And it did things to me. Because they weren't just eyes. They were intense, and his irises are such a deep brown they almost looked black. And his jaw line... I could faint now just thinking of it. It's chiseled, and it was covered in this stubble several shades darker than his hair.

It was too much.

Hans was too much.

So I said the only thing I could manage. *I'm Cassie, your new neighbor.*

He didn't look happy. Not before I said it, and even less so after I said it. But he did reply, with what I've had to assume is his first name.

Hans.

Hans, the Scandinavian fantasy I didn't know I had. *Please, pretty please, swing me up over your shoulder and carry me off to your bedroom. We can pretend it's a Viking encampment. You're the main warrior dude, and I'm the princess you just stole from your enemy to claim as your own...*

I turn off the water and squeeze my eyes shut as I pat my face dry with a clean towel.

Of course, none of that stuff happened. Instead of stealing and ravishing me, Hans dropped my hand, slammed his truck door, strode into his garage, and hit the button to shut the overhead door without so much as a glance over his shoulder for a second look at me.

Quite the ding to thee old self-esteem.

But after that *wildly successful* first meeting, I figured I'd win him over with baked goods.

And thus began our yearlong game of cat and mouse.

Though, I'm not really sure who's who in our situation.

Because I catch glimpses of him. Hans pulling his truck straight into his garage, Hans pulling out of his garage, Hans walking back from his mailbox with strides too long and fast for me to ever *accidentally* meet him while heading out to check on my own mail—trust me, I've tried. So I know he's still alive. And that he still lives there. But he never answers the door.

Not once.

I turn off the light and enter my bedroom.

Stripping off my shorts and underwear, I toss my bra on the floor and dig out a pair of sleep shorts.

Technically the shirt I wore over to Hans's house is a pajama top, but with a bra, it looks like any other tank top. And it's not like he saw me anyway.

I turn off my bedside lamp and drop into bed.

Time to scroll recipes while I wonder if Hans actually eats what I leave for him or if he just throws it all away and returns the empty container.

CHAPTER 3

Hans

When the final light in her house turns off, I wait another forty-seven minutes.

She's always asleep within forty-five minutes, but I like to be certain.

With a groan, I push out of my chair and turn off the monitors. My knives are as sharp as they're gonna get tonight, and I have food to retrieve.

I look through the little crescent window at the top of my front door, double-checking that no new lights are on across the street, then I open the door and scoop up the rectangular glass container before shutting and locking it again.

As always, there's a yellow Post-it note on the top of the lid.

Chocolate chip zucchini cookies.

Even as I trace my finger over the lettering, I can feel my nose crinkling.

I've heard of zucchini bread, but not cookies. And the bread has me skeptical enough.

Rolling my eyes at myself, I carry the cookies into my little kitchen and set them on the counter.

After carefully setting the Post-it off to the side, the lid lifts easily, and with it comes the smell of chocolate and wet vegetables.

I sigh.

Instead of looking like normal cookies, these look like damp green hockey pucks that have lost their shape along the way. But when I lift one out, it surprisingly holds together.

It's also heavier than I expected.

"God dammit." I curse my growing need to consume it, even as I lift the cookie and take a bite.

My mouth pulls into a frown, but I force myself to keep chewing.

It's... not good.

I look at the puck, seeing a little clump of unmixed flour that I've bitten through, and I take another bite.

The overall wetness of the *cookie* is off-putting. But the taste is even worse.

I shove the rest of it into my mouth.

For someone who bakes so much, Cassandra is not getting any better.

I move to my fridge and pull out a stick of butter.

It's too hard to be spreadable, so I slice off little squares and set them on top of the second cookie, then take a large bite.

Slightly better.

Another bite, and some of the cookie juice drips onto my shirt.

"Fuck," I grumble around my mouthful of the shredded vegetable bullshit.

After shoving the rest of the butter-topped cookie into my mouth, I rip a paper towel free from the roll sitting next to the sink and wipe at my shirt.

I eye the other four cookies still left in the container.

I don't want to eat them.

They're hardly edible.

But I'm curious to see how Cassandra photographed them for her food blog.

It didn't take me long to find the blog, though I was a little surprised that she only started it after moving in next door. No matter how awful the creation is, she always makes them look appealing in the photo, but since she's gifted me a container of every item she's ever blogged about, I know the photos lie.

I don't want to eat the rest.

But I have to.

After moving to the cupboard on the other side of the fridge, I open the door and take out the half-empty jar of peanut butter.

I scoop out a spoonful and do my best to spread it over the top of the third hockey puck.

It doesn't make it better.

I grab my glass of water off the counter and chug it down, trying to loosen up the peanut and zucchini concrete sealing my jaw shut.

When I finally clear my mouth, I move back to the fridge, and this time, I take out a bottle of beer.

I crack it open and alternate between pulls from the bottle and mouthfuls of cookie until the last three are gone.

My stomach protests at the last bite, but I can't waste it. It doesn't matter how bad her creations are, my deep-seated need to consume every bit of Cassandra won't let me throw them away. And my tastebuds won't let me go through this torture twice. So, this has become our ritual. Cassandra leaves me something that lands somewhere on the scale of edible, and I binge eat it while standing alone in my kitchen, staring out the window over my sink and imagining I'm eating them in her house, with her next to me.

When all the awful cookies are gone, I tip the glass container over the sink, letting the little pool of green liquid drip out. Then I wash and dry it.

Once I secure the lid in place, I leave the empty container on the counter and pick up the Post-it.

I walk across the living room, turning off lights as I go, and step into my bedroom.

The bedside lamp is on, and it illuminates my actions as I pull open the top drawer of my nightstand.

Leaning down, I carefully stick the newest Post-it on top of the last one, adding it to my little stack of yellow paper squares.

One for every delivery from the girl next door.

CHAPTER 4

Cassie

"OKAY, BYE! BE BACK LATER!" I GRIN TO MYSELF AS I step out the front door, locking the handle as I go.

I don't have any pets. There's nothing alive inside the house, but I still say goodbye to my home whenever I leave. It's probably silly, but it makes coming back feel happier. Like the structure itself will be waiting for my return.

As I take the few steps down to the sidewalk that leads from my front door to my driveway, I glance across the street. It's a cloudy afternoon, but I can clearly see my neighbor's empty front step. No cookie container in sight.

I bite the corner of my lip.

So he was home, but he didn't answer the door. Again.

Or he got home after you were there.

Or he was in the shower.

Or he came home this morning.

I pull my gaze away from Hans's house and hurry the rest of the distance to my old sedan. The thought that Hans might be spending some of his nights at a woman's house has crossed my mind more times than I care to admit. And even though I have zero claim over my elusive, handsome neighbor, the jealousy in my gut is real.

CHAPTER 5
Hans

CASSANDRA BACKS OUT OF HER DRIVEWAY, NEARLY clipping her mailbox. Then she takes her time playing with the radio before she finally pulls away, turning off Holly Court and disappearing from sight.

I give her the usual eleven minutes.

She has a track record of forgetting things and coming back for them, but she never turns around if she's more than five minutes away. So, when that eleventh minute starts, I tuck the empty container under my arm and step outside.

I don't look around. I don't try to sneak over. Both of those things give away the fact that you're doing something shady. It's always best to act like you belong.

Plus, there's no one here to see what I'm doing anyway.

The lots on our little cul-de-sac are large, and beyond the edges of our mowed lawns is a thick forest of trees. Both leafy and evergreen. So unless someone is on one of our properties, or coming down our street, they wouldn't see me walking between Cassandra's house and mine.

They won't see me now, and they haven't seen me the dozens of other times I've done this.

My boots are quiet on the steps up to her front door, and I

use the duplicate key in my palm to unlock the handle. When it turns and the door opens, I shake my head.

"Why have a deadbolt, Butterfly, if you're not gonna use it?"

I set the empty dish, lid attached, on her literal welcome mat, wipe my boots off on said mat, then step over it and shut the door behind me, relocking the handle. Just because she should be gone for a while doesn't mean I won't leave everything how I found it.

It doesn't take me long to do my usual rounds, but I don't rush through them.

I tell myself it's because I want to be thorough. That I need to make sure every window is properly locked—twice, because I may have missed it the first time.

I don't dwell on the way I enjoy being in *her* space. I don't think about the way the air feels different in here. The way it tastes different in here.

The living room doubles as Cassandra's home office. On one side of the room, the gray couch faces a subpar TV mounted above a fireplace she never turns on because someone—me— keeps disabling the gas line because someone—her—has left it on unattended one too many times. She's thankfully given up on calling out the repair man, because I don't want to feel bad about her spending money on repairs when I'm only going to fuck it up again.

The other side of the living room has a bright white table tucked against the wall, topped with a small lamp, her work laptop, a ceramic cactus, and an empty floral-printed cup with a matching pink straw that looks big enough to fit half a gallon of liquid.

Walking through the kitchen, I make sure all the appliances have their cords fully plugged in and that they haven't tangled since I checked them three days ago.

I pull the stove away from the wall, making sure the connections and valves are just as I left them. They are.

Pushing the stove back into its place, I notice the fruit bowl next to her sink is overflowing. With zucchini.

A shudder runs down my spine, and I wonder if there's something I can do to them that would make them rot overnight so she's not able to make anything else with them.

I slide my hand into my pocket, ready to pull my phone out so I can search to see if such a thing is possible, but I stop myself. Because if Cassandra woke up tomorrow to a bowl of rotten produce, she would feel sad.

She'd probably frown. Potentially pout. And I can't be the cause of that.

I pull my hand free and let it linger on the railing as I climb the stairs to her second level.

This house is as old and shitty as mine, except Cassandra has actually put in effort to make her home cozy. She's painted the walls in every room. The kitchen is a bright blue, her bathrooms are teal, and her bedroom—I step into the small space—is a gentle gray with soft pink bedding and rugs.

I inhale, and that rare feeling of calmness settles over my shoulders.

Her bed isn't made; it never is.

I flip on the light in her attached windowless bathroom and glance around, making sure nothing has been left on.

The mirror is still slightly steamy—accounting for her wet hair when she left the house—and the mix of shampoo, body lotion, and hair products makes me want to roll around on her shaggy bathroom rug.

But I don't.

That would be weird.

Turning the light off, I move back into the bedroom.

The window faces the street, and through her open curtains, I can see the front of my house. But there's a tall tree in Cassandra's yard, meaning she doesn't have a good view of my front door, which I use to my advantage, ensuring she can't see me retrieving the offerings she leaves for me on my front step. I'm rarely off on my calculations, but if she were to stand right here, forty-eight minutes after turning off her bedroom

17

light at night, she wouldn't get a clear view of me opening my front door.

Still facing the window, I walk back—two steps, three—until I bump into her bed.

Then I sit.

This is her side of the bed. Doesn't take a genius, or an obsessed stalker, to figure that out.

I pretend it's morning. That she's just woken and sat up, and I look out through the window.

This is her view.

My home.

Me.

I take a deep breath and scoot over an inch, then another.

Is this exactly where she would be sitting?

Slowly, I reach down and unlace my boots, then pull them off one at a time.

Then I lift my feet onto the bed.

I've never done this before.

Never crossed this line.

So I've touched her bed before, run my hands over the cool cotton sheets, but that's nothing.

I lie back.

The mattress is okay. Not good enough for my Cassandra. But it's comfortable.

I settle my head on her pillow.

It's too soft. Too girly.

I look up at her ceiling. At the sparkly mini chandelier she installed over her bed.

This is the last thing she sees each night.

I close my eyes and pretend.

Just for two seconds, I pretend she's here with me.

18

My eyes snap open.

A vehicle is approaching.

I sit straight up, disoriented in a place that borders on familiar and wrong.

The lighting has changed.

The shadows have shifted.

I look at the clock on the nightstand.

"Fuck me."

I swing my feet over the edge of the bed and slide them into my boots, lacing them quickly.

"Did you seriously fall a-fucking-sleep in Cassandra's house?" I'm so mad at myself. I can't believe I fucked up this badly.

Not that it's any real wonder. The stomachache I got from those mushy-ass cookies kept me up half the night.

Eyeing the rumpled bedding at my side, I run my palm over it once more before I stand, the cotton cool under my touch.

I stay far enough back from the window so I'm not visible to anyone below, but from this angle, I can still see out. And Cassandra's car slows to a stop in the driveway, yards from where I'm standing.

"Shit."

Her garage is attached to the side of her house, connecting through the small laundry room off the kitchen, which is right below me. The overhead garage door works, I've checked, but unless it's snowing, Cassandra always chooses to park outside. For a reason only known to her.

I could sprint. I could get down the stairs, turn at the base of the staircase, duck into the laundry room, and slip into the garage, pulling the door closed at the same moment she slams the front door behind her. Then I could exit through the window in the back of the garage or wait for her to fall asleep and then go back through the laundry room, into the kitchen, and out the door that leads into the backyard.

I could do all of that. But that would require me to have moved by now, which I haven't. And I don't.

Cassandra steps out of her car, and my heart races for a reason other than the threat of getting caught. My heart is racing because she's close. So close.

She has an iced coffee in one hand and a Target bag in the other, and she uses her perfect hip to shove the car door shut.

A little midday shopping trip, playing hooky from work?

The angle blocks me from seeing the expression on her face, but her body language telegraphs the fact that she's trying to hurry. Either she really has to pee, or she's trying not to be late for a work call.

I honestly don't know if she would run upstairs to use the bathroom attached to her bedroom or if she'd use the other one downstairs. But I've watched her through the living room windows enough to know that it's not unusual for her to have a virtual work meeting at any time of the day, so I'm hoping that's what she's in a hurry for.

As she moves beneath the bedroom window to the front door, I slowly unlock the window latch. Thankfully, I test these often enough, so it's used to moving and does so silently.

Slowing my breath, I listen, and when I hear the front door open, I start to slide the window up.

By the time the front door slams shut, I've slid the windowpane all the way up.

The screens are still blessedly not in place. Cassandra removed them this spring to clean, but they're still piled up in the corner of her garage, not installed.

I lift my left leg up and over the sill.

"I'm home! I'm home!" Her voice echoes up the stairwell, and I freeze.

Is she telling the empty house that she's home, or does she somehow know I'm here?

I hear the crinkle of her dropping the shopping bag onto the floor, then the squeak of wheels on hardwood, and I picture her dropping into her little office chair.

So, a work meeting.

Half in, half out of her window, I stand motionless.

If I climb out now, I could crouch on the little section of roof right below the bedroom window, wait for her to finish her meeting and leave the living room, then drop down to the grass below. Or—

My phone vibrates with a text.

Very few people have my number.

Still standing with my leg out the window, I pull my phone out of my pocket and look at the message from K. It's a city, a location, and a time.

I know the place, and if I'm going to be there on time, I need to get on the road in the next thirty minutes.

The phone vibrates again in my hand. This time K is calling.

She never calls.

I squeeze my fingers around the phone, indecision warring for a moment before I accept the call.

I put it against the ear closest to the window, leaving the other one to listen for any movement from downstairs.

"Here," I whisper.

There's a pause. "Bad time?" Karmine's voice sounds amused.

"Not the best," I admit.

She snorts. "Fine. I'll talk to you after."

Rather than answer, I hang up and slide the phone back into my pocket.

We both typically work in life-and-death situations, so I appreciate the brief call. But *after* means she'll meet me at the location after I'm done. And that means I don't have time to wait for Cassandra's work call to wrap up.

Fuck me, I guess.

I can hear the muffled, tinny noise of many voices talking through a speaker and assume the meeting downstairs is just starting.

That's my signal.

I shift and slide my body out the window.

It's not until I'm lowering the window from the outside that I realize I should've checked and made sure I didn't leave any hairs on Cassandra's pillow. My strands are not the bright gold they were when I was a child, but the dark blond color is still nothing close to her wavy black strands.

Losing your fucking edge, Hans. Maybe it is time to retire from assassin work.

Standing to my full height, I reach up and grip the edge of the roof.

Just not tonight.

I heave myself upward and use careful steps to crest the center point of the roof before starting my decline, aiming toward the back of the house.

I know the sightlines Cassandra has from her work desk, so I'm able to avoid her view by aiming for the corner above her bathroom, dropping lightly onto the roof of the garage, then lowering myself to the yard behind. Staying to the side of the yard, I walk the thirty feet across the lawn and enter the woods behind Cassandra's house.

Then I start to jog.

I stay out of view as I work my way through the woods and around the end of the cul-de-sac until I finally emerge from the same woods behind my own house.

Now, it's time to work.

CHAPTER 6

Cassie

As the VP of sales gets the meeting started, I put myself on mute and casually roll my chair to the side a few inches so I can reach off camera without being noticed. Then, watching my own little video square—to make sure my actions stay off-screen—I pour my to-go iced coffee out of the disposable cup it came in and into my giant thermos cup. I don't need my coworkers knowing I blew off half the afternoon shopping and buying lattes.

When the transfer is complete, I slowly lean back and bring the pink straw to my lips. And I have to stop myself from rolling my eyes at how good it is.

The boss blathers on, something about the training we'll be doing soon, but I tune him out. As the head of HR for a global manufacturer, I usually have plenty to do to keep my days busy. But I finished all the paperwork for our newest hire this morning and wanted to treat myself a bit. The nearest Target is fifteen minutes away, and next to my favorite store is BeanBag Coffee, my favorite coffee shop. Stopping there might be the reason I was almost late to this meeting but—I take another sip—totally worth it. And lord knows I need all the caffeine to make it through what is proving to be a tremendously boring meeting.

I unmute myself to agree with what everyone is saying, then mute my microphone again and let my mind wander.

And, of course, my mind wanders straight to the empty glass container sitting on the corner of my little worktable.

I'm tempted to reach out, to run my fingertip along the edge, trace the corner, but I don't. I keep my hands around my cup.

But I do inhale.

I swear his masculine pine scent clings to the glass.

I noticed the way he smelled the one time I was close enough to detect it. I don't know if it's soap or deodorant or a faint cologne, but the memory of it haunts me.

I swear I can smell it at the most random times when I'm in my own home. When I'm nowhere near him.

And I can always smell it when he returns the containers.

The glass is always clean. It's always on my front step. And it's always the very next day after I leave it on his. Every time. Every freaking time.

But there's never a note.

No *thank you*. No *I liked it*. No *cease and desist*. And no Post-it proclaiming what's inside.

Always the same. Label removed, container squeaky clean.

I don't even know if he eats what I make.

Does he transfer the cookies into another container? Does he put them right in the garbage?

There's no way he ate all six of them between last night and this afternoon. Same as the times I've dropped off whole loaves of banana or pumpkin bread. So he must be transferring them into something else.

Maybe it's a respect thing? Like he wants to return my belongings to me as quickly as possible?

I take another long pull through my straw.

I try my hardest to pay attention to the slideshow that just appeared on the screen. Everyone gets so excited about these new product launches, and I appreciate that they want to include me, but really... I don't care. I'm not sure it's possible for me to care less.

Human resources is my job, not my passion, and learning about commercial building materials is of zero interest to me. It really is just a job I fell into that I happen to be good at. So... yeah.

I'm swallowing more of my latte when motion outside catches my attention.

Forgetting all about the meeting, I turn my head and watch as Hans pulls his pickup out of his garage.

CHAPTER 7

Hans

I STRETCH MY BACK WHEN I FINALLY CLIMB OUT OF MY front seat and bite down on the groan I want to let out.

Six hours of sitting in the car after the brief adrenaline jolt of nearly being found by my neighbor means my muscles are tight.

My neck protests as I roll it one way, then the other, before I walk around to the back of my truck.

The bar's parking lot is packed, but only a few people are outside the building, and none are close enough to watch me as I lower the tailgate.

Under the light of a yellowing streetlamp, I use my thumbnail to flick up a tiny hidden door in the bed, then press my thumb pad to the small black square beneath.

Nero Security makes some pretty good locks. And thanks to having plenty of time and money on my hands, I was able to utilize these fingerprint locks to secure several hidden chambers in my truck bed. The compartments conceal a multitude of weapons that would see me in prison for the rest of my lifetime if anyone were clever enough to find them.

But I have a fail-safe for that.

The lock clicks, and after I press down on the nearest section of the bed, a four-foot-wide piece pops open on a spring hinge.

This is my most used selection. And it's a *selection*.

Handguns, knives of varying lengths, a grenade... the usual.

My lower back twinges as I reach for one of the knives, and I decide that tonight is a night for ease.

I still take the knife, tucking it into the sheath at my side, but then I reach for the Glock. And the silencer. And three prefilled clips of ammo.

Pressing the lid closed, I make sure to hear the lock reengage, then I lower the tiny door to hide the thumbprint reader and flip the tailgate back up.

The summer air is thick with humidity, but the temperature has dropped to tolerable degrees, meaning no one will look twice at me in my black jeans and the nondescript dark flannel I put on over my T-shirt.

The flannel is unbuttoned, the open edges flapping a little as I stride across the parking lot, but my lowered arms keep the fabric from pulling too far back and revealing the shoulder holster I have on beneath.

I cut through the handful of intoxicated people standing near the bar entrance and smoking cigarettes, and enter the poorly lit building behind them.

The bouncer at the door slides a bored gaze my way, but I look every one of my thirty-nine years, probably more, so he doesn't ask for ID.

But if he did, I have one on me. It's not my photo or my name, but it's close enough to work.

Country music blares through speakers mounted to the ceiling, and I do my best to tune it out as I slant my body between groups of people, making my way to the back corner, toward the hall that disappears into the dark.

I enter the hallway.

And I move past the bathrooms, past the storage room, past the locked walk-in cooler. And I end up at the very end of the hall. And the final door, hiding the final room.

It's a room saved for *private parties*. Ones that are little more than coke fests and excuses to hire strippers and treat them like shit.

It's a room with another bouncer, this one looking slightly more alert than the man out front.

It's a room I know about but have never been in.

Until tonight.

My steps slow until I stop in front of the man guarding the door.

Inside that room, three men are waiting for another man to arrive with instructions. Because they have a bag of money, and the man they're expecting has a cargo shipment, and they need to know where to go pick up that cargo.

Except I'm not the man they're expecting.

And humans aren't cargo.

So they're about to die.

"Password?" the bouncer asks me.

"Candy cane," I reply.

It's the right answer, even if it's a stupid one. But I know it's right because Karmine texted it to me an hour ago after she got it out of the real seller.

And people don't lie to Karmine.

The bouncer reaches behind himself to twist the door handle. He only opens the door a crack, then he steps aside to let me pass.

I nod to him, unsure how much he knows about tonight's dealings and, therefore, unsure if I should kill him too or not.

Time will tell.

I push the door open with my left hand, gripping the edge of it as I do, and as soon as I've stepped through, I swing it shut behind me.

The music is still audible through the closed door, but not so loud I need to raise my voice.

"Gentlemen." I greet the three men who are certainly not.

Their heads turn at the same time, looking up at me from their seated positions around a beat-to-hell poker table in the center of the room.

"You the guy?" one of them asks.

"I'm the guy," I reply.

The man on the right moves his eyes up to my shoulder-length blond hair.

He starts to slide his chair back.

"What's your name?" the first guy asks.

But I keep my eyes on the man to my right when I answer. "Hans."

His face pales, even as he reaches down to his side.

He knows my name.

He knows he needs a weapon.

But he's not a professional.

I am.

My firearm, silencer and all, clears my holster before his fingers can even close around the gun tucked into his waistband.

Too slow.

The first bullet goes through his forehead.

The second goes through his heart.

The third—I shift my arm to the left—goes through the neck of the man straight across from me as he tries to duck down beneath the table.

The fourth—I move my feet, stepping to the right and angling toward the last man standing, changing the target I present in case he has a gun on me; but the barrel of his gun is still rising as I squeeze my trigger—bores through the bridge of his nose, passing through his brain, before exiting out the back of his skull.

Five seconds after stating my name, all three men are dead.

There's a gurgle from the man I shot in the neck.

Okay, dead or dying.

I move my position again, striding to the other side of the door, and press my back to the wall.

Silencers don't actually silence anything. The muted pops won't be audible out in the main bar, but the bouncer on the other side of the door will have heard them.

I stand still. Eyes on the door, waiting to see if he opens it. If he's on the side of the dead men.

But the door doesn't open. The handle doesn't turn. And there's no sound of fleeing footsteps.

Huh.

I slide my pistol into my holster and stride across the room. Reaching the table, I lift the duffel bag from below it.

These idiots don't usually have tracers in their money, but I do a quick sweep of the bag to make sure.

No visible tracers, but a pair of cheap, probably dirty handguns on top of the pile of cash. *Would've done more good in their hands than in a fucking bag.*

I strip all three of their guns, drop the firing pins into the duffel, then drop the rest of the pieces on the floor.

I'm not concerned about fingerprints. If I'm ever brought in by law enforcement, I'll just blackmail my way out. I have plenty on plenty of officials. Or I'll die at another assassin's hands. Either way, it's not worth the hassle of constantly cleaning up after myself.

Plus, letting people know it's me is kind of my thing.

Like my name.

Ever since I started down this path, I've used my real first name. Because I wanted people to know who they were afraid of. And if she ever heard the whispers, I wanted my sister to know I was coming. That I was trying.

She had the same hair color as me. And wore it the same length. So it stays.

It will always stay.

Because she's the reason I am what I am.

And she's the reason there are three fewer worthless souls on this planet tonight.

After taking one stack of bills out, I zip up the duffel and hold the handle at my side.

With silent steps, I approach the door and quickly pull it open.

The bouncer is still there, but he's moved a few steps up the hallway so his back is no longer directly in front of the door— probably hoping to avoid a stray bullet.

His hands are open and empty at his sides, a smart way to show me he's not a threat.

He gives me a wary look before glancing past me into the room.

He works down a swallow before speaking. "Looks like they had some sort of argument."

"Seems so." I nod. "Probably time for a new coat of paint."

I toss the stack of bills, and he catches it against his chest.

Then I walk past him. Back down the hall, through the still rowdy bar, and back out the front door.

No one pays attention to the duffel bag low at my side. No one pays attention to the single dude walking out of the bar. No one follows me.

When I've passed the first row of vehicles, I push all of the lingering air out of my lungs, dispelling the taste of being in a small room with a discharged firearm. Then I fill my chest with fresh air.

I'm not desensitized to death.

I know each life is important.

But I also know it's important to end some of them.

I'm not special. I'm just a man. But I'm a man with the means and the will to do what has to be done.

I'm aware the argument could be made that, based on my headcount, I also deserve to die. And I'm not hypocritical enough to argue against that justification. But until I find an opponent capable of ending my life before I can steal theirs, I'm not going to worry about it.

Ahead of me, a figure steps away from the shadows at the base of the streetlamp.

Her hair is pulled up into a messy knot on the top of her head, but even in the dull light, I recognize the violent red color.

She's dressed to work in black cargo pants and a tight black

31

tank top. And I know if I'd seen her twenty minutes ago, she'd have been sporting several weapons as well.

"That was quick." Karmine smirks, stopping on the far side of my pickup.

"No comment," I reply, moving to the tailgate.

She rests her elbows on the raised side of the bed as I lower the tailgate and retrace the steps to put my weapons back in their places.

She raises her brow at my silenced Glock, but she already answered her curiosity.

I wanted to be quick.

Before closing the tailgate, I drop the duffel into the truck bed and shove it so it slides to a stop in front of Karmine.

Moving so I'm opposite her, I lean against my truck the same way. Just two friends chatting in the parking lot after a night at the bar.

But there are three dead bodies inside the bar, so we shouldn't chat long.

"There's something..." She taps a blood-red nail against my truck, and it's like I can see her thinking. "Who's the girl?"

I blink once. "I don't know what you're talking about."

She rolls her eyes at me. "How are you such a bad liar?"

I clench my jaw, then huff out my exhale. "She's my neighbor."

Karmine's eyes widen. My answer catches her off guard.

The reaction makes my mouth pull into a half smile. "Nice to see I can still surprise you."

We met a decade ago. I was ten years into my quest for murderous vengeance, and she was only months into her journey of finding what to do with herself after surviving.

We were both at the same place for the same reason. It was personal for her. Every time is. Just like every kill is for me.

It's all so fucking personal.

The next time I ran into Karmine at a hit, she had four other

32

women with her. And they were out for blood. So I introduced them to my arms dealer.

And the third time I saw her, she was running a crew fifteen deep. All bad-as-hell women who'd clawed their way to freedom. So when Karmine asked if I'd like to share intel and take on some hits for her, I said yes.

I'd been on my own for so long that it was nice to have someone else do the hunting. Nice to not have to do every damn step on my own. Only they did more than I ever could. They gave the women they found safety. They gave them options.

I was always so focused on destruction, knew I was only ever good for killing.

Karmine's army is so much more.

And I'm happy to be a weapon for them to wield.

"Can't say I was expecting the girl next door." My friend breaks her stunned silence.

"It's not like that," I admit, sure she's jumping to all sorts of wrong conclusions.

"Right." She drags the word out.

"It's not. I don't even talk to her."

Karmine narrows her eyes, and I press my lips together.

"You were whispering when I called you earlier..." I watch uncomfortably as she puts it together. "Hans, tell me you weren't in her house."

"Look," I start, and I already know I'm gonna sound like a fucking creep. "I'm not doing it to perv on her or anything. I'm just making sure she's safe."

"By skulking through her house in the middle of the day? While she's there?"

"When you say it like that."

Karmine snorts. "Man, I know you're not like these assholes." She gestures her hand toward the bar. "But maybe you should try to spend some more time with normal people. Because you can't be doing that. You're good, but she's gonna catch you. And that'll go down real bad."

"I don't—She doesn't..." I scrub a hand down my face. "She wasn't there before. I fell asleep..."

Karmine drowns out my words with her full-body laugh.

After several long seconds, she finally takes a breath, and I level her with a bored look. "You done?"

She brushes a tear away from her eye. "Christ, Hans. You can't just Goldilocks this girl and expect a happily ever after."

"Goldi—" I shake my head. "I might be fucked in the head, but I'm not delusional. I know that's not where my story goes."

"What? Happiness?" The sad look she gives me makes my stomach hurt.

She knows my past just like I know hers. She knows what weighs on my shoulders. She knows I was too late.

Karmine's expression softens. "You've more than leveled the scales of justice. Shit, you've ended enough bad guys to single-handedly populate one of the circles of hell."

"And that means I win a white picket fence?"

She sighs, having no patience for my self-pity. "It means you can think about, I dunno, maybe not being such a fucking loser. Retire. Get a life. Try talking to the girl you're stalking. Ask her out."

"I'm not stalk—" I cut myself off because, by the definition of stalking, I think I probably am. So I change the topic. "Did you just tell me to retire?"

"I mean, not entirely. I still need you around on occasion. But why not go call up The Alliance bros? Throw hands with those fancy fucks. Change up the scenery a bit. You didn't have us help you save that mafia asshole for nothing. I know you always have a plan."

I lift a shoulder.

There wasn't really a grand plan other than wanting to help out those who have helped me. True, The Alliance hadn't realized they were helping me, considering they were hunting me, but they still helped to dispel human trafficking deals in their territory. And that was helpful to me.

Getting a life debt from Dominic Gonzalez was just a perk.

"You gonna retire?" I ask, deflecting the attention.

Karmine scoffs. "Fuck no. But I'm not as old as you. And, unlike you, I'm still getting some."

"Bravo," I say sarcastically.

"Don't be a dick because you're jealous. Human interaction is good for mental well-being. I don't care about your fucked-up backstory; any girl would be lucky to end up with you." She loosely flaps her hand in my direction. "Assuming they like the ruggedly handsome bad boy type."

"Thanks, Mom."

"Anytime, sport," she snarks back, then pauses. "I've heard some chatter. People looking for you."

"People are always looking for me."

"Yeah, but not like this. This sounds close." Karmine's voice is serious.

"Noted."

She's right, of course. This newest ring of assholes has been more active than ever. And that means they have someone with lots of money funding them.

And it's all the more reason to leave Cassandra alone. If someone's after me, I can't have anyone else around me to catch the shrapnel.

"Alright." Karmine straightens from the side of the truck, hand on the duffel bag. "You want a cut?" she asks, like she always does.

"I'm good," I answer the way I always do.

I don't need it. I already have more money than I could ever spend.

CHAPTER 8

Cassie

A MOAN YANKS ME OUT OF MY SLEEP, AND IT TAKES ME A second to realize it was my own.

I stare at the ceiling, and the frustration is instant because I can already tell I won't be able to fall back asleep. But I want to so badly because I want to finish that dream.

And let Hans finish me.

Groaning, I drag the bedspread over my face and press the soft fabric against my eyes. As though I might visually smother myself back into unconsciousness.

Maybe I need to hire someone to come sage my house. Or maybe I just need to go out into public more. Or join a dating site. Because this crush I have on my hot neighbor is getting out of control.

I know it's my brain playing tricks on me, but it was like I could feel his presence all afternoon. And I blamed the empty zucchini cookie container. But when I came up to bed, I swear his scent was blanketed across my room. As though I was conjuring him with wishes and hopes.

I squeeze my thighs together and groan again.

I can't even bring myself to scream into my pillow because that smells like him too.

Which is crazy. Because I know it doesn't. It can't.

Giving up, I toss my bedspread off and climb out of bed.

I slowly walk through the dark to my window and pull the curtains back, seeing that the sun has barely started to rise.

I look across the street, wondering if Hans is in there now, but I can't tell. I can never tell when he's home.

The drapes or blinds or whatever he has over his living room windows aren't blackout ones. Often, I can see a glow inside, but after the first few months of living here and trying to figure out his schedule, I came to the conclusion that the lights in his house are on random timers. Or at least some of them. And I only know about the random timer lights because my dad always tells me to get them. He worries about me as a *female living alone*. I appreciate that worry, I do, but I spend a lot of my time *at home*, and having lights randomly popping on and off would drive me crazy.

Crazier than I'm already going.

Feeling a little too much like a creeper, I step away from my window and try to put thoughts of Hot Hans out of my mind. And the only way to do that is to start my day.

With my hip leaning against the kitchen counter, the aroma of brewing coffee fills the house, and I feel a little of my sanity returning.

I'm scrolling through my phone, deleting emails, when I come across one telling me my self-purchased birthday present arrived yesterday. Or at least one of them. The other one should be delivered any day now.

Not caring that I'm still in my pajamas, since I won't see anyone anyway, I head to the front door and slip on my sandals.

It's been hot this summer, but the early morning air isn't stifling. I take my time making my way down the driveway to my mailbox.

I was in such a hurry to get on that call yesterday that I forgot to check the mail.

I spare a glance at Hans's house, wishing I knew the layout, specifically wondering if his bedroom window is the one on the

S. J. TILLY

far front corner, next to what has to be his living room, or if it's on the back side of the house. I'm assuming the single narrow window closest to the garage is his kitchen, so the house must go garage, kitchen, living room, bedroom—possibly plural—and bathroom.

Okay, wow, time to get a hobby.

I almost chuckle at my inner voice.

Getting a hobby has never been my issue. It's sticking to a hobby that's the problem. Bringing me back around to the point of this outing.

Pulling open my mailbox, I sigh when I see that the box is clearly too big for this rusty old thing, but the mail delivery person jammed it in there anyway.

"Would it have killed you to bring the box to my front step?" I grumble, knowing damn well my ass wouldn't have walked it up to the house either.

I work to wiggle the box out, one corner, then the other, getting it caught on the lip around the opening of the mailbox.

I wiggle it some more.

The one hobby I've found that I really like to do is baking. So I bought myself personalized recipe cards, multicolored pens, cute little food stickers, and other things I don't want bent or wrinkled. It would be great to just mash the corner of the box to release it, but I can't. I need to finesse it.

When finessing doesn't work, I give it another hard tug, and finally the box slides free, scattering a handful of envelopes onto the ground in the process.

"Crap."

I tuck the box under my arm as I bend down to pick up the rest of my mail.

CHAPTER 9
Hans

I watch through the window over my kitchen sink as Cassandra's front door opens and she prances out.

"Seriously?" I question the universe as she skips down her driveway, wearing practically nothing.

Each step has her tiny yellow silk shorts riding up her thighs, exposing the expanse of jiggling pale skin.

Cassandra takes the last step from her driveway to the road, and her foot comes down a little harder than before, which is highlighted by her unrestrained tits bouncing under her matching yellow silk tank top. The thin straps are barely enough to hold the soft fabric across her chest.

And I know the fabric is soft because I've touched it.

I've held it in my hands.

My fingers tighten around the glass I'm drinking water from, and I have to force them to loosen. But I don't look away. Even when she looks in this direction.

The kitchen is dark, and I have a film over this window that blurs the view of anyone trying to look in, so I know she can't see me. Which is why I continue to stand here staring while she turns her back to me and starts to struggle with something in the mailbox.

The wiggling. And shaking. And bouncing... It's too much.

This woman is too fucking much.

And when she finally yanks the item free and mail falls to the ground around her, she finally does it.

She bends over.

The tiny shorts are no longer shorts; they're barely underwear as Cassandra flashes me with an unrestricted view of the bottom half of her ass cheeks. The material pulled tight across her pussy. The bunching fabric right where I want to put my face.

I'm across the kitchen, across the living room, and have my hand on the handle of my front door before I realize what I'm doing.

I close my eyes.

I just got home. Walked in my door five minutes before she walked out hers. I just needed some water and a slice of bread before I crawled into bed.

I don't need to accost my neighbor in the street.

Releasing the doorknob, I move back into the kitchen and watch her sexy ass walk back up her driveway and into her house.

After I sleep, I'll replay her walk on my security feed.

For research purposes.

To make sure she locked her front door.

And the next time she leaves the house, I'll go back over and relock her bedroom window.

I don't need the temptation of knowing it's open.

CHAPTER 10
Hans

LEAVING MY TRUCK IN THE DRIVEWAY, I GRAB MY groceries and take the dozen strides to my mailbox.

It's been twenty-four hours since I watched Cassandra get her mail, and I'm still on edge.

Mostly because I can't get the sight of her bent over in those fucking shorts out of my mind. Probably doesn't help that I've watched the video of her doing just that two dozen times. And it definitely doesn't help that I'm severely lacking in sleep after the last couple days.

I keep my eyes firmly on my own mailbox, not sparing a glance at the box across the street.

There's more mail in mine than I expected, but half is probably garbage.

With the pile tucked under one arm, I walk through my garage and into the kitchen.

The cans in the bottom of my grocery bag clunk against the counter when I set it down, but there's nothing cold in the bag, so I ignore it and turn my attention to the mail.

I sort out the typical junk mail and find one flyer for new shingles that came from my man with connections to Italy, so I set that to the side. He's old school and doesn't like to use phones, but his information is usually good, so I don't mind the Cold War approach. It'll give me something to do tonight as I sort out the coded message.

The last item is a plain brown envelope with something thick inside.

I lift it, ready to take it to my safe room to check it for explosives, when I see it's addressed to Resident of 1304.

This is Cassandra's mail.

I pause.

This isn't mine.

I shouldn't...

My fingers are already pulling the little plastic thread to rip open the envelope.

I know I shouldn't, but this is for her safety. The packaging is suspicious. The address is not personalized. The contents...

I tilt the large envelope, and a book slides out.

It's square, maybe seven by seven inches, with a hardcover covered in a soft black fabric.

I tilt it in the light coming through the window, causing the silver lettering across the cover to shine.

Lust Shots.

And my blood thickens with an emotion I can't pinpoint.

Anger? Jealousy?

I open the book, and my stomach clenches.

Definitely jealousy.

It's Cassandra. On her knees. On a bed that isn't hers. And the gauzy little nightgown she's wearing is pretty much see-through.

I turn the page.

She's on her back, her head hanging off the foot of the bed, her arms draped down toward the ground, her dark curls pooling between her hands. She's not looking at the camera in this one; she's looking to the side. And she's wearing—

I grip the book tighter, and the spine creaks.

She's in a bra and panties. That's it.

The angle of the shot highlights her giant tits, mounded on her chest, held in place by black lace and underwires.

I turn the page.

She's standing in front of a full-length mirror. The shot is from behind, and she's still just in her underwear. This one is in black and white. And...

My breaths are coming faster.

My chest rises and falls as if I'm fighting for my life.

I turn the page.

Again.

Again.

All her. All my Cassandra. Spread out like a fucking centerfold.

For someone else.

My vision tints an ugly shade of green, and I storm out of my house, book in hand.

CHAPTER 11

Cassie

WHEN THE POPPING STARTS TO SLOW, I HIT THE button to stop the microwave and yank the door open.

Popcorn steam plumes out, but I fan it away and lift the bag by the corner.

It's Friday. I've logged off from work for the day. I've put my hair up and I've got my not-for-public little cotton shorts on, along with the worn T-shirt I got at the Grand Canyon years ago. This is my definition of comfort, and my plans consist of becoming one with the couch while I catch up on the newest season of my favorite true crime series. Because what's more relaxing than murder?

Pinching the bag tight so I don't drop it, I carry it over to the dining table, where I have my big red plastic bowl ready.

I've burned myself more than once opening these papery bags, so I carefully grab opposite corners with my fingertips and start to pull gently.

Then a loud pounding on the front door startles me so badly I jump and accidentally rip the bag in two.

Popcorn showers around me.

Dropping my grip with one hand, I slap my palm over my heart.

44

"What the hell?"

I stand for a second, wondering if I really heard someone knocking, when it sounds again.

I set the bag on the table amid the scattered popcorn and head toward the door.

"Cassandra!" My name booms through the closed door.

Wait.

Is that...?

A fist pounds against the wood again, and it shakes in its frame.

"Cassandra, open the door."

My heart keeps galloping but for a new reason.

Is that Hans?

And did he call me Cassandra?

Popcorn crunches under my slippers as I hurry to the door.

CHAPTER 12

Hans

IF I COULD FORCE MYSELF TO LET GO OF THE BOOK, I'D pick her lock and let myself in.

But I won't let go.

"Cassandra," I bellow a third time.

The deadbolt clicks, and the handle turns, and I step through the door as Cassandra opens it.

She lets out a squeak of surprise, but she doesn't try to stop me. Doesn't do anything except back up.

"What the fuck are these?" My voice is quieter than before. "Who took them?"

"Wh-what?" Cassandra blinks up at me.

Her eyes are wide, and her cheeks are flushed, and she looks so much like that first photo I want to shove her to her knees to teach her a lesson about playing with fire.

"Who did you take these for?" I seethe, still stepping forward.

I don't care who the fuck the man is. I'm going to kill him.

Cassandra continues to back away from me, moving into the living room.

"Hans, what are you—" Her question cuts off when she bumps into the back of her couch.

"This." I hold up the book. "This is what I'm talking about, little Butterfly. Who did you fucking take these for?"

She drops her eyes to the little black book in my hand, and her brows furrow for a moment before her eyes widen.

Guilty.

"Oh my god!"

Her gasp goes straight to my dick, which has been hard as stone since I first opened this fucking book.

She reaches for it, but I hold it up.

She's average height, but I'm not, so it's out of her reach.

"Tell me." My demand is ridiculous. She doesn't owe me anything. I have no rightful claim over her.

But I'm past being reasonable. And she's pushed me here.

"Where did you get that?" Her eyes bounce between me and the book.

"It was delivered to my house." I step closer, leaving only an inch of space between our bodies. "Now answer the question, Cassandra. Who took these?" Shifting my grip on the cover, I let the book flop open.

47

CHAPTER 13

MY MOUTH DROPS OPEN AS I TAKE IN THE IMAGE hanging from my neighbor's large hand.

It's me, but it's...

Wow.

The flush crawling up my cheeks deepens.

It's me, laid out on the prop bed from the photo shoot, with the fluffy comforter bunched up beneath me and my hands above my head, one of my knees bent to the side.

I had fun that day, pretending to be a model. Pretending I was a total sexpot. But I didn't get to see any of the photos. That's the deal. Trust the photographer, and she picks the best ones to put in the book.

And *goddamn*, that photographer earned every single dollar I paid her.

Hans shifts his grip, and the page flips, a new, equally provocative image revealing itself.

Then my brain glitches back into reality, and I remember what's happening.

Hans is holding the book.

He is here.

He's seen the photos.

And for some reason... he's mad.

I reach for the book, but his free hand darts out and grips my wrist, holding it between us.

He lowers his gaze from mine, and I know the moment he looks past the hand he's holding captive and to my chest.

His nostrils flare, and I swear his jaw clenches.

And in reaction, my already tight nipples harden further against my thin shirt. The fabric feels like sweet torture, and knowing he's looking sends a jolt down my belly to between my legs.

I try to remember what he was saying. I'm pretty sure Hans asked me a question.

But all I can concentrate on is his nearness. The heat of his body so close to mine. The way the skin on my wrist feels under his grip.

I inhale, trying to clear my thoughts, but it doesn't work. Because it just fills my final sense with him. This man and pine scent. The one that haunts me through this house whenever I think too much about him.

"Hans." His name comes out as a whisper.

He shifts closer, our hands now pressed between our bodies. "Who took the photos, Cassandra?"

Cassandra.

My name said in his voice... Why is it so sinful?

"Who?" he repeats.

"It was a photographer," I answer like a moron.

"Give me his name." Hans leans closer.

And I feel...

My body arches on its own against him.

He's hard.

For me.

Satisfied pride swamps me.

I don't know what's going on. This is the most Hans has ever said to me.

He's in my house. Barged in without an invitation. Shouting

my name. Because he's turned on. And…

Wait.

"Are you jealous?" I can't keep the inappropriate excitement out of my tone.

He lowers the hand holding the book.

I don't turn away from him, but I watch from the corner of my eye as he tucks the book behind the back cushion on my couch.

Then, with his hand empty, he reaches up and grips the base of my ponytail. "Don't push me, Butterfly."

His hold is tight, and with the smallest tug, he tips my head back.

My body lights all the way up.

He shifts forward again, not stopping until our bodies are flush and I'm thoroughly trapped between him and the back of the couch. "Tell me who took them and who you took them for. I won't ask you again."

With the hand not in his grip, I reach out and grab at his black T-shirt to steady myself.

His muscles bunch under my touch, and I realize just how solid he is.

I don't answer. I don't mean to *not* answer. I just still can't believe what's happening.

"You have until the count of three to tell me," Hans demands.

Holy hell.

"What happens on three?" I breathe out.

He presses his hips into mine. "Something you won't like, Girl. Now answer me."

I don't believe him.

I think I will like it.

My breath comes out faster.

I think I'll like it a lot.

"One." He lets go of my wrist and moves his hand to my hip, the other hand still gripping my hair.

His fingers press into my soft flesh through my baggy shirt.

HANS

With his hold on my wrist gone, I use that hand to grab his other side.

His shirt is not baggy. It's practically plastered to his toned body.

This man is freaking ripped.

"Two." Hans tightens his grip on my hair, and the tug is just enough. Just enough to drag a whimper from my throat.

"Cassandra," Hans growls.

"It was a lady." I hurry the words out. Not because I don't want the punishment; I want that very much, but I also want to tell him. I want to give him what he wants. "The photographer was a lady."

I stare up into his dark eyes as he takes in my answer.

Hans leans his face toward mine until I can feel his exhales puff against my skin. "Who are they for?"

"N-no one," I try to tell him, but it comes out sounding like a lie.

"Three."

Before I have time to process what's happening, his mouth slams down onto mine.

His lips are unforgiving.

Harsh.

Warm.

Fantastic.

Hans uses his grip on my ponytail to tilt my head, and I let him. I let him control me.

His tongue demands entry, and I open.

He tastes like...

I close my lips around his tongue.

He tastes like candy. Like sugar and fruit and childhood memories.

Hans groans and slides his tongue deeper into my mouth.

My mind is fuzzy with desire, but I still want more.

More contact. More skin. More Hans.

I slide my hands up his body, up his chest, over his bunching muscles, until I grip his shoulders.

Our teeth click together when we both open our mouths wider.

I must be dreaming.

I curl my fingers, letting my nails dig into his shirt, confirming this is real.

Hans rocks into me. His hard length digs into my belly, and I lift my leg, hooking my foot around the back of his thigh.

I don't know what I'm trying to do. But whatever my body is thinking, his is thinking it too.

The hand on my hip slides around to my lower back. Then lower still.

He palms my ass, but he keeps sliding lower until his hand is between my legs, cupping my pussy from behind.

Right as I tilt my head back to suck in a breath, he lifts me. With one hand. And sets me on the back of the couch.

My legs automatically spread, and Hans steps forward to fill the space between us.

His hold on me is almost too much. The hand in my hair, and the one beneath me, between my legs.

"Who are the photos for?" Hans releases my hair and drags his hand down my neck.

I try to elongate my spine, try to stretch my body in a way that will force his hand to my chest.

"Cassandra," he snaps this time.

"Me," I admit on a tortured moan. "They were a birthday present for me."

The fingers against my core flex. My thin shorts and panties are the only thing separating his touch from my entrance.

"Jesus," I pant.

He shakes his head. "You use my name while I'm touching you."

"S-sorry." I can't believe I just apologized for that.

The hand on my neck lowers until he's squeezing my breast. "Who are the photos for?"

He pinches my nipple through the fabric as he flexes his other fingers again.

"You." I claw at his shoulders and wiggle against the hand beneath me. "They're for you."

It's not even a lie. Every time I've fantasized about a man since moving in, it's been him. When the photographer told me to imagine someone I wanted to seduce, I pictured him.

"That's a good girl." Hans tugs on my nipple.

"Hans," I cry, so close to coming.

I don't want to be in this alone, but I'm not sure how to ask him to join me.

The look on my face must say it all.

Hans rumbles out a sound through his chest, then his mouth is back on mine.

This man has never said so much as a sentence to me before today. He's a complete stranger to me. But if he pulled that thick dick out of his jeans right now, I'd let him fuck me raw atop this couch.

My neighbor uses the hand under me to hold me in place as he presses his hips harder against mine, grinding against me.

Our groans meld together as we both feel the press of his length against my core.

I tilt my hips, urging his dick to press harder against my clit.

His teeth scrape against my bottom lip, and my body tenses, preparing for release.

Oh god, I'm going to come in my shorts.
And I don't care.

I tighten my legs around him, but then something vibrates against my inner thigh, where his pocket is.

Hans palms my other breast, its size filling his large hands, and I want him to pull on my nipple again.

His pocket vibrates a second time.

"Fuck." He pulls his mouth from mine.

We stare at each other while we feel it vibrate a third time.

Texts. This man is getting texts while I'm having the most intensely sexual moment of my life.

CHAPTER 14
Hans

CASSANDRA CANTRELL, THE THIRTY-YEAR-OLD BEAUTY next door, is blinking up at me with her trusting amber eyes, her mouth red and puffy from my kiss, and her body vibrating like it's ready to explode.

The girl who flutters through life, no regard for her own safety, is looking at me like she wants me to fuck her. Like she'd happily reenact any one of those photos, only this time with my dick buried inside her. One hole or another.

She's watching me like she's waiting for me to explain what's happening. To explain why it feels like this between us.

She's doing that, and I'm getting text messages. Which means someone needs to die tonight.

And because I have more deaths on my hands than bones in my body, I'm the man who's going to do it.

Karmine's words echo in my mind. The warning about bad actors closing in. And I know I have to leave.

"Hans?" Cassandra says my name, and I hate it.

Because I crave it.

I flex my fingers, taking in one last handful. "Lock your door."

A question starts to form on her sweet lips, but I pull my hands free.

Free of her chest. Free of her heat.

Then I step away, breaking the last contact between us, forcing her legs to unwind from my waist.

Cassandra tips backward.

Her arms go wide, she lets out a little shriek, and then she hits the sitting part of the couch with a little bounce.

Before she can right herself, I shove my hand between the cushions, then stride out of the room and out of her house.

I don't belong here.

CHAPTER 15

Cassie

STUNNED, I LIE MOTIONLESS, THE WRONG WAY ON THE couch with my feet in the air.

Did he just drop me?

The front door opens and slams shut.

Did he just leave?

I scramble to get upright, then crawl to the arm of the couch nearest the window.

Hans is already striding across the street, his long legs cutting the distance in seconds.

His truck is parked in his driveway, and he stops next to the driver's door.

He pulls his phone out of his pocket to check his messages. And I hate that I wonder if it's a woman.

He puts the phone back in his pocket, then opens the truck door. Before he climbs in, I see him toss something into the cab.

Wait... was that my book?

Still watching out the window, I stick my arm behind the back cushion, trying to find the *Lust Shots* book I saw him tuck there.

But I can't find it, because he definitely took it.

Hans, my neighbor, stealer of breath and nudie books, pulls out of his driveway.

I sink back onto my butt.

What the hell just happened?

CHAPTER 16
Hans

I slam the heel of my boot against the metal door.

The shitty lock crunches with the single hit, and the door swings open.

Bare bulbs hanging from the ceiling illuminate the four men as they jump up from the thin, soiled cots they were lounging on.

The room is square. Two cots against the two side walls.

Two men to my left. Two to my right.

"Who the—"

The world will never know exactly what that guy was going to ask, because the blade of my first throwing knife sinks hilt deep under his chin, in the center of his throat.

He crumples back onto the cot.

With my left hand, I throw across my body to the rear right corner of the room, toward the man positioned opposite the first. And the only man to have his gun drawn.

My aim is better with my right, but the second knife still hits its target. Lodging itself into the center of the man's forearm, it forces him to drop his gun.

I'm not looking for stealth tonight. I'm not here to be in and out as quickly as possible. I'm here for blood. I'm here to make these motherfuckers pay.

For what they're in the middle of doing.

For what they've done before.

And for what they prevented me from doing with Cassandra.

The man reaches for the knife penetrating his arm, and I can see in his expression that he's not going to pull it free on the first try.

He should leave it.

He should fight with it in.

But he's a fucking moron.

The two uninjured men are on either side of me.

And I have two new blades in my hands.

The man on my right lets out a shout as he stops trying to get control of his firearm and leaps for me.

With his hands empty, I snap my attention to the left. That man isn't ditching his gun, making him the biggest threat. And his gun has already cleared leather.

He pulls the trigger, and the noise is almost deafening in the small room.

The bullet hits dead center in my chest.

It knocks the breath out of my lungs, and I stagger back a step, but that's it, because I'm wearing a vest. Because, unlike these guys, I'm not a fucking moron.

You don't bring knives to a gunfight without a little planning.

Plus—I grin—shooting a man and having him not react is kind of scary.

And right now, I want to be scary.

The man's eyes widen, then drop to stare at the knife hilt sticking out between his third and fourth ribs.

His gun wavers and lowers, then he stumbles back a step, and I watch him concentrate on lifting it back up.

A body collides with my back, and arms circle my neck in a bruising squeeze.

Perfect.

I use the new man's momentum to spin us, just in time for the stumbling guy to fire.

Two more shots echo inside the small room, and the body behind me jolts as he takes the friendly fire in his spine.

The man with the gun lets out an alarmed sound, and through the ringing in my ears, I can hear his gun clatter to the floor.

The arm around my neck is still squeezing, but not as hard. He's not dead yet.

I spin the final knife that's still in my hand so I'm gripping the handle instead of the tip of the blade, then swing my arm down and back, slicing through the man's upper thigh and his femoral artery.

I withdraw the blade immediately, giving the vital blood coursing through the artery a path of escape.

The man's arms fall away from my neck.

One dead.

One seconds from death.

One with a knife between the ribs.

One finally pulling the knife free from his arm.

Him first.

He tries to throw the blade at me, like I did to him. But he's not me, so the flat edge of the knife thuds against my chest and falls to the floor.

If it wasn't so fucking pathetic, I'd laugh.

"Really?" I ask, wanting more of a fight from these men. Needing it.

Without looking, I fling my final throwing knife down and back, hearing the meaty thud of it entering the body of the man who's bleeding out on the floor.

The man before me pales, like the idea of me being weaponless is somehow more intimidating.

I hear a creak from the cot behind me, and I know Rib Guy is trying to get up. Probably hoping to use his last breath to kill me.

He can try.

I'd love to make this an actual fight.

I lunge forward and capture Arm Guy in a bear hug, barreling us both to the floor.

He's big. As big as me. Maybe heavier.

My shoulder catches the corner of one of the cots, so I'm slightly off-balance when he swings a haymaker at my face.

I lean back, moving with it, but that off-balance bit has me leaning too far, and his fist slides across my throat.

The hit isn't hard enough to kill me, but it's enough to fucking hurt. And enough to seize up my throat muscles.

I punch the man once in the face, hard enough to stun him, then straddle his sprawled form.

My breath is still stuck in my lungs, but I know the air will come, so I don't panic.

Instead, I grab the front of his shirt to lift him, then smash his head back against the concrete floor.

I can hear movement behind me. Can hear Rib Guy picking up his gun from the floor. Can hear his ragged breathing, his left lung probably fully collapsed now.

I slam Arm Guy's head against the concrete again, and his eyes roll back.

Rib Guy is moving forward now. I can hear him getting closer.

He's afraid to shoot from too far away.

Afraid to hit his friend again, like he did last time.

Pussy.

I lift Arm Guy a few inches off the ground. If his skull isn't cracked, it's going to be. But instead of rocking forward and slamming him down again, I let go of his shirt and drop my body backward.

A gunshot cracks through the room, the bullet flying over my laid-out form and sinking into the chest of Arm Guy.

Continuing my backward motion, I roll through a reverse somersault.

My booted feet connect with the floor at the same time my throat finally relaxes. I suck in a deep breath as I bolt upright.

Rib Guy is trying to track me with his gun, but he's wavering, blood loss and lack of oxygen taking its toll.

In one move, I reach between us with my right hand and grip his gun from the top, my palm covering the hammer, preventing it from working. With my left hand, I grasp the handle of the knife still protruding from his chest, and just like a moment ago, I use my motion to my advantage. Letting my right hand lead, I spin, yanking the gun from his grip and pulling the knife from his ribs. My back is to him for a split second, but he's not quick enough to do anything. Then I face him again, his pistol in my hand. My finger on the trigger.

"Might as well kill everyone with your gun." I squeeze the trigger, sending a bullet into his heart, point-blank.

With my eyes on his, I aim the gun to the side and put a round into the man who died seconds after I entered the room. Just for good measure.

CHAPTER 17

Cassie

"Hi, Hans. I wanted to ask you for my book back. And see if maybe you could kiss me like you did yesterday?" I blink into the mirror, then drop my head forward and groan.

I can't figure out what to say. And the more I practice it, the more ridiculous it sounds.

But that's just it. The whole thing is ridiculous. Because my neighbor, who hasn't said more than a single word to me since I moved in over a year ago, who has literally only ever mowed his yard when I'm not home or gotten his mail when I'm not near enough to even wave, who eats—or throws away—every baked good I've ever given him without so much as a thank you, *that* neighbor banged down my front door, stormed into my house, and demanded to know who I took the sexy photos for. Like a possessive boyfriend who found another man's boxers in my car.

But he didn't just demand to know. No, he counted to three. He lifted me with one hand, between my legs, and then manhandled me in a way I've only dreamed of.

Clenching my thighs, I lift my head back up and face my mirror.

I look good.

I put on just enough makeup to look like I'm not wearing any while covering the dark circles under my eyes. I'm wearing leggings instead of shorts, a tank top instead of a baggy shirt, and a soft bralette instead of no bra—which is my compromise for having to wear any sort of bra on a Saturday.

Basically, I picked the opposite of everything I was wearing last night.

I'm sure I'm overthinking it, but at least there's nothing about my appearance that can make him think I'm trying to recreate yesterday. But that's also why I wore my hair down, even though the summer humidity will for sure frizz my curls between my house and his.

I square my shoulders. "Go across the street. Get your book back. Tell him he's welcome to finish what he started. Then smile and walk back home."

Before I can chicken out, I head down the stairs.

After Hans did that little runaway act yesterday, I've kept an eye on his house. And I know he came home about an hour ago—just in time for dinner. And I know he hasn't left.

With one last deep breath, I slide my sandals on, then open my front door.

I'm only half hyperventilating by the time I get to Hans's door. But I can't turn around now, so I suck in a lungful of air and knock against the wood.

The sound is quiet, muted, like the door is made of something denser than mine, but it's loud enough for someone inside to hear.

If he's actually going to open the door for the first time ever.

Only a few seconds pass before I hear the deadbolt unlock.

Oh god, it's happening.

When the door swings open, I start to talk. If I pause, I won't speak at all.

"I came to get..." The rest of my words bump against each other inside my chest.

Hans is in loose-fitting sweatpants and a tight-fitting T-shirt.

Jesus Christ. I want to put a steaming mug into his hands and stick him in a nineties coffee commercial.

Then I notice the exhausted look on his face. "Are you okay?"

He nods, and I watch as his narrowed eyes lower to my empty hands.

I bite my lip.

All the other times I've knocked on his door, it's because I've brought him food. Now that he actually answers, I have nothing to offer.

Is he hungry? Is that why he actually answered the door?

Ohmygod, stop it. I don't need to offer him anything. I'm here because the man stole my book.

"I would like my book back," I say in what feels like a very mature tone.

Hans shakes his head.

Umm...

I hadn't really considered him not agreeing.

"No, you won't give it back?" I clarify.

He just holds my gaze.

"You can't just keep it." I lift my hands, fingers spread, in a *what gives* gesture. "It... was expensive," I blurt out. Even if I shouldn't need a reason. Because it's mine.

Instead of replying, Hans steps back from the door, giving me my first view into his house. And I have to press my lips together to keep from smiling. Because from here, I can see that my guesses were correct.

The front door opens into the living room, like mine does. And off to my right is a little hall that must lead to the bedrooms. Right ahead of me is a doorway that must lead to a basement, and to the left is the kitchen, then the entrance to the garage.

Hans is stalking off to the right, toward the bedrooms, hopefully to get my book. But he didn't ask me to follow, so I'll just stand here and wait.

It's a little dated. Not much in here but the usual furniture. Basically, a typical *single dude* setup.

Except above the couch, mounted to the wall, is a... sword.

Huh.

I glance around at the rest of the room.

A remote and a glass of water on the coffee table. A standing lamp next to the couch. A TV, bigger than mine, in the corner of the room, angled to the couch. Nothing expensive looking, but the pieces look sturdy and well kept.

I don't require wealth from the hot man who kisses me like he wants to own me.

Hans reappears from the short hall, holding his wallet.

"What are you doing?"

Hans pulls a wad of cash out of the folded leather, and it looks like a bunch of hundreds. "How much?"

His voice snaps me out of my daze. It's scratchy and quiet.

He sounds awful.

"Oh geez, are you sick?" I press my hands against my chest, suddenly feeling bad for bothering him.

Hans lifts his chin.

"Your throat?" I ask, assuming it hurts too much to talk. "Have you taken anything?"

His brows furrow.

"That's a no." I roll my eyes. "Have you had dinner?"

Expression not changing, Hans slowly moves his head from side to side.

"Okay, um, I'll be back in five. Maybe ten. Just"—I wave my hand toward his couch—"leave the door unlocked."

Before he can refuse me, I hurry away.

I'm not worried about Hans getting me sick. I mean, he had his tongue in my mouth yesterday. So if I'm going to catch it, I'm going to catch it.

But feeding people is my love language.

And thief or not, Hans looks like he could use some love.

CHAPTER 18

Hans

I STARE AT THE CEILING FOR A SOLID MINUTE BEFORE I move back to the couch.

Cassandra, my obsession, the worst baker I've ever met, is going to come back with *who knows what* to make me feel better because she thinks I'm sick.

I'm not sick. I'm just struggling to speak because I got popped in the larynx last night by a man I was in the process of killing.

I never should have opened her mail.

Settled back into my usual spot on the end of the couch, I watch through the living room window as Cassandra exits her house, makes it a few steps outside, turns around, goes back inside, comes back out, this time pausing to lock her door with her bundle of keys, then hurries back toward my house.

She's dressed casually. But if she thinks skin-fucking-tight leggings are less provocative than shorts, she's as wrong as she is tempting.

I grit my teeth, silently telling my dick to chill out.

I can't sit here tenting my pants.

I shouldn't even let her back into my house.

There are so many reasons why getting close to her is wrong.

So many reasons for me to jump up and lock my door. Tell

68

her to stay away from me. Tell her to sell her house and move across the country.

But I can't turn her away.

Because I don't want to hurt her feelings.

And I don't actually want her to go.

I want her to stay.

Cassandra hops up my steps and knocks once on the door before turning the handle.

Like she requested, I left it unlocked.

The door cracks open an inch, then swings in, allowing her entry.

"Hey," Cassandra greets me shyly. Which is almost laughable since she was just here, and she's back because she boldly inserted herself into my night.

She shuts the door and pauses her hand next to the lock.

It was satisfying watching her go back into her house for her keys to lock her door. Because her safety is paramount. But watching her decide if she should lock herself into my house is amusing.

With a small shake of her head, she decides and leaves the door unlocked, then toes off her sandals next to the door.

"Okay." She crosses the living room toward me, stopping on the other side of the plain coffee table I currently have my feet on. "I brought a few things."

Cassandra sets an honest-to-god picnic basket on the coffee table. It's wicker, with two arched handles, a lid, and a red and white checkered lining that folds over the top edge of the basket.

I lift a brow.

Her cheeks turn a soft shade of pink. "It was my grandma's."

Cassandra folds the handles down and pulls the lid open.

"I don't know that she got it from anywhere special, but she kept my grandpa's ashes in it for the longest time." I lift the second brow just as she darts a glance up at me. "Not like *in* the basket. He was in an urn. His ashes..." Her hands go up in a stop gesture, and she takes a breath. "Pretend I didn't tell you that."

69

I have to work to hold my features steady and not smile as I give her a nod of agreement.

"So." She reaches into the basket, and I stare down her shirt as it gapes open. "I have ginger ale, cough drops, these fizzy tablets you can put in a glass of water—" She sets the items down on the table as she names them. "I brought my favorite tea, stuff to make a hot toddy, and soup."

I pull my gaze away from her tits to see her plunk down a frosty block of something next to the bottle of whiskey.

"The soup is still frozen," she rattles on. "But if you don't mind me in your kitchen, I can heat it up for you."

I lean forward and pick up the cold plastic. "What kind?" I scratch the words out.

"Italian wedding. It's homemade. Not sure if you've noticed, but I like to make food." She gives me a smile that's so vulnerable and happy I let the edges of my mouth tip up the smallest bit.

"I've noticed."

My voice cracks, and her smile pulls into a grimace. "Okay, that's enough talking." She takes the soup from my hands, then scoops up the whiskey, lemon, and honey until her arms are full. "I'll get the soup started. You rest."

I should really stop her.

For her sake. For my tastebuds' sake.

But instead, I crack open the can of ginger ale and prepare myself for what should be an interesting Saturday night.

CHAPTER 19
Cassie

I BITE MY CHEEK TO STOP MYSELF FROM SQUEALING.

I'm in Hans's kitchen.

Like his living room, it's not flashy. The counters form a U along the side of the room closest to the road, and at the back of the kitchen, under a window showing the backyard, is a small dining table.

It's remarkably clean. Not even a pile of mail on the table. And, not for the first time, I wonder if Hans is in the military. Or if he was.

Not the time, Cassie. Focus.

I debate for a second but decide that the stovetop is the best way to go for heating up the soup. I could try to do it all in the microwave, but it's frozen solid and the stove just seems easier. Then I can use the microwave to heat water for the toddies. Because I'm having one too.

It doesn't take long to find a pot with a lid in the cabinet next to the stove. I have to run hot water over the outside of the Tupperware, but then it only takes a little shaking and squeezing to slide the frozen block of soup into the pot.

I set the lid in place and turn the burner to medium heat, then turn my attention to the drinks.

There was a large glass measuring cup next to the pots, so I fill it with a couple cups of water and put it in the microwave.

The appliance hums to life, and I start to look for utensils.

The first drawer I pull open has hand towels. The next has takeout menus and mini packets of soy sauce and hot mustard. I've never seen him get food delivery, but apparently Hans likes Chinese food. Not that that's a revelation. Who doesn't?

I pull open the next drawer over and pause.

It's filled with knives. Probably a dozen of them, all perfectly nestled in a layer of foam.

They don't look like any of the knife sets I've seen before. They're thinner, like the ones I've seen people use to slice up fish, and they're a dull black, but they look expensive.

Maybe Hans is a chef too.

I take out the smallest one, needing it to slice the lemon, then move on to the next drawer and finally find what I'm looking for.

As the soup heats, I take the hot water out of the microwave and pour it into two mugs I found in an upper cupboard.

The mugs were next to matching white plates and bowls that clearly came together as a set. Another staple of bachelor life.

I add the honey to the hot water first so it can dissolve, then pour in the whiskey, a squeeze of lemon, and a shake of cinnamon.

I take a sip from one of the mugs and hum my approval.

Hot toddies are delicious and not just for sore throats. They're also good for giving you courage when you're inside your hot neighbor's home.

I let my gaze rove over the kitchen again.

There's something about this place that makes it feel like a rental or a cabin. It has the energy of a place that no one really lives in full time. The single set of dishes. The lack of clutter or art or decorations.

But I know Hans lives here. Sometimes it seems like he's gone for days at a time, but he's not gone enough for this to be anything other than his primary residence. He's probably just traveling for work. And now that he's acknowledging my existence, I should probably ask him what he does for a living.

The warmth of the mug in my hand reminds me he's not feeling well.

I'll ask him another time.

I'm taking another sip when my nose twitches.

I look over to the stainless-steel pot, and tendrils of smoke are seeping out around the lid.

"Ahh!" I rush the few feet to the stove.

My fingers touch the handle of the lid for just a moment, but I jerk away because it's an all-metal lid with a metal handle and it's scorching hot.

"Shit," I hiss while shaking out my hand.

I know I saw hot pads in one of these drawers.

A noise sounds from the other room, and I can picture Hans getting up from the couch to come investigate.

"It's all good!" I shout. "Stay there!"

Yanking open drawers, I find the hand towels and use one to pull the lid free.

A plume of smoke comes out of the pot.

"*How?*" I question the universe as quietly as possible.

I set the lid to the side and use the towel to fan at the smoke.

It disperses and thankfully doesn't set off any alarms.

Looking into the pot, I see the culprit.

Frustrated, I scowl at the mini meatball stuck to the side.

Only I would burn frozen soup.

To prove my point, a large chunk of frozen broth still floats in the pot.

And I know exactly what happened. The pot got hot, the block of ice tipped against the side, and instead of melting out of the ice and dropping into the broth below, the meatball decided to sear itself to the metal.

Using one of the spoons, I scrape at the burned meatball. "Why couldn't you just behave?"

When it finally breaks free and drops into the soup below, I realize I probably should have tried to scoop the burned parts out.

Whatever, too late now.

I bite my lip, eyeing the lid, but decide to leave it off.

Leaving the soup to finish melting and heating, I grab the mugs and head into the living room.

Hans's gaze is already on me.

"Soup's almost ready," I say, crossing the room, noticing that it smells like smoke in this room too.

I also notice that Hans is trying not to smile.

CHAPTER 20
Hans

SHOULD'VE KNOWN IT WOULDN'T BE AN ENEMY THAT gets me, but rather, pretty little Cassandra burning my house down from the inside.

I lift the spoon to my lips, pretending that I don't notice Cassandra standing there staring at me.

The scent of burned meat overwhelms any other pleasant aroma the soup might give off, but I keep my features relaxed as the first taste hits my tongue.

I take a second bite, then take pity on Cassandra and look her way.

"Okay?" Her expression is so hopeful it twists something in my chest.

"Yes." I nod. "Thank you."

Her mouth pulls into a bright smile, and tension drops from her shoulders. "Oh, good." She points at my empty mug. "Would you like another?"

I nod and watch her ass in those fucking leggings as she sways back into the kitchen.

I lied to her earlier when she asked if I'd had dinner. I had two ham sandwiches. I'm not the least bit hungry. But I can't turn down her food.

My fingers flex around the spoon as I take another bite.

Even assuming it wouldn't be good, I couldn't turn down a chance to consume something she made.

As she walks back into the living room carrying two mugs, I wonder if there's a way I could ask her to write Italian wedding soup on a Post-it for me. It feels wrong to not have this meal documented like the rest.

But then Cassandra sits on the couch next to me, and I accept that this meal isn't like the others. This isn't me standing in the kitchen, choking down what she'd left on my front step. This is me sitting two feet away from her gloriously soft body.

Nothing has changed. I still shouldn't have her here with me. Shouldn't let her anywhere near me. But I can't find it in me to make her leave. Because deep down, I want her to stay.

"Figured I'd have a second too." She gestures her mug to me as she sets mine on the coffee table. "It is the weekend, after all." Then she settles back into the couch, drink cradled in her hand. "What're you watching?" Her brows furrow beneath her curly bangs.

I want to brush her hair aside and trace my finger over the cute wrinkles that form across her forehead when she makes that expression.

"What language is that?"

What...?

My brain catches up, and I turn back to the TV.

Oops.

It's a Swedish film. In Swedish.

I don't usually slip up like this, showing someone something about myself by accident. I don't need her knowing I speak Swedish. Or Italian. Or Spanish.

Pretending I misheard her, I pick up the remote to exit out of the movie, then hand the remote to Cassandra.

"Oh, I didn't mean..." She tries to give it back to me, but I pick my spoon back up and gesture to my throat.

If I'm stuck faking this cold and eating burned meat soup

instead of feasting on her body, I'm going to use the few advantages it gives me.

Sighing, she clicks through the available titles, stopping on a documentary about secret societies.

I can feel her watching me for a sign of how I feel, but when I don't say anything, she selects it.

Cassandra sets the remote on the coffee table, then props her feet next to it, mirroring my position. "I've been meaning to watch this. And if you don't like it..." She takes a sip of her drink. "Too bad. You had ample opportunity to object."

I smirk around my next bite of burned soup. Butterfly has a backbone.

CHAPTER 21

Cassie

Hans finishes his bowl of soup. Then his second, eating the rest of what I brought. But when I started to stand up to go wash his bowl, he waved me to keep sitting.

So I did.

And after finishing my second whiskey drink, I let myself sink back into his couch.

The piece of furniture isn't much to look at, but it's incredibly comfortable. Not a cheap hand-me-down at all.

I turn my body so my side is against the back of the couch, then lift my feet onto the seat between us.

I'll just stay until the end of the show. Then I'll go home and let Hans rest.

As the host of the documentary talks about the victim traveling to Europe, I think about the movie Hans had been watching and wonder what language it was.

And then my lids start to lower.

CHAPTER 22
Hans

I GATHER THE DISHES FROM THE COFFEE TABLE, decades of training keeping my movements silent.

I set them in the sink, next to the soup pot, then circle through the house, securing the front door and double-checking the rest of the access points.

Finally, when the only light left on is the lamp next to my bed, I return to the living room and bend down to scoop Cassandra's sleeping form into my arms.

CHAPTER 23
Cassie

HEAT SURROUNDS ME, AND MY HEAD SAGS TO THE SIDE.

My eyes are heavy when I try to open them.

"Hush." Hans's deep voice vibrates through my body. "Go back to sleep."

CHAPTER 24
Hans

I STAND NEXT TO MY BED, HOLDING CASSANDRA against my chest.

She fell back asleep in the twelve seconds it took me to get from the couch to here, and I don't want to set her down. I don't want to lose the weight of her in my arms.

Having her this close...

Heat simmers through my veins, and I hold her tighter.

In response, Cassandra lets out a sigh that sounds so content I feel it in my bones.

Just set her down. You can climb into bed and have her back in your arms in moments.

Accepting that I have to, I lower her to the mattress.

Cassandra makes a soft sound, then rolls onto her side.

Her hands grope at nothing, so I grab my comforter—which I'd flipped back before picking her up—and tuck it around her shoulders.

Her fingers drag the fabric up to her face, pressing it against her mouth.

Then she settles.

And she looks so right, so at home, curled up in my bed.

It's the perfect sort of torture. Because now I know what it could be like.

Just like knowing what her mouth tastes like. Or knowing how much heat radiates from her hot little pussy when she's worked up.

Now I know the sight of her under my blankets.

I know it, and I'll never be able to forget it.

My heart squeezes, and I do the only reasonable thing I can. I take a photo of her with my phone, strip down to my boxer briefs, turn off the lamp, and climb into bed behind her.

I don't bother pretending, don't bother waiting. I move straight to her and press my front against her back, spooning her body with mine.

Cassandra lets out a deep exhale, melting into me.

The pressure in my chest intensifies.

What is it about her?

I've been with women. Lots of women. Some of them have been stunning. Some sweet. Some probably had the potential to be great partners. But I wasn't interested. It never even crossed my mind to bend my concrete boundaries or to consider retirement.

Retirement.

I circle my arm around Cassandra's waist, my forearm against her stomach and my hand tucking back between her soft body and the mattress.

I tuck my other arm under the pillow.

This feels so right.

I let my eyes close and think of the word again. Retirement.

I don't think I'll ever completely retire. You don't really leave this life, not with your heart still beating.

And I won't lie and pretend I hate it. Won't pretend something deep inside me doesn't love it. Doesn't revel in the violence. But I don't need to do every hit Karmine sends my way. She has plenty of girls who could do what I do. I've been doing it for so long—searching for justice and forgiveness, for so fucking long—it's just become *what is.*

But now...

I sigh.

Right now, nothing has changed. People are still after me. They might always be after me. And until I can guarantee the safety of those around me, nothing will change.

I can't keep her.

She's not mine.

Anger claws at the base of my skull, wishing things were different.

Wishing I was different.

Only tonight, I try to convince myself as I press my nose against her hair.

Only for tonight.

CHAPTER 25

Cassie

T<small>HAT HEADY PINE SCENT</small> I <small>LOVE FILLS MY SENSES AND</small> pulls my mind the rest of the way out of sleep.

Hans.

The heavy arm across my side isn't my own. The heat at my back, the breath against my hair, the hardness against my bottom... It's all Hans.

I take a slow breath and crack my eyes open, trying to keep my body still.

I'm in bed with Hans.

I am in a bed, with Hans.

I take another slow inhale.

A faint memory of his arms around me dances through my brain, and I have to assume he carried me in here. Which, one, I would love to be awake for that, and two, should probably worry me as much as the second sword he has mounted to the wall I'm facing.

But it doesn't.

Hans's decorating skills may need a little help, but this mattress is the most comfortable thing I've ever lain on.

With the smallest movements I can manage, I nuzzle my face into the pillow.

This pillowcase is made of the softest cotton, and the pillow's thickness provides the perfect amount of support.

It's like his couch and his knives. And, now that I think about it, his truck. All nice. All well taken care of.

I can't help but wonder what he thought when he was in my house the other day. Did he like all the color and decor, or does he hate it? Does he prefer living a minimalist lifestyle?

Not that he spent much time looking around.

The length pressed against my ass twitches.

I freeze.

Suddenly, it feels imperative that I get out of here before the man behind me wakes up.

What we did in my living room was hot. Like super hot. But it was also an *in the moment* thing. But waking up with his big dick twitching against my ass... I don't know how to be cool about that.

Not to mention, the man is sick. He needs to sleep so his body can recover.

I start to carefully slide from his grip.

I'll sneak out of here and save us both the uncomfortable experience of waking up together.

CHAPTER 26

Hans

HER BREATHING SHIFTS AND I KNOW SHE'S AWAKE.

I keep my body relaxed against hers. I don't want to make her feel weird by giving away that I've been lying here, watching her sleep, for the last thirty minutes.

She nuzzles her face against the pillow, and I wonder if she might just fall right back asleep.

But then her whole body does some sort of shimmy. And her ass wiggles against the hard-on I've had since waking.

I look over the top of her head, focusing on the wall and forcing myself to stay relaxed.

When she finally notices my cock pressed into her, Cassandra stiffens.

Slowly, she starts to climb out of bed, like she's trying to be sneaky or not wake me, but she accidentally pulls the blanket off my shoulders. Then she bumps the bed frame, shaking it.

She hunches her shoulders as she tiptoes out of the room.

My eyes are open, my head is turned toward her, but she doesn't look back.

She must step on every squeaky floorboard in the house on her way to the front door, only to make more noise gathering her picnic basket.

Shaking my head, I wait until I hear the front door open and close before I climb out of bed and follow her steps.

I don't know why she snuck out.

And I don't know how she could possibly think she was being quiet. Her exit could've woken me from a coma.

But whatever her reasons, I need to let her leave.

It's for the best.

CHAPTER 27

Cassie

BLOWING OUT A BREATH, I EYE THE FRONT OF HANS'S house.

I'm pretty sure he's home since I haven't seen him leave since I snuck out of his bed this morning. And I know I shouldn't bother him. I've done enough of that already. But...

I glance back at my car and bite my lip.

CHAPTER 28
Hans

MY KNIFE SLOWS TO A STOP AGAINST THE SHARPENING block as I watch Cassandra climb out of her car, even though she just climbed into it a moment ago.

What's wrong, Butterfly?

She puts her hands on her hips, indecision evident in her body language. She looks at my house, back at her car, then back to my house.

Her teeth press into that plump lower lip, and I feel it in my balls.

It's worse now. Now that I know what it's like to touch her. To feel her against me. Because now, when I see her on the screen like this, it feels even more distant. Even further from reality.

But then she takes one step down her driveway. Then another, and another, until she's crossing the street.

I let my knife drop to the workbench and stand.

I've always ignored her knocking at my door. Always.

Until last night.

And since she hasn't left the house today, she probably knows I haven't either.

And since I carried her to my bed last night rather than wake her up to send her home, I can't really ignore her. That would be rude.

Excuses.

With long strides, I exit my safe room, leaving my surveillance and voice of reason behind as I secure the door.

I'm through the false wall and up the stairs before Cassandra knocks the first time.

And I'm pulling the door open when she knocks the second time.

In a bright yellow sun dress, she looks like some kind of summer fairy. And even more beautiful in person.

"Can I borrow your car?" Cassandra leans forward a little as she asks, like the question tumbled out of her unexpectedly.

I blink at her.

Borrow my truck?

I think of my truck. The fake registry in the glove box. The hidden compartment under the rear bench seat. The dozens of weapons and explosives hidden in the bed.

"No." My voice is stronger than it was yesterday, the injury already healing.

"Um." She blinks back at me. "Please?"

"What's wrong with yours?" I counter.

"Won't start." She lifts a shoulder. "I tried ordering a ride from the different apps, but no one is out this way." She grimaces. "And if I don't leave in the next few minutes, I'll be late."

The town we live in isn't tiny, but it's small enough and just far away enough from the bigger suburbs that the different taxi services rarely run here, and there is no public transportation.

Which is good, because if I witnessed her getting into the back of a stranger's car, I'd have my sniper rifle out and aimed at the back of the driver's head before you could say psychotic.

She shifts her weight in her little white tennis shoes.

I take her in again. Casual shoes, pretty dress that stops a couple of inches above her knees, big leather purse slung over her shoulder, hair pulled up into a curly ponytail, glossy lips...

"I'll drive you."

Her face brightens. "You will?"

I nod. Because apparently, I will.

"Thank you, thank you, thank you." She hops twice, and I want to shove my face in her tits.

But I don't. I just nod my acceptance of her thanks, then gesture for her to back up. "Let's go."

"Do you, I don't know, need to get anything?" Cassandra glances down, then notices that I'm already wearing my shoes. Or tactical boots, to be more exact.

I glance down at myself too.

My black pants bunch a bit at the tops of the boots, and that, combined with my black nylon belt and black T-shirt, makes me look like a fucking mercenary.

Practice prevents me from fidgeting. And getting changed now would only draw attention to what I'm currently wearing and questions about why I put it on if I wasn't willing to leave the house dressed like this.

I don't have a mission tonight. No plans to utilize all the pockets hidden in my pants. But I like to be prepared. And anytime I'm sitting in my room downstairs, watching my monitors and sharpening my knives, I make sure I'm ready to go, should the need arise.

"I'm good," I reply and pull my keys from my pocket.

Cassandra spins around and walks ahead of me to the front of my garage.

I click a button on my key fob to open the overhead door, and we wait for it to rumble open before going to our respective doors.

It's not until we're climbing into my truck that I think to ask, "Where am I taking you?"

Cassandra pulls her door shut and answers while reaching for her seat belt. "Dinner at my parents' place."

CHAPTER 29

Cassie

HANS SLOWLY TURNS HIS HEAD TO FACE ME AS THE truck rolls down his driveway.

I bite my lip, refusing to look at him, worried that if I do, he'll throw the truck into park and demand I get out.

Not that he requires eye contact to kick me out.

"Your parents?" His voice, though much better than it was yesterday, is still a little scratchy, making him sound more serious than his already serious tone.

"Yes," I kinda squeak. "But you can totally just drop me off. They're in St. Paul, and I know that's a bit of a drive, but I'll pay you for the hassle, and I'm sure I can find a ride that will bring me back this way."

It's Sunday evening, so there won't be much traffic, and we'll get there in like thirty minutes, but I don't want him to think I can't pay for his time. I never expected him to offer to drive me.

Then again, I can't really picture him letting me take his truck alone either, now that I think about it.

Hans lets out a sigh, and I chance a glance at him just as he turns out of the driveway and presses down on the gas. "You're not going to pay me."

He doesn't sound excited, but I still relax. If he was going to kick me out, he'd have done it already.

It's not like my parents would be mad if I had to cancel on them, but they would worry. And that worry would turn into phone calls and questions and suggestions that I just don't feel like listening to.

"I am going to pay you," I insist, then keep talking before he can argue. "Would you like me to tell you directions as we go or put their address into your GPS?"

CHAPTER 30
Hans

"Just tell me," I clip out before she can reach for the screen on my dashboard.

I don't actually need her to tell me where to go; I know exactly where her parents live. But if she starts to type the address into my truck GPS, she might see that particular location already labeled as CP. And she's a clever enough girl that she might realize it stands for Cassandra's parents. I sort of doubt that's something she'd be cool with.

Changing the topic from addresses, I add, "You can let me keep the book as payment."

Out of the corner of my eye, I see her crossing her arms. "If I say no?"

I slide her a look. "I'll keep it anyway."

"Hans."

"Cassandra," I mimic her stern tone back like I'm in fucking middle school.

I glance at her again, and she narrows her eyes. "Why do you call me that?"

"It's your name." I play dumb.

"Yeah, but it's my full name. Everyone calls me Cassie."

"Well, then you shouldn't have introduced yourself as Cassandra," I lie.

Her face does that cute scrunching thing she does when she's thinking. "I did?"

I force my focus back on the road.

"You did," I lie again.

"But I never..." She trails off.

"Maybe if you figured out your own name, then your mail would be addressed correctly, and that sex book would've been delivered to the right house."

"Sex book?" Cassandra sputters a laugh. "They are tasteful boudoir photos."

"They're a taste of something," I grumble.

"What was that?" She turns toward me as she asks, causing the skirt of her dress to ride up her thighs.

"What part of St. Paul are we going to?" I try to distract us both.

"It's by the science museum. You ever been?"

I shake my head, trying to imagine a scenario where I take myself to a museum for... Well, for any reason.

And just like that, the little voice I tried to lock in my basement reminds me just how different we are. How different our lives are.

"You totally should," she starts, then spends the next ten minutes telling me all about the exhibits there and how often her parents took her growing up.

Her memories sound so fond, and I can't help but think of my childhood. My parents took us places. I remember loving the zoo. But based on Cassandra's descriptions, I can imagine how much my sister would've loved trying to gross me out in a body parts exhibit.

My sister was always going back and forth between wanting to be a doctor or a veterinarian. She wasn't squeamish about cuts and scrapes. Never shied away from potential gore. Blood and guts weren't my thing.

Until they were.

"That's probably why my parents chose to move near there."

I missed the last part of what Cassandra said, but I make a noise of agreement anyway.

"How long have they lived there?" My voice sounds scratchy, but I'll blame that on my recovering throat and not wistful memories.

The rest of the ride is filled with Cassandra explaining how her parents decided to move to a retirement community. How she went on tours with them, the mishaps of a moving truck with a flat tire, and how her parents' ninety-year-old neighbor, Harold, hits on her every time she's there.

Me and Harold are gonna have a problem.

Cassandra's hands fly up. "Turn here!"

The panic in her actions is unwarranted since I was already lifting my hand to flip on my blinker, but, of course, she didn't notice that. Which is good.

I follow her directions through the large complex of buildings, parking lots, and well-manicured lawns.

Having looked it up, I know this place has everything from regular apartments to full nursing care, so residents can just move buildings as they age.

It's nice. If you're into this sort of thing.

Even with this new talk of *retirement*, I don't really see myself living to the age of ninety. Hell, at this rate, if I hit fifty, I'll be fucking lucky.

Cassandra has me pull into a spot labeled for visitors next to her parents' building.

"Seriously, thank you so much for the ride. I really—"

I turn off the engine.

Cassandra pauses unbuckling herself. "What are you doing?"

She really thought I was just going to drop her off and let her fend for herself to get back home.

She's pretty. But she's a fool.

"I'll wait," I tell her.

"You'll... You'll stay for dinner?" Her tone is a mixture of shock and hope.

"No, I'll wait." I settle back in my seat. "Go eat with your parents, Cassandra."

I should've opened the window before I turned off the truck, but I'll do that after she leaves.

A small choking sound leaves her throat. "You can't just sit in your car."

Heaving out a breath, I turn and face her. "You aren't getting a ride home from some stranger, Butterfly. It's dangerous. Now get out of the truck and go inside. I'll be here."

She mouths the word *butterfly* before shaking her head. "You're coming with me."

"No—"

She cuts me off. "I literally cannot go enjoy myself while you sit out here roasting like a potato in an oven."

"Potato?" I look down at myself. I know my outfit isn't the height of fashion, and I might not be as chiseled as I was in my twenties, but *potato*?

She shoves at my shoulder. "I didn't mean you look like one. I just like food analogies." She fans her face. "Seriously, I'm already baking in here. Let's go."

With that, she unclips her seat belt, opens the door, and slides out of my truck.

Yeah, sure, let's go have dinner with my obsession's fucking parents.

If Karmine could see me now.

I shouldn't be seen with Cassandra in public.

I shift my eyes to the rearview mirror, looking for anyone suspicious.

But I also don't believe anyone is following me. The men after me aren't like that. They aren't going to watch me to learn my patterns. When they find me, when they get eyes on me, they'll come for me. Hard. And then it'll be me or them. Nothing in between.

Cassandra stands on the sidewalk, waiting for me.

Yearning battles with reason as I remember the feeling of waking up with her in my arms.

I open my truck door.

CHAPTER 31
Cassie

I PART MY LIPS AND TRY TO PULL IN A SILENT GULP OF air. I'm going to blame my thudding heart on the heat and the flight of stairs and not on Hans at my side.

Hans, my neighbor, who only started talking to me this weekend. Who pulled my hair and gripped me between my legs with his big hands. Who ate my soup. Who stole my birthday book. Who slept with his body pressed against mine.

His booted feet hardly make a sound on the hallway's industrial carpet beneath us.

I try to sneak a look at him.

I've felt his body, clutched it, but still, seeing him like this is almost... jarring.

He looks so strong with his biceps filling out his short sleeves and his chest muscles stretching the fabric of his T-shirt.

I never really had an opinion on guys with long hair, but I've decided I like it. I like it a lot.

Thinking of his hair, I press my lips together and glance up at it.

He has it pulled back into a low, messy bun like he always does, and I want to pull it free. I want to tug on his hair the way he tugged on mine.

I move my eyes to his face and find him staring back at me.
Caught.

"You're really handsome." I admit the obvious.

His lips part. But he doesn't reply. He just looks stunned. And that makes me feel a little less embarrassed about him catching me looking.

"Ready?" I ask, stopping in front of my parents' unit.

He shakes his head. "Probably not."

I grin at his answer and pull the key for their door out of my bag.

CHAPTER 32
Hans

WHEN CASSANDRA LIFTS THE KEY LIKE SHE'S GOING TO unlock her parents' door, I make an executive decision and reach up, knocking on the door.

She pauses with the key in the air. "But I—"

"I doubt your parents are expecting you to have a guest. I don't really want to surprise them by just walking in." I'm aware of the irony of feeling this way, but I don't care.

Cassandra rolls her pretty eyes at me. "Oh my god. It'll be fine."

Before I can think better of it, I dart my hand up and grip her ponytail.

Her mouth pops open.

"Watch the attitude, Girl." I give the command quietly, but there's no mistaking my tone.

"Or what?" she breathes. "I don't think your punishment worked last time."

"No?" My cock starts to thicken. "I'm sure we can find your limit."

She leans toward me, increasing the pull I have on her hair.

She presses her hands against my chest. "Promise?"

A low growl rumbles behind my ribs. "Cassandra."

She keeps her eyes wide as she looks up at me. "You want to count to three again?"

I lower my face toward hers, then I hear a lock click open.

Releasing her ponytail, I straighten and face the door.

Cassandra is still turned toward me when her mother pulls the door open.

"Oh geez, did you lose your keys again?" Mrs. Cantrell asks her daughter.

I watch my neighbor's flushed cheeks darken further with embarrassment as she shifts to face her mom.

"I didn't lose my keys, thank you very much." I love the sass in her voice. I hope she tries that tone on me soon.

"Then what are you—Holy hell!" Mrs. Cantrell slaps a hand to her chest when she notices me.

"Mom!" Cassandra sounds offended, and it takes all my effort not to laugh out loud.

Her mom runs her eyes up and down my form once before lowering her voice to her daughter. "Are you in trouble?"

Cassandra tips her head back and shakes her head.

"What?" Her mom defends her assumption. "He looks like security."

"Someone called security?" an older male voice says from behind Mrs. Cantrell.

"No, Honey, it's Cassie."

An older man steps up beside his wife, filling the rest of the doorway.

Side by side, you wouldn't mistake these two for anyone except Cassandra's parents. All three of them are the exact same height. And even though Cassandra has the same hair as her mom, she gets her eye color from her dad.

"You in trouble, Cassie?" he asks.

Cassandra puts her hands up. "Oh my god, no one is in trouble."

She's barely finished speaking when her dad steps forward to pull Cassandra into a hug. But her hands are still up, so her arms get stuck between them.

"Hi, Dad," she huffs good naturedly.

"Nice to see—" Just like his wife, Mr. Cantrell reacts with a jolt when he finally notices me. "Oh, Jesus!" He steps back from Cassandra and puts his hand to his chest.

Mrs. Cantrell gently smacks his arm. "That's who I was talking about."

Mr. Cantrell faces me. "Whatever it is, I'm sure she did it."

"Dad!" Cassandra presses her hand against my side, trying to get me to move. "You know what? I think they've finally lost their minds. Let's go back home."

"Home?" her mom gasps. "You're living with him?"

Cassandra stares up at me and whispers, "Help."

"But you're doing such a good job," I whisper back.

The corner of her mouth twitches.

Then the door across the hall swings open.

"Is that my Cassie?" An ancient man steps into the hallway.

"Hey, Harold." Cassandra lifts a hand and waves.

Unlike the Cantrells, Harold notices me immediately. "Well, well, well." He folds his skinny arms across his chest. "You my competition, then?"

I dip my chin.

"You willing to fight for her?" He narrows his eyes, bunching his bushy brows on his forehead.

I make a show of clenching my right hand into a fist. "I've never punched a geriatric, but I'm not strictly against it."

Harold grins widely. "I like you." He leans to the side to look at Cassandra's parents. "I like him."

"We like him too," Mrs. Cantrell replies, pretending they know who I am.

Cassandra snorts, and then something starts to beep inside the apartment.

"Okay, okay, everyone in." Mr. Cantrell steps back from the door and waves us into their apartment. "That's the egg bake."

"I've got it," Mrs. Cantrell calls over her shoulder as she hurries toward the kitchen.

"Alright, kids, take your shoes off, then come eat." Cassandra's dad follows after his wife, and I notice they're wearing matching red slippers.

My body is still a bit sore from the last job, so it takes some work not to groan as I lower down to one knee and start untying my first boot.

Cassandra drops her purse onto the floor, then bends to untie her tennis shoes.

"They seem nice." I can't help myself.

We're nearly eye level like this, so I can perfectly see the expression she gives me as she deadpans, "They seem insane."

"That too." I smirk, then switch so I'm on the other knee.

Cassandra shakes her head, moving to untie the other shoe. But as she does, she turns more of her back to me.

Bent at the waist, the back of her skirt has come up so far I can see the bottom half of her lacy white undies.

"That's *one*, Butterfly."

Cassandra turns her head toward me at my low words and sees where I'm looking.

She snaps to standing, smoothing her skirt down. "Sorry."

My fingers itch to slide up the back of her bare thigh. To feel that lace under my hand. But I can't right now. Because her parents are just feet away.

I stand and leave my boots next to her tennis shoes, the size difference as extreme as our height difference.

Before she can step away from me, I hook a finger in the front of her dress, holding her still. The warmth of her cleavage surges through my body.

"I swear, if you wear this dress out of the house and flash your sweet ass to anyone else like that..."

Cassandra shakes her head. "No. Never."

Her chest rises with a deep inhale, and I have to force myself to step back.

I pull my finger free of her dress just before her dad sticks his head around the end of the short hall and tells us to hurry up.

CHAPTER 33

Cassie

HANS PRESSES HIS PALM TO MY LOWER BACK, MAKING me walk ahead of him.

Every step brings us closer to my parents, and I'm realizing what a massive error it was to let Hans come here with me. They're going to ask so many questions and assume so many things, and it's going to be a disaster.

I slow, causing Hans to apply more pressure to my back.

"What is it, Butterfly?" His voice is low, but it still sends a shiver down my spine.

The nickname is enough to pull my mind away from the edge of stress. "Why do you call me that?"

Hans circles his thumb on my spine. "Ask me later."

I nod. "Okay." Then I square my shoulders and step into my parents' eat-in kitchen.

Before I can try to properly introduce him, my mom cuts in, setting a steaming dish onto the center of the round table. "Hope you like breakfast for dinner. Cassie didn't tell us she was bringing a *friend* with her, otherwise we would've asked for food preferences." She cuts her eyes to me when she says friend. And I accept that it's a freaking miracle she said that rather than just calling him my boyfriend.

"I eat everything." Hans's rough voice fills the room.
I have to stop my eyes from rolling back.
I eat everything.
Jesus take the wheel.
"Good." Mom's face lights up. "Cassie's father is the same way." She smiles over at Dad, who is placing a pitcher of orange juice and a carafe of coffee on the table. "That's how I first caught his attention. With my cookies."
Hans makes a noise that sounds suspiciously like a snort.
"Not true." Dad grins. "It was the way you filled out the seat of your pants."
"Dad!" I shriek.
Mom hits him with her oven mitt. "Oh, stop it."
Dad just shrugs. "Cassie is old enough to know the truth now."
"Now? I'll remind you I'm thirty, but I could've gone the rest of my life without knowing that." I add my age for Hans's benefit. I don't want him thinking I'm too young for him.
"And how old are you, young man?" Dad calmly turns his attention to Hans, like he hadn't jumped the last time he looked at him.
"I'm thirty-nine, sir," Hans answers formally.
My dad nods. "Good age."
Thirty-nine. I memorize the information.
"Name?" Dad prompts.
"Hans," my neighbor responds, holding his hand out.
Dad shakes it.
"Alright, alright. You can grill the boy while we eat." Mom gestures to the table. "Everyone, sit."
I snicker at my mom referring to Hans, the larger-than-life man, as a boy.
The man in question surreptitiously slides his thumb down the back of my arm, and I know it's his way of warning me that he heard my laugh.

S. J. TILLY

Knowing which chairs my parents always sit in, I move to one of the other two and direct Hans to the last chair.

Mom jumps right into dishing food onto everyone's plate, starting with Hans.

When she's done, everyone has a square of cheesy sausage egg bake, two slices of crispy bacon, and wedges of salted heirloom tomatoes.

"Dig in," Dad commands, already shoving a forkful into his mouth.

Hans stays silent as he takes one bite, then a second and third.

I don't know if he's feeling uncomfortable about the situation, but it's not stopping his appetite.

Hans pauses and looks up from his plate, tomato speared on the end of his fork halted halfway to his mouth. "This is delicious," he tells my mom before looking at me. "Take it this is where you get your love of cooking from?"

Warmth floods my chest as I nod. "Mom had me helping her before I could even reach the counter. I had to stand on a box."

"It was a wooden crate." Mom corrects me before she smiles at Hans. "So, our Cassie has cooked for you? Did you know she has her own food blog?"

I try widening my eyes while she's talking to get her to stop, but she doesn't take the hint.

"It's just for fun," I tell her and Hans, referring to my blog that practically no one follows.

"You do such a good job at it," Mom insists.

I'm trying not to grimace when I look over at Hans, hoping he's not holding back a laugh at the idea of me with a blog. But when I meet his gaze, he's looking at me seriously.

"I'd like you to show me."

I swallow. "Okay."

Why is that so sweet and so dirty sounding?

"Where did you two meet?" Dad interrupts my dirty thoughts.

108

"Um, well, Hans is actually my neighbor." I don't know why that fact makes my cheeks flame red, but it does.

"Oh, really?" Mom picks up her mug, and I can see her trying to remember what the houses near me look like. "You buy the one at the end of the street?" she asks Hans, referring to the unoccupied house.

"I'm in the house directly across from Cassandra's." Hans uses my full name, as he always does, and I don't miss when Mom widens her eyes.

But Dad just nods. "Makes sense."

Wait, what?

"What do you mean?" I ask.

Dad lifts his brows. "Well, you work from home and don't ever go out to actually meet people, so someone falling into your lap was really the only way this was ever going to happen."

I groan. "Thanks a lot. But there isn't anything *to* happen. We aren't dating or anything." My stupid blush is back. "It's just that my car wouldn't start, and when I asked Hans if I could borrow his truck, he offered to drive me."

Dad smirks. "I wouldn't let you drive my truck either."

"So—" I talk over the old man. "I invited him to come up for a meal as a thank-you. Please don't turn it into torture."

"What's wrong with your car?" Mom jumps back into the conversation.

I shrug. "Who knows. I'll get it figured out. I just didn't have time to do it today without canceling on dinner."

"How are you going to get to the airport tomorrow?"

At her question, I can feel Hans turn his attention to me.

"I'll figure it out." I don't know why I bother lowering my voice, everyone is obviously listening.

"I'm sure Hans wouldn't mind driving you," Dad helpfully chimes in.

"No, that's not—"

"I'll drive you." Hans cuts me off.

I lift my eyes to his. "You don't—"

He cuts me off again. "I'll drive you."

The hard look in his gaze tells me it would be a mistake to argue. "Okay," I whisper.

Mom clears her throat. "You all packed?"

I shake my head. "Not yet."

"Where are you going?" Hans hasn't turned his attention away from me.

"Um, Mexico." I try to smile. "It's for work."

"Where in Mexico?" Hans's tone has gone hard, like maybe he already knows the answer.

CHAPTER 34

Hans

WHEN SHE SAYS THE NAME OF THE CITY, I NEARLY DRAG her over my knee.

I'm no stranger to the country. It's beautiful. The people are kind. The food is some of my favorite on earth. But that city, that particular city, has been labeled the most dangerous city in the world the last three years running. Specifically for cartel violence and kidnapping for ransom. That city is not somewhere I want my Butterfly going. Ever. And definitely not without me.

But those facts aren't something the average person would know. And if it wasn't for my *fascination* with my beautiful neighbor, I wouldn't know it either. But when I did my *research* on Cassandra, I did my research on the company she works for too. They have branches all over the world, but their biggest and newest manufacturing facility is in this particular city.

As someone who works in human resources, I didn't think there would be any threat of her having to go there. That's for product development people, maybe the salespeople for training.

But apparently, I need to up my game. Tap her phone. Hack her emails.

If I'd known about this more than a day in advance, I could've found a way to make sure she couldn't go. But now...

"And where do you work, Hans?" Mrs. Cantrell asks.

Since I'm still staring at Cassandra's profile, I watch her slowly turn to face me. She's clearly curious about my answer but can't really admit she doesn't know.

In all fairness, I've never asked her about her job either. I just know the answer because... well, because.

"I'm a health inspector." The lie is one I've had ready for years.

I don't have to use it often since I don't interact much with people outside my real profession, but I know more than enough about the inspector world to answer any question Mrs. Cantrell, or anyone else, might ask.

"Bet you go to some interesting places," Mr. Cantrell says around a bite of bacon. "Explains the clothes."

"Dad, there's nothing wrong with his clothes," Cassandra argues.

I feel a spark of warmth at Cassandra defending me.

Mr. Cantrell shoves the last bite into his mouth, holding his hands up. "I didn't say there was. But a getup like that usually means military or construction. Health inspector isn't exactly construction, but being in kitchens and basements and wherever else, you probably need durable clothes that clean easily."

I lift a brow. He was paying closer attention than I figured. "You military?"

"Army communications. Served right out of high school, retired around your age so the wife and I could move back here and start a family." His expression is nothing but soft as he looks at his daughter.

I'm not intimidated by a man in his seventies who used to serve in the army, but I am aware that I shouldn't underestimate his observational abilities.

"Our little miracle baby." Mrs. Cantrell smiles at Cassandra.

"Yeah, yeah." My neighbor shakes her head. She reaches for the metal spatula and gestures toward my plate. "Would you like another slice?"

I look down and see I've finished every bite.

I believe Cassandra learned her love for food from her mom. But, and I'll take this to my grave, her mother's food is delicious rather than barely edible, so I nod.

A large slice of egg bake is set on my plate, and I waste no time digging in.

"How about your family?" Mrs. Cantrell asks. "Do your folks live around here?"

A twist of pain catches me off guard before I answer truthfully. "They passed away. A long time ago."

Cassandra's indrawn breath does something to settle that bit of pain.

"I'm so sorry to hear that." Mrs. Cantrell's voice is full of compassion.

I dip my chin, wanting to look at Cassandra but not quite daring to. I know she has big feelings. And her one inhale is enough to tell me that she's going to have a look on her face that will make me want to drag her into a hug. Right here. At the table with her parents.

So long as they don't ask me—

"Any siblings?" Mrs. Cantrell asks the only question I don't want to answer.

It would be so easy to lie.

I should lie.

"I had a sister. We lost her a long time ago too." I set my fork down, needing a moment of stillness.

Cassandra tries to muffle a whimper at my side.

Mrs. Cantrell hovers her fingertips over her mouth. "Were they all in an accident?"

I almost smile. How different my life would be if it had been as simple as that.

"Mom," Cassandra hisses.

"No accident." I'm in it now. And a part of me feels like I owe it to my family to be honest right now. "My parents died of pneumonia."

"Oh Lord," Mrs. Cantrell lowers her hand to press over her heart. "At the same time?"

"Oh my god, Mom! You can't ask that."

I reach over and set my hand on top of Cassandra's, where it sits on the table between our plates. "It's alright." I finally meet my neighbor's eyes, and they're as full of emotion as I knew they would be. "It was twenty years ago." I turn back toward her mom. "A week apart."

Cassandra's hand tenses under mine, so I flex my fingers around hers.

Mrs. Cantrell wipes at her cheek. "Oh, Hans. I'm so sorry. I shouldn't have asked."

Before I can tell her it's okay, and before Cassandra can remind her that she said not to ask, Mr. Cantrell leans forward.

"What happened to your sister?"

"Dad!" Cassandra slaps her free hand down on the other side of her plate.

When I meet the older man's eyes, I have a gnawing suspicion that he wasn't just communications.

"She was murdered." The words drag against my throat on their way out.

What I don't say is that we found her body two months before my parents gave up on living. And how, for four long weeks before that, we hadn't known where she was. Hadn't been able to find her or the people who stole her.

Both women at the table make sounds of distress.

I turn to Cassandra. "It's okay."

She's shaking her head, and I watch one tear, then another, drip off her lashes. "It's not okay." She looks at her dad, vibrating with those big feelings. "You can't just ask people stuff like that."

"I'm fine." I tell her the lie.

She stares up at me, not hearing. "I'm so sorry, Hans. We shouldn't have—"

"Cassandra." My tone is stern, finally stopping her flurry of words. "It's okay."

I watch her lower lip tremble.

"I'm okay." That's closer to the truth.

Cassandra sniffs, and another tear rolls down her cheek, then she pushes her chair back and stands. "We'll just be a minute," she tells her parents, then grabs my hand and pulls me the way we came, around the corner and down the short hall to the front door.

"You don't need to—" But she stops me by throwing her arms around my waist, holding me tightly.

My body stiffens. All my muscles still, with my arms held out wide.

Then I feel her chest hitch against mine, and I let old instincts take over. I hug her back.

With my arms wrapped around her, I lower my face to the top of her head and breathe.

Her feminine scent fills my lungs.

"I'm okay." I whisper it this time.

Because I'm starting to realize that I'm really not. The loss of my family two decades ago is still raw. Even my memories...

I can't think about any of them without thinking about their deaths. How they died. How I couldn't... didn't save any of them.

I close my eyes and hold Cassandra tighter.

The last hug I received was from my father. The night before he let the illness take him.

It wasn't an embrace like this.

It was frail. Shaky.

And it ended with him pointing to a carved wooden box at the side of his bed.

A dying man's wish.

"I'm so sorry." Cassandra's voice is a mumble against my chest.

I inhale her compassion, letting it trickle into the empty corners inside me. I rub my hand up and down her side. "Thank you."

She shakes her head against me, and her back hitches against my hold. "I should've stopped them."

I wrap my arms tighter around her. "Hush, Butterfly." I press my lips to her hair. "Please stop crying."

She sniffs.

"Want me to tell you why I call you that?" I ask her.

Cassandra nods.

"Because you remind me of one. Beautiful. Mesmerizing. Too fragile for this awful world." I slide one hand up to palm the back of her neck. "A pretty little butterfly I can't help but want to protect."

She sniffs again, then leans back just enough so she can look up at me. "Is that really why?"

I nod. I thought it the first time I saw her.

"That's really nice." Her wet lashes glitter. "I'm not fragile though."

I swipe my thumb across her cheek, catching a tear. "You're like spun glass."

The side of her mouth pulls up. She thinks I'm teasing her, but I'm not. She's the most precious thing to me.

Cassandra brushes at my shirt. "Sorry for crying all over you."

"It's alright."

Her hand stills against my chest. "I always wanted a sister."

I place my hand over hers. Not sure how to answer.

"What was her name?"

I close my eyes.

It's been so long... It's been so incredibly long since I've said her name.

"Freya." I say it so quietly that I can barely hear the hitch in my voice.

My throat burns, and I have to swallow twice before I can pull in another breath of air.

Cassandra tips her forehead against my sternum, and I'm sure she can hear my thudding heart.

116

"Freya," she repeats. "It's a pretty name."

I nod my agreement, even though Cassandra isn't looking up at me. Hearing someone else say my sister's name is... I fill my lungs again. It's cathartic. It... it makes her real, having someone else say it. Like not every part of her is gone.

CHAPTER 35

Cassie

A TIMER BEEPS BACK IN THE KITCHEN, AND I FORCE myself to step back from Hans.

"Sorry." I apologize again, brushing my hand over the damp spot on his T-shirt, which is thankfully not super noticeable on the black material.

"Please stop apologizing." Hans lets his hands slide away from my body.

"Sorry," I automatically reply before I can catch myself. Then I use my fingertips to wipe away the lingering tears under my eyes.

I don't know why I responded like that. It feels like an overreaction, but I'm not certain it was. The man I've been crushing on for a year, who I've been getting very close to in the last couple days, just told me his whole family is gone. And that he lost his only sibling in one of the worst ways.

His overbearing actions make more sense now. His impulse to control.

Too fragile for this awful world.

My heart aches even more at his explanation.

Hans reaches out and brushes back a loose curl stuck to my damp cheek.

"It suddenly smells like cinnamon rolls in here." His voice is gentle, and when I finally look up at him, his expression matches.

I sniff one last time. "Mom always makes them as dessert when we do breakfast for dinner."

He gives that loose strand of hair a gentle tug. "Probably could've told me that before you fed me a whole second serving."

I brush at my eyes again. "Maybe I wanted more cinnamon rolls for myself."

Hans narrows his eyes at me, and I feel the sadness start to dissolve around us.

He steps forward, bumping his body into mine. "Get back to your chair, Girl."

A genuine smile pulls at my mouth. "Or what?"

When Hans reaches for me, I jump back and hurry to the kitchen.

CHAPTER 36

Hans

CASSANDRA AND HER MOM ARE STILL SAYING THEIR goodbyes when I finish lacing up my second boot, her mom giving advice on what to pack in her carry-on just in case her main luggage gets lost on the way to Mexico tomorrow.

After our little sidebar in the hallway, the rest of the evening was filled with light topics and a surprisingly fun game of Scrabble, which I won.

Cassandra accused me of cheating, but when I won the second game, too, she settled for giving me adorably fake dirty looks.

Scrabble. With my sexy neighbor and her parents. What has my life become?

I brush off my knees as I stand to my full height and find Cassandra's dad watching me.

I can tell that he wants to ask me something.

He glances at the women, then steps closer to me, keeping his voice low. "Did they catch the people who hurt your sister?"

His jaw is tense, and I can see it in his eyes... the dread that I'm sure every parent holds deep in their chest. The worry of what *could* happen.

I think of the men responsible.

Bent limbs. Slit throats. Entrails trailing across the floor.

I hold his gaze and answer with the truth. "They got what they deserved."

He nods once. "Good." Then he looks over at his beautiful daughter. "Keep an eye on her, yeah?"

I suppress the inappropriate urge to smile but once again answer with the truth. "I do."

Giving her mom one last hug, Cassandra turns to me. "You finally ready to go?" She laughs at her joke as I pull the door open and usher her out into the hall.

Her steps are bouncy, which is her normal way of walking, so when she bumps into my side for the second time, she doesn't notice my hand sliding into her bag.

And as she uses her hands to tell me about the time her mom's suitcase burst open on a baggage carousel, she's too animated to notice my attention is pulled down low and off to my side.

While she finishes her story, I download my location tracking software onto her phone.

As we exit the building, I place my hand on her back, and she sways into me, just like I knew she would.

The sky is right on the edge of darkness, so when I reach across my body and slip the phone back into her bag between us, the colorful case is hardly visible.

CHAPTER 37

Cassie

"So..." I drum my fingers on my knees as the highway hums below us. "Do you have a girlfriend?"

It's dark inside the truck, but when I glance at Hans's profile, I can see his brows rise.

"What part of me having my hand on your hot little pussy makes you think I could have a girlfriend?" His tone is dry.

My face flames at his choice of words, and I shift in my seat.

But if he's going to be direct, then I will too. "Well, it was probably the part when you got a bunch of text messages, dropped me over the back of the couch, and rushed out of my house."

He waits a beat. "Oh."

I press my hands between my thighs. "Was it a woman texting you?"

"Yes."

His answer spears through my chest, and I regret asking.

"Now ask me if it was personal or for work." The tone of his voice tells me the answer, and that spear evaporates.

"Oh." I repeat his response from earlier. "Is the woman your boss?"

Hans huffs out a breath. "Feels like it sometimes."

We slow, and Hans takes the exit to our little town.

I want to ask if health inspectors usually get called out to job sites on a Friday night, but a different question comes out of my mouth. "Have you slept with her?"

His head jerks in my direction like he can't believe I asked that. "No."

I roll my lips together. "You're sure?"

"I tend to remember who I've slept with. Our relationship is strictly professional."

The sound of the blinker is loud inside the truck as we make our way closer to our neighborhood.

It only takes another minute before I break the silence. "Sorry. I didn't mean to pry. It's none of my business."

I mean, it kind of is my business if he has a girlfriend because I don't want to be the other woman. But I believe him.

Hans doesn't say anything at first, but I hear the steering wheel creak under his grip. "Have you slept with any of the men going to Mexico?"

"My coworkers?" My face pulls into a disgusted expression, and I see Hans glance over to catch it. "No."

"You sure?"

He's trying to be a pest, so I drop my voice and do my best impression of him. "Watch the attitude, Grizzly Bear." I can hardly hold in my laugh at the look on Hans's face. "So you can dish it out but you can't take it?"

He shakes his head while he turns onto our street. "Grizzly Bear?"

"You started the whole animal thing." I shrug. "And if you're gonna prowl around all gruff and angry..."

"Gruff and angry," he repeats slowly.

"Like a bear," I confirm. "But then I guess when you're being all sweet and stuff, you'd be more of a teddy bear."

Hans slows to a near stop as we reach the spot where our driveways meet the road. I almost think he's going to pull into my driveway first to drop me off, but then he turns down his.

Okay, so no front door service.

He presses a button on the dashboard, and the garage door ahead of us starts to open, but he parks the truck in the driveway rather than pulling into the garage.

I unbuckle my seat belt as Hans turns off the engine. "Thank you again for the ride. And for putting up with my parents." Hans turns toward me but doesn't say anything. "If you're serious about bringing me to the airport tomorrow, I need to leave at like five thirty." My smile falters. I hate getting up early. "But if you don't want to, that's okay. I can totally figure it out."

"Cassandra," he says in that grizzly tone.

"Okay, okay." I lift my hands. "You'll drive me."

Neither confirming nor denying, Hans opens his car door and starts to climb out.

Alrighty then.

Jokes on him when I start ringing his doorbell at five in the morning to make sure he's up.

I turn to my door and reach for the handle.

Then I shriek as large hands grip me under my armpits and haul me backward across the long bench seat.

"Hans!"

He stops when my butt is right on the edge of the seat and my legs are stretched out straight in front of me.

"That's two," he says against my ear.

My breaths are coming fast now.

Hans slides his hands down my sides, then around to my stomach, hugging me with my back against his front.

"When are you gonna learn that there are consequences for being a brat?" His voice on my neck causes my skin to prickle.

"Hopefully right now."

Teeth graze my ear, then Hans drags me the rest of the way out of the truck.

My heels automatically dig into the seat, trying to stop my fall. But I don't fall. Because Hans is holding me.

My legs drop down in front of me, but I'm too high up for my shoes to reach the ground.

Excitement flares inside me.

This is that gruffness I was referring to. I just didn't tell him how much I love it.

"That's three, Cassandra." Keeping me plastered to his front, Hans walks us toward his garage.

And then I feel it.

The hard length pressing into my ass as I bump against him with every step.

I can't stop my groan or the way I grip his forearms.

In response, Hans holds me even tighter.

We step over the threshold into the garage, and the darkness consumes me. I hadn't noticed that there's no overhead light on. No glow of anything.

The night sky didn't feel that dark while we were driving, but there's nothing to help relieve the black before my eyes.

"All fucking night," Hans grits out. "Teasing me with this fucking dress."

Instead of turning toward the entrance to the house, he keeps going straight back.

"Flashing me those goddamn white panties."

He shifts his hips as he steps, pushing his dick harder against me.

"Think you can have those tits in my face all night and I'll just ignore it."

"I-I didn't mean to." Arousal and delicious panic swirl inside me.

It's so dark. I can't see anything.

The laugh Hans lets out isn't amused.

I stretch my hands out. "Hans."

We have to be close to reaching the back wall.

One arm lets go of my waist. I open my eyes wider, trying to see, but the next thing I feel is that arm pressing down on the top of my own.

Hans clamps his arm around my chest, trapping my arms down so I can't reach out. So I won't be able to stop us before we run into the back wall.

"Wait!"

"Trust me," he rumbles.

I don't fight his hold. And he takes another two steps. Then he stops. And the arms around me release.

Another shriek leaves my lips as I drop. But his large body is still behind me, and I only fall a few inches before my tennis shoes land on some sort of rubber mat rather than the hard concrete floor.

I shift to turn around to face Hans, but when I try to twist, my hip bumps into something.

In the complete dark, Hans stopped us just inches away.

"I told you to trust me." He grips my wrists and forcefully sets my hands on the surface in front of me. "I won't tell you again."

It's some sort of counter. It's a little higher than a normal kitchen counter, and it's made of smooth, cold metal.

"Don't move."

"Don't—" Before I can ask, the heat at my back disappears as Hans steps away.

But he doesn't go far.

Hands tug my dress up, twisting it into some sort of knot at my lower back, exposing my lower half.

I have one second to hold my breath before a palm lands against my bared flesh.

"Ah!" My body jolts, and my hands move, gripping the edge of the counter.

The hand is still there, rubbing a circle over the lacy material that half covers my butt cheek. Where he just slapped my ass.

It feels nice. Soothing the sting. It feels—

I yelp again as his other hand smacks down on the other side.

"I should make this pretty ass so sore you won't be able to sit still on that plane tomorrow." His first palm slaps back down again. "Should make it so you think of me every time you sit for the entire week."

This is the first time I've been spanked. The first time anyone has tried anything even close.

And, god help me, I love it.

I arch back against him and moan his name.

"My dirty little Butterfly." His fingers grip my ass, squeezing.

I reach back, trying to grab his arms. Trying to grab some part of him. Needing to touch him too.

Hans pushes his body forward, pinning me firmly between him and the bench. "I told you not to move."

Before I can put my hands back, he's grabbing them.

"Such a naughty girl." His chest rises and falls behind mine, showing he's not unaffected. Then he steps back again, only this time he pulls my hands back so they meet at my spine. "If you can't hold still on your own, I'll help you."

Sweet Jesus, this is new too.

I pull against his hold. Not to break free, but to see how much force he'll use.

His grip tightens. "Stop struggling and spread your legs."

My knees are ready to give out, but I do what he says.

His grip shifts so he's holding my hands with just one of his.

"Good girl." Lips press against the side of my neck just as his free hand reaches around the front of my body to cup my sex.

My body tenses, then melts.

His fingers press and rub against the lace while his groan reverberates through my body.

"Fuck, Butterfly. You've soaked through your pristine little panties. I should probably take them off."

"Oh my god." My arms strain against his hold. "Hans. Please."

"Since you asked so nicely." He drags his fingers away from my core.

The heat of his body leaves my back, but I'm so flushed I don't even feel the cooling night air anymore.

"Don't move." The hand holding my wrists behind my back flexes. "I expect you to listen this time, Girl."

I nod in the dark.

Then he lets go of my wrists and slips his fingers under the top band of my underwear at my hips.

I sway, but I twine my fingers together, keeping my arms where he left them.

"That's my girl."

Hans drags my panties down, one inch at a time.

The lace scrapes over my skin, stretching as the elastic pulls over the widest part of my hips. Then down more. Peeling away from the dampness between my legs. And lower.

Hot breath brushes over my damp skin, and I realize he's crouched down behind me.

I blink, but all I can see is black.

Hans stops when my underwear is at my knees, the wide stance he requested stopping him from taking them all the way off.

He slides his hands up the outside of my legs, the roughed skin feeling so decadent against my soft thighs.

"Fucking perfect." He palms my ass again, only this time his face is level with it, and I'm suddenly very grateful for the dark.

But then his fingers dig into my flesh, getting a good grip, and he spreads me.

There.

"Wh-what are you doing?" I gasp even as I feel his exhale on my most private parts.

"A bear's gotta eat," he growls.

My mouth opens, but the breath gets stuck in my lungs when I feel Hans press his face into me.

I don't have time to process what's happening before his tongue flattens against my entrance from behind.

He's spreading me farther, lapping at me, feasting on me.

My hands release their hold of each other, and I reach forward, gripping the edge of the countertop. "Oh, fuck."

Hans makes a noise, but I can't focus on it. I can't focus on anything. Because he's dragging his tongue up, between my...

"Oh, fuck," I pant again, arching my back, shoving my ass farther into his face as he licks up and over... *oh my god.*

Hans pulls back, his hands and mouth leaving me at the same time, and I can't stop my whimper.

"If you're not gonna behave..." A metallic sound follows his words.

There's a tug at the material around my knees, then it drops away completely.

Did he just cut my panties off?

"Hands." It's a one-word command, and based on his voice, I can tell he's still lowered behind me.

I don't know what he has planned, but right now, I'd do anything to have him finish what he started, so I straighten up and put my hands behind my back.

Lacy fabric twists around one wrist, then the other, tying them together.

My hot neighbor just cut my underwear off and is using it like a rope to tie me up.

"That's better," Hans sighs. Then he smacks my ass again.

I jolt, shuffling forward an inch, until my hips are pressed to the cabinets in front of me.

His hand soothes the sting, and I let the counter hold me up.

Without warning, Hans spreads my cheeks again and...

A cry of surprise escapes my throat.

He's... oh Jesus, he's licking my... my...

"Such a pretty little asshole." Hans pulls back just enough to say the words, then his tongue rubs against my rear entrance again.

Hands trapped behind me, I lean my weight forward.

My legs are starting to shake.

He's still...

Fuck me, why does this feel so good?

My breaths are coming hard.

S. J. TILLY

Still spreading me open, he slides his thumbs down until they're on either side of my slit, and I can feel them slide through my slickness.

"My dirty Butterfly." Another lick. "Getting so wet when I lick this little hole." Another pass of his tongue. "Bet you'll get soaked when I fuck it."

"Ohmygod." My hands twist against the lace.

I never thought...

I've never even...

"Hans." My cry echoes around the empty garage.

One hand shifts, and his thumb pushes inside my core.

We both moan as my pussy clenches around him.

He's not touching my clit. His licks never reach that far forward. But I'm seconds away from coming as his tongue works in circles.

I clench around his thumb again. "Hans, please."

He pulls his thumb out of me and slides it up to where his mouth is.

"Please what, Cassandra?" His thumb presses against the ring of muscle. "What are you begging me for?"

Hans applies more pressure, and the tip of his thumb pushes inside me. Where nothing ever has before.

I groan.

"Relax," he commands.

And I try. With my body throbbing, I try.

Behind me is the sound of movement, and I can feel him stand back up.

The change in position twists his thumb, and I tense.

"Relax that sweet ass." His free hand cracks down against my cheek.

I startle, but then I do as he says. And he slides his thumb in another half inch.

"Please," I beg again.

The sound of his zipper is so loud in the empty room, it's like I can feel it on my skin.

"Use your words, Butterfly. Tell me what you need."

I feel dizzy.

I'm so ready to explode.

"Inside me." I feel like I'm going to choke on the words. "I need you inside me."

His thumb pulls out, then pushes back in. "I already have a finger buried in your ass." He pushes it deeper still, and dots of light start to spark in my vision. "What else do you want?"

Embarrassment tries to overcome my lust, but I tell him. I tell him what I need more than I need my next breath. "I need your cock, Hans. Please."

His body moves closer to mine, and I feel his jean-clad legs against the back of my bare ones.

"Where do you want it? Here?" He jiggles his thumb in my ass, and my clit starts to throb. "Or here?" Something warm and hard slaps up against my core.

I nod my head.

"Words." He slaps his dick against my pussy a second time.

"There." I'm almost sobbing now. "Put it in me there."

He rubs the head of his cock up and down my slit once, my dripping arousal coating him instantly.

Then he starts to push in.

He's so thick. So much to take.

My shoulders hunch forward, and I focus on breathing.

Hans holds still, with just the tip inside me, as he still rocks his thumb in and out of my ass.

I can't...

It's too much.

I'm stretched everywhere.

I can't take it.

"So tight," Hans grunts.

Then he thrusts forward, sinking every inch of his cock inside me.

CHAPTER 38
Hans

THE CRY THAT CASSANDRA LETS OUT MIGHT BE A scream, but I can hardly hear her over the rushing of my blood.

Her pussy is so fucking wet. So fucking tight.

I can't stop. I can't slow down.

I don't want to.

Pressing my fingers into her flesh, I bury my thumb as deep as it will go in her snug asshole and slam my hips into her.

Wet slapping sounds fill the space around us, and I wish the overhead lights were on so I could see every fucking jiggle.

She's making so many sounds.

Moans and whimpers and unintelligible words.

But I'm too far gone.

"That's it." I pull out and shove back in. "That's my good girl."

She whines. And then I fuck her with my thumb. Pushing it in and out of her little hole with the same speed as my dick.

"Hans. Hans." She's panting my name.

And goddamn, I wish I had an audio recorder in here. I want to hear her like this every night.

I want to own her.

I want to consume her in every way.

I thrust my hips forward as far as they'll go, then press even harder, burying my thumb to the final knuckle.

I need every hole.

With my free hand, I reach up and slide my fingers up her throat, over her chin, and press my first two fingers into her open mouth.

Cassandra seals her lips around my fingers. And something clicks inside me.

She is mine.

I fight against the tightness in my balls. Fight the need to fill her with every drop of my seed.

Not yet.

Her tongue swirls around my fingers.

I drag my hips back, pull my thumb halfway out, slide my fingers from her mouth, then push in. Everywhere.

Heat. Pure heat fills me.

Cassandra's pussy starts to flutter around my length. And I know she's almost there.

I press my forehead to her shoulder. "You ready to come, Butterfly?"

She nods and moans around my fingers.

I drag my hand away from her mouth.

"Tell me," I demand.

"Yes," she cries. "I'm so—"

I slap my hand down against her ass one last time. And when her body clenches in response, I shove as deep as I can, my cock skewering her insides.

And instead of soothing the smack, I reach around and pinch her clit.

The reaction is immediate.

Her hands, trapped between our bodies, claw at my stomach.

Her pussy convulses.

Her ass squeezes my thumb.

And she comes.

She comes so fucking hard I have no choice but to follow her over the edge, my release pumping out of my cock and filling her channel.

Grunting, I pull my hips back, then shove them forward, jiggling my thumb and rolling her clit between my fingers with the other hand, dragging her orgasm out to match mine.

"Hans. Oh. Fuck." Cassandra's little cries are the sweetest thing I've ever heard.

When her knees start to wobble, I slowly slide my thumb free, then wrap my arm around her waist. And when her body gives a violent twitch, I slide my hand up from her pussy to her soft belly and help hold her upright.

I press my open mouth to the side of her neck. "Fuck."

She lets out a sound between a choke and a laugh, making her pussy clench around my dick one last time, drawing the last drops out of me.

"That..." Cassandra shakes her head. "That was amazing."

My lips pull into a smile against her skin. "I knew you would be."

"Did you?" Her chest is still heaving, like mine.

"From the first time I saw you." I admit the truth before I can think better of it.

Her hips wiggle against me. "I thought the same thing."

Her response shouldn't feel like such a surprise, given how readily she's melted under my touch.

The thought that we could've been fucking like this for the past year flashes through my mind. But behind it comes the flashes of all the reasons we shouldn't have done even this. Same reasons why I shouldn't have gone to her parents' place. Or banged on her door when I found that book in the mail.

But standing here, cock still buried in Cassandra's sweet heat, I can't find it in me to regret any of it.

Because she is mine.

CHAPTER 39
Cassie

Hans presses his lips to my neck in a soft kiss, then he pulls back, unwrapping his arms from my waist and letting his length slip out from inside me.

I'm still too unsteady to do more than lean against the tool chest. But when I feel his release dripping out of me, I shuffle my legs together.

That was... probably a bad idea. But since I have long-term birth control taken care of, in the form of an implant in my arm, it's only a bad idea for every medical reason other than having a baby.

Hands tug at the destroyed underwear tied around my wrists, and a moment later, the fabric slides away.

Freed, I bring my hands in front of me, bracing myself so I can stand straighter while I catch the rest of my breath.

He slides one of his hands along my hip, like he's helping hold me in place, then with the other, still gripping the ruined panties, he startles me as he reaches between my legs, dragging against my pussy in one swipe, wiping away some of the mess.

I let out a sound of surprise, but Hans just makes a shushing sound.

Awkwardness tries to creep in around me, but I'm still too blissed out to worry too much about it yet.

Hans undoes whatever he did to tie up my dress so the skirt falls back down, covering me up.

Carefully, testing out the soreness between my legs and a foreign soreness in my rear, I turn to face Hans.

It's still too dark, but with the garage door open behind him, I can make out his outline against the slightly brighter night outside.

His hands gently close around my wrists, where they were tied, and I wonder if bears can see in the dark.

His fingers brush over my tender skin.

"Did I tie it too tight?" His tone is full of concern, and it's such a contrast from the man who just filled me so full a few moments ago.

I have to wet my lips to reply. "No, it's... I liked it."

He makes a sound low in his chest, and the whole of what just happened finally sinks in.

My mouth pulls into a smile.

I can't believe I just had sex with my hot neighbor... In his garage.

"Good thing no one else lives on this street," I joke, wondering how loud I was and how far sound travels.

Hans's silhouette turns to look out the garage. "We'll close the door next time."

Next time.

CHAPTER 40
Hans

NEXT TIME.

No matter how stupid or dangerous it is, I know there will be a next time. I won't be able to stop myself.

I slowly release her hands. "Get some sleep, Butterfly. We have an early morning."

She takes one tentative step, then another.

My chest fills with something hot as I watch her uneven gait as she makes her way to the mouth of the garage.

Cassandra stops and looks back through the dark at me. "Night, Grizzly Bear."

Not able to stop myself, I let out a low growl.

Her mouth breaks into the widest smile, and it hits me right in the heart.

Then she hurries away, with a quick stop at my truck to snag her purse.

CHAPTER 41

STEPPING THROUGH MY FRONT DOOR, I GLANCE UP AT
the sun-shaped clock hanging on the wall above my little worksta-
tion and sigh. I should've packed before I left for dinner, but I'm a
procrastinator at heart, so it's no surprise I didn't. So now I need
to pack before I drop onto my bed and relive everything that just
happened.

As I climb the stairs, my muscles twinge.

It's been a bit since I've slept with anyone, but I have. I'm not
a virgin. But that—I try my best to clench my pelvic floor muscles
as I hurry up the last few steps—was the hottest thing I've ever
experienced.

Turning, I head straight into my bathroom.

The shower turns on with a hiss of water, and I let it warm up
while I strip off what remains of my clothing.

I glance out the bathroom door, toward my bedroom, toward
the windows that look out over Hans's house.

Is he showering me off his body right now? Or is he already in
that comfortable bed of his, falling asleep?

CHAPTER 42
Hans

THE SENSOR READS MY PALM, AND THE DOOR TO MY safe room unlocks.

I ignore the monitors, step past the wall of firearms, and pull open the closet at the back of the room.

It takes me a second to find it, but the spoof laptop is where I left it. Slender ceramic knives exactly where I left them, hidden within.

If shit gets loud, I'll be able to get a gun off someone. But I like having my own weapons at the ready.

CHAPTER 43

Cassie

ONE PEEK OUT MY FRONT WINDOW SHOWS MY neighbor's house already alight with life.

When my alarm went off at four, the only thing that kept me from snoozing through it was the fact that I'd be starting my day with Hans.

Hoisting my work-branded backpack onto my shoulders, I look around the living room. "Okay, bye! I'll be back on Friday," I tell my house, then flip off the light and open my front door.

And then I scream because a man is standing on my front step.

"Who were you talking to?" Hans's deep voice is loud in the early morning quiet. But to be fair, my shriek was probably louder.

I press both hands over my heart. "What the hell, Hans?"

He takes a step closer.

I'm still blocking the doorway, but he looks over my head into my house. "Who were you talking to, Cassandra?"

"What—" I realize he must've heard me saying goodbye.

I don't really want to answer him, but I think I'm starting to know Hans well enough to know he's not going to just *let it go*.

Hands still over my heart, I admit, "I was talking to my house."

He tips his head down so he can look into my eyes. "Pardon?"

I press my lips together.

"Your house." He proves he heard me by slowly repeating what I said.

"Yeah." I drop my hands. "It's not that weird."

"Sure it isn't." Hans leans in farther.

For a split second, I think he's going to kiss me, and I start to close my eyes, but then he leans past me and picks up my suitcase.

I try to hide my embarrassed disappointment.

I wasn't totally sure what last night meant for us, *but apparently it doesn't mean that we're people who kiss when they see each other.*

Hans raises a brow as he lifts the suitcase, noticing how heavy it is. And that's fair. I definitely maxed out the weight limit.

"Alright." I move out onto the front step and pull my front door shut, locking it behind me. "I'm ready."

My suitcase has wheels on the bottom and a handle that telescopes out the top to make it easy to drag around. But Hans doesn't use either of those features. He just carries it by the top handle, all the way down my driveway, across the road, and up to his truck.

He makes it look easy. Whereas I'm already starting to sweat just from carrying my backpack. Which is also filled to the max.

I'm an over packer. It's just who I am.

Hans's truck is still parked in his driveway, and he stops at the rear passenger door, opening it.

The back seat is small, a bench style, like up front, with a small amount of leg room.

After setting my suitcase on the seat, he turns and holds out his hand for my backpack.

I slip it off one shoulder, and before I can get it down the second, Hans grabs the strap and lifts it off me.

This feels so... intimate. Which is weird considering—I glance at his closed garage door—what we did last night.

But now, with the sun breaking over the horizon, surrounding us with light instead of total darkness, this feels very relationship-y.

"Up." Hans's voice snaps me out of my daze, and I find he's already opened my door for me.

As Hans drives us out of the neighborhood, my anxiety about traveling starts to hit me.

I'm not a terrible flier. I don't hate planes, but I also don't ever look forward to boarding one. And leaving the country by myself adds another level of stress. I know I'll be meeting my coworkers when I land, but I'll still have to navigate customs alone, and I've never had to do that before.

I force my lungs to fill steadily and watch the world pass out the window while we ride in silence.

If I'm being completely honest, I'd admit that I'm pretty nervous about this trip.

I like to be prepared, so when my company announced this sales meeting and where it was being held, I did a search online. Mostly to check the weather so I knew how to dress, but I also like to see what a place is famous for. Maybe a certain type of food. Or a landmark. There's always something.

And it didn't take more than five seconds to find what this place is famous for.

Violence.

The city is famous for freaking violence.

I swallow.

I'd been so tempted to tell my parents—so I could have someone to share my worries with—but if I did that, they would've lost it. And I don't need them panicking the whole time I'm gone.

Plus, it's not like I can just refuse to go. It's a mandatory trip. And I'm there representing human resources. How bad would it look if the head of HR doesn't go because they're scared but allows everyone else to go?

I can picture my mom now... *"If everyone else jumps off a bridge, would you do it too?"*

Well, yeah. If it's between that and the unemployment line, I just might.

I blow out my breath.

There's no way my company would be sending everyone there if it was actually dangerous. Those news stories were probably exaggerating.

I brush away a stray thread on my knee, then press my hands between my thighs.

I packed two outfits for each day—one business casual, one business fancy—since I'm not sure how dressed up people are going to be, which is another reason for the heavy luggage.

For today, I picked something in between—black pants, black flats, black silk shirt. The universally accepted all-black outfit of corporate life.

A large hand settles on my thigh. "You okay?"

"Yep!" I answer too quickly, with a voice that's too bright.

With my hands still between my legs, Hans uses the pad of his pinkie finger to lightly brush against the skin around my wrist. It's tender but so faintly pink most people wouldn't notice.

"Did I hurt you?" The question is so quiet I barely hear it.

I turn my attention to look at Hans. "No." I lift my hands, turning my wrists around to show all sides. "See? All good."

Last night, the skin was a little raw, but I rubbed some aloe on it, and now you wouldn't even know I was tied up with my own underwear less than twelve hours ago.

Hans makes a humming sound as he merges onto the highway that will take us to the airport.

Needing to distract myself, I grasp for something to say. "So... got a big week at work?"

He shakes his head and asks his own question. "Do you speak any Spanish?"

I think back to the three months of online lessons I did four years ago. "Not really."

"Not really?" The hand on my thigh gives a little squeeze.

"Okay, not at all. I can say the word for bathroom. And beer. Which just makes me sound like an asshole." Hans's mouth twitches, and I don't know if he's trying not to smile or trying not to frown. "A few years ago, my parents bought me that expensive software people use to learn a new language for my birthday, but I didn't stick with it." My shoulders sag. "That's kinda my thing."

"Learning languages?"

I shake my head. "No. Quitting."

"Explain."

Feeling self-conscious, I push my hands back between my legs, careful to avoid touching Hans's hand in the process. "I have a... tendency to start new hobbies but not follow through." I sigh. "Like Spanish. And German. And knitting. And target shooting. And pottery."

It's a depressing list, and it's a lot longer than just those things, but I think I got my point across.

A finger taps against the back of my hand, and I lift my gaze from my lap to look at Hans.

He flicks me a glance. "What about your food blog?"

Unexpected emotions press against the backs of my eyes.

My mom brought up my blog at dinner last night, but I didn't think Hans would remember. Or ask about it again. He said he wanted me to show him, but I figured he was just being nice.

I scoot my hand up, stopping when it touches Hans's. "That one I've stuck with."

"What made you start?"

I scoot my hand over so my pinkie is covering his.

I'm looking at his big hand below mine when it blurs.

My hand instinctually jerks back, but Hans catches it before I can move an inch.

He moved so fast I couldn't even track it. But now his hand is fully on top of mine, trapping mine between my thigh and his palm.

"You're quick."

His hand flexes. "What made you start your blog, Butterfly?" he asks me again.

"I've always loved food. I mean, you met my parents. They're great at making stuff. So I figured baking was something I wouldn't get sick of." I lift my shoulders. "I've been thinking about doing the blog for a few years. I just never pulled the trigger."

"What changed?"

CHAPTER 44

Hans

WHY'D YOU START YOUR BLOG RIGHT AFTER MOVING IN across the street from me?

"You," Cassandra says casually, but the answer slams into my chest.

CHAPTER 45

Cassie

I BITE THE EDGE OF MY LIP, NOT BELIEVING I JUST admitted that.

"Me?"

Hans looks so surprised, it's worth the bit of ego I have to shed sharing this next part. "Yeah, so, I always wanted to—start the blog—but I didn't want to waste the stuff I made. And it's not like I can just make a single cookie. Recipes are bigger than that. And I need extra to make sure I have a good one for photos. Ya know?"

Hans nods slowly.

"Well..." I sigh. "I was embarrassed about not being good, and I couldn't bring myself to ask any of my previous neighbors if they'd want anything. And for the last, I dunno, several years, I've worked from home, so I didn't have an office or something to bring them to."

"You didn't have someone to share with," Hans says, putting it together.

I nod, even though his eyes are on the road. "I did my first posting the weekend after we met. I thought, maybe, a guy who lived alone wouldn't mind some extra food now and again." I bite my lip. "I don't know if you remember—"

CHAPTER 46
Hans

BANANA SCONES.

"I made banana scones."

She says it like I haven't memorized the entire history of her blog.

Like I haven't read through the entire thing, top to bottom, countless times.

Like I don't open her blog every time I have trouble sleeping.

Like I could have possibly forgotten.

I incline my head. "I remember."

CHAPTER 47

Cassie

"YOU DO?" I TRY TO TAMP DOWN MY EXCITEMENT. "I mean, I guess you would. The first time the stranger from across the street leaves a container of food on your front step is probably memorable."

"They were good."

I wiggle my fingers under Hans's hand. "Can I ask you something?"

"Uh-huh."

"Will you tell me the truth?"

Hans slides me a look. "Maybe."

I take a deep breath and ask, "Do you eat the stuff I leave for you, or do you throw it away?"

CHAPTER 48

Hans

I THINK ABOUT THE BANANA SCONES THAT WERE RAW IN the middle and charred on the outside. I think about the angel food cake that was salty. I think about the wet zucchini cookies I inhaled over the sink.

"I eat all of it." I keep pressure on Cassandra's hand, and it moves with mine as I slide my palm up her thigh until I can feel the heat radiating off her pussy.

It takes focus to stop there. I want to do more. Want to grip her *there*.

The woman I've been *focused on* for over a year just admitted that she started her blog because of me. She made that food *for* me.

And I want to devour her for it.

I want to strip every shred of clothing from her body and tell her how much she means to me. I want to feast on her flesh and tell her I'll eat anything she makes me.

But we're about to pull into the airport. And as much as it would simplify my life, I can't make Cassandra miss her flight.

CHAPTER 49
Cassie

"You do?" My voice is breathy.

Hans eats my food.

And his hand is so warm over mine. And it's so close to touching me *there*. Which I want him to do, but I'm glad he isn't. Because I don't want to walk through TSA with damp panties.

"Always." His tone is so honest.

We start to slow, and I look out the windshield to see we've already arrived.

I watch his profile as he slows and pulls his truck to the curb in the departures lane.

"When I get back, I'll bake you something."

He puts the truck into park and looks at me. "I'd like that."

Before I can say more, Hans shoves his door open and climbs out.

And just like that, all my earlier travel stress flares back to life. But rather than begging Hans to take me back home, I follow him out of the truck.

He's already got my suitcase on the sidewalk next to him, and he's holding my backpack out for me to put on like a jacket.

I slip one arm through the first strap, then the other, before turning back to face Hans again.

He moves his hands to my shoulders, adjusting the backpack.

"I get back Friday afternoon, but my dad is planning to pick me up."

Hans nods, adjusting the straps again.

"Thank you for driving me this morning." I wet my lips. "I really—"

Hans slips his fingers under the straps and yanks me forward, my chest bumping into his. "Be careful, Cassandra."

"Wh-what?"

He pulls me tighter against him, even though we're already touching. "Be fucking smart. Stay with your group. Don't go anywhere alone." He leans down, his face inches from mine. "Promise me, Butterfly."

An overwhelming sense of comfort fills me, his concern acting as a balm for all my worries. "I promise, Grizzly Bear."

He narrows his eyes. "Such a brat."

Then his mouth is on mine. Claiming mine. Invading mine.

I grip his sides. His T-shirt warm from his body. His hard muscles flexing beneath the fabric.

He pulls back.

"Hans." I can't stop myself from pushing up on my tiptoes.

His hold on my straps shifts, and he's helping me stretch up to reach him.

My tongue brushes over his lips, and he parts them.

This time it's me. I'm the one claiming him. I'm the one wrapping my arms around his back. I'm the one tasting him.

A car horn honks farther down the lane, forcing us to break the kiss.

"I should go," I whisper.

Hans uses his hold of me to set me back a step. "Remember your promise."

He drops his hands from my shoulders and, after reaching for my suitcase, pulls out the telescoping handle for me.

I grip the handle tighter than necessary. "Bye, Hans."

"Behave yourself, Girl."

CHAPTER 50
Hans

I FLEX MY JAW AS I WATCH CASSANDRA WALK THROUGH the glass doors into the airport.

I want so badly to grab her and haul her back into my truck. But I don't do that. Instead, I climb behind the wheel.

Cassandra has already disappeared out of view when I merge into the lanes of slowly moving cars leaving after dropping their passengers off.

I follow the traffic out of the departures area.

I keep my speed steady with everyone else.

I stay in the far lane as we all head toward the airport exit.

I flip on my blinker.

I follow the sign directing traffic that wants to *return to terminal*.

I follow the looping road until I join the cars heading into the airport again.

But instead of taking the lane for departures, I follow the signs for parking.

The ramps are crowded, but I find a spot between two other pickup trucks.

After turning the engine off, I unbuckle, then twist around and press a hidden button behind my seat.

The rear bench seat silently unlocks, and with minimal effort, the whole seat lifts on a hinge to reveal a compartment within.

I drag my nondescript black backpack out, then reach for my folded suit jacket.

I wait until I'm out of the truck to shake out my jacket and put it on.

Black leather boots, dark jeans, gray T-shirt, black suit jacket, and boring black backpack. I look like every other upper management douchebag heading out for a week of sales meetings.

Making it super easy to blend in at the airport.

No one questions me.

No one even looks twice at a man flying with just a backpack. Seasoned travelers have their packing down to a science.

Three changes of clothes.

Minimal toiletries.

A laptop containing four throwing knives.

A passport and airplane ticket for a man whose name isn't Hans Eklund but who looks *just* like me. And who has TSA PreCheck, so I, or whoever this man is, don't even have to take off my shoes to go through security.

Picking my backpack up after its uneventful trip through the X-ray machine, I make a stop in the first shop I see.

Since I purchased my ticket last night, I don't have much of a game plan for when I get where we're going. At least, no real plan beyond *follow Cassandra*.

I grab four bags of beef jerky, a bag of peanuts, bottle of water, two packs of Skittles, and a magazine about cars that will either work as a cover or as a fire starter. Whatever turns out to be more useful.

CHAPTER 51

Cassie

THE PILOT HITS THE GAS, OR WHATEVER IT'S CALLED IN a plane, and we start to speed down the runway.

I know the jostling is normal, but I still hate it.

Rather than turning my head to look out the window at my side, I close my eyes and think about Hans and that kiss we shared.

We might not be people who kiss when they see each other, but it turns out we're people who kiss when they part ways.

Hans would've made it back home already. I wonder if he went back to sleep or if he stayed up to start his own workday.

CHAPTER 52
Hans

My plane taxis into position, our pilot letting us know we're next to take off.

I pull my hair free from its tie and lean my head back against the seat, closing my eyes.

My conversation with the Cantrells fresh in my mind, I think back about how this all started.

CHAPTER 53
Hans
(AGE 19)

"YOU REALLY THINK THAT'S GONNA WORK?"

My sister rolls her eyes at me. "It's a dance club. It's not like I'm trying to get into the CIA."

"Why not just go to an eighteen-plus place?" She turned eighteen last month, a few days after graduating, so she could get into those with her actual ID.

"Because those places are fucking lame. You'd know that if you ever came out with me."

"No thanks."

I don't have time for partying. I'm too busy taking summer classes so I can graduate earlier than the rest of my classmates and get started on the life I want.

"Nerd," she sighs, but I know she doesn't mean it.

"It doesn't even look like you." I hold up the driver's license.

Freya twirls, her short silver dress flaring out, her blond hair shiny around her shoulders. "They aren't gonna look that close."

"Mom and Dad will kill you if they find out." I state the obvious.

"Which is why I'm going to tell them I'm staying at Kay's house tonight." She snatches the ID out of my hand and tucks it into her handbag. "And I am." She sets the bag on her dresser, then snags a pair of sweatpants off the floor and pulls them on, the baggy material covering the skirt of her dress. "We're just going out first." She tugs her favorite T-shirt on next, the tie-dye pattern forming a flower across her chest.

I shake my head. "Good luck."

Not wanting to be a witness to Freya lying her way past our parents, I head to my room.

I don't bother mentioning that getting in trouble with the law could mess up her plans to attend veterinary school at the University of Minnesota. Knowing her, even if she got kicked out of college, she'd still move up north. She's talked about nothing else since she heard about all the lakes they have, saying she's sick of living in the desert.

I shut my bedroom door and sigh.

It's a little weird being back here after getting used to living on campus. But we don't have classes on Monday, so I decided to spend the weekend at home.

Free food and free laundry are hard to turn down.

Plus, I have to admit, it's kinda nice to be around my family again.

I eye my bed.

I'm a little tempted to blow off studying so I can lie in bed and watch some crappy TV. But I don't.

Dropping into the desk chair in the corner of the room, I flip my *Health Law and Policy* book open.

I've always wanted to be a lawyer. Probably watched too many movies growing up. But righting wrongs, being the good guy, eventually being my own boss... What more could a man want?

I RUB MY EYES AND LOOK AT THE CLOCK ON MY nightstand. Just after six, and I didn't go to bed until after two.

I start to roll over, intending to go back to sleep, but my

mom's voice, pitched higher than usual, filters into my room through my closed door.

My parents are early risers, but not on Sundays. And Mom never raises her voice.

A pit builds in my stomach as I toss my blankets off.

In my pajamas, I head out of my room.

When I reach the top of the stairs, Dad's voice speaks over Mom's.

"Tell her we'll call her back. We need to call the police."

The pit turns into dread, and I hurry down the stairs, my bare feet quiet on the carpet.

"You heard him. Yes. Okay."

I turn the corner into the kitchen in time to see my mom hang up the phone.

"Give it here." Dad holds his hand out, and Mom gives him the handset.

He dials three numbers, then puts the phone to his ear, his free hand settling on my mom's shoulder.

They haven't seen me yet, so I stay where I am, listening.

"Yes. I need to report—" Dad's voice hitches, and Mom presses her hands over her mouth. "I need to report a missing person."

A missing person.

"... Eklund... My daughter..."

My sister.

"She was last seen..."

Freya is missing.

I take a step back.

"Comet, yes, the club." Mom's shoulders are shaking, and Dad's knuckles whiten around the phone. "We didn't know she was going..."

I did.

I knew.

"Her friend just got home ten minutes ago. Her parents thought the girls were in bed." Dad's head sags forward. "Kay thinks they were drugged. She doesn't remember how she ended up at another friend's house. But—But Freya, my girl, she wasn't with her."

Freya got separated.

"I know it hasn't been twenty-four hours." Dad's tone changes. "I will call the mayor—"

I should have stopped her.

Mom turns away from Dad with a whimper and spots me.

I don't hear the rest of what my dad says because Mom rushes toward me and throws her arms around me, hugging me tighter than she's ever hugged me before.

THE COP GIVES US ONE LAST LOOK BEFORE HE STEPS out the door, shutting it behind him.

The only reason he's even here is because Dad has money.

The cop asked questions and wrote down our answers, but I don't think he really believes she's missing and not just partying.

There's no news.

No signs of Freya.

She's been missing since yesterday morning.

MY FIST POUNDS AGAINST THE LOCKED BACK DOOR.

Comet is closed, doesn't open for a few more hours, but cars are parked in the employee lot. And if the cops won't get us any fucking answers, I will.

I pound my fist again.

Finally, it opens.

"Forget your key?" the man asks before he realizes I'm not a fellow employee.

HANS

Before he can slam the door in my face, I stick my foot out, keeping it open. "I need to talk to someone."

"Look, kid, if you lost something, you gotta wait till we're open. Then you can check the lost and found."

The darkness that's been bubbling inside me since I first heard my mom's worried voice expands. Filling more of my soul.

I shove the guy back.

Surprise is the only reason I get him to move. He's got fifty pounds and twenty years on me, but he still stumbles.

Then he rights himself and pushes me in the chest. "I'll fucking end you, you little shit. Get the fuck out."

I shove his hands away. "I'm not leaving until I talk to someone."

The man steps into my space. "You rich pricks think you can do whatever the fuck you want." This time when he pushes me, he pushes me hard, and I clip my shoulder on the edge of the shelving unit next to the doorway.

He probably saw my car parked outside the door. Saw the luxury model and figured I'm here because I'm just another spoiled shit trying to get his way.

"My sister was taken!"

I shout it.

I shout it with all the rage and worry and anguish inside me.

"Someone here saw it!" Heat fills my eyes.

But I don't care. I don't care if he sees me cry. I don't care if he punches me. If he breaks all my bones. Nothing will stop me from finding Freya.

The man freezes, his eyes widening, before they flicker away and back.

He knows something.

"Who?" I hiss, stepping into his space. "Who has her?"

His head is shaking before I finish asking. "I don't know anything about any girl."

He's lying.

I grab for his shirt, but he swats my hands away.

161

"Tell me!" My voice breaks. "She's only eighteen."

"Just like I told the cops, I don't know what the fuck you're talking about." He raises his voice, and something about it is off. Like he's doing it for someone else, not me. "You need to go."

My breaths are coming heavier now.

"Who?" I whisper.

"Out. Now." He's still talking loudly, pushing me backward toward the door. Then his voice drops to a whisper, just like mine. "Marcoux."

I step out into the daylight, and the door slams shut in front of me.

"Dad?" I keep my voice quiet, not sure if he's awake.

None of us have gotten any sleep since...

His head lifts from where it rested against his desk.

It takes his eyes a moment to focus. "Hans? Come in."

I step through the threshold. "I... I have a name."

It's a different officer this time, and the sympathy on his face looks as fake as his hair.

"So..." He glances down at his notepad, like he can't remember what I said twenty seconds ago. "You went to Comet, without telling anyone you were going, and then bullied some employee into giving you this *name*." He says *name* like the one I gave him is alien, not French.

"I didn't bully him," I snap. "And I'm nineteen. I don't need to tell people where I'm going."

"You do when it interferes with a police investigation."

"What investigation?" I throw my hands up. "You haven't done anything!"

Dad settles his hand on my leg. I don't know if it's for comfort or to keep me from attacking the cop.

"I understand this is a trying time." The fucking prick isn't even trying to sound like he cares anymore. "But you need to let us do our jobs. And chasing after rumors"—he holds up his notepad where he supposedly wrote the name down—"doesn't help."

I keep my jaw clenched as he rises from the other couch.

"We'll be in touch." He dips his head to Mom, who's been sitting on my other side, then he sees himself out.

Mom doesn't acknowledge him. She doesn't do anything.

The cop called the name a rumor. But Dad had heard the name Marcoux before.

It's not a fucking rumor.

Fifteen years ago, when I was just four and Freya was three, we moved here from Sweden. Dad had an investment opportunity that utilized his mining experience, so he sold his company, and we came to the US. And in a bid to familiarize himself with Arizona, he took to reading the local paper, cover to cover, every day. He never stopped.

Which is how he knew about the uptick in gang activity in the Phoenix area in the past year. And he remembers Marcoux. He especially remembers it because the very next day, the newspaper published an article recanting the Marcoux name. He remembered it because it screamed of corruption.

It didn't take Dad long to find the article, saved in a stack in his office.

He found it and read it to us.

The statement claimed that the previous story was an editorial error and that the name *wasn't* associated with the recent violence, drug use... or human trafficking.

It was that last part, those last two words, that broke Mom.

She hasn't spoken since.

LIGHTNING CRACKLES ACROSS THE NIGHT SKY, AND THE responding thunder covers the sound of my car door slamming shut.

I thought I'd be scared. Thought my hands would shake. But that void inside me has grown since Freya disappeared a week ago.

Seven days.

Seven awful days.

Mom has been catatonic.

Dad isn't eating.

No one is sleeping.

I haven't been back to my dorm. Haven't been to my classes.

Finding Freya is all that matters.

And the men inside this bar know where she is.

They have to.

I tuck the keys of my Porsche into my pocket and walk across the cracked blacktop toward the front of the bar.

There's no bouncer. No one checking IDs. It's a shitty bar in a shitty part of town filled with shitty people. A person would have to be crazy to go in if they didn't belong.

Crazy. Or desperate.

The front door is propped open, and I step through into the low-ceiling space filled with cigarette smoke and the scent of stale beer.

I dressed in a plain T-shirt, a dirty pair of hiking boots, and my oldest jeans, hoping to blend in, but I still feel eyes on me.

Ignoring the instinct to turn and run, I keep my head up and move toward the bar.

It's definitely a rough crowd, but it doesn't look like a straight gang hangout. There's too much variety in the patrons to have them all be part of the Corsican mafia. Maybe the intel I picked up wasn't as good as I thought. Or maybe it is. I'll find out soon enough.

With each step I take, the tension builds in the air.

There are pool tables on my left, low tables on the right, groups of people standing where there's space, and more standing at the bar.

A few people bump my shoulders, but I don't react to them. I just keep moving.

I don't know how to fight. And I don't know what sort of weapons these guys might have. All I have is a switchblade in my pocket that I bought at a truck stop.

But I won't let that stop me.

When I reach the bar, the bartender is already staring at me.

I stop in front of the scarred top across from where he stands.

"You lost, kid?" the old man asks.

"Not lost. Just need information."

He huffs. "Information isn't free."

I take my wallet out of my pocket, fatter than usual, pull a hundred out, and set it on the bar top. "I need to know who likes to take girls from Comet."

The bartender lifts a brow as he slides the hundred across the bar and shoves it into his apron.

"Well?" I prompt.

He lifts a shoulder. "Never heard of Comet."

I grind my teeth. "The nightclub."

His expression doesn't change. "Not really my thing."

"How about Marcoux? You heard that name before?" I keep my volume conversational, but I know I've hit my mark when I hear several chairs scrape against the floor at once.

That void inside me spreads as I turn, putting my back to the bar, facing off with the four men moving to stand before me.

"You got one chance to get the fuck out of here." The man in the front of the group tips his head back so he can look down his nose at me.

I passed six feet last summer. Gained a couple more inches since. So these guys don't have height on me. But they have muscle. I'm just a skinny nerd who spends too much time studying to work out or eat correctly.

But things are different now.

Now, I have nothing to lose.

And I'm fucking hungry.

I square my shoulders. "You got one chance to tell me who steals girls from Comet."

The three men in back snicker, but the one who spoke first doesn't. "You think you're tough?"

I shake my head. "No. But I need to find my sister."

The snickers stop.

"If your sister is gone, accept it and get gone yourself."

I swallow.

This man isn't going to tell me anything.

My wallet is still in my left hand. I raise it slowly, so I don't startle anyone, and pull out the nineteen hundred dollar bills I have left.

Bribery won't work. But I need a distraction so I can get at least one good hit in before these guys kick my ass.

"Free money!" I shout, then toss the bills into the air.

The people closest to me, who'd been watching the interaction, lunge toward the valuable pieces of paper, getting between me and some of the bad guys. But no one is blocking the leader, and he lunges for me.

I jump to the side, dodging his first swing.

Before he can strike again, I kick out as hard as I can.

As the underdog, I'll use any advantage. Including fighting dirty.

My kick doesn't hit his knee like I'd hoped, but the steel toe of my heavy boot connects with his shin.

I don't give him a second to catch his balance. This time, I'm the one to lunge.

Shouts break through the buzz of adrenaline in my ears, so I think another fight might have broken out, but it's not enough.

I duck down so my shoulder connects with the asshole's

stomach and use all my weight and momentum to push him backward.

Right into a big, tattooed dude in a leather vest, who was about to take a shot in his game of pool.

I can't see the table as I fall to the ground. But based on the way Vest Guy spins around, we fucked up his shot. Just as I'd hoped.

Vest Guy slams his giant fist into the face of the asshole I shoved into him.

And just like that, everyone is fighting.

Already on the ground, I roll under the pool table and crawl out the other side.

This is my best chance to leave. Sneak out without getting hurt. But I need a lead. I need something, someone, to chase next.

I climb to my feet and dodge bodies until I spot one of the other three guys who came over to intimidate me.

I cut the distance and slam into his back, circling my arm around his throat. "How do I find Marcoux?" I shout into his ear over the roar of the crowd.

He tries to headbutt me, but I've seen enough movies to tuck my head in by his neck, so he doesn't have the range to hit me hard enough to dislodge me.

I tighten my hold on his neck. "Tell me."

We crash into other bodies, tables, stumbling together.

"You can talk, or I can strangle you." I squeeze harder, even as I grunt when one of his elbows gets me.

One of his hands taps against my forearm. Not trying to claw me off like before, but like he's ready to speak.

I loosen my arm enough for him to suck in a breath but not enough to let him go.

"Where is he?"

"He—" The man coughs. "He's the money. Ground guys would've grabbed her."

I don't know how much of what he says I can trust, but it makes sense.

"Where do I find them?" Acid rolls in my stomach. "Where do they keep the girls?"

He's not denying that they're human trafficking.

"Fuck you!" His outburst comes a heartbeat before a sharp pain in my side.

I jump back, releasing my arms from his neck, and see the knife held in his hand.

He turns toward me, his face still red from lack of oxygen. "You're gonna pay for this." He holds his knife up, the tip of it already red with my blood. "And you'll never find your fucking sister." He takes another step, and I bump into a table behind me. "If she's not dead yet, she'll wish she was."

He pulls his arm back.

And I spring forward.

The switchblade in my hand sinks into the soft flesh of his stomach.

He was so focused on my face, waiting for pain to fill my features, that he forgot to watch my hands.

He drops his knife, his hands grabbing at the hilt over my own. But I keep walking forward, keep walking him back, until he hits the bar.

"My name is Hans. And I'm coming for Freya."

Releasing my grip, I take a quick step back, then melt into the frenzy and find my way to the door.

I'll find her.

I have to find her.

ANOTHER WEEK.

Another dead end.

Another fight that ends with me needing stitches.

A THIRD WEEK.

I can see Mom wasting away as each hour passes.

Dad is trying to hold it together. He's on the phone every day.

But no one has news.

I have a cracked rib from last night. And a black eye that my parents are too distant to notice.

My feet scuff along the sidewalk as I near the line for Comet.

I've been here every night when I haven't been starting fights that I keep losing.

I know she isn't going to be here, but what's left of my soul just wants to be close to her. Close to her last known location.

The line moves forward, and I think about that night.

I think about what we said to each other.

She didn't straight out ask me to go with her, but the invitation was there. And I didn't go.

I could've gone.

If only I'd have gone.

But I didn't.

I didn't go with Freya, and the last words I ever said to her were *good luck*.

The bouncer sighs when he sees me, but we've done this routine. I hand him a couple hundred dollars, and he lets me in.

It's not like I'll be trying to get a drink at the bar. I'm going to do what I always do—stand against the wall, staring into the crowd, willing the darkness inside me to hold off just a little longer. Just long enough for me to find her.

MY MOTHER'S SCREAMS WAKE ME UP.

They're unending.

They're agony.

And I know.

I know they found my sister.

And I know she's dead.

I scramble out of bed, but my legs don't hold me.

I crash to the floor.

I can't breathe.

My lungs won't fill.

I can't...

Pain and sorrow and the heaviest sense of failure collapse on top of me.

I didn't get to her.

I didn't save her.

Mom's wails continue to curl through the house.

My face feels contorted.

My mouth is open but no sound comes out.

Freya.

My baby sister.

She's gone.

She's never coming home.

TODAY WAS MY SISTER'S FUNERAL. AND IT KILLED MY parents.

It killed a part of me too.

Standing here, alone under the glow of the moon, next to Freya's freshly filled grave, I know I'll never be the same.

I'll never be the man I planned to be.

I'm going to end up as someone else.

Someone darker.

TWO MONTHS LATER, I STAND IN THE SAME SPOT AND stare down at my mother's grave, buried next to her daughter.

Dad stands at my side, coughing between silent sobs.

After Freya's body was found in Vegas, abused and discarded, her cause of death labeled as a drug overdose, Mom gave up.

The doctors said it was pneumonia, and maybe it was, but she'd lost her will to live.

The reality of what happened to Freya, how she suffered her last weeks, days, hours... it was too much.

My dad is sick too. I can hear him struggling to breathe at night when I'm walking through the empty halls of our house.

He's not going to get treated. I don't have to ask him to know that he won't.

And standing here, again, looking down at the women who meant the world to both of us, I don't blame him.

I don't take it personally that I'm not enough to keep him here.

A rare raindrop lands on the dirt.

I'm not sure I want to stay in this world either.

"HANS." DAD'S VOICE IS BRITTLE, BUT I HEAR IT AS I pass his room.

Pausing my steps, I press my hand to his door, and it swings open.

Dad is in his bed, face pale, cheeks sunken in as he fights his way through a coughing fit.

It's been exactly one week since Mom's last breath, and he looks ready for his.

He lifts his hand, a small movement gesturing me in.

We haven't talked. Not to each other. There's nothing to say.

The first few times someone came to our door, offering

condolences, bringing food, I answered. I kept a passive look on my face. But then I couldn't anymore.

I couldn't hide the rage that filled me.

I couldn't say thank you.

And then the people stopped knocking.

My feet are quiet on the thick rug covering the floor. It's shades of red. Embroidered flowers of every shape and size. Mom picked it out. It was so *her*.

I stop at the foot of the bed.

If this is going to be our goodbye...

I swallow.

I'm not sure how much more I can handle.

I don't know how much my heart can endure.

But as I look at my father, I realize he's already gone.

I place my hand on the blanket over his foot. "It's okay, Dad."

His chin quivers, and his chest shakes with his inhales.

"Come here." He raises an arm.

Slowly, I move to the side of the bed, then bend down and gently hug his shoulders.

A hand rests against my back.

This is it, then.

When I pull back, his eyes slide over to his nightstand.

I follow his gaze.

Sitting next to the framed photo of him and Mom on their wedding day is an ornately carved wooden box.

I recognize it. It was my grandfather's, given to my father. And now to me.

I stand before it.

The latch doesn't lock, and the hinge has been kept oiled, so it opens smoothly.

The overhead light is dimmed, but it still glints off the blades inside the box.

Dueling knives.

Antiques.

But sharp as hell.

I close the lid and reset the latch.

Lifting the box into my arms, I turn back to face my dad.

He holds my gaze, his eyes showing more life than I've seen since the morning everything changed.

His mouth opens. Closes. Opens again.

Then he gets out the final words I'll ever hear him say.

"Make them pay, Hans." His inhale is scratchy. "Make them suffer."

I DON'T HAVE A FUNERAL FOR MY FATHER, BUT I BURY him next to his wife.

And when the paperwork is done and my bags are packed and in the trunk of my car, I walk back through the house one more time.

There's nothing left here but misery and grief.

I stop in front of my sister's bedroom, turning the handle and opening the door.

I don't step into the room.

I don't take any of her things.

That's not who I am anymore.

But I do give her a silent promise.

I swear to her that I won't stop until every one of the men responsible is dead.

Then I turn and head back down the hall. Back downstairs. Into the kitchen. I pull the stove out from the wall and finish loosening the gas line. With a final twist, I sever the line.

I don't need the insurance money. As the sole survivor of the Eklund mining fortune, I don't need another penny so long as I live. But I don't need anyone coming after me for arson either. So I'm making it look as close to a faulty gas line as possible. People will be suspicious, but I'll be long gone.

And if my sister isn't coming home to her room, then no one will.

Next to the front door is the three-wick candle Freya picked out for our mom last Mother's Day. Mom never lit it, claiming it was her favorite scent and wanting to have it forever.

I pull the book of matches I took from Comet out of my pocket.

As the flame crackles to life, I carefully light each wick.

The warm vanilla scent, Mom's favorite, starts to fill the living room as I close the front door behind me.

That night, long after the flames are doused and the house is ruined, I kill a man for the first time.

Nineteen, with blood on my hands and my entire family gone, all I have left to live for is vengeance.

I flex my fingers around the hilt of the antique knife.

I've always heard the saying *what doesn't kill me, makes me stronger*. But what if both things are true?

The real me died with my sister. But I'm still here. Still alive. Still breathing.

I'm just someone else now.

Someone who has the means to wage a war.

CHAPTER 54
Hans

My EYES OPEN ON AN INHALE.

That was just the start of it.

The first killing of hundreds.

The first day of the past twenty years.

The seat belt light turns on, and the flight crew tells us to prepare for landing.

It's been two decades since I've allowed myself to feel.

My right hand reaches across my body to brush over the spot where a faint scar remains from that very first fight. The man who got in a swipe while I was choking him.

It was the first scar of many, but it's barely even visible anymore.

But him? I went back for him.

He was the first man I killed.

The first of many in Phoenix.

Then more in Vegas.

Then more in LA.

I trained.

I found teachers who would show me the quickest way to kill.

Found others who would sell me what I needed.

I went overseas. Went to France. Killed more men. Ones who pulled the strings.

Killed so many I have bounties on my head from half a dozen countries.

I never found Marcoux.

He had come and gone before I got to the top of the organization. He was the money man. An investor. A businessman who profited from the sale of human beings.

I didn't find him. But I found his first name. Gabriel.

I can't rest until he's dead.

But—a small smile pulls at my lips—neither can he.

CHAPTER 55

Cassie

My hands tremble a little as I hand my passport to the customs agent.

I wish I wasn't still feeling so nervous. I landed. I got my luggage. I'm on time. I'll find my coworkers in just a few minutes.

But my body doesn't seem to accept that. And with the amount of sweat trickling down my back, I won't be surprised if I get detained for suspicious activity.

"What brings you to Mexico?" the man behind the desk asks.

"Work," I croak.

He lifts a brow, holding my passport up so he can look at the photo and then back at me.

He does this for several seconds.

The pressure is too much.

I lift my hands and fan my face, the summer heat permeating the indoors. "Sorry." I keep fanning myself. "I don't like flying alone, and I'm stressed out and hot, but I promise I'm just here for work."

The man stares at me for another beat before he smirks and hands the passport back to me. "You're good, Ms. Cantrell. Welcome to Mexico."

My entire body sags in relief, and the man's smile grows into a grin.

If I wasn't so obsessed with my growly big-dicked neighbor, I might ask this guy for his number.

"Thank you." I slip the passport into an interior pocket in my backpack, then zip it up, making sure there's no way for it to fall out or for someone with skilled fingers to lift it. "Thank you," I say again, then drag my suitcase—with my backpack attached to the handle—away.

It doesn't take long before I spot a group of people I recognize standing next to the sign for transportation. It makes me feel a little better, but there's a part of me that wishes Hans could've come with me. I still barely know him, but his *don't fuck with me* attitude just makes me feel safe.

I square my shoulders and plaster a smile on my face.

I'll see him soon enough. Time to face reality.

CHAPTER 56

Hans

I DON'T EVEN BOTHER SIGHING WHEN I SEE THE HOTEL Cassandra's company has her staying in.

The bus pulls through the *open gate* leading onto the property, and I follow.

I saw my Butterfly through one of the side windows of the bus, so I know she's in the middle and not in the rear seat, which would be the only place she could realistically see me from.

Her company didn't even spring for a coach bus. They're in a fucking rented-out school bus. No tinted windows. Just clear glass and a front and rear entrance begging someone to hijack them.

The gate guard nods to me, and I nod back as I drive through, but what I really want to do is pull one of my knives out of my bag and throw it through his eye socket. Or at the very least roll down my window and shout *¡Haz tu trabajo, maldito idiota!* But I don't do any of that. Because he obviously *is* a fucking idiot. But also, his not doing his job makes this easier for me.

I back my rented car into a spot in the middle of the little parking lot.

There aren't a lot of vehicles here, so hopefully that means they have a vacancy. And if they don't, well, I have enough cash to create one.

I watch through my windshield as Cassandra's coworkers drag their luggage off the bus.

Cassandra is next. I can see her red suitcase before I can see her.

A man reaches up to take the heavy bag from her, and I shove my door open.

She smiles at him, and I put a foot outside.

He grins back at her, and I'm reaching for my laptop.

I stop myself and take a deep breath through my nose.

My girl isn't going to let him touch her. And I don't want her to have to struggle with her bag. And I can't just walk up there and join their fucking week of meetings.

My foot stays planted on the blacktop outside my car, but I stay where I am. Memorizing the face of the man helping my girl.

I won't kill him just for that, but that's his strike one. And if he reaches three, his punishment will be much different from Cassandra's.

I rip open one of the bags of Skittles and shove a handful into my mouth.

I chew slowly and wait until everyone is inside.

I wait until the bus parks in a corner of the lot.

I wait for the bus driver to finish his cigarette and enter the hotel.

Then I get out, walk over to the bus, slap a magnetic tracker in the rear wheel well, and finally enter the hotel, requesting a room with a view of the parking lot.

CHAPTER 57

Cassie

"ALRIGHT, EVERYONE, WORK IS OFFICIALLY OVER!" OUR
VP of sales lifts his arms at the front of the bus.

The cheer is mostly enthusiastic, but I don't think I'm the
only one that is completely over this trip.

I'm over people. It's hot. My deodorant has been working
overtime since before we landed on Monday. It's Thursday afternoon. We leave for the airport tomorrow morning, and all I want
to do is take a cold shower, then lie naked on my hotel bed.

"Just settle in, and we'll be at the distillery in..." He looks at
his watch. "A little over an hour."

I fight the groan that tries to come out of my throat.

There isn't air conditioning on this bus. Or if there is, it
doesn't work. So that means I need to sit through the next hour
with the back of my thighs sticking to the seat beneath me. *Great.*

At least our group is small enough for everyone to get their
own little bench seat. If I had to sit shoulder to shoulder with one
of my coworkers, soaking up their body heat, I'd crawl out the
emergency hatch in the ceiling and end it all.

Slouching down, I put my knees against the back of the seat in
front of me. My knee-length skirt drapes open beneath me, and

the small amount of airflow against my bare legs is worth the risk that Suzanne across the aisle might see my underwear.

The bus rumbles away from the manufacturing plant, where we've been every day for training seminars, and merges onto the main road we take to and from our hotel. But instead of turning toward the hotel, the way I desperately want to go, we turn the other way.

I get that they're trying to do something fun for our last night, but a distillery... How could anyone think that copious amounts of hard liquor the night before we all have six a.m. flights is a good idea?

My stomach roils just at the thought of boarding a plane hungover.

I don't have anything against drinking. I enjoy it when the mood strikes. But I won't be partaking today.

It's the final night. One last night before you get to go home. One more night until you can see Hans again.

Making an effort to push away my sour mood, I watch the scenery beyond the window.

I'm a little embarrassed over how much time I've spent thinking about Hans this week. Especially since there's a chance he'll go back to ignoring me.

We're nearly out of the city when the bus jerks to a stop, causing me to slide farther down in my seat.

A few people make noises of displeasure at being jolted, and I struggle for a moment to right myself.

I'm about halfway back on the bus, sitting in the same place I have every other day, but through the big windshield, I can see the top of the van in front of the bus. They must've stopped suddenly at the red light, forcing our driver to hit the brakes.

Bad drivers are truly everywhere.

I start to lean back in my seat when someone up front screams.

Like *screams.*

Then more people scream.

I hear a shout, and then the bus lurches straight into the back of the van, pushing it forward a few feet.

"What—" My words are cut off when a bang rips through the air.

The screaming gets louder. And our bus driver is slouched over in his seat. His foot must come off the gas because we stop pushing the van into the intersection.

My heart is racing.

What the hell just—

Over the screams, I hear the distinct sound of breaking glass before a stranger climbs the steps at the front of the bus. Holding a gun.

I slap my hands over my mouth.

Oh my god.

A second man follows him onto the bus.

Oh my god!

"Stay where you are!" the first man shouts. His accent is strong, but there's no mistaking his demand.

The second man is reaching for the bus driver.

I press my hands harder to my mouth.

He's going to drag him out of the seat so he can drive us off. Because that first bang was a gunshot. They killed the driver.

We're being kidnapped.

The first man holds his gun higher and snaps something at one of my coworkers up front.

This was my fear. And now it's happening.

The gunman's still yelling at someone, but then he whips his head over to look past where I'm sitting.

Toward the back of the bus.

He straightens his gun arm like he's going to shoot.

I squeeze my eyes shut and brace for the loud noise as more screams fill the bus.

But there's no gunshot.

I open my eyes.

Then widen them.

The gun drops from the man's hand as he reaches up to his face. His fingers grab at the slender hilt of a knife protruding from his eye socket.

Under my hands, my mouth pulls into a grimace.

The man drops to his knees, then out of sight.

"What the fuck?" I whisper into my palms.

Hands still over my mouth, I turn my head and see another man, a new man, walking up the aisle of the bus from the open rear door.

He's large. Tall, with broad shoulders wrapped in a black long-sleeved shirt.

His face is covered in a black knit ski mask that makes him look sinister, but the thick material does nothing to hide his defined jawline.

In a blur, one of his hands whips forward, and something flies from it.

There are more shouts. More cries of fear. But I can't focus on anyone else. And I can't look away from the new man. Because peeking out around the bottom of his mask is hair. Long dark blond hair.

Still striding forward, the man nears where I'm sitting. And when he reaches me, when he passes my seat, he turns his head my way.

Just for a heartbeat.

A split second.

But our eyes connect.

My stunned ones to his intensely dark ones.

My heart skips.

"Hans?" I gasp the name against my fingers.

But the man doesn't stop.

He doesn't acknowledge me. He just keeps moving.

My head turns to follow him.

Something inside me urges me to go after him. To be near him. But...

It can't be him.

Can it?

I hadn't noticed the gloves on his hands until he puts them on the back of two seats, one on each side of the aisle, and swings himself forward.

I stand, needing to see.

The masked man swung over the man on the floor with the knife in his eye.

I'm not great with anatomy, but the man is on his stomach, and blood is pooling around his face.

I don't think he's gonna make it.

There's a grunt, and I snap my eyes back up.

The second man, who was dragging the driver out of the seat, is pulling a knife out of his neck.

The ski-mask man, our hero, who might be my mother-freaking neighbor, must've thrown that knife too.

Second Man presses his free hand over the bleeding wound in his neck, then he lunges, knife first, toward Ski Mask.

This time, I'm the one who screams.

Faster than I can track, Ski Mask avoids the wild swipe by dodging down and to the right.

Second Man still has his arm extended.

Ski Mask lets his right arm lead, shooting up and to the left, cutting across between them and stealing the knife back from Second Man.

Because I'm staring—because I can't look away—I see the knife spin in Ski Mask's hand so the sharp side is pointed back toward Second Man.

Bringing his arm back down, Ski Mask steps forward as he slams the blade into Second Man's chest.

Second Man stumbles backward, crashing into the controls at the front of the bus.

Not stopping, Ski Mask slams his palm forward, against the butt of the knife, sinking it farther into Second Man.

It all happened in seconds.

My mouth is hanging open.

Someone up front pukes.

And Ski Mask doesn't stop.

Gaping, I watch as he grips the shirt of Second Man, who's gone limp, and tosses him down the bus steps. The door at the bottom of the stairs is still open from when the bad guys broke it.

New shouts sound from outside the bus.

More bad guys.

Ski Mask ducks down and picks something up off the floor.

I see a glimpse of a gun, then he's following the body of Second Man down the stairs and off the bus.

Gunfire erupts outside, and as everyone crouches down in their seats, I move onto my tiptoes.

I need to see.

I need to know.

CHAPTER 58

Hans

FUCKING IDIOTS.

I pull the trigger again, this bullet sinking through the skull of the man behind the wheel of the van.

They're all fucking idiots.

The morons trying to steal a bus full of people.

The morons who organized this idiotic trip.

A man groans from the back seat, and I turn my aim to put another bullet into his torso. The first two didn't work fast enough.

Two dead on the bus. Two more that I shot out on the sidewalk. And these two, trying to get away.

Shoving the driver to the side, I reach into the van and put it into neutral.

I toss the empty gun onto the floorboard and take the assault rifle the driver dropped on his lap.

Jogging, I circle back to the bus. I've only been off it for thirty seconds, and this ground crew is dead, but more could be coming.

I bound up the blood-stained stairs and lock eyes with Cassandra. The only person who's standing rather than hunched down.

Did she not hear the fucking gunshots?

From the front of the bus, I point a finger at her. "Sit. Down."

I don't have to work to make my tone angry and intense.

I am angry.

I'm fucking pissed that she was this close to violence.

This fucking close to being taken.

Rage boils inside me.

I want to drag her off this bus and leave everyone else to their own fate.

But she probably wouldn't like that. And since I escalated the situation, I'll finish it.

Needing to clear the aisle, I grab the dead asshole by his feet and drag him to the top of the stairs, then shove him down them, his body landing on top of his dead asshole friend.

Out of the corner of my eye, I see one of the corporate yuppies reach for a pistol lying on the floor between the seats.

I yank my third throwing knife from my belt and toss it so it lands buried in the floor between the man's outstretched fingers and the firearm.

"Don't be fucking stupid," I snap at him, and he cowers back into his seat.

Now to get everyone to safety.

The bus driver is dead, and he deserves more than me pushing him to the floor, but it's the best I can do under the circumstances.

Stepping over his body, I climb into the driver's seat.

The bus is still in drive, and with the van in front of us in neutral, I'm able to depress the gas and push it out of the way.

Now that the gunshots have stopped, people are starting to gather around. And I probably have about two more seconds before someone starts to live stream this shit.

I take a hard right at the light and speed up for a dozen yards before slamming on the brakes.

The people in the seats behind me shout in alarm, but the motion forces the rear door to slam closed.

Nothing about this piece of shit bus is bulletproof, but I don't need an open back door inviting fucking trouble.

My foot moves back to the gas, and after we've gone a few blocks, I turn again.

Toward the US Consulate.

CHAPTER 59

Cassie

SUZANNE IS WAILING LOUDLY IN HER SEAT ACROSS from me.

I should probably try to comfort her or Bob—who is rocking and crying in the seat ahead of me. But I can't look away from the man driving our bus.

His head and face are still covered with the ski mask, but the more I stare at him, the more I try to catch another glimpse of his eyes in the oversized rearview mirror, and the more I'm convinced that the man who just killed *several* people is Hans.

I swallow.

But how would that even be possible?

Okay, so I've felt his muscles. I've sensed that edge of danger that surrounds him. Maybe I can believe the *how*.

But why?

Why would he be here? In Mexico. Specifically in the exact location as me.

The bus rocks around a turn, and a car horn blares, but the man behind the wheel never loses control. He just keeps driving.

I can't wait anymore.

I need to know.

And I need to... move.

I feel too hot.

Too... flustered.

Too—

Oh god, am I turned on right now?

I start to stand, intending to just walk right up to the front, but the bus swerves, making me sway hard enough that I sit back down.

When I look up, I swear I can see the man under the mask glaring at me through the mirror.

I narrow my eyes, trying to make out the color again. But I'm too far away.

We make another turn, but this time, it's wide, and we're driving the wrong way down the street.

A few people let out screams, and I'm tempted to roll my eyes at them. Clearly this man is a good guy—or at least good in the sense that he just saved us. Even if he did do it by killing a bunch of people. He's not kidnapping us from the kidnappers; he's rescuing us.

Two of the wheels bump up onto the curb, and then we're screeching to a stop in front of a large building surrounded by a large fence—I look out my window—with a large American flag flying in the courtyard between the gate and building.

The moment the bus comes to a complete stop, the man behind the wheel rises. "Get inside the fence." He's talking to the VP sitting in the front seat. "Tell them who you are."

When my colleague doesn't answer, the man in the ski mask leans toward him and shouts, "Now!"

When the VP nods, the man in the mask strides down the aisle.

"Get inside," he commands the rest of us.

His voice is deep. Filled with intention.

It's not exactly the same as the one that has whispered against my ear, but...

The man doesn't stop when he passes me. Doesn't even look at me. Just rushes past, kicks open the rear door, and jumps out.

There's more shouting, only this time it's coming from outside. From the armed American soldiers rushing toward the gate we're parked in front of, and I realize that the man parked this way to get us as close as possible. To get us inside the US Consulate quickly, where it's safe.

I push to my feet.

Everyone is moving now, staggering to the front of the bus, exiting with their hands up and running toward the gate.

But as soon as Suzanne gets up, I slide across the aisle and climb over her seat.

I press my face to her window. I need to see.

There's too much street traffic. Too many cars and people.

I can't...

Then I see him.

Dressed all in black, with his back to me, across the four-lane road, is a man heading into a narrow alley.

With my heart thundering behind my ribs and my blood pulsing between my legs, I watch him reach up and pull the ski mask from his head.

And I watch familiar long hair tumble free.

CHAPTER 60
Cassie

Just as the oven timer stops beeping, my phone starts ringing.

I throw down the hot mitts I was putting on and reach for my phone on the counter.

Seeing that it's my mom, I almost don't answer. They just left here an hour ago, after spending the entire day with me since picking me up from the airport.

"Hi, Mom." I don't hide all my exasperation.

"I know, I know, we were just there." She repeats the thoughts I just had, and I can hear my dad sighing in the background. "I just wanted to check in, see if maybe you changed your mind."

"Thank you, but no. I promise I'm okay."

She spent the day trying to convince me to come spend the night, and tomorrow night and probably the rest of my life, with them in their little apartment.

I obviously refused.

It's Saturday. I was supposed to fly home from Mexico yesterday, but after the whole *bus highjacking* on Thursday, the authorities made us stick around an extra day to give statements.

It was weird, and stressful, and long, and... confusing.

"Well, if you decide you want to come over, you are always welcome," Mom reminds me.

"I know, Mom. But I just want to try and get back to normal."

"If you're sure."

"I am," I sigh. "It was freaky." Seeing three men die, and hearing more get shot, should be more than freaky... but that's a worry for intrusive thoughts later. "But it's not like I was personally targeted. No one is coming after me. And even if the guys who attacked us wanted to travel all the way to Minnesota to steal me, or whatever the plan was, they're all dead," I try to reason.

"Except the man in the mask," Mom argues back.

I glance through the big picture window in my living room to Hans's house. "He helped us, Mom."

When we gave our statements, I lied. I told the police officers the man in the mask had blue eyes and tattoos on the visible part of his neck. And that the tiny bits of hair I could see in the mask eye holes were black.

I gave my parents the same description.

I don't know why I lied.

No, that's another lie.

I lied because a part of me believes that the man in the mask is Hans.

I still don't understand how it's possible. I only know what I saw and what I felt when I saw him. And if it is him... If there's even a chance that the man who saved our lives on that stupid, sweaty bus was Hans, then I can't let him get in trouble for it.

My coworkers were all pretty rattled, so I don't know if any of them even noticed his long hair or his eye color, but my contradicting eyewitness should confuse matters enough that no one will come looking for my neighbor.

Mom exhales. "I know. I'm just worried about you being alone in that house."

"I'll be fine." I roll my lips, then add, "If I need anything, Hans is just across the street."

She makes a sound of agreement. "Okay, fine. I'll let you go."

"Thanks. I'll call you tomorrow, okay?"

"Okay. Good night, Cassie. I love you."

My dad shouts his love through the phone.

"Love you both."

Ending the call, I set my phone back on the counter.

I often wonder if having siblings would've made my parents less involved in my life, but I don't think it would've mattered. They are who they are. And, annoying or not, it's nice having people who care.

My eyes wander back to the front windows.

Hans doesn't have that.

There's obviously a lot I still don't know about his past, most of it, really, but I know his parents are gone. I know his sister is gone. That she was murdered.

I bite my lip.

If it really was him in Mexico, if Hans really is the man who so swiftly and violently saved us, is that because of his past?

My nose twitches as an unpleasant scent hits it.

"Oh shit!" I spin around and snatch the hot mitts off the counter before yanking open the oven door.

A mixture of steam and smoke billows out, and I use the mitts to fan it away.

"Damn it." Lifting out the tray, I can see the darkened edges around the too-flat cookies.

"No!" I whine, knowing I've burned them.

After shutting the oven door, I turn it off and set the tray on top of the stove.

A few of the chunks of sweet corn that are sticking out of the cookies caught fire. There are no flames now, just smoke trailing from the burnt little chunks.

I look at the Post-it note I already filled out for Hans—the words mocking me. Charred sweet corn cookies indeed. The charring was supposed to only be from when I flash seared the fresh sweet corn. A little note of umami flavor to the sugar sweetness. Not charred to within an inch of its life.

My eyes start to sting, and I realize how hazy it is in the kitchen.

I groan. The last thing I need is my smoke detector going off.

I reach over the sink and open the window behind it to let in some fresh air.

Even though night has fallen, it's still warm outside. But the little breeze is immediate, and the haze starts to lessen.

I still stand here, waving the oven mitts around, trying to bring in more fresh air.

It's dark out, and with the lights on inside, I can't see through the window into the backyard, but I'm thankful my house backs up to the woods. The number of times I've had to wave smoke out of my house is a little embarrassing, and I'm glad no one can see me.

The clock on the back of the stove shows that two minutes have passed since I pulled the cookies out of the oven, but the recipe says to let them sit for five before transferring to the cooling racks.

At this point, it doesn't really matter what I do with them, but I'm still going to stick with the recipe.

I let my eyes close as I breathe through my frustration.

Along with needing to hone my baking skills, I need to figure out what to do next month.

My company is giving everyone who was on that bus the next two weeks off, fully paid, but it doesn't take a lawyer to recognize the huge pile of shit that will no doubt hit the fan.

Our names were supposed to be kept confidential, but with social media and those job networking sites, it hasn't taken the news outlets long to narrow down the people involved.

I have no desire to talk to the media about what happened, but I can think of at least four people right off the top of my head who will jump at the chance.

Even if the company can survive the scandal, I don't know that I want to deal with it.

My cheeks puff out with my exhale, and I accept that I should start looking for a new job on Monday.

I've got a little money saved, but not enough to survive being jobless for more than a month or two. And I'm all too familiar with how long the hiring process can take.

A crack sounds from outside, and my eyes snap open.

I stand totally still, listening, but I don't hear anything else.

Unnerved, I slowly step away from the open window.

It's nothing.

It certainly isn't the Mexican cartel coming to get you.

Just stay calm.

I take another step across the kitchen, toward the door that leads outside.

I don't go out onto my little back patio much, since I'm more of an indoor girl, but I do have a small slab of concrete behind the kitchen, big enough for a grill I never use.

My gaze flicks back to the window.

"It's nothing." I stamp my foot as I say it.

A branch fell out of a tree because it was dead, or a bunny, maybe a coyote, stepped on a stick. The noise was literally nothing.

But if I don't check, I know I won't be able to sleep.

Huffing out a breath, I move to the storage bench sitting next to the door and yank it open.

I may not go outside much, but I keep all my things right here. A pile of knitted winter hats—my last failed hobby. A rain jacket that's too tight on my arms. Two and a half pairs of flip-flops. Oversized grill tongs. And... I pick up the beginner crossbow sitting on top of it all. Then I wince over the fact that I left it sitting in there loaded, arrow already notched into place.

It's not heavy duty, only meant for target practice, not for hunting. But it does have a high-powered flashlight attached to it.

And holding it will make me feel better about opening the back door.

It's shaped like a short shotgun, with a pistol-type grip and trigger in the middle of the length. So I put the butt to my shoulder and hold it in place with my right hand, my pointer finger resting next to the trigger, then I use my left hand to swing the door open.

Darkness.

I forgot to turn on the flashlight feature before I opened the door.

There's a small pool of light on the grass from the open kitchen window, but there seems to be no moon at all tonight.

My left hand fumbles for the little button on the side of the bow, then I find it.

And I flip it on.

Brightness flares in my vision, and I blink it away to see a man sprinting across the lawn toward me.

A stranger.

I stumble backward.

And I pull the trigger.

I don't even mean to.

I didn't even aim.

I just reacted.

But before I can shove the scream out of my lungs, I watch the arrow land. Right in the center of his throat. Sinking through the soft skin.

He falls on his next step and smashes down onto his knees.

Shock and fear fight for space inside me as I slam the door shut and lock it.

That did not just happen.

I drop the empty crossbow and rush to the window, sliding that shut too.

I try to look through the window, then remember it's too dark.

I hustle back to the door and flip on the switch for the exterior light I completely forgot about two minutes ago, then go back to the window over the sink.

Maybe nothing really happened.

Light floods the yard, illuminating the man.

"Um." I press my hands together.

In the middle of my yard, maybe twenty feet from my back door, is the stranger, clawing at the arrow protruding from his neck.

"Umm!" I say it a little louder.

Then he pitches forward.

"Umm!" My voice jumps an octave.

I flip off the light.

Ohmygod, ohmygod, ohmygod...

I spin away from the view and run across my house to the front door.

I'm in a pair of short sleep shorts and a thin tank top, and I have to press a hand over my boobs to keep them from bouncing all over the place, but I don't stop running for anything.

Not my shoes. Not my keys. Not anything. I just rip open my front door and run straight across my front lawn toward Hans's house.

CHAPTER 61
Hans

THE SHOWER CURTAIN FLICKS WATER AT ME AS I SHOVE it open to grab my towel off the rack on the wall.

I kept my distance after jumping out the back door of that bus, but there was no way I was going to leave her there without my protection. So I stayed an extra day too.

My flight home left twenty minutes after Cassandra's, but with my lack of checked luggage and the speed of my driving, I made it home—truck parked, garage door closed—eight minutes before Cassandra's parents pulled up to my neighbor's house with their daughter in tow.

I braced myself for my girl to storm straight over, demanding an explanation. But that didn't happen.

Maybe because her parents spent all day at her house.

Maybe I just imagined her gasping my name on the bus.

Maybe she didn't put it together.

I have the towel over my head, squeezing water out of my hair, when I hear something.

I lower the towel and stand in stillness for a moment.

Then I hear it again. The sound of my name being shouted.

I've taken two steps when the knocking starts.

"Hans!" Cassandra's voice is panicked. Scared.

I cut across the living room.

"Ha—" Her shout cuts off when I open the door.

CHAPTER 62

Cassie

"Ha—Holy shit!"

My gaze scans the bare skin in front of me, down to the towel wrapped low around Hans's hips.

Hans opened the door practically naked, and I don't know what to do with myself.

A large hand closes around my forearm, and he pulls me into his house, slamming the door behind me. But I can't look away from his... body.

And all the scars.

"Cassandra," he snaps. "What happened?"

I force my eyes up to his and swallow. "I think I killed someone."

He doesn't even flinch. "Explain."

With nothing else to hold on to, I twist my fingers in the hem of my shirt. "I, um, I heard something in the backyard, after—after, um, I opened the window. And then—"

Hans frames my face with his warm hands. "Breathe, Butterfly."

I stare into his dark gaze, appreciating his damp hair and the way a piece hangs across his forehead. It makes him feel normal.

I take a breath.

"I opened the back door to see." His jaw works, but he stays quiet. "I was holding my, uh, crossbow. And when I turned the light on, there was—" My heart rate spikes. "There was a man running straight for me."

"What man?" His voice is even.

"I didn't recognize him. Hans..." I reach up and grab his wrists. "I shot him. It was an accident. I didn't mean to pull the trigger. But he scared me and I stumbled. And I..."

"Where is he now?" His thumbs brush across my cheeks.

"My backyard," I whisper. "I think he's dead."

"Did you call anyone yet?"

I shake my head. "I... I didn't even think about that. I just ran over here."

"Good girl." Hans leans in and presses his lips against my forehead. Then he pulls back. "Do you trust me?"

I nod. Because I do.

He presses another kiss to my forehead. "Good. Come with me."

Hans lets go of my cheeks to grab one of my hands, then pulls me with him to the door that leads to the basement.

He yanks it open, and we descend.

My bare feet are a little sore from running over here, catching a few pebbles when I crossed the street, but when we reach the bottom of the stairs, the cool concrete floor soothes my soles.

Hans lets go of my hand so he can resecure his towel, but he doesn't stop walking, so I follow him across the unfinished basement to... a wall.

My lips purse, starting to form the word *what*, but then he presses his hand to the wall, and a door-sized panel swings outward.

Behind the secret door is a hidden door made of metal that looks sturdy enough to survive a bomb.

Hans lifts his right hand and sets it on a black rectangular screen embedded in the wall next to the door.

My jaw drops.

Is that a freaking palm reader?

There's a heavy-sounding clunk, then the thick metal door opens inward.

Wow.

Hans guides me toward the pitch-black room, and as soon as I step foot inside, lights automatically turn on above me, filling the large room with an even glow.

Extra wow.

My mouth opens even wider.

The room is big. Like bigger than it should be, based on the size of the house upstairs.

I can't tell whether the walls are made of concrete or metal. But one entire wall is covered with a sort of rack system with hooks. And hanging from those hooks are guns. A whole-ass wall of guns. And are those... grenades?

The door shuts behind Hans, and I hear the quiet whirl of fans turning on.

"The life support systems automatically come on when a body is in the room." I look up at the ceiling, then over to Hans. He tips his head to the side as he walks past me, like he's thinking about what he said. "Well, an alive body."

"Um, has there been an unalive body in here?"

I probably shouldn't ask that. If this were a movie, I'd be yelling at the girl to turn around and run out of the scary bunker.

But this isn't a movie. This is my life. And this is my neighbor who calls me Butterfly and drives me to the airport. And who I'm now ninety-nine percent sure was the man on the bus in Mexico.

"Not in this house."

Not in... Oh, right. Dead bodies.

My eyes follow Hans as he opens one of the four doors lining the far wall, revealing a closet.

More scars mark his back, with one particularly long line of raised flesh two inches away from his spine.

"You have other houses?" My question comes out breathy.

"A few," Hans replies, then he drops his towel.

And *holy ass cheeks*, this man is built like a Viking god. Battle marks and all.

Even though I've had his tongue, fingers, and cock inside me, I haven't seen him naked. Not even shirtless. Until right now.

When he bends down to pull on a pair of black boxer briefs, I get a glimpse of his balls hanging down between his legs, and I have to brace my hand on the wall.

Lord have mercy, why is that hot?

When he starts to pull on a pair of black pants, like the ones he wore to dinner at my parents', I drag my eyes away to look around the rest of the room.

Opposite the weapon wall is what I can only describe as a monitor wall. Like something out of one of those Jason Bourne movies. Rows of screens, all turned off at the moment, mounted above a counter that runs the length of the wall.

"Wait, did you say you have a few houses?" I ask as I walk over to stand behind the rolling office chair centered in front of the monitors.

"We'll talk about it after. Okay?"

I turn back in time to see Hans lacing up a pair of his boots, black T-shirt already in place. "After?"

Righting himself, Hans moves to the weapon wall.

He slips a shoulder holster off a hook and shrugs it on.

I watch in fascination as he selects two matching handguns, doing that thing people do in the movies to check the clips, then shoving them into the spots on the holster. Then he grabs a long knife in a fabric sheath and attaches the whole thing to his belt.

"You're like Batman," I whisper. He's only missing the cape and mask.

Hans shakes his head. "Nah. My parents got rich off mining."

His tone is dry, and it sounds like he's joking. But I guess I don't know the Batman lore that well because I don't understand the joke.

"Wait." It suddenly dawns on me what he's doing. "You're going over there."

Hans nods, then gestures for me to move so he can pull the chair out.

I do, and then he points. "Sit."

I comply.

Hans grips the back of the chair and turns me to face the monitors.

I don't see a way to turn them on, but then Hans flips up some hidden panel in the counter and a keyboard appears before me.

He taps a few keys, and the screens come to life.

I lean forward, trying to get a closer look, since most of the screens are split into four quadrants.

"What..." Then I recognize what I'm seeing.

A view from Hans's front door, at eye level. A view of the street. A few more of what must be Hans's yard. My house.

Lots of views of my house.

"I'm the only person who can get into this room from the outside, but you can exit the room anytime you want," Hans says.

I tip my head back to look up at him. "Are you obsessed with me?"

Hans blinks once, slowly. "Cassandra, I need you to listen." *Oh my god, I think he is.* "You aren't trapped here, okay?"

I nod, but I'm still thinking about the fact that he's obsessed with me.

Hans points to the monitors. "You can watch me through these so you can see when I'm coming back. If something happens, and I don't come back—" Hans sets a phone down in front of me. "Call the contact A3."

His words are like a bucket of ice water on my skin. "What do you mean, not come back?"

"Just a precaution." He points to the phone. "Now, tell me who to call."

"A3," I repeat. "Who is that?"

"His name is Dom. He owes me. And if he doesn't answer, try A2 or A1." He pauses. "In that order."

When he starts to step away, I reach for him. "Please don't go."

He grips my hand in his. "I'll be right back, Butterfly. Stay here."

And then he's gone.

The heavy door shuts behind him, and the locks slide into place with a thud.

Oh Jesus.

I tap the phone to make sure it's not locked. Because if he *doesn't come back* and I don't have a way to make a phone call, I'm going to start finally freaking out.

But the phone isn't locked.

And I can see the home screen. And the photo saved as the background is... me. Asleep in his bed.

I bite down on my lip.

He's totally obsessed with me.

CHAPTER 63
Hans

THERE'S ONLY ONE QUESTION I NEED ANSWERED. WAS this man coming for Cassandra, or was he coming for me?

Either way, if he's not already dead, I'm going to kill him.

CHAPTER 64
Cassie

My eyes bounce from screen to screen, but I can't find Hans. And I can't hear anything, so I don't know if he's still in the house.

I should've told him my front door is unlocked.

Not that he needs to go through my house; he can just go around it to get to the body.

I reach over with my right hand and pull on one of the little hairs on my left forearm. Then I make a face when it hurts.

Okay, so I can still feel things. Then why am I not stressing the fuck out about killing someone?

I'm almost certain the man I accidentally shot with an arrow is dead. And I'm almost certain I should be having a meltdown. Questioning my morality. Begging forgiveness from a god above. But I'm not.

And, well, he shouldn't have been there.

I can't think of a single innocent reason why a man could be sprinting for me, through my backyard, in the dark.

A shiver skitters up my arms.

I've never been one for scary movies. And that moment—the light flicking on and revealing him—is going to wake me up at night.

I wrap my arms around myself—this room is shockingly cold —and scan the screens again for Hans.

Nothing.

He should've crossed the street by now.

My attention snags on a mostly black screen.

There.

It's hard to make out dark movement on a dark background, but it looks like—I lean closer to the screen, causing the edge of the counter to dig into my stomach. Hans is running. Through his backyard and into the woods. Literally in the opposite direction of my house.

"What the hell?"

He disappears.

I look around at the other screens, trying to find him again.

Hans isn't leaving. He wouldn't bring me down here, then load himself up with weapons just to run away into the forest.

Pretty sure.

Palms on the counter, I push myself up, then cross over to the main door.

One of the screens shows the empty basement beyond the door, so I know no one is lurking there, but I need to know...

I grab the lever handle and depress it.

It moves, and I can hear the heavy sound of the locks disengaging.

Not locked in.

I pull the door open just a few inches, then shut it, and the locks do their automatic thing again.

"Okay." I blow out a breath. "Trust the process."

Keeping an eye on the monitors, I cross to the back of the room and open the first door on the back wall. The closet Hans got his clothes from.

The shelves are lined with stacks of clothing. All in shades of black and gray.

I grab a black hooded sweatshirt. Hans doesn't have much body fat, but he's tall and built, so when I pull the garment on, it's spacious enough for my chubby frame. It's also so long it's the same length as my shorts.

I snag a pair of socks and stuff them in the hoodie pocket, then shut the closet.

I keep glancing at the monitors, but since I'm already up, I can't stop myself from checking the other doors.

The second door reveals a closet full of duffel bags and boxes of electronics.

The third door reveals a closet full of nonperishable food. Mostly bland-looking things, packs of stuff I've seen in camping stores. But there's also a half-full case of Skittles, the bright-colored packaging jarring next to everything else.

I take a pack.

Moving to the last door, I open it and feel that chill roll across my skin again.

Behind the fourth door is another door. A heavy metal one, just like the one we came through to get in here. But this one is leading the other way. Toward the backyard. Where nothing else should be.

I slam the *closet* door shut and hurry back to the chair.

The wheels slide around a little bit as I pull the oversized socks onto my feet.

A handful of the views on-screen are of the dilapidated house at the end of our little cul-de-sac, but I don't spend time looking at those feeds. I don't know why he has cameras on that place, but he's not going there. He's going to my house.

My house, which is featured in the majority of the camera angles.

I reach up and touch the screen that shows my large living room windows.

Since it's dark outside and lights are on inside my house, it's easy to see straight inside. I can see my couch, part of my work desk, and part of the opening that leads into my kitchen.

Hans has sat right here—I grip the chair armrests—and he's looked right into my home.

Heat swirls in my belly.

My reaction to Hans has always been *more*.

I've been more interested in him than I should be.

I've focused on him. Wondered about him. Fantasized about him. Thought about stripping down in my bedroom window just for the hope that he might see me. And want me.

I never did it, but I wanted to.

And *this*... Him watching me. Or whatever this is. I know it's not right.

And I know it's not right for me to feel so fucking good about it.

But I don't really feel like fighting it.

I know who I am. And I'm a lot.

My scattered attention span. My attempts at baking that I know are nowhere near as good as my mom's. My ultra-curvy body that I have no intention of changing.

All my relationships have been surface only. Fun while they lasted but nothing special.

My parents raised me to have good self-esteem. And I mostly do. But a part of me has just assumed I'd be one of those *single forever* women. And I was okay with that. I accepted it.

I look around at the other screens, wondering if he can see into my bedroom.

My core muscles tighten just thinking about it.

Could he see me touching myself?

Would he have sat here, gripping that big dick of his, jerking off while he watched?

My eyes bounce around as I look for my bedroom window, but I don't see a good view of it.

I move my attention back to my living room and yelp.

Because Hans is there.

Inside my house.

CHAPTER 65
Hans

I cross Cassandra's living room and flip the deadbolt on her front door.

Assuming she's watching and not disobeying by leaving my safe room, I stop in front of the picture window and hold up my hand with my fingers spread, letting her know I'll be back in five minutes.

Then I turn and head back toward the back of her house.

The man outside is most certainly dead.

My pretty little Butterfly shot him straight through the Adam's apple.

I believe it was an accident, but it's still a damn good shot.

Even though I should be leaving, I move into the kitchen. There's something in here for me.

On the counter, next to the stove with the tray of burned cookies, is a Post-it note. Just like all the other ones stacked in my nightstand. And I know she was going to give it to me.

I read the words.

Charred Sweet Corn Cookies.

"Ah, Christ." I shake my head. "Why, Butterfly?"

I nudge one, and it slides across the pan. At least they aren't stuck.

It feels dry, and when I pick it up, little pieces fall off. But I'll take my cookies crumbly over wet, like the last batch.

Opening wide, I shove the whole thing into my mouth.

My throat closes involuntarily, the intense campfire taste over-whelming my senses. But I chew.

Needing a little help, I step to the sink and turn on the tap. I bend and put my mouth under the stream and gulp some water.

Then I shove another whole cookie into my mouth.

What the fuck is wrong with me?

Not wanting to dirty one of Cassandra's containers, and not willing to leave them behind, I stack the cookies to make them easy to carry.

I can hold eight in my hand, but she made a full dozen.

I work to swallow the burned corn, then I cram two more cookies in.

I've tasted Cassandra at the source. I don't need to settle for her awful baking anymore. But that doesn't matter. If anyone so much as thought about eating what she made for me, I'd slice their stomach out of their body.

I duck my mouth back under the faucet.

The water helps to dissolve the mashed-up cookies in my mouth, and I'm finally able to get them down.

With my stack of eight cookies in one hand, I stride back to the front door and scoop up a pair of Cassandra's tennis shoes. It's her favorite pair. The ones she always wears when she's leaving the house for errands, so I know they're comfortable.

I hesitate for a split second as I consider bringing them to my nose, but then I remember that she might be watching through the window, so I shove them under my arm instead.

I've already shown her too much of my hand with the whole *surveillance* thing. I don't need to add shoe sniffer to the list.

Flipping off the backyard light, I exit out the back door.

Not having camera angles in her backyard was clearly a fucking rookie mistake, but I utilize that now so Cassandra can't see me use my own set of keys to lock up her house.

Though, again, the fact that she's currently sitting in my safe room, looking at all the live feeds I have of her house, has probably tipped her off to the fact that I've invaded her privacy.

Are you obsessed with me?

My feet are silent in the grass as I circle around the back of her house in complete darkness, having memorized every inch of her property.

Yeah, Cassandra Lynn Cantrell. I'm obsessed with you.

Getting to her driveway, I jog the distance to my house.

When I first checked out what happened, I circled through the woods. Because I needed to know if the man was alone or if he was part of a force trying to hit my location—and Cassandra just happened to hear the wrong thing at the wrong time.

But since it appears as though the man was by himself, now it's about speed. Because I doubt this is about Cassandra. I'm certain this man was coming to confirm my location.

I jump up the steps to my front door and use my free hand to unlock it.

Once inside, I go straight to the kitchen.

It takes me seconds to snag a Ziploc bag and shove the cookies in, then cross the house to my room, put the Post-it on the stack with the others, pull two backpacks out of my closet, shove the cookies into one, then head back downstairs.

CHAPTER 66

THE MOMENT HANS APPEARS ON THE SCREEN SHOWING the rest of the basement, I jump up from the chair and rush to the door.

I pull it open just as Hans opens the outer door. And I still at the sight of him.

His hair is still loose, drier now and slightly wavy, and he has a backpack hiked over each shoulder.

With the brighter basement lights behind him, he has an almost otherworldly look.

His eyes move down my body.

My look is less *otherworldly* and more *I stole your sweatshirt*.

He lowers his eyes to my hands and the half-eaten bag of Skittles I'm holding.

Oh, right, I also stole his candy.

Hans doesn't give me time to step back. He hooks his hand around the back of my neck and slams his mouth to mine, sliding his tongue between my lips.

He groans.

Like *groans*.

The fingers on my neck flex, and he cups the back of my head with his other hand.

He's only touching me above the shoulders, but it feels like he's consuming me.

I dig my hands into his firm sides.

He licks into me. "Fuck." He pulls me closer. "Goddamn Skittles." His mouth consumes mine. "Fucking seductress."

His grip on me tightens, then he pulls back.

"We gotta go."

I nod. Then come back into the moment. "Wait, go where?"

Hans swings one of the backpacks off his shoulder and pulls my favorite tennis shoes out of a side pocket.

I automatically drop them to the floor and start to shove my feet into them.

As soon as my second heel slips into the shoe, Hans grabs my hand and pulls me out of the strange surveillance room.

A tiny part of me was wondering if Hans would try to keep me down here, so him guiding me out of the room is a good sign. But then I remember the way he ate my ass in the garage last weekend, so Hans locking me up and keeping me as his little sex pet might not be a bad thing.

Hans pauses to make sure both doors close behind us, then we're back to moving.

I follow him up the stairs, through the kitchen, and into the garage.

Like last time, the garage is pitch black, but Hans keeps his hold on my hand and guides me to the pickup truck.

I hear the door open, but no light comes on.

"Climb in."

"I can't see."

"Oh, right." Hans says it like he didn't realize there is zero light in here.

His hand leaves mine, and I hear his footsteps across the floor, then the garage door starts opening.

It's dark outside too, but there's enough ambient light to illuminate the truck in front of me.

I climb in and am closing my door just as Hans opens his.

He tosses the two backpacks into the back seat, then gets in himself.

"So..." I start as he turns the truck on. "Can you see in the dark?"

Hans turns his face to me. "What?"

"You walk around like you can see everything when I can't even see my hand in front of my face."

He shrugs and puts the truck in reverse. "I just have things memorized."

Memorized.

Hans backs out of his driveway, then right up mine, stopping with his rear bumper a few feet from mine.

Ah yes, my car that won't start.

"Stay here," Hans tells me, then jumps out, leaving the engine running.

Watching him circle around to the back of the truck, I realize I never got an answer when I asked where we were going.

Hans lowers the tailgate, and I watch him open a panel I didn't know was there in the side wall.

He pulls something free, then slams the panel shut and jogs off around the corner of the garage.

My eyes widen.

Is that...?

Just before he disappears into the dark, he gives the plastic a shake, and it unfurls into what can only be described as a body bag.

I bite down on the completely inappropriate urge to laugh.

A man with a basement full of guns and camera angles of my house, who also keeps body bags in his truck, has to be a red flag. Right?

I stay turned in my seat, my eyes glued to where I last saw Hans.

If he's running into the backyard with *that*, then the man must be dead.

On cue, Hans reappears with an *occupied* man-sized bag slung over his shoulder.

It hasn't even been a minute.

He must be good at bagging bodies.

Hans stops at the back of the truck and bends forward with a heft of his shoulder, causing the body to thud into the truck bed.

The impact reverberates through the vehicle, and my mouth pulls into a frown.

Ew.

Hans slams the tailgate back into place, then pulls a retractable cover across the top of the truck bed, blocking anyone's view of what's inside.

He opens his door, but before getting back into the truck, he takes a little bottle of hand sanitizer out of the pocket in his door and slathers his hands with it.

"Safety first," I try to joke.

Hans drops the bottle back into the pocket, then climbs in. "Can never be too careful."

"From the number of scars you have, I'm guessing you learned that the hard way." I clamp my mouth shut, but Hans just lifts a shoulder.

"The hard lessons are the ones you usually heed more."

I think about that and have to agree.

Hans drives us off our street, through our little neighborhood, and toward the main highway.

"So..." I drag the word out. "Is there a reason we're taking the corpse on a joy ride? Do cops like delivery service on murder victims?"

"We're not involving the cops."

His words shouldn't bring me such relief, but I don't want to spend my life in prison for accidentally killing someone.

"But what if people ask—"

Hans is shaking his head before I finish. "Nothing happened for them to ask about."

"But—"

"Nothing happened, Cassandra. No one died in your yard. You want to talk about it, we can talk about it. But you only talk to me, okay?"

I roll my lips together, then nod. "Okay."

"Far as the world is concerned, all that happened was you came over to my place, and we decided to go to a hotel for the night."

"Hotel?"

Hans turns us off the highway and onto a side road. "We need a little space from Holly Court."

I don't think I've been down this road, and from the looks of it, there's not much out here.

"When you said you had other houses..."

"Not local," Hans answers. "I had a condo downtown, above my club, but the manager and her family live there now." He taps his fingers on the steering wheel. "Several months ago, the ownership transferred to an overseas entertainment company, so no one should be going there looking. And if anyone does, I have good security."

I repeat the first part back to myself. "You have a club?"

"I just own it. I don't run it."

"Like a nightclub?" I don't know why I'm so hung up on this.

"More of a venue. Concerts and stuff."

This doesn't sound like the sort of thing Hans would like. "Why?"

He drums his fingers on the steering wheel. "All sorts of people are always coming and going from a place like that. Can hardly tell who's who half the time."

His answer is cryptic. And I feel like it might have something to do with the reason he has body bags stored in the back of his truck.

I swallow, thinking about the body bouncing around in the back of the truck. "The guy I killed... He was a bad guy, right?"

I don't know why I expect Hans to know the answer to that, but I want to feel better about not feeling bad.

"He wasn't good," Hans replies. "But I need to get some more information."

"How do we do that?"

He pulls his phone out of his pocket. "I gotta make a few calls."

I pat my hoodie pocket, knowing that's where I put the phone when I was still in the basement.

How did he...?

The phone starts to ring, and I see him look down at it for a second, like he's deciding something, then he puts it to his ear.

Was he going to put it on speaker and then decided not to?

Even though the audio is going through the phone, it's still connected to the truck, so the screen on the dashboard shows the call is being made to someone named K.

"Karmine," Hans greets. "I have a situation."

K is for Karmine.

Then I hear the unmistakable sound of a female voice on the other end of the line.

The jealousy I feel is so instantaneous I don't even have time to register what I'm doing until I'm doing it.

My finger presses the screen on the dashboard, switching the audio to the truck.

It clicks over, the speakers humming with silence from the other end of the line.

"Hans?" the feminine voice prompts.

I cross my arms and glare at Hans's profile.

He glances at me, and from his expression, I can tell he doesn't understand what's going on.

"Give me one sec," Hans says, then reaches for the mute button.

"You called me!" Somehow the woman says it in a way that makes it sound like they know each other well. Like she's dealt with this sort of behavior from Hans before.

He drops his phone into the little cubby on the dashboard. "What's wrong?"

"Who is she?" My arms stay crossed.

"Karmine. She's a... colleague."

I turn in my seat so I can glare at him harder. "In health inspecting."

This time, when his eyes dart over to me, he reaches out and grips my forearm. "Stop that." He pulls, dislodging my crossed arms. "Don't be mad at me." He slides his hand down until he's holding my hand in his. "Karmine and I work together... helping good people and hurting bad people."

"Have you slept with her?" I snap.

I have no right asking him that. No right to feel this territorial over a man I've slept with once. But if he's gonna be obsessed with me, he'd better be obsessed with *only* me.

When Hans lets go of my hand, I suck in a breath.

If he's going to stop touching me while he admits to having slept with her, I'm going to hit him.

"That's fucking one," Hans growls.

He presses the button to unbuckle my seat belt.

I try to slap his hand away, not sure what he's doing, but he catches my fingers and shoots a glare of his own my way. "That's two."

He drops my hands and, keeping a grip on the wheel with his left hand, leans over so he can reach across my body. He hooks his hand around the front of my waist, and then he drags me across the bench seat toward him.

"Put your seat belt on," Hans bites, acting like he's not the one who just unbuckled me.

But my heart has started racing, and my chest feels warm, so I do as he says and buckle the strap across my lap.

When I finish, Hans grips the far outside of my thigh, his fingertips digging into the soft, bare flesh. And I love it.

"I have never slept with Karmine." He looks down at me, the headlights illuminating a straight road ahead of us. "I haven't touched another woman since you moved in across the street. Got it?"

His intensity is intoxicating.

"Got it," I whisper.

"I like your jealousy, Little Girl. But it's unnecessary." He grips me harder. "Now, unmute the call."

Satisfaction blooms inside my chest.

He's not trying to hide the conversation from me. And he doesn't want to let go of me long enough to unmute it himself.

I believe him.

I lean forward and tap the screen.

The woman must be able to hear the change because she speaks immediately. "What's wrong?"

"Possibly little. Possibly scorched earth."

"Explain." The woman's tone is all business.

CHAPTER 67
Hans

I flex my fingers against Cassandra's leg. She isn't going to like me sharing this, but if there's anyone I can be fully transparent with, it's Karmine. "I have a body that I need identified."

"You back home?"

Cassandra tenses at Karmine's question, probably not liking that she knew I was out of town.

"Yeah." I resist the urge to smile. I always dreamed of a world where my Butterfly would let me touch her. It never occurred to me to fantasize about her being possessive of me.

And I fucking love it.

I slide my hand over the top of her leg, then shove it between her bare thighs.

She follows my unspoken command and presses her legs together, squeezing my palm between her warm flesh.

Karmine makes a humming sound. "Sandra is on a job in New Mexico with the R Team." Sandra is her go-to for finding IDs, and if she's working with the Rescue Team, that means they intervened in something big. "And I'm on a hit with the K Team in Utah."

I grunt my approval. The Kill Team in action is always good for humanity.

"Can you keep him on ice?" she asks.

"No. It can't wait." I sigh. "I'm on my way to The Alliance Kill House."

I can feel Cassandra's gaze on me, but I need to pay attention to the road now. I know we're getting close.

"I'm letting you know because I think this might be what you warned me about." I refer to Karmine's warning that people were looking for me.

"Shit, man. Was he at your house?"

"Not exactly. He was at my neighbor's."

Karmine lets out a low whistle. "The girl you're stalking?"

I keep my eyes forward. "I'm not stalking her."

"Uh-huh." I can hear her damn eye roll. "You get the guy before he could touch your porridge?"

"Porridge?" Cassandra whispers, but not quietly enough.

"I'm not fucking Goldilocks," I grumble to both of them. "Can we focus?"

It's silent for a beat, then Karmine snickers. "She with you?"

I glance over at Cassandra, and she bites her lip, pretending innocence.

I sigh. "Yeah, she's here."

Karmine's laugh is more of a snort this time. "If you didn't want me to out you, you shouldn't have put me on speaker."

"That was me." Cassandra squeaks out the admission. "Sorry about the invasion of privacy."

I shake my head. Only she would apologize in this situation.

"No worries. Just one question." Karmine is talking directly to Cassandra now. "Are you with Hans willingly?"

"Um, yes?" she says like it's a question. "Sorry, are you asking if he kidnapped me?"

"Yes." Karmine doesn't mince her words.

"Oh, well, thanks for checking. But I'm happy with Hans."

I push my hand farther between her legs until I'm able to slide my fingers under her closest thigh.

I can't get her close enough.

I can't touch enough of her.

"Okay, then." Karmine accepts her answer. "So, what happened? Did you get him to say anything before he died?"

"I didn't—"

"That was also me," Cassandra cuts me off. "It was an accident."

"Well, this keeps getting more and more interesting."

I lean down and press a kiss to Cassandra's hair. "I'll give you the particulars later, but the man was in Cassandra's backyard, acting like a fucking predator. When she came over to tell me what happened, I swept the woods around our houses. No sign of anyone else, so I think he must've been a scout. But he had no ID on him. And I need to know who he's working for."

"You do have a lot of enemies," Karmine adds helpfully.

"He had a phone on him. I've disabled it, but I'll see about digging through it to see if he reported anything."

"Either way, if they're on your street, they've found you." She says what I already know, but it twists something inside me.

I just got my Butterfly. Finally got to touch her. Hold her in my hands. But if they've found me, then my life living on that quiet little cul-de-sac is over. And...

My lungs hitch.

She can't live there either.

I've put her in danger.

I've done the one thing I never wanted to do.

Small hands close around my forearm.

I look down, and all I can see are her fragile fingers against my body full of violence.

And I hate myself for bringing her into this.

It was never my intention.

But in reality, the moment she moved in across the street from me, that was it for her.

Even if I'd never become obsessed. Even if she'd never baked me a single thing. She still would've been across the street from me. And that man would've been in her yard tonight.

Spots of red trickle into my vision.

If tonight had happened, and we hadn't built this bond between us, what could've happened then?

You could've moved after she bought 1304 Holly Court.

Then I remember Mexico.

How I almost lost her only days ago.

How that had nothing to do with me. And how if I hadn't been there...

"Hans." Cassandra's voice is quiet as her hands slide up and down my arm.

My chest is heaving.

If I hadn't been there.

I was too mad about the whole situation to appreciate how scared I was. I was too angry to even think about what the world would be like if Cassandra Cantrell's light had been snuffed out.

It was so close.

She was so fucking close to slipping out of my grasp.

"Hans, Baby." One of her hands slides over to press against my chest. Pressing over my racing heart. "It's okay. I'm right here."

Another swell of emotion fills my body.

Baby.

No one has ever called me by an endearment.

No one except Cassandra when she called me a grizzly bear.

No one has ever had the right to.

No one I wanted to hear it from.

Her knee presses into my thigh as she turns toward me, and the arm not reached across between us twists around mine, hugging my arm to her body even as my fingers dig into her thigh.

Until now.

I force my lungs to fill, my expanding chest pressing against her palm.

"Call me that again," I rasp.

Her hand moves in a small circle. "Baby?"

I nod.

"It's okay, Baby." Cassandra presses a kiss on my shoulder. "I'm right here. I'm safe."

Her sweet breath is close enough for me to taste.

My favorite girl with a mouth flavored like my favorite candy.

My exhale is rough, but my next inhale is smooth.

Her hand makes another circle over my heart. "That's it. You're good, Baby."

She kisses my shoulder again, then rests her temple against it.

My muscles start to loosen.

I take another breath.

I've never had a breakdown, or whatever that just was, in front of anyone before. But if decades of working to rid the world of evil has taught me anything, it's to embrace the good.

I haven't had much good. But the woman next to me, she's my good in this world.

And losing her would destroy me.

After a moment, Karmine breaks the silence. "What do you need me to do?"

My voice is steady when I speak again. "I'm going to need intel. When we find out who he works for, we can cross it with names on incoming shipments."

"They might be expecting you," Karmine points out. "If there are breadcrumbs to follow, we'll have to assume it's a trap."

"If we're ready for it, then it's not that good of a trap."

She huffs but doesn't disagree.

I don't want to throw myself into a setup. But I also don't want to spend the rest of my life hiding.

I'm not exactly sure how to make that possible with all the different people out there who would love to kill me. But I can't give up the woman at my side. Can't give up how she makes me feel.

"Alright, I'll send you what we get for any upcoming deal in

North America. As soon as you have details on the dead guy, send them my way."

"Will do."

"When are you dropping the body off?"

The mile marker sign I've been looking for flashes in my headlights.

I lift my foot off the gas and start to depress the brake. "Now."

"I know you guys came up with a little truce or whatever that shit was at the restaurant. But maybe hurry the fuck up."

A small smile tugs at my mouth. "I don't plan to linger."

Karmine ends the call, and when a narrow gravel road appears on our right, I turn down it.

We sit in silence as the tires crunch down the path. There are no signs, nothing to signal that something important is back here. But there is. And if we were able to drive through the property, we'd see crushed cars, piles of shit you'd expect in a junkyard. And a building. An unassuming building that looks as run down as the rest of it.

But it's not run down.

It's a cover.

And it belongs to The Alliance.

An organization run by three ruthless men. Nero, the unhinged devil who has been the known leader of The Alliance for years. King, the rich guy turned mobster. And Dom, the head of the Chicago mafia who married his way into the deranged family last fall.

They aren't good men. But they aren't exactly bad either. Not by my standards, at least.

They did, however, spend a year or so under the impression that *I* was behind the recent increase in human trafficking.

It was an honest mistake. My name gets thrown around a lot.

But my name was mentioned in relation to the *transactions* because I was showing up and killing all the men, not because I was in charge of selling the women.

Usually I wouldn't mind the confusion.

Confusion is good. It's easy to get lost in.

But it became obvious that The Alliance guys weren't going to sit back idly while shit went down in their territory. And I don't expect to die of old age, but I didn't really want one of them to put a bullet in my brain because of misinformation.

So, last Christmas, when I happened to be in Chicago for a hit, I also happened to get wind of an ambush that was planned for the mafia leader and his new wife. It also just so happened that Karmine was in town, too, with some of her closest friends.

We didn't get there in time to prevent the ambush, but we did get there in time to kill the attackers. And while Karmine's army obliterated the opposition, I found myself doing a little field triage that saved Dominic Gonzalez's life.

Of course, he was too close to death to know I was even there, so when he'd recovered, I found my way into crashing a dinner The Alliance men and their wives were having at a little restaurant.

The grenades were just a precaution. I only wanted to pass on a message.

And that message was simple. I wasn't the man they were hunting for.

It's been more than seven months since that night. And I haven't heard any whispers from them. Neither that they believed me nor that they're still looking for me. So I'm not really sure whether it worked.

I'm leaning toward *it worked*. But I'm not quite willing to bet my life on it.

Not yet.

Cassandra lifts her head from my shoulder, seeing the same thing I do.

A chain link fence, with a gate padlocked shut.

CHAPTER 68

Cassie

HANS SLOWS AS HE PULLS THE TRUCK OFF THE ROAD TO the right, then turns the wheel and makes a U-turn before backing the truck up to the gate.

He puts the truck in park, then turns toward me.

His eyes bore into mine. The night's darkness hides the color but not the intensity.

I think he might say something, but instead, he grips my face and presses his lips firmly against mine.

"I'll be five seconds."

Then he's out of the truck.

Twisting, I watch him run the few steps to the tailgate and yank it down. He slaps something I can't see, and the cover on the bed retracts, swiftly rolling up and disappearing into another hidden compartment.

Hans grips the end of the body bag and drags it to him, then hoists it onto his shoulder like it's a bag of pet food and not an entire man.

Without ceremony, Hans turns and practically throws the body over the locked gate. Then he slams the tailgate shut and rushes back to the driver's seat.

Unlike the drive out here, Hans doesn't drive at a sedate pace.

He speeds back down the gravel road, causing plumes of dust to follow us.

He hardly slows when we reach the main road, but he doesn't lose control on the turn, and when the tires catch on the smooth pavement, he floors it.

CHAPTER 69
Hans

I PICK MY PHONE UP AND OPEN MY CONTACTS.

Here goes nothing.

I hit A1.

This is the last man on the list I'd want my Butterfly calling, but also the first choice for tonight. Because he feels like someone who will act immediately and save the thinking for later.

As the ringing fills the cabin, I place my hand on Cassandra's lap, and she grips it with both of her own.

CHAPTER 70

Nero

SITTING AGAINST THE HEADBOARD, I LOOK AT THE notification on my phone.

What the fuck?

Then the screen changes, showing a call from an unknown number.

Extra what the fuck. That shouldn't be possible.

My jaw tenses as I flip the yellow comforter off my legs and climb out of bed.

I have no idea what this call means, but I tired Payton out an hour ago and I'm not about to wake her.

Unknown mocks me on the screen until I step into the hallway and close the door behind me.

Then I accept the call.

But I don't say anything. I'm not playing a fucking guessing game.

"Nero." The voice that comes through the line is... familiar. "It's Hans."

There isn't much that surprises me anymore, but it takes me a full heartbeat to accept what I just heard.

"You the reason my sensors just tripped at The Junkyard?" I stride down the hall, heading toward my office.

"Yeah." I can hear that he's in a vehicle. "I need you to look at something for me."

"Is that right?" I deadpan. "Why not stick around? Have a chat with my men when they show up?"

"Funny, but I wasn't sure what sort of reception I'd get. You guys didn't exactly say you believed me."

"I dunno, explosives are usually pretty convincing." I'm still a little salty about him standing feet away from my fucking wife covered in grenades.

"I knew I wouldn't have to use them. You three seem *mostly* civilized."

I hate that I'm tempted to smile. "That why you think I'll help you now? Because I'm *mostly* civilized."

I take the stairs down to the main level two at a time.

"I think you'll help me because The Alliance has proven they don't allow human trafficking in their territory. And whoever is closing in on me is doing it because I keep fucking up their deals."

We always thought Hans was behind the new trafficking ring, but with what we found out last December, we've done more digging. And it does appear as though he's telling the truth.

At least one thing is certain: everywhere he goes, people die.

"What did you drop over my fence?" I ask.

"A body. I need it identified, and my usual guys are out of town."

"Guys," I snort.

Dom's wife told us all about the army of women that Hans showed up with to blow away the hit team that was about to kill them.

Then I process what he said, and I stop on the threshold of my office.

Out of town.

"Do you fucking live here?" I don't even bother to hide my shock.

We've heard Hans's name all over the Midwest, but we've also heard it from guys we know in the South. And out West. And on

235

the East Coast. It never even occurred to me that he might live *right fucking here*. In the Twin Cities.

Hans makes a humming sound. "Probably take me about thirty-five minutes to get to your place from mine. But that's the thing, I can't really stay there anymore. Because this guy was at my house."

I look to the ceiling.

Thirty-five minutes.

Dom is gonna have a fucking field day with this.

"And what?" I ask. "You want us to just take care of your little problem? You make too many enemies out there slitting throats that you can't kill them all on your own anymore?"

I can hear his sigh. And it's annoying.

"I don't need a rent-a-militia. I just need this guy ID'd quickly. Dom owes me a favor. Dom is Alliance. You are Alliance..." He trails off.

"So *I* owe you a favor?" I growl into the phone.

"That's kinda how it works."

I might be back to hating Hans.

"Look," he starts with a placating tone that doesn't do anything to lift my annoyance. "If I had the time to drive to Chicago and dump the body onto Dom's private elevator, I'd do that. But I'm kind of in a hurry. And I thought maybe we could be friends."

Not missing the way he casually mentioned that he knows how Dom's penthouse is set up, I let out a loud groan and make it last for several seconds before I reply. "Fine, dick. But if you want me to call you tomorrow with information, you'll need to send me your fucking number."

I hang up before he has a chance to try and recite his number to me. This isn't a fucking spy movie. If he does that, I won't remember shit, and he'll never get what he wants.

And neither will we.

I heave out a breath and dial another number.

"What?" Dom answers on the third ring.

"Get your ass to Minnesota."

CHAPTER 71

I ABSENTLY TRACE MY THUMBS BACK AND FORTH ON
Hans's hand.

I can accept that I have no idea what's going on, but clearly,
I've found myself in the middle of *something*.

Everything I've overheard rolls around in my mind as we
quickly drive toward the faint lights of downtown Minneapolis
off in the distance.

I couldn't find my way back to where we just were if I tried.
But considering Hans called it a kill house, and that Karmine
woman basically told Hans to get away from it quickly, that's
probably for the best.

I also think about Karmine's comment about Hans being
back home.

I decide to just ask. "That was you in Mexico, right?"

I look up and watch Hans work his jaw for a moment before
he sighs. "That was me."

"And you just so happened to be there? In the same city as
me. Right behind our bus. Even though you made no mention of
going on such a trip when you dropped me off at the airport?"

His fingers flex around mine. "Yeah, well, I told you to be
careful."

"Me?!" Indignation fills my chest. "How much more careful could I have been? I was sitting on a bus."

"Sitting on a bus in one of the most dangerous cities in the world."

I toss my hands up. "That was for—"

"Don't," Hans snaps.

I think he's yelling at me for arguing with him, but his hand darts up to grab mine. Then he forcefully presses my palm into his thigh. Making me touch him.

His *don't* was because I let go of his hand.

God, he really is crazy.

I squeeze his thigh.

Maybe I'm a little bit crazy too.

"That was for work," I try again, saying it calmly.

"You shouldn't have gone." He still sounds so upset.

"I didn't have a choice. It was a mandatory meeting."

"There's always a choice, Cassandra."

"Oh?" I try to cross my arms, but Hans still has my hand closest to him trapped against his thigh. "And what was your choice? You killed those guys on that bus pretty easily."

"You're already at two. Don't push me."

Heat blooms in my core as I remember him dragging me across the seat earlier.

His punishments are not punishments. So I keep pushing.

"You have your own body bags. That's not normal, Hans."

"I never pretended to be normal."

I slide a look up at him. "You told my parents you were a health inspector."

Hans glances at me. "Health inspectors *aren't* normal."

I press my lips together to keep from smiling. "Did you just make a joke?"

"I'm deadly serious."

The click of the blinker fills the car as Hans merges onto another highway. We're back around actual traffic now, with Minneapolis looming in front of us.

Hans squeezes my hand, then lets it go. "Will you grab the backpacks from the back seat?"

I have to release my seat belt to turn and reach them. And as soon as it clicks open, Hans hooks his arm around my waist. Like if we got into an accident now, he'd keep me in place just through sheer will.

The backpacks look nearly identical. The only difference is that one has a small orange tag attached to the top handle.

I set them both on the seat next to me, and he points to the one without the tag.

Instead of handing it to him, I unzip it. "What do you need?"

"My shirt."

I look back at him and the black T-shirt he's wearing, noticing the shoulder holster with two guns I'd somehow forgotten about.

"Is your shirt dirty?" I ask, thinking maybe he got some *dead guy stuff* on it.

My mouth pulls into a frown. That'd be gross.

"No, just need a costume change."

"Costume?"

Instead of replying, Hans lifts one knee until it's pressed on the underside of the steering wheel, holding it in place, then uses both hands to remove his shoulder holster.

"Oh my god, what are you doing? Let me help."

Hans sets the holster, guns included, on my lap. Followed by the sheathed knife from his hip.

Then, still driving the truck with his knee as we cruise down a highway that is *not* empty, he reaches behind himself, grips the collar of his T-shirt, and drags it up over his head.

"Hans!" I reach for the wheel, but it's unnecessary. We don't so much as swerve within the lines.

And then he's shirtless.

And I'm speechless.

He's so perfect. By not being perfect at all.

Scars. Muscles. Chest hair I want to nuzzle my face against.

Warm fabric hits me in the face, and I catch his shirt as it falls into my lap.

"Rude." I ball up the material.

"It's rude to stare."

I look past Hans to the SUV riding in the lane next to us. And the woman who's staring across at my topless man and not at the road.

Leaning across Hans, I press my middle finger to the glass.

"Cassandra."

I lean back into my seat, chastised, but the woman speeds up, so I consider it a win.

Then I look up and see the crooked smile on Hans's mouth.

"She was looking," I defend.

He shakes his head, his loose hair fully air-dried and shining in the dim light of streetlamps. "You're a menace."

I shrug, then pull his backpack onto my lap. "What shirt?" I push around the pile of dark clothes.

"Here," he says, reaching into the backpack and pulling out an item by touch.

He's back to steering with his knee, shaking the shirt out.

It's a gray button-down, and it's surprisingly not wrinkled.

I snag a corner and rub it between my fingers. It's super soft and a little stretchy. Definitely some sort of anti-wrinkle material. Great for people who run around with bags of clothes in their truck.

Hans starts to pull it on.

"Can I at least steer for you?" I ask.

"You can do my buttons."

I lean out of the way as he stretches his arms to get the shirt to sit on his shoulders correctly.

When he has it how he wants it, Hans grips the steering wheel with his left hand and drapes his right arm across the back of the seat behind me.

Twisting toward him, I grip a button in one hand and the other side of the shirt in the other, then start.

I let my fingers brush over Hans's skin. And I trace one scar for every button I do, loving the freedom of being able to just touch him like this.

I leave the top two buttons undone.

Fuck, he's so hot.

Pressing my hand to his chest, I smooth down the row of buttons. But my eyes keep trailing down. To the noticeable bulge at the front of his pants.

"Thank you." Hans's voice sounds rougher than usual. Then he nods to the other backpack. "Your turn."

I switch the bags so the one with the orange tag is closest to me. "My turn for what?"

"Change of clothes."

I look down at myself. At my bare legs, my shorts hidden beneath the hoodie I clearly stole from someone bigger than me. "Where are we going?"

"The Syndicate." He says the name of a nice hotel, and I suddenly feel uncomfortable about looking like such a goober.

"Why so fancy?"

"I like their room service."

A flare of anger hits me. "You take a lot of women there?"

"Cassandra." He's back to using his scolding tone, but I've flipped past reason.

"What's in here?" I rip open the zipper of the second backpack and see clothing that definitely doesn't belong to Hans. "I'm not wearing your stash of skank clothes."

His head jerks over to look at me.

I'm not used to these waves of awful jealousy. I've literally never felt anything like this before.

It's all consuming.

It's more than I know what to do with.

"I can't—"

I was going to say *I can't be reasonable about wearing someone else's clothes,* but the arm on the back of the seat hooks around my shoulders, and Hans presses his hand over my mouth.

"You are going to listen to me for one fucking second before you finish that sentence. The backpack is full of *your clothes*, Cassandra Lynn. Your *actual* clothes." My eyes widen. "I'm a sick fuck. I've crossed some pretty big lines when it comes to you. I won't pretend otherwise. And I never wanted to drag you into the mess that is my life, but I still wanted to have you." He uses his hold on me to pull me into his side. "I wanted to fucking keep you, Butterfly, from the moment I met you. And on the off chance something like tonight happened, I needed to be prepared. So, yeah, I took a few of your things. But now you have what you need." He takes a deep breath and lets it out. "So be a good girl for me and find something to put on. Or don't." He shrugs against me. "You're a beautiful woman. People won't question what you're wearing. But I'm a big creepy dude. If I showed up dressed in tactical black, dragging a girl like you behind me, people would assume I'm one of the trafficking assholes I've dedicated my life to killing."

I reach up and gently touch the hand over my mouth.

Hans takes another big breath. "Please don't ever tell me you *can't*."

Twisting into him, I dislodge his hand and wrap my arms around his body. It's an awkward way to hug someone. But... I have to do it.

Please don't ever tell me you can't.

He thought I was going to say I can't be with him. That I can't stay. That I can't do this.

I squeeze my eyes shut.

The only thing I can't do is give him up.

For a year, I've been dreaming of what it would be like to have his attention. And it turns out I have all of it.

Now I can't settle for anything less.

Hans presses his arm against my back, holding me to him.

"You're not creepy." I sniff into his side. "Even if you were stalking me."

"It was hardly stalking." He leans down and presses a kiss to my head.

"You just said that backpack is filled with my clothes." I try to look up at him.

Hans presses his hand to the back of my head, keeping it against his body. "It was more like watching over you."

"Uh-huh, sure."

"Do you have any idea how many times you left with your back door unlocked? Or fell asleep with your ground floor windows open?"

I bite my lip, thinking of the times I thought I did that but then would wake up to everything locked up tight. I figured I was just losing my memory. "That was you?"

"Or the times you left for work with your hair thing plugged in."

"Hair thing?" I try to lift my head again, but he doesn't let me. "My blow dryer?"

"Yeah, that." Our bodies shift together as he takes an exit. "It's a miracle you made it into adulthood."

"Hey!"

"That gray hair your parents have, I bet that's all from you."

"I'm not that bad." I huff.

"You are," he argues.

I try to pinch his side, but his body is too firm.

His hand leaves my head, then there's a smack against my ass, the cheek exposed with the way I'm twisted.

I let out a squeaky sound.

Hans's hand moves back to my head too quickly for me to sit up.

"Pretty sure the gray hair I have is because of you too," he gripes.

"Those are probably because you're so old," I grumble, feeling defensive.

Another smack to my ass.

"Hans!"

He's too quick, back to pinning me.

But I know how to play dirty.

I lift my hand like I'm going to try and push myself away from him, but instead, I lower it right over his dick.

CHAPTER 72

Hans

THE WARMTH OF HER HAND MIXED WITH THE PRESSURE of her palm has my cock hardening the rest of the way.

"Dammit, Butterfly." I lift my knee to hold the wheel, then press my left hand down on top of hers.

I need more pressure. I need all of her.

She nuzzles into my side. "Did you really break into my house?"

Is it breaking in when you have a key?

"Did you really not know?" I ask instead of answering, even though I already admitted the truth.

Cassandra shakes her head, but the movement slows. "Sometimes, I'd swear I could smell you." She moves her hand beneath mine, massaging my length.

I shift my hips. "Smell me?"

"Yeah." She turns her head into my body and inhales. And it lights me on fire.

She knew what I smelled like.

I have to lift my hand back up to the steering wheel to take a turn.

We're close to the hotel now. So close. But I can't get there quick enough.

"What do I smell like?" I'm doing my best to watch the road and not nut in my pants, so my voice is strained.

"Like pine trees." She breathes me in again. "And man."

I grunt, spotting the sign for the hotel ahead.

I slide my hand down Cassandra's back and pat her ass. "We're here."

Her fingers squeeze me through my pants one last time, then she sits up. And I allow it.

Cassandra looks over at the backpack filled with her clothes. "I forgot to change." She starts to dig through the clothes I've selected, then slowly turns to me, lifting out a pink lace thong and matching bra. "Do you know how long I looked for these? I wore them like once, and then, poof, they disappeared. I thought I was going crazy."

I lift a shoulder. "Oops."

"Oops?" She lets out a snort. "It's a good thing you're cute."

Cute?

She stuffs the underwear back in the bag and zips it up.

"Guess I'm crazy too," she mumbles.

"You're not crazy." I feel unreasonably angry hearing her say that about herself.

Flipping on my blinker, I turn into the parking ramp just before the hotel. They have valet parking, but I don't let other people drive my truck.

Cassandra turns to me and lifts a brow. "No? I killed a man tonight." She ticks the points off her fingers. "You have a room in your basement full of weapons and cameras aimed at my house. I watched you throw a dead body over a fence in the middle of nowhere. You've admitted to stalking me. You followed me to Mexico, where I saw you kill two men, but I know you killed more. Raging jealousy had me ready to fight more than one woman tonight. And now I'm happily going with you to a hotel for the night rather than calling the police, like I probably should have when I first shot that arrow." I don't like this list. "Oh, and I gave a fake witness testimony to the Mexican police."

I glance at her as I drive through the rows of parked cars. "Fake testimony?"

Her fingers play with the strap of the backpack. "I said you had blue eyes and black hair."

I back into an empty spot, then turn to look at her. "Why would you do that?"

She bites her lip in that way that makes my blood heat. "I wasn't positive that it was you, but I was pretty sure. And... I didn't want them to find you."

I turn off the engine and stare at her.

It's been twenty years since I've loved someone.

But I recognize the feeling.

It's like hearing a song for the first time after years and years but remembering every lyric the second it starts.

It's a heavy sort of comfort. But it also terrifies me.

I unbuckle my seat belt.

Cassandra was my obsession.

My Butterfly to love at a distance.

A pretty creature on the other side of the glass.

I never wanted her to know me.

Never wanted to take the chance of trying.

Because her rejection... It would crush me.

I'd known that much. Known that if she was afraid of me, it would smother the last bit of humanity I still held.

From afar, I could pretend. I could dream. I could fantasize and prepare. But never believe any of it could be real. Never think I'd ever have her close enough to touch.

I made a point to never get close enough to touch.

Cassandra reaches up and brushes her fingers along my jaw.

Not once, not ever, did I think she'd reach for *me*.

And now I'll settle for nothing less than all of her.

CHAPTER 73
Cassie

THERE'S SOMETHING GOING ON BEHIND HIS EYES. Something intense.

And I'm irritated that I don't know his expressions well enough to know what it means.

But Hans doesn't say anything, just reaches past me to grab the backpacks, lifting them easily up and over me.

As he flings his door open, I shift and slide out after him.

Of course he doesn't let me just drop down to the ground—he catches me around the waist, lowering me slowly.

I expect him to start walking toward the hotel, but Hans moves to the rear door and opens it.

I'm on the other side of the door, so I don't see what he's doing until he slams it shut.

And then my jaw slackens.

Because he's pulling on a worn leather jacket. Mixed with his boots, long hair, and shirt that's not buttoned all the way to the top, he looks like a literal rockstar.

Unaware of my throbbing libido, Hans slings a backpack over each shoulder—which somehow doesn't look out of place, then gestures for me to go.

I stop in front of the truck and hold my hand out for Hans.

His eyes snap down to my hand, and I watch him swallow before he grips my fingers with his own.

His hold is tight, like he's worried I might say *just kidding* and pull my hand back.

I glance up at his profile.

He really is stupidly handsome. And vigilante killer or not, I can't believe he didn't have a woman in his life already.

But thank fuck he didn't. If I'd had to witness a girlfriend coming and going from his place, I'd probably have moved.

Together, we step off the parking ramp and turn down the sidewalk.

The historic hotel is only a dozen yards away, and that's when I remember what I'm wearing.

I halt, pulling Hans to a stop with me.

He looks down at me, but I just hold up a finger.

I use the toe of one shoe to pull off the other, then lift my foot and pull off the oversized sock I stole from Hans's basement bunker. Shoving my bare foot back into my tennis shoe, I repeat the process with the other.

With both socks off, I shove them into the hoodie pocket and tug the sides of the hoodie down even more, ensuring it covers my sleep shorts entirely.

"What are you doing?"

Not dropping his hand, I step back to let him see. "I'm your drunk hookup for the night."

He lifts a brow. "Huh?"

"You picked me up at *your club*." I smirk. "But my high heels were killing me, so I switched into these." I point at my feet. Without the bulky socks bunched at the top of my shoes, I look much less *memorable*. "And I got too cold in my skimpy outfit, so you gave me your hoodie. Because you're a gentleman." I bat my eyes.

"Because I'm a gentleman," Hans repeats.

"Yep." I start walking, pulling him along with me. "Until we get to the room, of course. Then you're going to fuck me like the brat I am."

CHAPTER 74

Hans

THEN YOU'RE GOING TO FUCK ME LIKE THE BRAT I AM.

In the middle of the sidewalk, I drop Cassandra's hand and grip the back of her neck, forcing her to a stop.

She looks up at me, and I want to see her just like that—wide-eyed and full of mischief—with my dick stuffed down her throat.

Cassandra presses a hand against my chest and sways into me.

"Girl." My jaw is so tense I barely get the word out.

Her stance softens, and the sides of her mouth pull up. "Yes, Daddy?"

Fuck. Me.

My cock throbs, and every muscle in my body tenses.

I pull her closer and slide my hand up the back of her head until I'm gripping her ponytail. "That's three."

Her lids lower, and I don't think she's faking the intoxicated look this time.

She's perfect.

Then her other hand slides out of her hoodie pocket, and three little spheres are in her palm. Red, yellow, and orange.

My grip tightens as she lifts her hand and pours the Skittles into her mouth.

"Cass—"

She opens her mouth, sticking her tongue out. The candies sitting there.

For me.

"You *are* a fucking brat."

I seal my mouth to hers.

Her tongue pushes into my mouth, and I swipe mine across the top of hers.

The Skittles slip off her tongue, igniting my tastebuds.

The kiss is sweet. And filthy. And nostalgic.

Cassandra tugs at my jacket.

"Hans," she pants.

I keep my grip on her hair, holding her still as I pull back. Then I let her see the Skittles on my tongue before I swallow.

She lets out a small whine, and my dick strains against my zipper.

"Come," I demand, even as I start striding toward the hotel, dragging her with me.

She has to take quick steps to keep up with mine. But I slow when we near the front doors of the hotel.

I slide my hold back down to her neck, then down around her shoulders as we step inside the building.

Cassandra instantly falls into her *drunk club girl* routine, leaning her weight into my side.

Our footsteps echo around the black and gold lobby, and she sways to the quiet jazz music playing overhead.

Cassandra shifts her shoulder against my side, and then she slides her hand into my pocket. With a fucking giggle.

There's a man, about my age, working the front desk, and his eyes are locked on Cassandra's bare legs. And if this douchebag doesn't stop staring at my woman, I'm going to need a second body bag tonight.

I clear my throat loudly and slide my hand from Cassandra's shoulder to the back of her neck in a blatantly possessive move.

The man finally looks at me, and I feel a small amount of

satisfaction at the way he takes a small step back, his animal instincts reacting properly.

"G-good evening." The man remembers his job.

I skip the pleasantries. "We need a room."

"No problem." The man focuses on his computer. "How many nights?"

"Five nights," I snap.

Cassandra turns into me and places her hand on my stomach. "Just five?" she teases.

Teases.

Her hand starts to trail lower, and I slap my free hand down over hers, keeping it still.

The man clicks his keyboard, but I don't miss his eyes jumping between us.

"Grab my wallet, Little Girl." I keep my gaze on the man, but my attention is all for Cassandra.

She wants to play this game, I'll play.

Her hand twitches against my stomach, and I know if mine wasn't over hers, she'd be gripping my shirt.

My wallet is in my pocket where her other hand already is. I know she can feel it. I know she could pull it out without an effort. But she slides her fingers deeper into my pocket, scratching her nails across my upper thigh, moving toward my dick, before she grips the leather and pulls it free.

I tighten my fingers on her neck.

The man tells us a total.

Controlling the move, I use my other hand to slide her palm down my stomach to my belt buckle.

Behaving for once, she curls her fingers around the metal and keeps them there. Keeping herself right where she belongs.

She has to wiggle her arm out between us to hold my wallet up. Rather than handing it to me, she uses her thumb to flip the folded leather open and holds it still for me.

I flex my hand on her neck, showing my appreciation, and use my free hand to pull a credit card out.

Like all my documents, it's not my name. But the name on the credit card matches the name on the driver's license also in this wallet.

I hand the credit card over for the man to run.

He hands it back to me with the room keys, and I don't wait for more.

I've been here. I know how to find the elevators, and our room number is written down on the little paper card holder. And if I catch him looking at my girl again, I'll snap.

Cassandra sways against me as I walk us to the elevators.

I keep my grip on her as we wait.

I keep my grip as we ride up two floors.

I keep my grip on her as I walk her down the hall.

I keep my grip until we're in the room, with the door shut and locked behind us.

Then I let go.

CHAPTER 75

Cassie

WHEN HANS RELEASES ME, I STUMBLE FOR REAL BEFORE I catch my balance and face him.

There's a lamp on somewhere in the room behind me, casting shadows across Hans's face.

He steps toward me. And I take a step back.

With his second step, he drags his jacket off.

I step back.

Another step, he's tying his hair back.

My skin tingles, and I step back.

Another step and he's unbuttoning his shirt.

I'm not afraid of him.

This is exactly what I want.

But when a man that looks like that, like he might pull your soul out of your body through your vagina, you back away.

Hans frees the last button, and I bump into the mattress.

His shirt hits the floor, and he stops.

Eyes boring into mine, Hans kicks his shoes off while he unbuckles his belt.

He steps out of his shoes. And shoves his pants down his hips.

They pool at his feet, and he steps out of them. Steps closer. In nothing but straining boxer briefs.

My mouth has gone dry, all the moisture pooling between my thighs.

Hans grips the bottom of my sweatshirt. "Arms up."

I do as he says.

When cool air hits my stomach, I know my tank top is being pulled off too.

The hoodie passes over my head. And I'm left in just my little sleep shorts. No underwear.

I feel so exposed. More exposed than I've ever been to him.

Even with him watching me...

"Have you seen me naked?" I ask him, my voice a rasp.

"I couldn't." His hands close over my rib cage. "I couldn't cross that line."

I grab his forearms to steady my shaky legs. "You couldn't?"

He inches his hands up and runs his thumbs along the underside of my tits.

My nipples are so hard they hurt.

"I was never going to touch you." He moves his hands to cup my breasts, his thumbs brushing over my nipples.

"Never?" I dig my fingertips into his arms.

I can't imagine this never happening.

Can't believe the world would be so cruel.

"You deserve the best life, Butterfly." He lowers his mouth to suck one peak into his mouth.

My hands automatically go to his hair, finally feeling the silky texture as I dig my fingers into the strands.

He moves to the other side, sucking that nipple between his lips.

"Hans!" I call out.

He releases my breasts. "You're calling me something else tonight."

Something else?

Then I remember.

My lungs catch.

He liked that?

Hans lets go of me, then jerks my shorts down, letting out a groan when he sees I'm not wearing anything underneath them.

I reach for his waistband.

He snatches my wrist in the air.

I lean into his hold, my fingers extending. "I wanna touch it, Daddy."

His lids lower, and a wave of power crashes into me.

"You can look at it." He slides his tongue across his lower lip. "Get on the bed."

I scramble backward.

This is normally when I'd feel the most self-conscious. Completely naked in the light.

I know I'm a big girl. It's not a secret. And Hans might have a body built for fighting, not an inch of softness on him. But I can see his obsession for me glowing in his eyes.

Maybe this level of fixation is dangerous, but it's exactly what I need. Because I know he craves me. I know, because I can see it in his heaving chest, that he likes the way my stomach looks when I lean back on my elbows.

I am his addiction.

And I've never felt more desired.

Standing at the foot of the bed, Hans starts to lower his last piece of clothing.

The base of his dick is the first thing revealed.

Thick, surrounded by golden hair, I want to wrap my fingers around it.

Doing exactly what I want to do, Hans reaches into his boxer briefs and grips his length.

I watch him stroke himself once, then he pushes his boxers the rest of the way off.

My breathing increases as I take in all of him.

He's so freaking good looking I feel like I'm in a porno.

His hand squeezes at the base of his cock.

I know I've had that inside me. But I'm honestly not sure how.

Hans strokes his cock. Long, slow movements, and I can't look away from the tip as it starts to glisten.

He lifts one knee onto the bed, then the other, until he's kneeling at my feet. But his hand never stops moving.

"Spread your legs, Little Girl."

My eyes nearly roll back.

Jesus help me.

I've been wet since he called me that in the lobby.

When I don't move quickly enough, Hans leans forward. "Now."

I drop my knees open.

Hans lets out a rumble as he drops forward. His hands land on the mattress on either side of my hips, then he lowers his face and drags his tongue up my entire slit.

I drop onto my back and moan.

My hips lift, following the sensation, but he's already crawling up my body.

"Brats don't get eaten out." Hans uses his knees to push my legs wider.

I reach up and cling to his shoulders. "What do they get?"

He reaches down between us, and I feel the head of his cock pushing at my entrance. "They get fucked. Hard."

Hans slams his hips forward, cramming his cock inside me.

CHAPTER 76
Hans

CASSANDRA CRIES OUT AS SHE STRETCHES AROUND ME.

Her pussy is so wet it's dripping onto my balls.

Her fingers claw into my back.

And her needy whimpers skitter across my skin.

I lower onto my left elbow, hooking my forearm beneath her neck and gripping her opposite shoulder, keeping her in place.

I draw my hips back, then I shove them forward. Giving her my entire length.

With my right arm, I reach down and hook her knee over my elbow, spreading her wide.

Another thrust, and she arches her back, gasping when I hit even deeper.

Our mouths meet, and I can still taste the candy on her tongue.

I roll my hips as I lick between her lips.

And every time I shove my cock inside her, she makes a sound. Moaning and mewling at the intrusion.

"Do you get it now?" I growl as her perfect body bounces beneath me. "You're all I see, Cassandra."

She rolls her hips to meet mine.

"The only fucking woman I want."

She's getting wetter with each thrust.

I tighten my hold on her shoulder and rock my hips deeper. "That's it, Little Girl. Let me in."

Her body tenses.

"You like that?" I'm practically panting. My heart is fucking racing.

I have my Cassandra, here, in the light.

She wraps her arms around my neck. "I love being your little girl."

"Fuck." I press my lips to hers. Our breaths combining as one. "You're so good." I lick into her mouth. "So perfect. My Cassandra."

When I pull back, she stares up at me. Eyes shining. "My Hans."

My cock starts to leak.

"My everything."

I release her leg and slide my hand between our bodies.

"You only get wet for me." My fingers slip across her clit. "I'm the only one who gets to touch you."

The heat around my cock starts to clench.

"That's it, Little Girl." I rub quicker circles as my hips thrust harder. "Tell me what I want to hear, and you can come."

"Only you." She slides her hands up into my hair, tugging it, holding my head close to hers.

I groan.

"Only you can touch me," she promises.

I'm right there. Almost over the edge. But I need her to say the rest. "And?"

Cassandra lowers a hand between us, and I feel her fingers next to mine, swiping through her slickness, brushing against the base of my cock.

"And." She lifts her fingers to my lips. "I only get wet for Daddy."

I suck her fingertips into my mouth, the taste of her pussy coating my tongue. And I start to come.

My cock swells and my balls pull up, and I'm filling my little Butterfly as I moan around her fingers.

CHAPTER 77
Cassie

HAN PULSES INSIDE ME.

The size of him, the stretch of him. The pressure of his fingers against my clit. And the heat of his mouth as he licks my fingers clean is more than I can handle.

The orgasm slams into me, and I have to press my mouth to Hans's shoulder to muffle my scream.

CHAPTER 78

IT'S LATE, OR RATHER VERY EARLY IN THE MORNING, when I finally step out of the bathroom, freshly showered and wearing the pajamas Hans conveniently stole from my house and put into the backpack he prepared for me.

After Hans played my body like a professional musician, we ate room service burgers, sitting half-dressed on the bed.

I insisted that Hans shower first since I was still working on my food and because I knew I'd take longer. And now I feel like me again.

I find Hans sitting up in bed, scrolling through a phone, wearing nothing but boxer briefs, with the blankets around his waist.

Climbing in on the other side, I scoot over and lie on my side, facing him.

Hans sighs while he powers down the phone. "I'm gonna have to go back to the house tomorrow if I want to break into this phone."

I assume that must be the one he got off the dead guy.

Hans slips it into a black pouch and sets it on the nightstand.

And I scrunch my face. "What's that?"

He looks where I'm looking. "Oh, that's a faraday bag. I

disabled all the features on the phone that matter, but this will ensure no one can track it here."

"So, cool spy shit," I say nonchalantly, like all of this is normal.

"Cool spy shit," Hans agrees.

He shifts down the bed so he can lie on his back. But when he reaches for the lamp, I place a hand on his side and stretch my neck up to look past him. "And what's that?"

I point to the empty Ziploc bag on the nightstand, sitting next to the phone bag, filled with crumbs.

Hans looks at the bag. "That... was cookies."

"What cookies?"

"The cookies you made for me." Hans glances at the bag, then back to me. "Sorry, I should've let you take a few pictures first."

"Pictures...? Wait, those were the corn cookies?"

He nods.

I look back at the bag. "You brought them with you?"

Hans nods again. "I wasn't gonna leave them."

"But... All of them?"

His nod is slower this time.

"And you ate all of them," I clarify. "All twelve."

Hans rolls to face me, leaving the lamp on behind him. "You made them for me. I saw the Post-it." His tone is defensive.

I tuck my arm under my pillow. "Well, yeah. I'm not mad you ate them. I'm just surprised you *finished* them. They were burned."

"You make them for me. I always finish them." Hans says it simply.

I know he told me once before that he always eats what I bring over. And I didn't necessarily think he was lying, but seeing the evidence of it is something else.

"Thank you." I place my hand on his chest, and he shuffles closer so he can hug my arm to his body, my forearm flat against his chest. "We don't have to talk about it right now..."

His chest expands with a deep inhale. "You can always ask me anything, Butterfly. I'll always answer."

I hold his eyes, hoping he can see the truth in my gaze. That I just want to know. That I'm not going to judge him.

"Are you an assassin?"

He's quiet for a beat. "I don't get paid to kill people. I do it because I want to."

CHAPTER 79
Hans

I TELL CASSANDRA EVERYTHING.

I tell her about Freya. About that morning and every awful week after.

I hold my Butterfly while she cries—for me, for my sister she never knew.

I tell her about my parents. About their funerals. And I tell her it's okay when she says my parents should have stayed for me. Hug her when she says they should have fought for me.

I tell her about burning my family home down. I tell her about the literal fortune I inherited. I tell her about the investments I made and all the properties I own.

I tell her about hunting down every man associated with Freya's death. How I traveled continents. Leveled compounds.

I tell her about Gabriel Marcoux. How I never found him. And I place her hand on my side, letting her feel what's left of my first scar.

I tell her about the first time I met Karmine. And every time after. I tell her about the other women, the ones who have joined Karmine's army. How I work with them. How we've been destroying trafficking rings one hit at a time.

I tell her I moved to Minnesota because of Freya. That she was going to attend college here and that it was her dream to live somewhere with lakes and seasons. And I tell her how glad I am that I did.

I twine my fingers through Cassandra's when I tell her that I read her blog, Cul-de-sac Culinary with Cassie. That I've read it all the way through a dozen times.

I let her kiss me then. With her surprised smile and tears on her cheeks.

Then I tell her about The Alliance. I tell her why Dom owes me a favor. And how even though Nero said he'd help, they're still dangerous men to be wary of.

I tell her I have a lot of enemies. And that it could be any one of them who sent a man to find me. How it was just bad luck that she opened her door. But also that if she hadn't, the man might have been able to identify me. And if that had happened, when he came back, he wouldn't be alone.

I tell her the truth. That I'm good at what I do. But that if they'd hit my house with enough men, when I wasn't expecting them, I could've died.

I tell her she may have saved my life tonight.

And that I'd give my own to keep her safe.

And it feels good to tell her.

It feels good to share my story.

It feels good to trust someone again.

CHAPTER 80

Lifting my hand to his cheek, I lean forward and gently press my lips to his. "You're a good man, Hans."

He shakes his head, but I kiss him again.

"You might do it through unconventional ways, but you make the world better."

His dark eyes stare into mine. "I've killed a lot of people, Cassandra."

"I killed one tonight." I rest my head back on my pillow and shrug. "Some people deserve to die."

Hans watches me. Like *really* watches me.

I'm a privileged girl from the suburbs. I've never physically hurt anyone before tonight. I've never thrown a punch. Never even slapped someone. And I've never seen a dead body outside of an open-casket funeral.

But I've watched enough documentaries. I listen to the news. I know there are some really awful people in this world who do really awful things. And I know—*I know*—Hans isn't one of those people. He isn't bad.

Sure, according to polite society, I should be much more alarmed by all this. By the fact that I'm lying in bed with someone who admitted they kill because they want to. That I took a man's life tonight. That I may very well be in danger and on the run in the immediate future.

But really, what's so bad about all that?

We only live once, as far as we know, and I wasn't doing anything with my life.

I wasn't saving anyone. I wasn't bringing justice to wrongdoers.

I wasn't unhappy, but I wasn't thriving. I've just been existing. Looking for my passion. Something to inspire me.

My parents raised me to understand that there are consequences for our actions, repercussions we need to face when we do something wrong. And the men Hans has killed... Their wrongs are unforgivable. They earned their punishment.

Hans is their punishment.

And Hans is my passion.

Lying on our sides, facing each other, I feel a sense of rightness. Like this is where I belong.

When Hans told me the details about his past, about his family, it broke my heart.

I can't fix it for him, no one can bring them back, but I can be here for him now.

"You're a good man," I say again.

Hans's throat works on a swallow, then he grips my shoulders and forces me to roll away from him.

I don't fight it, because I can feel him move with me. And as soon as I'm facing the other way, he presses his body to mine. His front to my back.

"My Butterfly." Hans presses a kiss to the back of my head. "My girl." He circles his arm around my waist. "My light."

His words seep into my heart.

"My Grizzly Bear." I hug his arm. "My man." I melt into his body. "My stalker." I smile.

Sleep finally starts to take me, the weight of the day pulling me under, when Hans whispers two more words.

"My love."

CHAPTER 81

Hans

"I'M TAPPING OUT," CASSANDRA GROANS, LEANING back in the sole chair.

We slept past noon and ordered another round of room service. Only this time we ate at the desk in the corner instead of on the bed. And I made Cassandra use the chair while I just leaned against the wall.

If I hadn't been so busy hating the employee who checked us in last night, I would've asked for a suite.

Cassandra was already interested in me when she thought all I could afford was one cheap, run-down house. So I know I don't need to impress her with fancy hotel rooms. But it would've been nice to give her something special after yesterday.

I eye what's left of her club sandwich. "You're not gonna finish it?"

She presses her hands to her stomach. "It was huge. I'm too full."

It was huge. I'm too full.

My blood simmers, and I drag my gaze from her plate up to her face. "That's one, Butterfly."

Her mouth drops in an indignant expression. "What? I didn't

even do—" Then her lips press together, and she rolls her eyes. "I was talking about a sandwich."

"Doesn't matter. You still said it."

She pretends to be annoyed, but I can see the smile she's fighting. "You're ridiculous."

"Probably." I lift a shoulder. "Can I finish it?" I point to her leftovers.

She smirks. "It's all yours, Baby."

My balls tighten as I reach down and pick up the food. "One and a half."

Cassandra lets out a full laugh, and I grin as I shove the last bite of her sandwich into my mouth.

It tastes better than I know it should. But that's because it's hers. She had her hands on it. Her mouth on it.

I lick a smudge of mayo off my fingertip.

From the few meals we've shared, I think it's safe to say my obsession with consuming her food doesn't just apply to her home bakes, but also to anything she's eaten herself.

My eyes move to the crumbs on her plate.

Cassandra seems to let a lot of my bad behavior go, but licking sandwich crumbs off a hotel plate might be too much.

I'm still considering it when my phone rings, making the decision for me.

I pull it out of my pocket and set it on the table between us. A1—Alliance One, Nero's designation—fills my screen.

I answer and put it on speaker. "Quick work."

"Had my best guys on it," Nero replies. And I wonder if he's talking about him and King. "So, the dead guy—nice shot, by the way."

"Thanks," Cassandra responds automatically, then slaps a hand over her mouth.

There's a beat before Nero speaks again. "Well, this just got more interesting. You a part of the hit crew that saved Dom and Val?"

"No," I reply before Cassandra can.

Nero hums. "Then who are you?"

He still addresses his question to Cassandra, but I still answer. "No."

"Alright, we can circle back to that." I can hear Nero tap a keyboard. "So, our dead guy has ties to a branch of the Corsican mafia." Dread twists in my gut. "Word is that some French fuck with a bunch of money is back in the game, and he hired a crew to take you out. I personally haven't heard of him before—"

"Gabriel Marcoux." I speak the name I think of every single day.

Nero pauses. "That's the one. You know him?"

I stare at the table. "I killed most of the men under him."

"When?"

"Twenty years ago."

"Why?" Nero's tone is too curious.

"You don't need to know that," I grit out, and a soft hand settles on top of the one I have fisted on the table.

"Maybe not. But as you know, I can find out. So if we're building trust here..." Nero trails off.

I loosen my fingers, and Cassandra immediately intertwines hers.

I let out a breath. "His men kidnapped and murdered my sister. He was in charge at the time, behind the scenes. But he disappeared before I could get to him."

Nero makes a low, angry sound at my admission before adding, "And now he's back."

"Now he's back," I repeat, because it must be true.

"So... want help killing him?" Nero offers, catching me off guard.

My first instinct is to refuse, but refusing help from a group as powerful as these guys would be stupid.

"I need to be the one who kills him," I say slowly.

"Oh, we'll let you do the heavy lifting. But we can offer extra hands."

I tip my head to the side. "Are you offering me The Alliance?"

"Nothing is free."

"Exactly."

Nero heaves out a breath. "Diamond Dom owes you a life debt, and he'd be happy to get that off his back. Which would cover part of what I'm offering."

"Part," I repeat. "And then what? I owe you a favor and we just keep trading?"

"Don't knock it till you try it." He says it like he's no stranger to trading favors. "Plus we could always use another boogeyman at our disposal."

"Boogeyman?"

Nero snorts. "What? You think your name makes people think of fucking sprinkles and ponies?"

"Sprinkles and ponies?" Cassandra snickers.

I shake my head, then direct my attention back to the phone. "What exactly is your plan?"

"What makes you think I have a plan?"

"You wouldn't be offering me a spot on the A Team if you didn't already have some sort of plan."

"Yesterday, you sounded like you knew where I lived."

"I do." It's not a big secret. Nero is a rich business owner, as well as one of the leaders of The Alliance. He has a big house in a rich neighborhood not far from Minneapolis.

"Come over."

I squeeze Cassandra's hand. "My girl is with me."

Nero makes a sound of dismissal. "And my wife is here. You're not fucking cool."

I roll my eyes. "I'm not bragging. I'm trying to tell you that if you cross me and she gets hurt, I will end you."

"Yeah, yeah. Death and destruction. I got it."

I shake my head. "We gotta stop at my place first. Then we'll head over."

"Try not to get killed." Nero ends the call.

CHAPTER 82

HANS HAS BEEN VERY CALM SINCE WE LEFT THE HOTEL.

He casually drove us to an apartment building not far from where we live, and he had us get out of the pickup truck and into a Prius.

It's the least likely car I could imagine Hans driving. But that's probably the point since we're driving back into our neighborhood, and no one who's looking for either of us would look at this silver hybrid.

Hans makes a few turns and pulls over to the side of the street behind a giant pickup truck with the name of a construction company on the back.

I know we're close to Holly Court, but I honestly don't know all the little streets around ours to pinpoint our current location. With the thick trees between lots, it's hard to tell sometimes.

The house we're parked in front of is under construction, with half of a garage attached to the front of it. Through the partially framed walls, I can see a few guys milling around inside, but no one is paying attention to us.

Hans turns the car off, then faces me. "I don't want you to come, because there's a chance we might run into trouble. But I'm not going to leave you here alone, so you're coming with me."

I eye the house. "We're going inside?"

"No, we're going behind," Hans says, then pushes his door open.

Well, that was cryptic.

I follow him out of the car.

Hans is back in his all-black getup, minus the gun holster and knife, and I'm in a pair of pink jean shorts and a worn boy band T-shirt. Both items of clothing I instantly recognized as things I'd misplaced months ago. I'd said a silent thank-you to my mom for teaching me to only keep clothing I like and to donate anything that doesn't fit anymore. I can't imagine what I'd do if Hans had packed a bag full of stuff that stopped fitting two sizes ago.

Meeting Hans on the sidewalk, I take his offered hand.

Side by side, we probably look mismatched. The girly girl and the intense assassin. But my palm fits in his perfectly.

CHAPTER 83
Hans

CIRCLING THE HOUSE WITHOUT INCIDENT, I WALK Cassandra to the far corner of the yard.

Like our houses, this one butts against thick woods. But this patch of forest is the same patch of forest behind the *abandoned house* at the end of Holly Court.

And the couple that lives here spends all their free time on cruise ships, so they don't spend much time in their yard. And they've never ventured past their mown lawn. So they haven't noticed the trail I carved, allowing a person easy access from one property to the other.

I duck under the low-hanging, untrimmed branches of the lilac bushes that line the back of this yard and enter the forest.

Tall grass brushes against my calves, and I make a mental note to grab the other bag I put together for Cassandra.

I love the way she looks in her tiny shorts, but my dick twitches at the thought of her dressed in matching tactical blacks.

"What is this?" Cassandra whispers from my side when she sees the narrow path in front of us.

"This is called being prepared." I keep my voice just as quiet.

A finger jabs into my side. "Who's the brat now?"

I should be focused. And I am. But I'm also smiling. And that's weird.

CHAPTER 84

Cassie

THE TREES ARE THICK ENOUGH THAT THEY BLOCK OUT a lot of the afternoon sun, but ahead of us, brightness signals that we're almost through.

The trail we were on ended a few yards back, so I carefully follow Hans's steps through the underbrush to the edge of the tree line.

Hans lets go of my fingers and holds his hand palm down, lowering it a few inches toward the ground.

I have no idea what the fuck that's supposed to mean, but I stop walking.

He stands completely still for several long seconds, listening or waiting for something. And I take the time to look around.

Before us, in an overgrown yard, is a dilapidated gazebo.

At one point, it was probably a great place to hang out. Sitting on the benches that line the circular interior, sipping coffee while raindrops bounce off the shingled roof. Or having sex with your hot neighbor in the privacy of the backyard.

I push away the urge to reach out and grab Hans's perfect butt, and look around at the rest of the property.

It looks like the lawn hasn't been mown all summer, and the paint is peeling off the back of the house.

I narrow my eyes. Why does the color of the house look so familiar?

Hans startles me by crouching down and rushing out of the woods and across the few yards to the gazebo.

I expect him to go around it, maybe hide behind the railing, but he steps into it. And... lifts a panel in the center of the floor.

What the hell?

Staying low, Hans looks over his shoulder and gestures for me to come forward.

Following his lead, I try to make myself small as I cross to him.

"You first."

At his command, I look down at the black hole in the center of the gazebo floor.

"Um..." I whisper my hesitation.

Hans pulls a flashlight out of his pocket and aims it down, revealing metal rungs.

Oh, well, so long as I don't have to just jump in.

Forty percent of me rebels at the idea of climbing down into some dark pit behind a random abandoned house. But the other sixty percent of me is soaking up the rush of adrenaline.

Abandoned house.

My eyes dart back to the house, and my mouth pops open.

That's why I recognized the color. This is the abandoned house at the end of our cul-de-sac.

"Butterfly."

Right. The pit.

"Okay, okay."

It's awkward to get my feet lined up, but once the soles of my tennis shoes connect with the rungs, I lower myself into the ground.

CHAPTER 85

Hans

I FOLLOW CASSANDRA INTO THE TUNNEL AND DRAG THE lid back over the entrance while still aiming the flashlight down.

The air is damp and cool, but I walk this path once a week, checking for signs of disturbance and making sure the exit stays clear, so I know there are no critters living in here.

The tunnel structure was built offsite in custom-designed sections, and then when the city received a *surprise* grant to upgrade the sewer system, and all the roads were torn up, there was a three-day period when some extra heavy machinery showed up.

That machinery tore up a path between the back of my house and the abandoned house. *Something about a bad septic tank.* And because I'm a good neighbor, I made sure new sod was laid the moment they finished filling the dirt back in.

My neighbors got upgraded utilities, and I got a new exit strategy. A win-win for everyone.

The tunnel isn't wide enough for two people to fit side by side, so I hand Cassandra my flashlight and move ahead of her.

The glow she points at my feet is more than I need to make it through the couple of curves. I've taken this path with light, no light, holding my breath... But I've never taken this path with someone.

We stay silent as we go, but when my steps slow, Cassandra leans around my side and shines the flashlight forward.

"The other door." She's still whispering, but I can hear the understanding in her tone.

When I left her in the safe room last night, I know she went through the closets because she put on my sweatshirt and stole a pack of Skittles. I assumed she must have also opened the final closet door, revealing the back entrance to the safe room. Which is where we are now.

Same as the other door, this one has a palm reader mounted to the wall beside it. I place my hand against the surface, and we listen while the locks disengage.

There's no such lock on the entrance at the gazebo. But I do have a way to flood the tunnel with a substance that will render anyone inside unconscious. So there's that.

CHAPTER 86

THIS IS... INSANE.

Hans goes into the room first, and he strides around the space like he's checking to make sure nothing is out of place.

I step into the room on shaky legs because I am becoming embarrassingly flustered.

This shouldn't be sexy.

Making so many enemies you have to build an actual escape tunnel that goes from your hidden Batman room to an old moldy gazebo shouldn't be a turn-on.

And yet, here we are.

Hans flips on the wall of monitors, reminding me of how much time he's spent stalking me, and my core throbs.

Unaware of the fact that I want him to fuck me on this floor, Hans pulls out the chair at the work bench. "I need to grab some things. If you want to sit here, you can keep an eye on the screens."

Knowing we need to focus, I do as Hans says and drop into the chair.

I look at all the feeds, eyes stopping on one house in particular. "So that abandoned house?"

"I own it." Hans's answer is simple. "Or technically, a company does, but it's my company."

"So when you told me about all the houses you own..." I glance over at Hans as he pulls bags out of the middle closet.

He pauses to look up at me. "I didn't mean to not tell you. I just don't really count that one since it's as shitty on the inside as it is on the outside. It'll need to be leveled when someone wants to live there."

"Hmm." I turn back to the screens. "Did you buy it just so you could do the tunnel thing?"

"That was a selling feature. But my plan was to actually buy all three houses on the street and live in undisturbed peace. But then the old lady across the street kicked the bucket while I was out of the country killing some people, and when I came home, a pretty little distraction had bought the house before I even knew what happened."

"And aren't you glad I did?" I say tartly, mad at myself for being so annoyed that his plans didn't include me. Even though that would've been impossible because we hadn't met yet.

A hand grips my ponytail and tips my head back.

I expect him to laugh at me or count. But he stares down at me with a serious expression. "You buying that house was the best thing that ever happened to me."

Everything inside me softens.

Hans doesn't just throw words around. I know he means it.

I blink up at him. "Best decision I ever made."

He pulls my head back a little farther, eyes locked on my lips. "Good."

My head is nearly level with his hips.

I open my mouth, wide.

His grip tightens on my hair. "That's two, Butterfly."

Heat shoots down my spine. And I slide my tongue out. Inviting him to do something about it.

Hans reaches up with his free hand and traces the tip of my tongue with his finger. "We don't have time for three."

He rubs that same fingertip against his lips, then lets go of my hair and backs away.

For the first time ever, I kind of hate him.

Shifting in my seat, I can accept that sucking his dick, right here and right now, might not be the best idea. But goddamn, tell that to my lady bits.

I'm wondering what my punishment would be if I slid my hand down my shorts and took care of myself real quick when movement catches my attention.

I lean closer to the screen. "Uh, Hans."

"Just two more minutes."

"No." I point at one of the screens. "We've got company."

A van pulls to a stop between our houses, parking just before my driveway. The design on the side looks like a logo for an internet company, but it's not the one we use out here.

Hans stops behind me, one hand on the back of the chair, the other on the counter as he leans in.

The driver is visible through the windshield, and as we watch, four men exit the vehicle.

The van is the only attempt they seem to be making at a cover, because all four men have guns in their hands.

I expect the group to walk up to Hans's house, but they break off into pairs, two heading this way and two toward my house. And in both cases, one man walks to the front door and the other circles around to the back of the house.

Hans doesn't have a view of my backyard, but we watch the man circle Hans's house. I don't know what he's looking for, but he just looks around before ending up back at the front door, where his partner is already trying to break in.

I can feel my pulse picking up while excitement and stress swirl in my stomach.

Hans does that thing that has the keyboard appearing, then he taps a few buttons.

A speaker buzzes to life, and unfamiliar male voices float into the room.

"... told you the scout is dead."

"All he needed to do was to get eyes on the fucker. How do you mess that up?"

My hand balls into a fist. How dare he call Hans a fucker.

"Because clearly"—the first man shakes his head—"Hans saw him first."

The second man shrugs. "Okay, so Hans killed him. He's gotta be long gone by now."

The first man grunts and shoves his shoulder into the door. "The fuck is this thing made of?" he grumbles, then goes back to the lock.

"I'm just saying, Hans, the fucking ghost-man killer dude, isn't going to be sitting inside waiting for an ambush." Second Man shakes his head.

I glance up at Hans and silently admit the man is right. Hans is standing.

There's a loud clunk through the speaker. "Finally," First Man grunts and pushes the door open. "And don't be a dumbass, he's obviously split town. We're just here looking for clues."

Second Man gestures across the street where—to my horror—the other two men have already busted down my front door.

An indignant sound leaves my lips, and Hans moves his hand from the back of the chair to my shoulder.

The audacity.

Fuming, I move my gaze back to the first monitor just in time to see these two assholes enter Hans's house.

Hans taps a few more keys, and some of the outdoor cameras are replaced with views inside the house.

"What are we gonna do?" I whisper.

Hans taps more keys, and the audio switches to inside the house as well.

Guess we're going to stay and watch.

My pulse jumps up a beat. "Do you have any cameras in my house?" I ask, hoping he does so I can see what the men are doing over there.

The hand on my shoulder squeezes. "No, sorry."

I sigh, fully aware that should be a good thing. Then another thought occurs to me. "Do you have cameras in your garage?"

"No, sorry." Another squeeze as Hans repeats the same apology. Both of us bummed we don't have a recording of the first time we had sex.

Focus, Cassie.

We watch on the monitors as the men inside Hans's house do a quick walk-through, checking every room.

When I see Second Man, the one who circled the house, head to the basement, I tense.

But Hans doesn't change his stance. He doesn't reach for a gun or turn out the lights.

Of course Hans was correct to not panic. The man peeks into the corners of the empty basement before turning and jogging back up the stairs.

"Not so much as a box down there," Second Man shouts across the house as he stands in the living room. "This can't be his full-time house."

That comment makes me feel a little sad because this *is* Hans's full-time house. Or has been for a while, at least.

From what Hans told me, up until very recently, he had both the good guys and the bad guys after him. Everyone either fearing him or hating him. So it's no wonder he hasn't felt comfortable enough to settle down and make a house a home.

I lean toward his warmth.

And now, as we watch them pull out drawers and dig through every inch of his place, it's clear this won't be his house anymore. Even if he kills the main bad dude, this location has been revealed. Hans said it himself; he has lots of enemies. He'll never just be able to live in a cozy neighborhood like this and not always be looking over his shoulder.

Second Man snickers as he reaches for the sword mounted on the wall above Hans's couch. "Don't mind if I do."

It takes him a second to get it down, but as soon as he does, he starts swinging it around like an idiot.

On another screen, First Man is digging through Hans's bedroom. When he moves toward the nightstand, Hans straightens beside me.

The man pulls open the drawer and bends over it, digging around the contents.

Second Man's voice sounds from a different part of the house. "I'm gonna check the garage."

"Okay," First Man calls back. Then he mutters, "What the fuck is this?"

He straightens, and a stack of yellow Post-it notes is in his hand.

The hand Hans has on the worktop balls into a fist. "That's it," he growls.

"What's—"

Before I can finish asking, Hans strides across the room. Opens the door. And storms out into the basement.

I open my mouth to shout after him. To ask him what the hell he's doing. To tell him to grab a gun or a knife or something. But I don't want to yell and be heard by the intruders.

The door swings shut, locking between us.

"Charred sweet corn cookies," a male voice says, confused. "Is this supposed to be a code?"

Slowly, I turn back to the monitors.

Those are *my* Post-it notes. The ones I handwrote for each baked good. The ones I gave to Hans.

And First Man is touching them.

My eyes dart around to find Hans on the screen.

He's already climbing the stairs.

Second Man is still in the garage, looking around. But he could step back into the house at any moment, and then it will be two on one, and Hans is unarmed.

"Please be careful."

But Hans doesn't slow down. He doesn't move cautiously.

He takes the steps three at a time and flings the door open at the top. Leaving it open, he strides across the living room. Hands opening and closing into fists at his sides.

The man in the garage doesn't come out. He doesn't see Hans or sound the alarm.

Meaning First Man has no idea what's coming for him.

CHAPTER 87

Hans

My boots are silent on the carpet as I step into my bedroom.

"Those are mine."

At the sound of my voice, First Man spins around.

And then I see them. My pristine squares of paper have been pulled apart, crumpled into two uneven stacks. And... Is that one torn?

The red that usually spots the edge of my sight flares bright across my vision.

He freezes, just for a second, but I use that second to grab the notes out of his hands.

First Man recovers quickly, reaching for the pistol he holstered.

Accepting they're already damaged and needing to keep them close, I shove the Post-its into my mouth and bite down, holding them there as they protrude from my lips like a mouthful of hay.

The man's gun has cleared leather.

He's big. We're nearly eye to eye.

I don't have a weapon on me. But that doesn't matter.

I am the weapon.

And I'm angry.

Before he can lift his gun, I jump forward, throwing my weight into my fist as I slam it into the man's sternum.

His diaphragm contracts, stopping his ability to breathe and preventing him from calling out for help.

My left hand is already in motion, and I jab at that perfect spot on the inside of his right arm, a few inches up from his elbow. The one holding the gun.

My hit connects with his biceps brachii trigger point, and his grip on the gun releases.

He tries to get away from me, stumbling to the side. But I step with him.

First Man's back hits the wall parallel to my bed, and I pin him there with my left hand.

I can feel the moment the muscle under his lungs starts to relax, and he tries to take a breath.

Before his airway can open, I twist my body and slam my elbow forward against the front of his throat, feeling his windpipe give way under the impact.

His eyes bulge, but the Post-its clenched in my teeth remind me of what he's done. What he took from me.

I slam my elbow forward again.

This motherfucker ruined the first thing I ever received from Cassandra.

He's destroyed one of the few things that are precious to me.

Still trying to get away from me, his head bangs against my wall. Against the flat side of the katana mounted there.

I dart my right hand out to the side of his head and grip the sword's handle.

My swords are not decorations.

They were made to be used.

I move my left hand from his chest to grab a fistful of his hair.

I pull him away from the wall, just a few inches, while my right hand twists the handle of the katana. Only stopping when the sharp side is facing out.

Then, with my grip on his hair, I press his head back, holding him still as I drag the sword toward me.

The razor edge slices through flesh, slips between his vertebrae.

He touched something Cassandra touched.

Life fades from his eyes.

I keep him pinned in place, continuing the motion, slicing through muscles and tendons and arteries.

He touched what's mine.

With a final pull of my right hand, the weight below the man's neck falls away, and I'm left with a head in one hand and a sword in the other.

CHAPTER 88

I'M STANDING, LEANING OVER THE COUNTER, FACE practically against the screen, watching every movement Hans makes. And I'm panting.

Pant-ing.

I press closer.

Hans just beheaded a man.

He drops the head on the carpet, the thud audible through the speakers.

I should be disgusted.

Hans turns around, sword in hand, and I finally get to see all of him.

A wildness glows in his eyes.

His shoulders are bulked with exertion.

And he's covered in blood. The red droplets dripping off the edges of the Post-it notes clamped in his teeth.

"Holy fuck," I whisper into the room while fanning my face.

It's like Hans can hear me because his eyes move to the hidden camera as he reaches up to take his treasured Post-its out of his mouth.

My breath fogs the screen, and I'm seriously considering

licking it when the speakers crack from a door being slammed elsewhere in the house.

I force my eyes away from Hans and see Second Man walking through the kitchen, the door to the garage closed behind him.

His brows are furrowed as he approaches the open basement door.

He still has Hans's other sword in his hand, but the point is down and he's using it like a walking stick.

Second Man stops at the top of the stairs and calls down, "I told you, there's nothing down there."

"Wrong." Hans's voice sounds a second before he steps into the living room.

Second Man whirls to face him.

Hans doesn't slow as he crosses the room.

With his left hand, he stuffs the stack of Post-its into his pocket, and with his right hand, he holds the blood-soaked sword, point aimed up and out.

He twists his wrist, and the blade twirls in a macabre dance.

There's still blood on his face, and a few strands of hair have come free from where the rest are tied back.

He looks intimidating as hell.

Second Man's eyes widen, which is the correct response.

But then he lifts his stolen sword in front of him, even though it's clear he doesn't know how to use the weapon.

This guy doesn't stand a chance.

Sorry, sir, the correct reaction would have been to run. Away. As fast as you can.

My fingers touch the screen as Hans spins the blade once more. But this time, when it twirls upward, he reaches across his body to grip the handle with both hands.

In one smooth motion, Hans takes the final step and clashes his sword against the one in Second Man's hands.

Second Man's sword jerks upward, the impact of Hans's too much for it to withstand.

As Second Man's hands lift with the new trajectory of his weapon, Hans lifts his own arms as a follow-through.

Second Man takes a step back to catch himself, and Hans keeps his momentum, swinging the sword all the way up and then back down at his side.

It's so fast. So pretty.

And then Hans twists his wrists again, changing his grip so the blade is pointed directly at Second Man.

Without a single hesitation, Hans thrusts his sword forward, straight through Second Man's chest.

I'm practically on top of the workbench now. Breathing heavy.

I just watched a sword fight!

Hans uses his sword like a toothpick in a grape and maneuvers Second Man so he's standing with his back to the stairs. But from the way the man is slumped, I think Hans is supporting his weight.

With a shove, Hans sends the man falling backward down the stairs, but he doesn't release the sword, so it slides free from the man's body as he falls away.

The thud of the body tumbling down the stairs is loud in the speakers.

Hans kicks the basement door shut, with him still on the other side of it.

I find the screen showing the street, but everything is the same. The driver is still sitting there, head bobbing slightly like he's listening to music. And I can't see any signs suggesting where those other two guys are in my house.

I kinda hope Hans kills them too. And not just because they work for that human trafficker asshole, but because they're going through my things. I won't be able to wear any of my clothes again, not knowing what they touched. Or use my dishes. I'll have to freaking burn it all. And that pisses me off.

In the living room, Hans drops to his knees next to the coffee table.

He reaches underneath it, doing something, and then a piece of wood in the center of the table flips open.

Hans lifts the newly revealed rifle from its hiding place.

"Well, that's clever."

From his knees, Hans rolls himself over his shoulder in a move I've only seen in movies, ending up back on his knees next to the big window on the front of the house.

With one hand, he unlocks the window and slides the pane up. Giving himself just enough room to set the barrel on the windowsill.

I can't stop my smile.

He's about to sniper the shit out of those other guys.

Hans lifts something small and black to his mouth.

His voice is low when he speaks, sounding a little off. "You guys are gonna want to see this."

He drops the black thing, some kind of walkie-talkie he must've grabbed off the first dead guy, and lowers his eye to the scope.

It really was the smartest thing to say. Gets the curiosity of the other guys without alarming them.

My front door is hanging open, broken, and my eyes are on it when both men step into view, preparing to walk out of the house at the same time.

The leading man is one step away from the threshold when his head snaps back and red mist fills the doorway.

The man behind him freezes for one second, then turns to dive back into the house.

But Hans is quicker.

A second crack of gunfire fills the speakers while the last man falls to the floor, lifeless.

"Damn."

Having also heard the gunfire, the driver slams on the gas, but he had it in drive, and he's facing the end of the cul-de-sac.

He's got to be the worst getaway driver in history.

The van nearly tips as the driver speeds around the circle in front of the abandoned house, no way out except back between the houses.

I glance back at the screen with Hans.

The angle of the camera means I can't see Hans's face, but I can see him shake his head as the van careens back our way. I'm certain he's rolling his eyes.

I look back to the street view just in time to see the van's windshield crack, red splattering it from the inside.

CHAPTER 89

Hans

WATER DRIPS OFF MY CHIN, SOAKING INTO MY T-SHIRT.

My shirt has plenty of spatter on it, too, but that's hard to see on the black fabric. Unlike the blood that was all over my face.

I took one minute to scrub my face and hands clean before heading back downstairs. It's going to be hard enough to get back to our car unnoticed after what I'm about to do, having my face covered in blood would make me way too memorable.

I use the toe of my boot to shove the dead man off the last few steps and onto the basement floor.

There's no point in checking the bodies for identification. I know who sent them. And now we really need to get to Nero's.

I'm not one hundred percent sure they won't turn out to be a bunch of pricks, but there aren't many places that are safer than his fortress.

While I'm opening the outer door to the safe room, the inner door swings open.

Cassandra stands before me, her eyes blazing and her cheeks flushed.

My eyes dart to the monitors.

She watched.

I reach up and brush my thumb across the front of her throat, feeling her wild pulse.

I don't like her this close to violence, but I do like her this close to me.

"Do you still trust me?" I have no right asking her this after what she just watched, but I ask it all the same.

She nods, her head only moving the smallest bit. "I do."

A flash of her in white fills my mind.

Soon, I'll have her saying I do *in another way.*

I drag my thumb down her neck, then move into the room and pick up the bags I pulled out of the closet earlier.

First is the backpack of tactical clothes for Cassandra, next is a duffel bag with documents, more clothes, and the few things I don't want to leave behind.

Moving to the wall, I grab my favorite set of throwing knives and clip the holder onto my belt. Then a Glock and four full clips go into the duffel.

Last, I move to the desk, open up a cupboard locked with a palm-print scanner, and withdraw the little black book of Cassandra's boudoir photos. Those go into a hidden pocket inside the backpack.

With everything I need gathered, I slide my arms through the backpack straps, then hook the duffel over my head so it hangs cross body. It's a more conspicuous look than when we came in but worth it.

"I can carry something," Cassandra offers.

I point to the flashlight sitting on the edge of the bench. "You're in charge of the light."

Gentle fingers pick up the military-grade flashlight while I reach for the keyboard.

It only takes a few clicks to open the program I need.

I glance at my girl, taking in her beauty and remembering she said she trusted me, then I press three keys simultaneously.

One second passes and a warning beep sounds.

Another second, another beep.

A third second, and the ground below our feet vibrates.

The screen showing Cassandra's house now shows a ball of fire.

Cassandra gasps. "Did you just blow up my house?"

CHAPTER 90
Cassie

HANS PRESSES HIS LARGE HAND AGAINST MY BACK. "Yes."

Yes. He just says yes.

His hand applies pressure. "And we have about fifteen seconds left before mine blows."

So much for always telling my house goodbye.

Then I register the rest of what he said and hurry to the exit.

My hands are still trembling from watching Hans in action upstairs, and it takes me two tries to get the flashlight on. When it illuminates the tunnel, I run.

The ceiling is low, the walls are narrow, and I hate running, but I felt that tremor from my house across the street. I don't want to be underneath Hans's house when it explodes next.

My heavy breathing is echoing through my ears, but I hear Hans behind me when he says, "Two... One..." Then he loops his big arm around my waist.

As soon as he has a hold of me, the world around us shakes. Our feet stop, and Hans pulls me into his body, bending over me. Shielding me.

But when there are no loud cracking sounds, and the tunnel stays intact, Hans urges me forward.

CHAPTER 91
Hans

CASSANDRA HOLDS MY HAND THE WHOLE JOG THROUGH the forest. And by the time we're climbing back into the Prius, we can hear sirens.

We stay quiet, and I drive the speed limit for the few minutes it takes to get to the apartment building where we swapped vehicles.

I park in the opposite corner of the parking lot from my truck, and we take the long way around. Several people are outside, looking at the thick smoke rising from a few miles over. None of them are turned our way, but this way, if anyone notices us, they'll just see two people walking through a parking lot, not suspiciously jumping out of one vehicle and into another moments after two houses blew up a few blocks away.

I toss the bags into the back seat and open the passenger door for Cassandra.

Her cheeks are still pink, and I wonder if she's gonna be mad at me for burning down her house.

I hate the idea of her being mad at me.

With my hands on her hips, I help her into the truck, then shut the door and stride around to my side.

When I open my door, Cassandra has slid into the center seat.

302

I'm taking it as a good sign, because if she was angry, she wouldn't want to sit next to me. Right?

Needing to touch her, I place my hand on Cassandra's thigh as I drive us out of the parking lot.

She tenses under my touch.

Instead of pulling my hand away, I grip her harder. "Butterfly, I'll never hurt you."

"I know." Her voice is breathy when she replies.

I glance down, and she has her hands gripped together in her lap.

"I'm sorry you had to witness that," I tell her.

She squirms.

"And I'm sorry for blowing up your house."

"Hans—" She puts her hand on my thigh.

"Just don't be afraid of me." Panic creeps into my chest, and my lungs start to burn. "I couldn't take that. Please don't—"

"Oh my god, shut up." Cassandra shoves my hand off her leg, and before I can stop her, she unbuckles her seat belt.

"Cassandra!" I snap. "Buckle up now."

She twists toward me. "No."

"You—" I start. But I stop because she's reaching for my belt.

Delicate fingers jerk at the buckle, pulling it free.

"What—What are you doing?"

She undoes the button and jerks the zipper down. "Watching you..." She struggles to pull my hardening cock out of my pants. "God, Hans, I'm so fucking turned on. I can't take it."

Using both hands, she gets my dick free.

I make an unintelligible sound, not believing what's happening.

"Just let me do this," she begs.

Then she wraps her hand around my base and lowers her head into my lap.

When her lips wrap around the tip of my cock, I can't stop my hips from lifting.

"Fuck," I groan and nearly drive us into the ditch.

I force my eyes to stay on the road. But all my attention is on the girl who is suddenly sucking my cock like it's the only thing she wants in life.

"Goddamn." I shift my hips again, and Cassandra takes me a little deeper.

I'm barely even in her mouth. Haven't hit the back. And I'm fighting not to blow.

Her tongue slips around the head, flicking over the tip, licking up the precum seeping from my dick.

"Fuck. Cassandra. Fuck." I grip the steering wheel tighter.

I take a turn I don't need to take, just so we can stay on a side road. If she does this on the highway, and someone sees... I'd have to kill them.

She moans, and I feel her cheeks hollow as she literally sucks my cock.

My eyes start to roll back.

I snap them back open.

I need to remember I'm driving a fucking vehicle.

Cassandra shifts her hips, twisting on the bench seat and lifting her foot so it's on the seat and her knee is up. Spreading her legs for me.

Holding the wheel with my left hand, I reach across with my right and grip her shorts-covered pussy.

Her whole body writhes at my touch, and her lips slide farther down my dick.

I can hardly focus, but I undo her shorts one handed, and she spreads her thighs wider.

I take a second to glance down.

"Jesus."

Her panties are exposed, her body is contorted so she can suck my dick while her pussy is practically begging me for attention.

I shove my fingers under the band of her panties and slide them lower.

And I groan, deep and long, because she's fucking soaked.

Her pussy is so damn wet my fingers slide right inside her heat.

As my fingers push deeper, Cassandra arches her neck and takes me even deeper.

"This from watching me?" I growl, fucking her with my fingers, pushing them in and dragging them out. "This pussy get drenched watching me kill those men?"

She nods. On my dick.

If I had a free hand, I'd press down on the back of her head.

Her tongue rubs at my length, and I groan again.

"Fuck." I can't stay quiet. "You feel so fucking good."

Her pussy is gripping at my fingers. Her saliva is dripping down my dick.

I flex my hips and hit the back of her throat.

She gags, and her muscles tense around the tip of my dick. But instead of pulling back, she pushes deeper.

"God, Butterfly, you're a fucking freak."

Her hips shift against my touch while she slides her mouth up my length. "Sorry," she pants. But her lips never leave my dick. They're still brushing against the tip, getting covered in precum with every word. "I'm sorry. I can't help it." Her back arches, and she closes her lips back around my length.

"You can't apologize with my dick in your mouth." I shift so my knee is against the bottom of the wheel, keeping it steady, then press my left hand to the back of her head. "But you can apologize by swallowing."

Cassandra moans and lets me shove her head deeper.

I push my pointer and middle finger into her pussy, as far as I can. She moans again, and I grip her ponytail, dragging her mouth back up my dick.

I hold her there. At my tip.

"Yeah," I grunt. "Suck Daddy's dick. Make him come."

Her body shudders, and I press my thumb to her clit.

With my hand like this, I'm practically gripping her pussy

from the inside. I rub my fingers against that sensitive spot inside her and circle her clit with rough movements.

Cassandra is writhing and moaning, and I'm about ready to explode.

"You ready, Little Girl?" I can hardly get the words out. "You ready to fucking take me?"

She makes a noise that sounds like a yes, or what yes would sound like if your mouth was full of cock and you were moaning from pleasure.

I push my hand firmer against her pussy, my pinkie brushing against her cute little asshole, and she clamps down around me.

Cassandra comes all over my hand, and her orgasm sparks mine.

My balls squeeze, and the first shot of release coats her tongue. Then I push down on the back of her head, and she takes it.

She swallows and chokes and pulls against my grip to go even deeper.

My vision goes blurry for two beats, and I forget we're in a moving vehicle as I come so hard it almost hurts.

My body feels like it's vibrating, and I have to tell my fingers to let go of her hair so I can grab the wheel.

Without my hand holding her in place, Cassandra takes me deep, one last time, then licks up my length as she pulls her mouth up my dick. She sucks as she goes, making a wet popping sound when she releases.

I'm tempted to leave my fingers buried in her pussy for the rest of the drive, but I drag them free from her heat and shove them into my mouth as she starts to sit up.

Her flavor hits me, and that, mixed with the strong scent of sex in the truck, makes my cock twitch one final time.

Cassandra snickers, then leans down to lick the drop that just leaked out of my tip, and my entire body jerks at the contact.

"Christ, woman," I mumble around my fingers.

She sits all the way up this time, and when I look at her, affection fills every inch of my being.

There are tears on her lashes. Her lips are swollen and pink. Her always untamed hair is extra messy with loose curls pulled free from her ponytail, and her wavy bangs are all pushed to one side. And she's smiling. Full-on smiling. Teeth showing. The tip of her tongue visible in her open mouth.

All I ever wanted was to have her nearby.

Never dreamed...

I soak in the feeling of this happiness.

I'm going to marry this girl.

CHAPTER 92

I'M STILL IN THE MIDDLE SEAT, CLUTCHING HANS'S hand as we drive through a neighborhood like nothing I've ever seen before. Well, except maybe in magazines when they show celebrity homes.

The houses are gigantic, set way back from the street, and each property is surrounded by tall fences.

I've only just learned about The Alliance, but I guess this is the type of place they live in. Or at least one of them, since we're going to a house owned by a guy named Nero.

I know he has a wife named Payton and that his *business partner* is named King. And since this is the first formal meeting between them, Hans suspects King will be in attendance too.

The guy Hans saved last Christmas is named Dom, but he lives in Chicago, so Hans isn't sure whether he'll be here too.

I also found out that Hans rigged both of our houses to blow by using some sort of igniter thingy between the gas stove and the wall. He claims it was super safe, that he checked both of them every week, and that there was no worry about it ever blowing up on its own.

I probably could've learned more details about the whole

house explosion thing if I hadn't spent the first half of the car ride giving Hans a blow job, but honestly, I have no regrets.

With anyone else, I'd probably be embarrassed about how turned on I got watching him kill people. But considering he's the one who just casually ended five lives in the span of a few minutes, it's not like Hans can really judge me.

Plus, making him fight for control like that was amazing.

One hand between my legs, the other pushing my head down to take him deeper, while he drove with his knee and tried not to crash the truck...

I shift.

Okay, so even though I came so hard I had to change my underwear and my shorts when we stopped at a gas station, I'm still worked up enough that I'd happily climb over and impale myself on Hans's lap if we weren't about to pull up to someone's house.

"You okay?" Hans asks, misreading my discomfort. "I don't want to leave you at a hotel alone, but if you don't want to come with, we can figure something out."

I put my hand on top of his, where it rests on my lap. "No, I'm totally okay. Promise." I squeeze his hand. "Just thinking about earlier."

He slides me a look full of heat. "Dirty girl."

I grin, and he shakes his head, then starts to slow the truck.

My eyes widen when I see the gate we're turning toward. The other driveways have had gates, too, but this one seems... *extra*.

Instead of just a call box, there's a pillar big enough to hold a couple of men.

Just as I think it, two men step into view from behind the bricks.

They're dressed similarly to Hans, and they're holding guns.

Hans pulls the truck to a stop in front of the closed gate, and one of the guys gestures for him to roll down his window.

Hans does.

From the other side of the gate, the man holds up a phone.

He must've taken a photo or is on a video call with someone to get approval because a few seconds later, he nods and the gate starts to slide open.

Hans keeps his window down as he drives through and slows when he comes even with the guard.

The guard keeps his gun at his side. "Stop in front of the house, exit the vehicle, and wait for the bosses."

Hans doesn't look like he's going to reply, so I call out a "thank you" before he drives forward.

I try to keep the shock off my face as we near the house. It's so fancy.

My teeth dig into my lip as I look down at myself.

Tennis shoes, new pair of jean shorts, same band shirt, hair slightly tamed, but still a mess.

I hope these guys dress casually. Though something tells me they don't.

Hans puts the truck in park where the driveway curves in front of the house and turns off the engine.

He heaves out a breath and turns to me, lifting his hands to cup my face. "I'm trusting them because I know at least some of our morals line up. But other than the times I've told you about" —he means saving that one guy and threatening to blow them up in a restaurant—"I haven't interacted with them. So, if this turns out to be a gigantic mistake, please forgive me."

His grip on my face is firm enough that it squishes my cheeks when I try to smile, but that just makes me smile more.

"Hans." I place my hands over his. "I think I'd forgive you just about anything."

He sighs.

"Unless you cheat on me," I tell him. "If you do that, I'll chop your dick off."

Hans gives me a soft smile that's completely inappropriate for what I just said. "Butterfly, no force on earth could make me touch another woman."

I swoon.

And the front door opens.

Our hands slide from my face as we look at the three men walking down the steps toward us.

They're all tall and built, like Hans.

And they're all handsome, each in their own way.

The dark-haired, dark-eyed one who looks a little feral. The one with rich brown hair and an air of arrogance. And the one with all the tattoos, buzzed hair, and an amused smirk.

The leaders of The Alliance.

And of-fucking-course they're all in suits.

CHAPTER 93
Hans

I HAVE TO TRUST MY INSTINCTS.

I have to trust these men will keep their word. That my woman is safe around them.

Opening my door, I exit the truck and pull Cassandra out after me.

She keeps her hand in mine as we move to stand at the front bumper.

I don't see any visible weapons on the three men, but I still take a second to focus on the weight of my throwing knives at my hip. If I've severely misjudged them and this goes bloody, I'm confident I can kill at least two of them before they take me out.

Which two will have to be based on proximity.

Dom strides ahead of the other two, stopping before me and holding out his tattooed hand. "Good to see you."

I lift a brow.

He lifts a shoulder. "And good to get this debt off my back."

Not wanting to lose contact with Cassandra, I shift my grip on her hand and press hers to my belt, like I did at the hotel.

Understanding what I want, she slides her fingers around the material, holding on to me.

Right hand free, I shake Dom's.

I don't miss the fact that he's trying not to grin, but I appreciate that he's keeping his eyes on me and off Cassandra.

King and Nero step up on either side of Dom.

This isn't my first time standing before them, but it is my first time on their turf. And it's a little unsettling.

"Hans." King dips his chin.

"King." I greet him the same way, then turn my attention to Nero.

All three of them are intense, but Nero is the wildcard. The most unhinged. Or at least that's what the rumors say.

"Mind if we search your truck?" He stares right at me.

I hold his stare. "If you can break the security, you're welcome to look."

He narrows his eyes at me, then he does something I don't like.

Nero holds his hand out to Cassandra. "I'm Nero. Welcome to my home."

Too nice for her own good, Cassandra smiles as she reaches her hand out toward Nero's. "Thank you, it's beautiful."

Her palm is an inch from Nero's when I reach out and grip Cassandra's wrist and lower it.

It's rude. And juvenile. But I can't help myself. I can't let anyone else touch her. Not yet.

Nero doesn't look offended. He looks like he understands. But Dom makes a noise of amusement.

King has already started to circle my truck, and thankfully, the other two men of The Alliance follow.

Cassandra tugs on my belt to get my attention.

I look down at her pretty face and speak before she can scold me. "I know." I take a deep breath. "I know."

The smile she gives me is so understanding my heart swells behind my ribs.

She presses her hand to my chest. "I trust you. Now trust yourself."

She didn't spend the past year watching my every move, like I did to her. But she still gets me. Still understands my moods. And she understands that I can't help how I feel about her.

I place my hand over hers and nod.

I've fought side by side with Karmine's army. I have no problem letting women do whatever they want. I know they're more than capable of taking care of themselves. But Cassandra is mine.

She's mine and that makes it different.

It makes me want to protect her. To stand between her and everything sharp in this world.

It makes me crazy.

We're just turning to follow the guys when Nero lowers my tailgate.

"Are you fucking kidding me?" he snaps.

And I can't stop my smile.

King barks out a laugh. "At least he has good taste."

"The best money can buy," I reply.

"On a fucking truck." Nero shakes his head as he puts his hands all over the locks that cover my truck bed, recognizing the thumbprint readers as one his company, Nero Security, produces. "A plain-ass fucking pickup truck."

"Sometimes it's better to blend in." I state the obvious.

King leans against the side of my truck and sighs. "You know he's not gonna let this go until you show him everything."

"I assumed as much." I look down at Cassandra.

She grips the side of the truck, opposite where King is, before letting go of my belt. "Go show off your toys."

It's ridiculous for her to hold on to the truck, like she might float away if she isn't touching me or something I own, but it makes me feel better. And I'm once again struck by how well she knows me.

Dom is watching us closer than I care for, but I move past him and stop beside Nero. "Promise you'll leave everything where you find it?"

Nero rolls his eyes. "I'm not gonna steal your shit."

Dom scoffs from my other side, and I assume there's some sort of joke I'm missing.

With no real reason not to, I press my thumb to the first lock, then the next, and the next, until all the compartments are open. Handguns, long guns, ammo, knives, gloves, climbing gear, rations, fake government employee uniforms—all on display.

The last little door I flip open is above the gas tank, and it's full of C-4.

I lift my hands. "Now before you get your panties in a twist, this is for self-destruct. If I wanted to blow you guys up, I wouldn't do it by driving myself, and my girl, onto your property."

King leans over the side of the truck to look closer. "How often do you find yourself needing to blow up your own shit?"

Cassandra snickers.

"You'd be surprised," I reply.

Dom reaches into one of the side compartments and pulls out the thick black material.

He shakes it out and lifts his gaze to look at me. "Really?"

I lift my shoulder even as Nero reaches to take it from Dom.

"See?" Nero pulls the zipper down a few inches, then slides it back up. "I told you he had nice body bags."

"Yeah, I fucking heard you the first four times." Dom snorts. "And I'll say to Hans what I said to you." He turns to face me. "A man who travels with his own body bags is either very meticulous or very insane."

I shrug again. He's not wrong on either account.

The front door of the house opens, and a woman I recognize as Nero's wife sticks her head out. "Pizza is at the gate." She calls across to us, then lifts her hand in a little wave to Cassandra. "Hi!"

Cassandra lifts the hand not on the truck and waves back. "Hello."

"Come on in." Payton opens the door wider.

Cassandra looks back at me.

I should let her go. I'm sure it's safe for her to be with Payton, but I'm not letting her walk into Nero's house alone.

I grip the tailgate and start to lift it closed. "We done?"

Nero tucks the body bag under his arm. "I've seen enough."

King straightens. "Not sure how a truck full of hidden explosives and all this other shit makes you feel more trustworthy, but it kinda does."

"It's settled, then." Dom slaps a hand on my back. "Let's go eat pizza."

On cue, one of the gate guards comes up the driveway in a golf cart–looking vehicle with a stack of pizza boxes on the seat next to him.

I circle around to Cassandra, and she takes my hand, squeezing my fingers.

Then we walk up the steps to Nero's house.

CHAPTER 94
Cassie

STEPPING THROUGH THE MASSIVE FRONT DOOR, I'M thrown into a world I didn't expect.

A world of color.

The space is giant and formal, but there's bright artwork lining the walls of the two-story entryway, along with side tables full of large rose bouquets.

Nero struck me as a black-on-black type of man, but this is not that. Not at all.

Hans's fingers flex around mine, and I reach across to grip his forearm with my free hand.

I know a part of Hans doubts his plan to trust these men, but they actually seem really nice. And I'm looking forward to meeting their wives.

When King enters the house behind us, stack of fragrant pizza boxes in hand, my stomach growls.

Hans jerks his gaze down to me, having heard my stomach rumble, and I can sense his immediate distress. From his look alone, I can tell he hates the fact that I'm hungry.

"Worked up an appetite on the way over," I whisper for only him to hear as I lean into his side.

His nostrils flare, and—as I'd hoped—his mind is sufficiently distracted from my growling stomach.

As a group, we enter a kitchen with massive white marble countertops and bright yellow cabinets.

It shouldn't work, but it's beautiful. And so is the brunette standing next to the island. She's the same woman who stuck her head out the door.

"Hi." She smiles while she greets me again and holds her hand out. "I'm Payton."

I give Hans a squeeze, then let go and move to the woman. Shaking her hand, I smile back. "I'm Cassie."

"So, you're with Hans?"

"Yeah." I bite my lips as our hands let go. "You're with Nero?"

She nods. "I know he can seem like a bit much, but he's really sweet."

Looking around at the cheery mansion, I find myself believing her.

There's even a dog lying on a plush bed in the corner. He's medium sized and adorable, and he lifts his head to look at the crowd but then yawns, stretches his furry legs, and shuts his eyes.

"That's Toto." Payton shakes her head. "Not much will disturb him from a nap."

I grin at the goofy dog, thinking I'm the same way.

Then two more beautiful women enter the kitchen from the far side. One has long blond hair, and the other has hair the same shade as King's.

All of the women are dressed much more casually than the men, though I can tell their clothes are expensive.

There's something else...

It takes my brain a second to realize what it is. They're all curvy girls, like me.

It shouldn't matter. It *doesn't* matter. But I'm just so used to being the biggest girl in the room, and there's something freeing about *not* feeling that way.

Payton gestures to me when the women stop at the edge of

the island. "This is Cassie. She's here with Hans." She points to the blonde first. "That's Savannah, King's wife. And this is Val, Dom's wife."

Val lifts her hand to wave, and I immediately notice her entire ring finger is covered in tattoos. *That's badass.* Then she lowers her hand, and that's when I notice her *belly.*

I almost blurt out something inappropriate, but I manage to press my lips together and stop myself.

I don't know why I'm so surprised to see that one of the women is pregnant. People have babies all the time. It's just that, having assumed I'd be forever single, I also assumed I'd never have kids.

Then I met Hans. And then I started to understand just how dangerous Hans's world is. So I just assumed that would also mean no kids.

And if I have Hans, I don't need anything or anyone else.

But these women live in that same dangerous world. And it doesn't look like it's stopping them from doing anything.

Nice houses. Babies...

Does that mean this is a possibility for us, too?

The tattooed man moves to stand next to his pregnant wife. "Cassie, was it?"

I nod as I feel Hans come up behind me.

Val looks up at her husband. "Did you not introduce yourself outside?"

Dom shakes his head, and the side of his mouth pulls up. "Hans was being a bit... territorial."

Two large hands settle on my shoulders, and I watch as all three women smile up at Hans.

I don't really like them looking at him because I know how hot he is, and I can't stand the thought of someone else having dirty thoughts about my Grizzly Bear. But these ladies all have their own super attractive husbands, so I force my hackles to stay down.

There's another round of introductions between the wives

and Hans, and the guys all officially say hello to me. The whole thing is a lot less awkward than I expected.

I know the three men run some crime organization. And I know my man has a scary reputation for killing lots of people. But it kind of feels like I'm at my boyfriend's holiday work party.

Then someone opens the first pizza box, and we all grab plates and seats around the U-shaped island. Hans and I seem to be the dividing line in the middle, with the women all seated next to me and the men on the other side of Hans.

"So." Savannah turns to me as I lift a slice to my mouth. "What do you do for work?"

I halt my hand, the pizza inches from my mouth. "Oh, well, I'm in HR, but my company went through some stuff, like, last week, so I think I'm gonna look for another job."

Hans shifts on his stool beside me. "You don't have to work."

Val snickers from her spot next to me. "Okay, so he's like the rest of them."

I'm guessing she means overbearing, so I nod and shove the pizza into my mouth.

Payton smiles. "Well, if the guys are gonna start working together, you could always help Aspen and me organize fundraiser events." Seeing my confused look, she clarifies, "Aspen is King's other sister and one of my best friends. You'll like her."

My confusion was actually over her just blindly offering me a job of sorts, but I appreciate her telling me who this other woman is too.

Val snickers. "And since Aspen is hooking up with my husband's second in command, it's only a matter of time before they become official, and she lives out her own *happily ever after.*"

Savannah snorts. "Any time I want to piss King off, I remind him that he's gonna have two sisters married into the Chicago mafia."

I smile and nod as I eat more of my slice. There are too many new names for me to keep up with. I feel like I need a chart, or a book, to keep track of them all.

Payton goes back to her original topic of inviting me to help with their fundraisers. "No pressure or anything. But if you don't go back to work and want something to do, we can always use the help."

"That'd be nice," I say honestly.

I've never planned any kind of big event, but I'm good at following directions, so I'm sure I could learn.

"Great!" She beams, then tips her head. "Wait, do you live here? I know Nero mentioned that Hans is somewhere in the cities..."

"Yeah, well, I mean, I do." I cringe. "But my house kinda blew up today."

"What?!" all three women gasp in unison.

The men's voices cut off.

"What did she say?" King asks.

Savannah glances at her husband, then back to me. "She said her house blew up."

"It's not so bad," I try to reason. "I wouldn't have wanted to go back in there after those men went through my things anyway. And I still have all my old photobooks and stuff in my parents' storage unit, since I bought the house after being in a tiny apartment forever and never got around to getting them out."

They all just gape at me.

That might've been an overshare.

"Wait, who blew up Cassie's house?" Dom asks, and I finally turn toward the men's side of the island.

Hans sighs. "I'm the one who blew up her house."

I place my hand on his thigh.

"Um..." Dom looks back and forth between us. "On purpose?"

Hans nods, and I rub my hand in small circles. I know he feels bad about it, but on the ride over, he explained that he did it to destroy the bodies and muddle evidence while also drawing the attention of the authorities since they'll douse it all with water and finish ruining anything that wasn't burned.

Honestly, I'm not upset about it.

It was probably overkill. But what do I know about corpses and evidence? And I really do have all my important things tucked away in the storage locker in my parents' complex. Plus, it turns out my neighbor with the sparse house is actually super rich, so he can replace anything I need.

If I'm lucky, maybe they'll make a documentary about it titled *What the Fuck Happened on Holly Court?*

Nero leans against the counter. "I think it's time to tell us what happened after I called you today."

CHAPTER 95

Hans

MY FINGERS TWITCH AT MY SIDES.

I hate that Cassandra isn't in the same room as me, but we came into Nero's office to look over the intel The Alliance was able to dig up on Gabriel Marcoux. And as much as I wanted to drag Cassandra in here with me, she looked happy talking with The Alliance wives. So now I'm in here, staring at a green and purple painting of a lion's head while Cassandra is somewhere else in the house.

"He owns three homes in the states, Texas, Arizona, and California. Then a place in Nepal and a property in France he built a few years ago that looks like a replica of the one that was burned down almost two decades ago." King rattles off the information as the large monitor on Nero's desk shows the exact locations of the homes.

"I'll have to torch that one too," I mumble as I look at the screen.

No one says anything because it should be no surprise that I'm the one who leveled his first home.

But I can't focus on that right now because my eyes keep moving to the sprawling estate highlighted just outside of Phoenix.

Back where it all started.

King clicks a few buttons to show Marcoux's financials, but then my phone rings.

When I see it's Karmine calling, I put it on speaker.

I plan to tell her I have other people within earshot, but she doesn't let me get a word out before she starts talking.

"Your man was just spotted in Dallas."

I stand up straighter. "Where?"

"Getting into some douchebag limo outside the DFW airport. One of my girls was there looking for someone else, but she called me when she recognized him from the photos I sent everyone last night. She wasn't in a position to follow him, so I don't know where he's going, but—"

"He has a house in Dallas," I cut her off, thinking back to the map we were just looking at.

"Since when?"

King returns to the previous screen and clicks on the details.

"He bought it last month." I relay the information.

"Good find," Karmine hums.

"Wasn't my find," I admit, just as King replies, "I do my best."

"My, Hans, what talented voice acting you've mastered." Her sarcasm is heavy.

"If you'd've taken a breath before you started talking, I would've warned you that I have you on speaker."

"Uh-huh, sure, make it my fault." She doesn't say it with any heat. "Let me guess. The Alliance bros?"

"Alliance bros?" King repeats under his breath, clearly not appreciating the term.

Dom leans toward the phone in my hand. "Dom here. I'm a big fan of your work."

"Aww, thanks." I can picture her dramatically pressing her hand to her chest. "I'm a big fan of your wife. She's kickass."

Dom smirks. "I know."

He was unconscious from blood loss when Karmine's girls took out the force that was trying to kill him and his wife. But I was witness to Val's shooting skills, and I have to agree with Karmine.

"Shall I assume Nero and King are there as well?"

King looks at me, then down to the K displayed on my phone.

"Safe assumption. Do we get a name to go with the letter K?"

There's a long pause. And I'm surprised by her answer.

"It's Karmine. And if you want my phone number, I expect to get all of yours in return."

Nero takes the phone out of my hand and, clicking on her contact, sends her a text with his number.

"Nero. The number you just got is mine."

"Got it." There's another pause. "You should have mine now."

Nero pulls his phone out of his pocket. "Got it."

Dom rubs his hands together. "I love it when armies collide. Now we just need a target."

"Give me a few hours to get more intel. I wouldn't be able to get any of the girls together for another twenty hours anyway. But if he sticks around town for more than some business dinner, we'll know."

"I just killed five of his guys," I cut in, remembering I haven't told Karmine about the houses yet. "And it wasn't exactly under the radar." Nero snorts, probably thinking about the exploding houses. "So he knows that I know he's after me."

"So, him being suddenly visible might be a trap." Karmine supplies the rest of my thought.

"That's what I'm thinking."

"Well..." I can hear Karmine tapping her nails against a surface. "If the force is big enough, it doesn't really matter how good the trap is. And you got all those big bads in one room..." She lets that hang as she ends the call.

Sliding my phone back into my pocket, I look at the three men. "Just like that?"

"Just like what?" King asks.

"Just like that, you go from hunting me to helping me?"

"Ridding the world of this Gabriel asshole helps everyone."
King lifts a shoulder. "And I'm not sure we were ever that good at
hunting you."

I think of all the times I had to dodge them and their men. "I
don't think you were as bad at it as you think."

"No?" King lifts his brows.

"I spent six hours in a fucking dumpster outside of the deal
you busted in Minneapolis last summer."

Nero makes an impressed face. "That makes me feel a little
better."

"Happy to help," I deadpan.

"If it makes you feel more trusting in our *sudden cooperation*,
we didn't just decide to loop you in yesterday." Dom slides his
hands into his pockets as he rocks back on his heels. "We've been
talking about it since January. But you didn't exactly have your
phone number written on that grenade you threatened us with."

I look around at their faces. "I'll be honest, I wasn't aiming for
some sort of team-up. I just didn't want to deal with you guys
trying to kill me every time I went out on a job."

Dom laughs. "Well, saving my life kinda put you on the fast
track to friendship. And these dummies do whatever I say, so—"

Nero jabs a punch at Dom's side, cutting him off.

"How about we figure out how to kill this French prick first?
Then we can make friendship bracelets around the campfire
after." King turns back to the computer.

I pull a different cell phone out of my pocket, faraday bag and
all, and set it on the desk. "This belonged to the guy in that nice
body bag. I've been a little too busy to crack it."

CHAPTER 96
Cassie

I'M TRANSFERRING THE CHOCOLATE CHIP COOKIES
from the cooling rack to the fancy wooden platter Payton set on
the island when I hear the men's voices.

They've been off making plans for the past hour, and I needed
something to do to help me feel less tense. Plus, making cookies
for a pregnant lady has got to earn me some friendship points.

The women are all so nice, asking me how I met Hans,
wondering how long we've been dating.

It felt a little silly to admit that the closest thing to a date
we've been on was dinner at my parents'. But they all thought that
was sweet. So then I told them about bringing him food for the
past year in hopes that he'd talk to me. Which led to them asking
what sort of food I like to make, which led to my blog, which led
to me offering to make something.

I slide the last cookie onto the pile and have to admit they
look pretty good.

Since I didn't want to try something new for a crowd, I went
with a recipe I have memorized—and that Payton thankfully had
ingredients for—my mom's classic chocolate chip cookies.
They're pretty standard, except she always flattens the balls of

dough on the pan, using her thumb to depress a circle in the middle, and then fills that with more chocolate chips.

If you like chocolate, they're pretty great.

And only a few of them look a little too done, so I put those at the bottom of the pile.

I set the empty pan in the giant sink and take a second to just appreciate the kitchen. Everything is top of the line. Practically begging me to use it. They even have one of those fancy espresso machines that Payton used to make us a bunch of delicious decaf lattes.

I'm still standing on the far side of the island, opposite the stools where we sat before, when King enters the kitchen first.

"Smells good." He rubs his stomach.

I wring my hands together in front of my stomach.

Even though I know things didn't always turn out great, baking for Hans helped boost my confidence a lot.

But now I know he ate everything because of his *infatuation* with me. I could have given him a container of gravel and he probably would have eaten it.

I twist my fingers tighter together.

Maybe baking was a mistake. I don't want to embarrass myself in front of Hans's new friends.

The object of my own infatuation is the last to step into the room, and his eyes are already locked on mine.

And just like that, the tension building inside me lessens.

It doesn't matter what anyone else thinks of my cookies, Hans will always love me.

Something warm wraps around my heart.

Hans will always love me.

The last of my tension vanishes, replacing itself with something so light I feel like I could start floating.

It should hardly be a revelation. Hans loving me. He's proven it so many times already in the limited interactions we've had.

And I love him too.

This big, crazy, domineering stalker of mine, he's just that. Mine.

He's still ten feet from the other side of the island, but he's coming to me.

He'll always come to me.

"Cassie made them," Payton says in a cheery voice as Nero reaches for one of the cookies.

And that's when Hans's expression changes. And he throws one of his knives.

CHAPTER 97

Dom

A KNIFE FLIES PAST ME.

Reflex has me jumping back and drawing my gun.

"Hans!" Cassie shouts.

And Toto starts barking his ass off.

Payton scoops up her dog, causing him to quiet, as Cassie hurries around the island to her deranged boyfriend, who has another throwing knife in his hand.

The first knife, the one that flew in front of my face, is buried in some sort of cutting board in the center of the island. The tip of the blade stuck in the wooden surface with the handle sticking up between Nero's outstretched hand and the stack of cookies.

Hans's jaw is clenched tight, and Cassie steps directly in front of him, putting both her hands on his chest. "Baby, we're guests here. I made these for everyone."

I move my gaze over to King and mouth the word *Baby*.

He just rolls his eyes and shakes his head.

"But you made them." Hans's voice is a growl, and I start to second-guess myself as I slide my gun back into its holster.

He might not be a *bad guy,* but this dude has probably killed more than any two of us combined. And he seems just as fucking unhinged as Nero. Maybe more. Which is saying something.

Nero reaches forward, and Hans twitches, like he's ready to throw the second blade. But this time, I doubt he'll be aiming for an inanimate object.

Little Cassie, in her band shirt and ponytail, reaches up and grips Hans by the face with both hands.

He slowly lowers his eyes to hers, and only because I'm so fucking curious, and listening so fucking hard, do I hear her whisper. "That's one."

I roll my lips into my mouth and bite down on them to keep from busting out laughing. She just fucking scolded the ghost man for throwing a fit over some cookies.

Goddamn, it's gonna be fun having them around.

Wood creaks, and we all look over to see that Nero just pulled the knife out of the board.

"Be careful," his wife warns him as he presses his thumb pad to the tip of the blade.

"Throwing blades, huh?" Nero asks, then balances the knife on the edge of his palm, testing the weight. "These are nice."

Hans slowly slides the knife he was prepared to throw back into the holder at his waist. "I know. They're custom."

Nero tosses the blade into the air and catches it.

"Be careful!" Payton hisses again. And rightfully so. I don't think any of us are qualified to fuck around with throwing knives.

Cassie lowers her hands from Hans's cheeks and turns back to face the rest of us, with her body directly in front of Hans. I'm not sure if she's trying to block us from going after him or blocking him from doing anything else crazy.

Either way, it's appreciated.

"You gonna give that back?" Hans nods his head to the knife in Nero's hand.

Nero uses his free hand to pick up one of the cookies that started this whole standoff. He takes a bite, then uses the tip of his blade to point at Hans's hip. "You gonna tell me what that pile of notes in your pocket is all about?"

I swear I hear Hans's teeth grind.

"Seems like *no* all around then." Nero grins around another bite of cookie.

I hadn't even noticed the corners of paper sticking out of Hans's pocket.

Cassie breaks the silence first as she uses her hand to shove the pieces of paper deeper into Hans's pocket. "He's a little particular about these."

"Oh?" I ask, not able to help myself.

She looks up at me. "Well, he beheaded the last guy who touched them. And that was only a few hours ago, so probably best not to poke the bear." When she refers to him as a bear, I watch Hans dart his gaze to her. "Plus, they're just notes from me. Nothing to do with the mission. Or whatever you call it. But, please"—she waves her hands toward the island—"have some cookies. I made them as a thank-you for the hospitality."

Before we split off into the office, we agreed that it was easiest, and safest, for the two of them to stay here for the night. Even with Val and me using one of the guest rooms, it's not like there's a shortage of space.

I see Savannah trying not to laugh as she reaches for one of the cookies.

Apparently everyone here is so used to absurd behavior we're just going to brush off the whole knife-throwing thing.

Val takes a cookie next, then King, and before I can move to grab one, Hans stomps around Cassie and picks up three. Then another two.

He hands one to Cassie, then shoves two into his mouth—at the same time.

"How'd you behead him?" Nero asks, still holding the small knife.

"Schmord," Hans replies with his mouth full of cookies.

"What was that?"

Hans stares at Nero while he chews. When he's swallowed enough to talk again, he answers. "A sword."

"Seriously?" I'm the one to ask it. Because *fucking seriously*?

Hans nods. "A katana." Then he shoves the third cookie into his mouth.

"You bring it with you?" Nero's eyes are way too interested.

I shake my head. This cheap bastard is gonna try to get a free sword out of Hans, and I give it a fifty-fifty shot that either Nero gets one or Hans tries to kill him with one.

And if those two go head-to-head in a fucking sword fight, my money is on the guy who looks like a damn Viking.

CHAPTER 98

With my hair twisted into two wet braids, I exit the en suite bathroom.

Hans is sitting on the foot of the bed we're sharing for the night, wearing sweatpants and nothing else.

I don't even have to think about it; I smile when I see him. He's just so handsome.

I'm in my usual pajamas of skimpy shorts and a loose tank top, but Hans drinks me in like I put an evening gown on after my shower.

This place is opulent enough that the idea isn't even that crazy. This guest room is bigger than the apartment I lived in for most of my adult life.

Hans pats the bed next to him.

The bed is taller than I'm used to, so I have to climb onto it, then I shift so I'm facing Hans with one knee bent on the mattress and one leg hanging off the end of the bed.

"How do they live like this?" I ask.

"They have lots of money."

I snort at Hans's reply. "That's obvious. I mean..." I wave a hand around. "It sounds like you've basically been living in secret, but these guys are just... *living.*" I purse my lips. "I'm not wording this right."

Hans adjusts his position so he's mimicking my pose, our knees touching on the mattress. "I get what you mean." He takes my hands in his, rubbing his thumbs against my shower-warmed skin. "Short answer, they have each other for protection. And along with all the men who work for The Alliance, Nero has a security company that has even more manpower. I could hire people to watch my back, I have the money, but I don't have the trust."

"What about Karmine? You said she had a bunch of people working for her."

Hans tips his head from side to side. "It's a little complicated with that group. Karmine is in charge because she started it all. But they're all partners. They're all doing what they do because they want to be there. They hire out for little jobs as a way to stay busy and make some extra cash." He squeezes my hands. "I actually have two of Karmine's watchers at your parents' place."

"My parents?" I question, then my eyes widen. "Oh man." I wince. "They really liked you after that dinner, but you're probably going to need to do some groveling when they find out what happened to my house."

Hans smirks. "It was a gas leak, remember?"

I roll my eyes, then sober. "Do you really think someone will go after my parents?"

"I don't." He continues to rub circles on the backs of my hands with his thumbs. "This is just a precaution. And when I told Karmine it was for you, she gave me a discount."

"Well, in that case." I heave out a breath. "I'm happy to delay telling them the truth, but my mom calls almost every day, and I haven't had my phone since I left it somewhere in my house after I"—I lift my hand and drag my thumb across my throat—"that guy."

Hans shakes his head and lets go of my other hand to reach into the backpack sitting behind him on the bed.

He pulls out a phone, then a little black case that's about six inches long with a zipper running around three sides.

He hands the phone to me first. "There might be a few photos missing, but it's synced up with your last backup. Same number too."

My jaw drops. "Seriously?"

Hans nods.

I grin at him. "It's kinda handy having a stalker."

"Brat," Hans says without heat. Then he looks down at the case in his hands.

"What's in there?" I ask, getting nervous the longer he waits.

He slowly unzips it, then opens the case.

I press my lips together at the site of two syringes. One small, one huge.

"What are those for?" I'm not sure I really want to know.

Hans holds my gaze. "I would like to put a tracker in you."

CHAPTER 99
Hans

CASSANDRA GLANCES DOWN AT THE SYRINGES, THEN back up to me. "Would that mean you can always find me?"

I nod as I search her eyes. "Will you let me?"

The thought of us being separated and not being able to find her has been clawing at my insides since the very first day we met. When I'd be out of town for hits, I would have nightmares about going home and her being gone. Missing. And ever since I stormed across the street with that book in my hand and got to touch her, got to put my mouth on her, that clawing sensation has turned into razors on my soul. And now that I've had her, now that I've made her mine, I know I wouldn't survive losing her.

I wouldn't be able to do what I did before.

Because no amount of death and destruction could soothe the loss of her.

"Okay," Cassandra says quietly.

"Okay?" I ask.

She bites her lip but nods. "I want you to be able to find me."

I exhale in relief and reach for her, running my hands up and down her thighs, feeling her warmth. The proof she's alive and with me.

Cassandra blinks at me with her big, beautiful eyes. "I don't know how you found me in Mexico, but if you hadn't—"

"You were never out of my sight," I tell her, not letting her finish that sentence. Because I *was* there, and we never have to think about what could have happened. Not ever.

"I don't think I ever thanked you for that."

I grab her hand and pull it to my mouth, kissing the back of it. "You don't ever have to thank me."

She swallows, then looks back down at the case. "Will it hurt?"

I kiss her hand again, then reach over and flip the lid closed.

She doesn't need to see the needle. The gauge is large, in order to fit the slender pill-shaped tracker, and I hate the answer I have to give her. "A little. But I'll use the small syringe to numb the area first. That will be the worst part."

She nods again and puffs out her cheeks as she blows out a breath.

I was worried she'd say no. Most reasonable people would. And I wasn't sure how I was going to handle that. But my girl has proven herself to be not so reasonable. And I'm grateful for it. Because I actually do know how I would have handled it. I would have badgered her until she let me. There is no other option.

I place my hands on her thighs, needing the feel of her skin under my palms. "There's a couple of places I can implant it. Usually, it goes in the back of the neck, the inner arm, or the upper thigh. It might be a bit sore afterward, but only for a day or so."

Cassandra lifts her right hand and touches the inside of her left bicep. "This is where the doctor put my birth control implant. Can you do it there? I remember it not hurting too much after."

I nod and lift my hand to brush over the skin where she's touching. I can feel the tiny piece of plastic under her skin, and it makes me wish I could put the tracker right under the surface, where I could see it any time I looked at her. "It will need to be deep enough that no one can easily feel it." I brush my thumb over the spot again. "And I'll need the tracker to be far enough away from this spot so your doctor"—*who better be female*—"won't notice it when she's replacing this one." I don't know how often that is, but I know it'll need to be changed out eventually.

She sets her hand over mine, where it's still gently holding her upper arm. "It's good for another year and a half, but..." Cassandra bites her lip. "What if..."

My chest starts to tighten. "What if what, Butterfly?"

"What if I didn't get it replaced?" she whispers.

That tightness squeezes even more. "What would you do instead?"

Her chest rises and falls. "Have your baby."

The binds around my heart snap, and the clenching muscle expands painfully.

Have my baby.

I reach for her face.

"You would do that?" My voice is choked.

She nods her head jerkily. "I want to."

My throat burns, and that spot between my eyes aches with pressure. "Wh-why?"

She reaches up and holds my face the same way I'm holding hers. The same way she did downstairs to calm me.

"Because I never realized how much I wanted to make a family until I met you," she whispers. "Because I love you, Hans. And because I'm pretty sure you love me too." She changes my life.

Because I love you.

Heat streams from my eyes. And I try to tell her that I do. That I love her with all my being. But only a strangled sound comes out before I crush my mouth to hers.

This woman.

This strong as hell Butterfly.

She is the reason I fought for so long.

She is the reason I didn't give up.

The reason I didn't lie down and die next to the rest of my family.

She has given me life.

Cassandra pulls me closer, tugging at my shoulders and my sides. Her fingertips dig into my bare skin, promising me this is real. That she's really real.

I roll us so she's on her back.

She wraps her legs around my waist and presses her heels into my lower back.

"I love you, Hans. My big, perfect Grizzly Bear."

I seal my lips to hers and swipe my tongue into her mouth, trying to taste the words as she says them.

Her hips rock up into mine, and I'm not close enough anymore.

I pull away and slide off the mattress so I can stand at the foot of the bed. Then I grip her sleep shorts.

Cassandra lifts her hips, helping me as I pull them off and toss them to the ground, leaving her bare.

My woman.

I grip her hips and drag her so her ass just hangs off the end of the bed.

My ribs feel like they're trying to press out through my skin. Like my heart has grown too big for my body.

I shove her thighs apart and see the shine of her arousal.

I push my sweatpants down and free my throbbing cock.

Cassandra lifts her knees, exposing even more of herself to me. "I need you to practice," she pants. "Practice putting a baby in me."

Fuck.

With one hand, I press down on her stomach. The skin there is so soft, so incredibly wonderful to touch. I can't wait until it's swollen large. *With my child.*

I grip the base of my dick with my other hand and line my tip up with her entrance.

I have to blink to clear my vision, but I watch Cassandra's

pretty face as I push inside her.

Her lips part and her back arches. And I keep pressing forward.

I keep pressing forward as her muscles tighten around me.

I keep pressing forward until my hips are flush against her and I can't push any deeper.

From here, standing above her with my dick all the way inside her hot pussy, I can see everything.

I can see her stretched around me. I can see her nipples straining against her thin shirt. I can see the flush across her chest. I can see the tears in her eyes.

And I can finally breathe.

I grip her hips and hold her on my length as I lean over her. "I'm going to fill you so full, every single night, that you'll be leaking my cum for the rest of your life."

She moans, and her pussy flutters around me.

I release her hips and grab her left arm, holding it straight out against the bed.

I rock my hips and reach for the case.

"I'll always be with you."

I take a tiny packet out and rip it open with my teeth, then smooth the damp wipe over her skin, sanitizing the area.

"You'll never be rid of me."

I withdraw the small syringe and bite the cap off.

"You'll never be lost from me."

I lean over Cassandra and push the needle into her skin.

"I'll always take care of you."

I depress the plunger, and her body tenses around me.

I know this part hurts. And the sting of the anesthesia is more pain than I ever want to cause her.

"Shh," I soothe her as I pull the needle free and set it back in the case.

She arches, but I hold her arm in place and gently rub my thumb over the injection site.

"I'll give you as many babies as you want." I slide out just an

341

inch, then slam back in. "As many as you can fucking handle."

"Hans." She reaches for me with her free hand and digs her fingers into my shoulder.

I keep her arm pinned but work my hips, sliding my dick in and out.

"It's Daddy, now," I groan. "When we're working to fill this belly, you're gonna call me Daddy."

Her body trembles. "Please, Daddy."

With my free hand, I tug down the top of her tank top, freeing her tits. And I shove my hips forward with more force and watch them bounce.

I close my fingers around one and wonder what she'll look like with these swollen too. I wonder if she'll let me suck on them, taste their sweetness.

My balls squeeze, and I decide that she will.

"You'll let me drink my fill of these, won't you, Little Girl?" I pinch her nipple and tug on it gently.

Cassandra nods and grips her other breast.

I pound into her harder. "You'll let me do whatever I want to this sweet little body."

"Yes. Anything you want." She pulls at her other nipple.

Her pussy is gripping me with every thrust.

"Because you know I need to own you," I grit.

She lets go of her tit and slides her hand down her stomach until she's rubbing her fingers against her slick clit.

"Because you know I need to consume every bit of you." I shove myself deep inside her.

I tug her nipple one last time, then let go and pick up the big syringe.

I line the large needle up with her arm.

"You're going to hold still, Butterfly." I rock my hips once. "You're going to make yourself come on my cock, right now, but you're going to hold still. Because you're a good girl. Because I need to do this. And because I love you too." I press the needle into Cassandra's flesh and inject her with the tracker.

CHAPTER 100

I LOVE YOU TOO.

I knew he did. I could feel it. But hearing him say it in that deep, gravelly voice, combined with the pressure in my arm as he plants his tracker in me, just like he's going to plant a baby in me... I explode.

Hans presses his forearm into my chest to keep my arm still while I writhe beneath him, bursts of pleasure shooting down my limbs.

"That's it." His hands are steady, but his breathing isn't. "That's my Butterfly." His body tenses. "Make me yours."

My legs tighten around his hips, pulling him deeper.

"You are mine." I reach my hand lower and let my fingers rub against the base of his dick.

Hans groans and pulls the syringe free from my arm.

I part my fingers and do my best to squeeze his dick right where we meet. "Because you love me."

His hips jerk, and I know he's right there.

I turn my head to look at my arm and the bead of blood forming on my skin. "And now you'll always be able to find me."

Hans drops his head and flattens his tongue against the inside of my arm. As he laps at my blood, he comes.

Hans moans against my skin as his cock pulses inside me, and it brings me right back to the brink.

I swipe my thumb over my clit while Hans licks at my arm and fills me with his release, and I follow him right over. Crying his name and milking him dry.

When I can't take any more stimulation, I pull my hand away from my pussy.

But Hans doesn't pull away. He stays like that, slowly rocking into me, our combined releases making the motion extra slippery. And he keeps his tongue against the small puncture in my skin, licking at it gently.

This is what heaven feels like.

He finally lifts his head to look at me. "Every part of you belongs to me."

There's a small smudge of red on his upper lip, so I reach up with my thumb and wipe it off.

Then curiosity wins, and I push my thumb between my lips.

His neck does a controlled roll, like he's fighting off a shiver over watching me take a taste.

I expect him to climb off and find me a towel, but he slides his arms under me in a bear hug and drags me up the bed, dick still hard inside me.

"Hans," I sputter his name.

He scoots me up until the back of my knees are at the end of the bed, then he rolls us over so I'm astride him.

"Hans," I sigh this time, but he just hugs me to him.

A warm hand slides up under the back of my shirt to rest on my spine. "I love you, Cassandra."

I'll never get tired of hearing that.

"I love you too, Hans."

I'll never get tired of saying that.

Closing my eyes, I press my face into his neck. "I feel a little cheated, like you've gotten to have us longer."

He hugs me tighter. "What do you mean?"

"I know I shouldn't be jealous of your... *watching* me. But I feel like you've gotten to experience more of me than I have of you." The hand on my back rubs up and down. "I mean, I definitely fantasized about you all the time. And wondered what you were doing. And checked out my window for glimpses of you whenever I could..."

Hans grabs one of my braids, with the hand not on my back, and gives it a little tug.

I lift my head to look down at him and watch as his eyes search mine.

"Did you really do all that?"

I don't stop my smile. "I did."

"Then I haven't had you longer, pretty Butterfly. We've had each other for a year. You and me and no one else." He slides his hand down my braid. "It's just the touching part that's new."

My smile turns into a grin. "It's the touching part that I love the most."

His hips flex, reminding me that he's still inside me.

I lean my head down and brush my lips over his. "I'm proud of you for sharing your cookies tonight."

He grunts, pressing his lips gently against mine. "I'm proud of you for making them. But the next batch is just for me."

I pat his chest, resting my head back on his shoulder. "Such a hungry bear."

CHAPTER 101

Hans

THE WORDS COMING OUT OF KING'S MOUTH BLUR INTO nonsense as my eyes lock on Cassandra walking out the front door of Nero's house.

She's...

I swallow.

God, she is fucking perfect.

And she looks like mine.

She skips down the steps and comes to a stop next to me in the driveway.

"Well?" She holds her arms out and turns in a circle. "What do you think?"

"I think I want to find a way to fuck you while you wear that."

Cassandra snorts, then slaps a hand over her mouth as her gaze darts over to the three Alliance men.

I trace my finger across the neckline of her shirt.

"You ready to go, Hans—I mean Cassie?" Dom smiles at his joke as he stops beside us.

I know he's trying to be funny, but I'm not the least bit offended.

Then Cassandra grins at Dom and says, "I'm ready."

I find myself suddenly wanting to punch the man.

Wisely, he steps back. "The vehicles are being brought around."

I nod, then turn back to Cassandra, taking her in from the tips of her toes to the top of her head.

I'm the one who bought everything and gave her the backpack with the clothing after breakfast, but even my fantasies didn't do her justice.

On her feet are black combat boots, laced up her ankles, just like mine. Tucked into them are black tactical pants, just like mine, with extra pockets going down the outside of her hips and thighs, drawing my eyes to her luscious curves. And tucked into her pants is a tight black shirt, just like mine. Only hers is the long-sleeved version. It's lightweight, so it won't be too uncomfortable when we land in the Texas heat. And the material hopefully feels like a nice bit of compression against the spot where I implanted her tracking device. The anesthesia would've worn off sometime while we were sleeping, and I saw the start of a small bruise earlier. I reach out and gently brush my fingers down the inside of her arm.

I don't ever want to be the cause of her pain.

I don't want her to feel any at all.

Cassandra presses her palms to my stomach. "You okay?"

I slide my hand up until I'm gripping the back of her neck. "I'm worried that bringing you with is the wrong choice."

She shakes her head. "I'm not staying here without you. No offense to any of these people, but I'd be so worried about you that I wouldn't be able to breathe. Please don't ask me to stay."

With my hand on her neck, I pull her to my chest, then wrap my arms around her. "I won't."

I can't.

She might be closer to danger by coming with me, but if something happened to her here while I was down in Dallas, I wouldn't be able to breathe either.

Karmine was able to confirm that Gabriel Marcoux spent the

night at his house in Texas, and she picked up chatter about a large sale taking place tonight in the city.

It could be real. Could be nothing. Could be a setup.

But we're going.

We're bringing men.

And I have a shipment of weapons meeting us at the airfield when we land.

CHAPTER 102

Cassie

I PAT THE DAMP PAPER TOWEL AGAINST MY CHEEKS before tossing it in the trash can.

The clothes Hans bought me are surprisingly breathable, but the late afternoon heat in Texas is no joke.

After unlocking the door, I step out of the little bathroom and back into the private airplane hangar.

I've never flown private before, and even though every seat was filled with intense-looking men that I don't know, it was fun.

We were halfway to Dallas when I realized that Nero was the one flying the plane, and that was a little alarming, but I can't fault his landing.

Now, all the men are getting ready, and I'm trying to stay out of the way. Apparently we're waiting for some other plane to land that's filled with guns and stuff. I sort of zoned out when they were talking about the details, but it sounded like Hans knows the guy delivering them.

Not sure how I should feel about Hans being friends with an arms dealer, but—I look across the hangar at Hans as he checks the clip of his handgun—glass houses and all that.

The hangar is basically one giant room with an overhead garage door big enough to drive a plane through. There are people-sized doors on the far side and on the back of the building, which lead to parking spots and are currently propped open for the cross breeze. Then on this side of the building is the restroom I just used and two other rooms that I think are offices.

The plane we flew here in is sitting in the middle of the hangar, and three black SUVs are parked across the entrance to the hangar in the strip of shade the building provides. And there are more SUVs out back, because there's no way all these people will fit in three vehicles.

I cross the concrete floor to Hans.

As soon as I'm close enough, he reaches his hands toward me, sliding them up and down my arms.

If I'm within range, Hans is going to touch me. And I love it.

"It's gonna be another thirty or so minutes," he tells me.

"Okay." I run my hand down his chest, loving the way his muscles tense under my touch.

My other hand pulls a crinkly package of candy out of one of my many pants pockets.

Hans's eyes light up, and he holds one of his palms out.

I tear a corner off the bag and pour Skittles into his hand. And he wastes no time lifting his palm and sliding the candies into his mouth.

"Why do you like these so much? I saw your box of them in your bunker, and then there were like three of these in every backpack." I shake a piece into my hand and put it in my mouth, sucking the candy shell to get the most flavor.

"First, it was a safe room, not a bunker." Hans holds his hand out again, and I pour more into it. "Second, they're good." He pops the Skittles into his mouth. "I don't remember my first time having them or anything like that. I've just always liked them. And they don't melt easily."

I pluck out a different color next and pop it in my mouth. "Have they always been your favorite?"

Hans nods while he chews. "Every Halloween, I'd trade my

chocolate candy to Freya for her Skittles. She was a tough negotiator, so I'd usually have to trade two for one, but it was worth it."

I smile and step into him, leaning against his body. "That's a nice memory."

Hans wraps his arms around me, and I love it, but after about five seconds, it's too hot.

I push against him and step back.

He looks down at me with his brows furrowed. "What's wrong?"

"Nothing." I fan my face. "I'm just a little warm."

The hangar isn't as sweltering as it is outside in the sun, but it's still hot.

Hans moves his hand to my back and starts to guide me to the closest SUV.

He lifts his chin, getting the attention of the man leaning against the front bumper. And the man steps forward.

Hans points to the vehicle. "Can you start it up and turn the AC on?"

My eyes widen with guilt. "No, Hans, I'll be okay."

The other man ignores me and nods. "Can do."

"Hans—"

"Butterfly." His voice is so gentle. "I love you."

I melt.

"Hans." My tone matches his. "I love you too."

"Then you'll get your sweet ass in that back seat and cool down. But leave the door open so I can see you."

Having a door open while blasting the AC seems like the most wasteful thing ever. But as a drip of sweat breaks free from my hairline, I decide to indulge us both.

CHAPTER 103
Hans

"The pilot just called to let me know they'll be touching down in ten," Cain's rough voice tells me through the phone. "Some dumb fuck stalled out on the runway, delaying their takeoff, but he made up some of the time in the air."

"That's not a problem," I tell him. "I know this was all pretty last minute."

"Usually is with you." His chuckle sounds rarely used.

"Can't argue." After hanging up, I slide my phone back into my pocket.

Ten to land, five to taxi here, another ten to unload and gear up. We should be on the road in under thirty.

I cross the floor to update the guys and glance over to the SUV where Cassandra is sitting.

As promised, the back door facing the hangar is open, and she's leaning against the far door with her legs stretched out in front of her across the rear bench seat. She's finished her candy and is doing something on her phone. Probably reading through her favorite recipe sites.

Determined to give this update and then go sit with her, I'm just turning my head away from my girl when the door behind her suddenly opens, and she's dragged back out of the vehicle.

CHAPTER 104

My stomach drops as I start to fall without warning.

I let go of my phone and throw my arms wide, trying to catch myself, but rough hands grip my armpits and harshly drag me backward.

My elbow hits the door frame, and my heel catches on the running board.

Panic flares alongside confusion, and I haven't even had time to scream.

But as I'm forcefully hauled away, I look through the open back seat of the SUV and see Hans sprinting toward me.

Understanding finally hits, and that's when I start to scream.

CHAPTER 105
Hans

CASSANDRA'S SCREAMS ECHO AROUND THE HANGAR, and I try to run faster.

No, no, no.

Men are shouting behind me, and I can hear their footsteps as they chase after me.

She can't—

They can't take her.

They can't have her.

My lungs are screaming after ten steps.

I need to move faster.

I break out of the hangar.

I can see her. I can still see her.

She's kicking and screaming and reaching behind her to claw at the face of the giant man carrying her.

The man carrying her.

I memorize his features.

I can't let him take her.

My gun is in my hand, but I can't shoot. I can't risk hitting her. If I aimed for him and accidentally killed her instead... I would immediately turn the gun on myself.

"Cassandra!" I shout, letting her know I'm coming.

He's only ten yards ahead of me.

I can get there.

But then. I see it. The plane rolling toward us. And the stairs being tossed open.

"No!" I bellow out my dread.

Someone steps into view on the plane at the top of the stairs and raises a gun.

The shots are loud, but I don't stop running.

I can't stop chasing her.

"Hans!" she screams.

Cassandra screams my name.

I'm closer.

"Cassandra!"

I'm getting closer.

And then a bullet rips through my thigh, and I fall.

My hands catch the pavement, and I roll. But I'm not quick enough. Because when I climb back to my feet and lift my head, Cassandra is being hauled up the stairs.

"No!"

She disappears into the plane.

I stumble on my first step, then shove the pain to the back of my mind and run.

"Cassandra!" This time my voice breaks.

My Cassandra.

The plane takes a ninety-degree turn onto one of the cross-ways, moving from the outside lane toward the runway.

It's getting farther away.

It's going to take off.

Someone pulls the stairs closed from inside the plane, but I can't shoot at them.

I won't be able to disable a plane at this distance with a handgun, and I can't chance damaging the hull. Can't chance doing something that would only cause it to falter midflight or crash during its landing. Not with my Butterfly aboard.

Footsteps surround me. The hit to my leg slows me enough for the other men to catch up.

"Don't shoot," I try to yell, but I choke on the words.

"Do not shoot!" Dom shouts from beside me.

The plane makes another ninety-degree turn, and it starts to pick up speed.

From this angle, we're looking straight at the windows on the side of the plane. I'm still running. I can't stop.

When I see Cassandra through the window, my heart seizes.

She shoves the man trying to hold her and lunges to the window.

Her hands press against the pane, and her eyes lock with mine.

And when I read my name on her lips, my soul splinters.

And when I watch a hand reach for her, see the glint of the syringe aimed for her neck, when I see it roughly pushed into her skin, the world around me turns red.

CHAPTER 106
Cassie

My palms slap against the window.

I have to see him.

I have to let him see me.

And there he is.

My protector.

My man.

Running across the tarmac. Blood streaming from his leg. And agony covering his face.

"Hans!" I cry his name as my heart breaks for him.

I want to tell him not to worry.

I want to tell him that I trust him.

I want to tell him that this won't be like before.

That no matter what happens, I don't blame him.

I don't regret knowing him.

Something sharp bites into my neck.

I'll never regret loving him.

CHAPTER 107
Hans

THE PLANE LIFTS INTO THE AIR.

My steps waver as I lift my head to watch it rise.

Cassandra is on that plane.

My heart is on that fucking plane.

I stagger to a stop and bellow my rage at the sky.

Not again.

Not fucking again.

I can't do this again.

A hand grips my arm. "We'll get her back." Dom steps in front of me. "Hans, we will get her back." He shoves me back toward the hangar. "Let's go."

I don't want to look away from the plane fading into the distance.

I don't want to, but I do.

Because it's time to do the hard things.

It's time to become the ghost assassin my enemies whisper about.

WE'RE STILL CLIMBING THROUGH OUR TAKEOFF WHEN Karmine answers on the first ring. "Was it a bust?"

"I need the army." My voice scrapes out of my throat.

"What happened?" Karmine switches to full alert.

"Marcoux has Cassandra."

She hisses a curse. "Send me the coordinates."

I watch the dot on my screen. "It looks like they're going to Phoenix. They're on a plane ahead of us."

"She have a tracker on her?"

"Subdermal," I tell her so she knows it's not a phone that can be found and switched off. "Just last night."

She knows what that means too. That the site of the injection will be visible.

"Where?"

"Her sleeves cover it." It's all I can bring myself to say. Because the words *As long as they leave her clothes on* won't form.

I can't say it.

I can't bear imagining.

Because that would be bad enough. The absolute worst. But if they suspected the tracker... I almost heave. They'd cut it out of her.

"How far ahead are they?" Karmine asks, forcing me to think of something else.

The men went as quickly as they could, but we needed to refuel and lost precious time.

"About eight minutes," I tell her, but we both know I can't just jump off this plane and get her.

Even if we could land at the same airport, we can't land second. We don't know what sort of weaponry they have. They could take out our entire plane before we even touch ground.

So I have to make assumptions.

I assume, based on their trajectory, they're headed to Phoenix.

I assume when they land, they'll take Cassandra to Marcoux's compound in the dessert.

I assume the satellite images King got are accurate.

I assume this is all a tactic to get me. And that they'll keep Cassandra alive.

"We'll get her, Hans," Karmine promises. "I owe you this."

She doesn't owe me shit. But I need her help all the same. "Just head to Cain's hangar in Phoenix. We'll gear up there."

"On my way."

I hang up and hit on Cain's contact.

It rings twice, and before he can speak, I start. "Change in plans. Couldn't wait for the delivery."

I wouldn't consider us friends exactly, but he knows this life well enough to know that a last-minute change in plans is not a good thing.

"Where are you headed?"

"To your city."

"What do you need?"

I tell him.

CHAPTER 108

MY HEAD HITS SOMETHING HARD, FORCING A GROAN
out of my throat.

The world jostles around me.

"Come on, bitch." An ugly voice tugs at my arms.

Fuck you.

I try to say it, but I can't get my mouth to work.

I'm so tired.

CHAPTER 109

Hans

THE PLANE SLOWS TO A STOP DIRECTLY IN FRONT OF the open hangar door, and I'm the first one down the stairs.

There's a catering van parked just inside the building and a line of SUVs parked along the side.

The ache in my thigh makes my steps uneven as I cross the tarmac and enter the hangar. But the bullet only tore through muscle; it didn't hit bone, and it exited out the back, so the quick shot of antibiotics and tightly wrapped gauze beneath my pant leg will do until I get Cassandra back.

Before I reach the van, the driver's door opens. And a man as tall as me, built like a weight lifter, with hair graying from age and experience, steps out.

Without a greeting, I follow him around to the back of the van, where Cain opens the rear doors, revealing an arsenal.

Dom, King, and Nero step up beside me.

"All of it?" I ask.

Cain dips his chin. "All of it."

King leans into the van. "Is that what I think it is?"

"Hans said there's a helicopter pad at the target," Cain replies as King drags the case closer to himself. "You might not need to use—"

"Oh, I'll use it," King cuts him off.

A feminine whistle sounds from behind us, and we all turn.

Karmine stands there, having entered on silent feet, her red hair twisted back into one long braid. "Hi, boys."

Then the side door opens, and a dozen of her soldiers walk through.

Their steps are as quiet as Karmine's were, and their presence is menacing.

They know who we're going after tonight.

They know the history.

My history.

And they want to kill him just as badly as I do.

As the women approach, the men from our plane join them, gathering around in front of me.

A sense of gratitude fills me, so large it nearly blocks out my fear.

Before me are the men of The Alliance, men of the Chicago mafia, Karmine's warriors, and Karmine herself, the only person I've called a friend in a long time.

I can't say thank you.

Can't bring myself to speak. So I just nod.

And they all nod back.

CHAPTER 110

Waking up after being chemically knocked out is not fun.

I had my wisdom teeth removed when I was twenty, and that's the only time I've ever been out for something. But I hated the feeling. And I hate it even more now.

But most of all, I hate the big motherfucker carrying me over his shoulder like I'm a sack of rocks.

I tried to wake up when I was jostled off the plane. I really did try. But I slipped back under.

Not this time though. I'm staying awake.

I force my eyes to blink.

The sunlight makes them water, but I keep blinking.

I don't actually know whether it's better to be unconscious or conscious for whatever is about to happen. But I know Hans will come for me. So I need to stay alive until then. And at least if I'm aware of my surroundings, I can maybe do something to help myself.

Sucking the inside of my cheek between my teeth, I bite down. Not hard enough to draw blood, but enough to cause pain.

I am staying awake.

Eyes still blinking, I turn my head and try to take in my surroundings.

It's hot, and the sun is still up, but it's lowering toward the horizon.

A horizon covered in... Is that a cactus? It blurs, then comes back into focus as many. That's a lot of cactuses. Cacti?

I work to steady my vision and see what looks like mountains, or maybe they're just ragged hills. And I can't tell if I see a fence or if my eyes are playing tricks on me.

Wherever I am, it's nowhere good.

I open and close my mouth. The movement helps to spark my senses. But with those senses comes nausea.

The shoulder digging into my stomach is making it hard to breathe, and when the monster carrying me starts climbing steps, the bumping around is too much.

I press my hands into the man's back and lift my head just in time to vomit up my stomach full of half-digested Skittles.

I pinch my eyes shut and feel tears dripping from my lashes as I heave again.

"What the fuck?" the man carrying me curses, and then my world turns again when he dips his shoulder, causing me to slide off.

I try to catch myself, but there's no way.

I crash into a railing and have the awareness to be grateful that he dropped me on the landing at the top of the steps and not on the stairs themselves as I land in a heap.

I manage to get up onto my hands and knees before I dry heave once more.

"Stupid bitch," the man growls, and I glance up to see him twisting around to look at the back of his pants.

I hope I puked all over him. I hope those were his favorite pants. And I hope he never gets the smell out.

He glowers at me, and it doesn't even matter that he might be considered handsome. He's a terrible human, so he's ugly as shit.

"I'm not sorry," I rasp out.

My throat hurts, and I'm so thirsty, but I still have just enough drugs in my system to help me feel angry instead of scared.

His giant hand wraps around my upper arm, and he jerks me up to standing. "Get walking."

I spit on the floor as I stagger to my feet, trying to get the nasty taste out of my mouth.

"Disgusting," the nearly seven-foot-tall man snaps and jerks me forward.

My arm gives a sharp zing of protest since he's squeezing right where Hans injected that tracker into my arm. But I force my arm to stay lax. I don't even want to think about what these people will do if they suspect there's a GPS tracker inside my body.

He drags me to an ornately carved door and shoves it open.

I didn't have time to appreciate the size of the building from outside, but standing in the entryway, with Evil Andre the Giant at my side, my eyes widen.

This isn't a house. It's a freaking palace.

Before us, the hallway stretches impossibly long, with giant two-story living rooms, or whatever they're called in a place like this, on either side.

It's impressive. But it's also gaudy as hell. The floors and walls are all some sort of shiny marble, and the ceilings have so many chandeliers it looks like a lighting showroom for villains.

"Come on," Andre snaps, dragging me farther into the home.

My feet slip on the smooth floor, and I realize my boots are missing.

I look down.

My shirt is untucked.

Another wave of sickness rolls through me. And I use my free arm to pat at my body.

I'd know if they did something to me, right?

They had to just be checking for weapons. Maybe took my boots off because...

More of my brain fog clears, and it's replaced by panic.

I have no idea why they'd take my boots.

I need to get out of here. Even if it means running through the desert in socks.

Hans will find me.

He'll always find me.

I don't remember Andre locking the front door after we came in. Which is good. I think.

I just need to get away from the man at my side.

Except he's so much bigger than I am. I'll never win in a fight.

My chest constricts, and I have to open my mouth to pull in a breath.

Don't freak out.

Focus.

I fill my lungs.

What would Hans do?

I picture Hans jumping through the back door of a hijacked school bus, throwing a knife through the eye socket of an unsuspecting kidnapper.

I picture Hans biting down on a stack of Post-its while using a wall-mounted sword to behead a man.

I picture him luring the other men into view with a stolen walkie-talkie before blowing away their skulls without hesitation.

I know what Hans would do.

Hans would fight dirty.

I do my best to fake a stumble, causing Andre to lean to the side to support more of my weight. Then I jerk my arm down as hard as I can.

The movement is sudden enough that he lets go and close enough in timing to my stumble for him to think I'm just falling. Meaning he's not completely on guard.

When Andre turns to get another grip on me, I turn toward him and knee him in his balls as hard as I can.

The strangled sound that comes out of him fills me with satisfaction.

But when I turn to run, my sock-covered feet slip on the smooth floor.

It's just a second. Just half a second before I catch my balance. But it's enough.

Andre grips my hair.

I struggle to keep my feet under me as my scalp screams in pain. But I can't fall. If I do, I have no doubt he'll drag me by my ponytail.

"I'm going to fucking kill you." I can hear the pain in his voice, and it's the only comfort I have when he drags me in front of him and backhands my cheek.

My eyes fill with tears.

I'm not crying.

I am not crying.

It just fucking hurts when a grown-ass man baby hits you.

He shakes me by my hair.

It also hurts when someone mean pulls your hair.

I reach up and cling to Andre's forearm, trying to hold my weight up with his arm and take the pressure off my scalp. It lessens the pain, just a little, and I'm able to stay on my feet as he drags me down the long hall.

When Hans pulled my hair, he knew how to make it feel good. And even with tears still trailing down my cheeks, I try to remember that. Try to remember that a good man can make anything feel good.

I won't let Evil Andre ruin hair pulling for me.

We keep moving down the incredibly long hallway. Men are visible, but I don't bother calling for help. There is literally no way to confuse me for a willing participant, and none of the men milling around with assault weapons are giving me so much as a glance.

Cool, everyone here is a piece of shit.

I hope Hans kills all of them.

Andre drags me through a doorway, and I stare at the tiny

room in confusion before the sound of doors sliding shut clues me in.

It's an elevator.

The ground beneath my feet starts to move, and I twist in Andre's hold to look at the floor indicator.

When it changes from one to two, I let out my breath.

Nothing about this situation is good, but I feel like going below ground would somehow be worse.

The number changes to a three as the elevator slows to a stop.

Andre doesn't give me any sort of warning; he just starts walking, painfully yanking my hair with every step.

I'd kill for my crossbow right now.

I try to pay attention. Try to focus on how many doors we pass and which way we're walking. But it all looks the same. Same stupid slippery floors. Same lack of taste.

I'm pulled to a stop as Andre opens a dark wood door. I barely get a glimpse of the room before he shoves me forward so hard that I fall. My hip connects with the floor first, and a jolt of pain shoots through my body.

Groaning, I roll onto my knees, readying myself for whatever is coming next.

But Andre doesn't follow me in. He slams the door shut between us, and I hear a lock turn. From the outside.

"You're such a little bitch!" I yell and frantically rub at my hip, trying to soothe the sting.

When the pain subsides enough to move again, I climb to my feet and take in the room.

It's an empty office.

And it's as pretentious as the rest of the house.

On one side of the room is a seating area with three high-back chairs covered in green velvet and a glass and gold coffee table, all on top of a patterned rug. On the other side of the room is a giant dark-stained desk in front of matching bookcases that cover the entire wall behind it. But the shelves are empty, and that might be the worst part about this room. Then again, it could be the orange silk curtains surrounding the wall of windows across from me.

It's like someone went into random furniture stores and bought the most expensive things they could find and expected them to work together.

Money really doesn't buy taste.

Of course, I think of Hans.

Sweet, quiet neighbor Hans. Who lives alone in a small house, has a normal vehicle, and wears plain clothes. But apparently has more money than I could even imagine.

Tears build in my eyes again, but this time, I can't blame Evil Andre.

I'm scared.

And I miss Hans.

I sniff and sniff again.

Be sad, but be productive.

Wiping the back of my hand across my cheek, I'm reminded I was hit in the face recently and wince.

Okay, tears can stay.

I turn back to the door I was pushed through and try the handle.

It doesn't budge.

I didn't think it would, but I had to try.

Trying to focus, I cut straight across the room and look out the windows. The landscape beyond is beautiful and harsh, with sand-covered hills and prickly desert plants.

I try to open the window, but there's no latch. They don't open.

When I press my face to the glass and look down, I can see nothing but sharp rocks two stories below me. And since I won't be able to get away on broken legs, I don't bother trying to break the glass.

With one last place to look, I walk through the sitting area to the other door in the room.

It's partially open, with darkness on the other side, and if it's not a bathroom, then I hope it's a secret tunnel out of here.

I press the door open. Not a tunnel.

Stepping into the bathroom, I shut and lock the door behind me, then turn on the faucet and cup my hands under the water.

I swish the mouthful around and spit it out. Then I fill my hands again and gulp down the cold water.

CHAPTER 111
Hans

WE'RE TEN MINUTES FROM THE TARGET, AND I'M IN ONE of the back seats, sitting between Nero and Karmine.

It's quiet, with everyone doing a final check of their gear.

And we have gear.

Cain pulled through. He'll still charge me for everything, but nonetheless, he pulled through.

I tighten the leg holster over my bandaged leg.

A glint of light draws my attention to Nero.

He slips his fingers through the carved metal and... I narrow my eyes.

Does this guy seriously have a set of diamond-encrusted brass knuckles?

I look away.

I don't have time to question Nero's weapon choices.

All my focus has to be somewhere else.

On someone else.

I touch my hand to the gun at my hip, then to my throwing knives, then to the extra clips and blades secured to my bullet-proof vest.

Eight minutes.

We all have our assignments.

Karmine's team will sweep the house, looking for anyone held against their will. The team with King will secure the perimeter before moving in. And everyone else is with me and Nero. But they all know that I get Gabriel Marcoux.

I get to kill him.

Seven minutes.

I set my hand on my final weapon.

I can't sit in a vehicle with it on my back, so it has to wait until we arrive.

Six minutes.

CHAPTER 112
Cassie

WITH MY SOCKS IN MY POCKET, I STEP OUT OF THE
bathroom barefoot and back into the empty office. I won't let
slippery feet slow me down again.

After digging through every cabinet, I found a small thing of
unopened mouthwash and used it three times. Then, because I'm
a nervous pee-er, I used the toilet as quickly as possible. It freaked
me out thinking someone with a key could walk right in. But I
didn't really want to add peeing myself to the list of terrible things
that happened today.

I also pulled my ponytail free and pressed my damp hands
against my scalp to try and calm some of the lingering pain before
loosely putting my hair back up.

I'm standing on the threshold of the room, wondering what I
can use to smash the mirror in the bathroom, when I hear the
click of the main door unlocking.

Before I have time to decide whether I should hide in the
bathroom or rush the door, it swings open.

Evil Andre steps in first, followed by an older guy.

The new guy gives off a super creepy vibe, and based on his
three-piece suit, which is over the top for anything less than a
wedding, I'd bet he's the owner of this awful house.

Andre shuts the door after them and then stands against it as a human blockade.

The suit, who looks like someone's sleazy uncle, stops a few feet away from me.

Too far for me to kick him.

"I'm Gabriel Marcoux."

But he is close enough for me to spit on.

So I do.

Andre steps away from the door like he's going to punish me for spitting on his boss, but Gabriel lifts a hand to stop him.

Andre obeys.

Gabriel pulls the fancy satin square out of his suit pocket and wipes at his chest. He's trying to look unaffected. But he's not good at it.

Sadly, none of my spit got on his face, but the message was received.

"You're the neighbor, aren't you?" He tosses the soiled kerchief to the floor. "And yet you're dressed like a member of *that whore's* little army."

"Pretty sure her profession is killing bastards like you, not whoring. But if you want to be a total fucking hypocrite and talk down about sex workers, go ahead."

He lifts a brow. "Hypocrite?"

"I have to explain it..." I shake my head.

I know I shouldn't goad him. But he's freaking me out. So it's sass or hiding in the corner, and something tells me I should be buying time.

I squeeze my hands into fists to stop myself from reaching up and touching my tracker.

"If you know me so well, Cassandra Lynn Cantrell." He spreads his arms in a *do tell* gesture.

I ignore him using my full name. "I know your interior designer sucks. And I know Hans is going to kill you."

Gabriel narrows his eyes. "My mother furnished this house."

"Sorry, but I'm pretty sure your mother hates you."

His jaw flexes. "You're acting like a child."

I cross my arms instead of responding.

"And the idea of Hans rescuing you with the help of his little harem is just as juvenile." He scoffs. "It's a suicide mission I'll welcome with open arms."

I don't miss the way he's always belittling women. This man hates females. Which tracks with him being *the worst*. And it means he'll never be afraid of Karmine's army. Even if he should be.

But a man like this, one who preys on those weaker than him, I bet I know what he is afraid of.

I bet he's afraid of Hans.

Afraid of ever finding himself one-on-one with the killer.

And right now Gabriel feels safe in this marbled prison.

He feels comfortable.

And I just can't allow that to continue.

My lips pull into a smirk. "Hans isn't with the women."

I suspect he's called Karmine for help by now, but that's not important for this conversation.

"So he's coming alone?" Gabriel mocks. "Even better."

I shake my head. "Not alone."

He starts to sneer, but I don't flinch. And I can see the moment he realizes I might be telling the truth.

Hans has always been alone.

Since the man in front of me ruined his life twenty years ago, Hans has been alone.

He's fought alone.

He's killed alone.

He's eaten his meals alone.

Spent his holidays alone.

My heart squeezes so hard for him.

For what he lost.

For what I can give him.

"What is she talking about?" Gabriel turns to Andre, whose face has gone pale.

"There, uh—There were men. With him in Dallas," Andre stammers. "I thought you knew."

Gabriel slowly shakes his head. "And how would I know that if you didn't tell me?"

"On the plane—You were on the phone with Kris—" Andre slices a glare at me, like it's my fault he didn't do his job.

I wink at him.

"Who?" Gabriel snaps.

Andre visibly swallows. "Um, I think the guy next to him might've been Dominic Gonzalez."

Gabriel's head rears back. "The head of the Chicago mafia? What the fuck would he be doing with Hans?"

"Maybe it wasn't him," Andre backpedals. "I don't know. I just saw the tattoos and hair..."

Both men turn toward me.

I don't have to fake my smile this time. "Oh, didn't you know? Hans is a part of The Alliance now."

"You're lying," Gabriel hisses at me.

I lift a shoulder. "Am I?"

I might be lying; I don't actually know the details. But the idea of it seems to be rattling this asshole's confidence, so I'm sticking with it.

Gabriel steps closer into my space. "I was going to let you sit up here, nice and comfortable, until we lured Hans out of whatever hole he lives in and killed him. Then I would have killed you with a bullet to the head. Made it quick. But I think I'll keep you instead. Put you to work." He steps back. "Radio Henrik. Tell him we have product for him to transport to the cells. And let him know he can be as rough as he wants." Gabriel's voice is filled with a terrible-sounding glee that fills my stomach with dread.

I stand still while they leave, but as soon as the lock clicks behind them, I rush back into the bathroom.

I cannot just stand here and wait for Henrik.

I pull open the top drawer of the vanity.

Nothing new has appeared, and still nothing hard enough to break a mirror.

Then I pause.

Fucking duh.

I yank the drawer all the way out and shimmy it loose.

I tip the contents into the sink and find the best way to hold it two handed, like a square baseball bat.

Then I look down at my bare feet.

If I put my socks back on and the bad guy comes to get me, I won't be able to run. I'll just have to be careful and accept the risk of cutting my feet.

Squeezing my eyes shut and turning my head away, I swing the drawer.

The mirror shatters on impact, but I keep my eyes clenched shut for another second before opening them.

Shards are all over the counter, but there's a perfectly pointy triangle of glass still sitting in the corner of the frame.

Using a washcloth I found earlier, I pry it out, then wrap the bottom half of the mirror chunk in the little towel so I can hold it without slicing my palm open.

I have a weapon. Now I need a plan.

I look around the small bathroom.

I could lock myself in here, but I have no doubt the man they're sending up would be able to break the door down in moments. And then I'd be stuck in the narrow bathroom with no way out.

But is standing in the main room, facing off, glass chunk to gun, really a better idea?

CHAPTER 113

Hans

THE BEEPING DOT ON MY PHONE IS STILL IN THE northwestern corner of the estate.

As we traversed the desert, I watched the dot. I haven't stopped watching the dot, watching Cassandra's location, since her plane disappeared out of my sight. But for the first time since getting to the house, she's not moving.

I can't tell what floor she's on, but over the past several minutes, it's looked like she's in one room. Pacing, moving a little bit here and there. But for the last forty-five seconds, she hasn't moved at all.

And I can't let myself think of all the reasons why that could be bad.

Ten yards to my left, Nero holds up his hand, letting everyone know it's time.

All at once, from every direction, forty men and women close in on Marcoux's estate.

Be brave, Butterfly. I'm coming for you.

CHAPTER 114

LESS THAN A MINUTE AFTER I GET INTO POSITION, THE main door flings open.

I can't see it; I can only hear it bang against the wall. What I don't hear is the sound of it closing again.

Heavy footsteps enter the office, and I hold my breath.

Please don't let this be a mistake.

The man stomps to the bathroom door.

It rattles in the frame.

"You think a little door will stop me?" He chuckles. "This is just foreplay."

There's a loud thud as he slams into the door.

I have to slap my empty hand over my mouth to keep from screaming.

Fear courses through my veins.

I've never been more scared in my whole life.

I don't want to be alone with this man.

There's a second hit, and the man grunts.

I lower my hand and pull in a deep breath.

A third hit is accompanied by the sound of wood splintering.

"Come out, come out, wherever you are," he taunts, stepping past the wreckage of the bathroom door.

And that's when I climb out from under the desk and run as fast as I can for the open door.

My bare feet slap against the floor as adrenaline spikes through my body.

The man shouts something, having seen me, but I don't look back.

I want to close the office door behind me. I want to lock him inside. But I can't risk slowing down.

The piece of mirror shines in my hand as my arms pump, and I rush through the doorway into the hall.

And that's when all hell breaks loose.

Somewhere below me, gunfire erupts.

A lot of gunfire erupts.

It's so much. So loud.

I can also hear glass shattering and men screaming, and it's the best sound I've ever heard in my life.

Because it means Hans is here.

CHAPTER 115
Hans

When we hit the house, we go loud.

We enter through every door and first-floor window.

We show no mercy.

We don't have any.

We don't need any.

Every man and woman fighting with me has hands covered in blood.

And that's okay.

Because vengeance is rarely clean.

CHAPTER 116

THE ELATION OF KNOWING HANS IS CLOSE IS overshadowed by the terror of knowing the man behind me is closer.

My lungs burn as I run as fast as I can down the hall.

The elevator is out of the question, not enough time, but there has to be stairs somewhere.

"Keep running, bitch!" the man shouts from not too far behind me. "This is my favorite part!"

A whimper catches in my throat.

I haven't even seen the man's face, but his voice is going to be burned into my memory.

Rooms blur by.

I just have to get to Hans.

I just have to find Hans.

He'll destroy this man for me. I know he will.

The man laughs behind me.

I feel like he's toying with me. Like he could have caught me by now.

I push my legs faster.

Just ahead, the wall on my left falls away.

Stairs.

I reach out with my left hand and, just as I pass, grab the railing that climbs up the wall.

My momentum whips me around until I'm looking down the stairs, straight at a woman with bright red hair, holding a gun pointed right at me.

"Down!" she shouts, and I let my legs collapse beneath me.

My butt hits the top step, and then she's shooting.

The bullets fly over my head as I bounce down a few more steps, and I hear a gurgled cry from the man who's been chasing me.

I duck my head, sliding down a couple more stairs, as the woman shoots once more.

My ears are ringing, but I still hear the thud of a body hitting the floor behind me.

I slide to a stop and open my eyes.

The woman is still standing on the landing, where the flight turns back to go down to the second floor, and from my spot on the steps, we're nearly eye level.

She lowers her gun and smirks at me. "Cassandra, I presume?"

A noise between a laugh and sob bursts out of me, and I scramble down the last few steps and throw my arms around the woman.

Her body tenses against mine, and I quickly let go and step back. "Sorry. Sorry." I brush the rogue tears off my face, forgetting and wincing at my bruised cheek. "You must be Karmine. It's *really* nice to meet you." I sniffle.

The intense woman looks at me like she isn't quite sure what to do with me, then she lifts a radio to her mouth.

The noise of gunfire downstairs has intensified, but I still hear her words.

"I have the butterfly."

CHAPTER 117
Hans

KARMINE'S VOICE PLAYS THROUGH MY EARPIECE, AND the world quiets around me.

Cassandra is safe.

I fill my lungs with air.

I won't be okay until she's in my arms. But that's fine. Because I still have some people to kill.

A large man peeks out from around a doorway ahead of me.

Like this guy.

The big man who carried my Cassandra, kicking and screaming, onto that fucking plane ducks back into the room he's hiding in.

He starts to shut the door like a fucking coward.

I take two sprinting steps, then drop into a baseball slide.

My boots hit the door just as it's about to close, forcing it to swing open as I slide into the room.

These stupid marble floors are good for something.

My target staggers backward from the door slamming into his shoulder.

He's holding a gun, but it's not at the ready.

Mine is.

My first shot goes into his right shoulder. Where ball meets socket.

He drops the gun.

My second shot goes through his right hip. Again, exactly where the joint meets.

It's a lot of pain for the body to stand against. Especially a body as big as his.

He drops to his knees.

Anger and disbelief contort his features.

I switch my gun into my left hand.

"You touched what's mine." I reach behind my back with my right hand.

"And now you'll pay." My fingers close around the grip of the katana secured to my back.

It pulls free from the sheath with a satisfying swoosh.

The man's eyes widen. And his mouth opens. And then he helpfully holds his hands up for me.

My blade arcs down between us, and I sever his hands from his body.

Nobody touches my Butterfly.

The man screams.

And I breathe a little bit easier.

Turning my back to him, I step out of the room and shut the door behind me, but not before locking the handle.

He'll bleed out soon enough.

CHAPTER 118

Cassie

KARMINE PULLS A SECOND GUN FROM A HOLSTER AT HER hip. "Here."

I look at it and then at her. "Um, I don't know—"

She shakes the handle end toward me in a hurry-up motion. "Just point and shoot. No matter what, it's gonna work better than a chunk of fucking mirror."

Oh. Right.

I drop the towel-wrapped mirror piece on the steps and take the gun.

Karmine flips a little thing on the side of the gun, exposing a little red dot. "It's live and loaded. Don't point it at my back, and follow me."

I nod and grip the gun tightly.

Karmine spins, and I admire how perfect her braid is as I follow her down the steps.

My feet are sore from running on these stupid hard floors, my butt hurts from the stupid stairs, my face aches, and my scalp is still throbbing, but being here, in the presence of this badass woman, I feel a little badass myself.

Karmine stops at the open entrance to the second level, standing guard, and waves me to go past her down the stairs.

I hurry down the steps on my bare feet and mentally pat myself on the back for taking my socks off. Boots would obviously be better, but I never would have made it to the stairs, to Karmine, if I was sliding all over the place.

I wait on the middle landing for Karmine to pass me, then follow her again.

The noise is louder down here. So loud I can feel the vibrations.

It feels like I've been dropped into the middle of an action movie.

The staircase we're on isn't a grand one ending in a foyer, but rather one that spits us out in the center of the house, in the middle of that endless hallway.

We're almost to the main level, and all I can see from here is a knocked-over decorative table next to a closed door and then the hallway disappearing on either side.

I'm right behind Karmine, and I take the last step without seeing the shattered porcelain all over the floor.

Little shards dig into the soles of my feet, but before I can recoil—or cry—the door opposite us flies open.

Karmine shoves me to the side just as bullets slam into the stairs we just descended.

"Go down!" Karmine shouts at me as she flattens herself against the wall, returning fire.

Down?

I look behind me and see that the stairs continue down into the basement.

Oh hell no.

I hesitate for one second, but then a hailstorm of bullets chips away at the steps above and I decide the basement is a perfectly fine place to go.

The first step sends bolts of pain through my feet.

I want so badly to reach down and brush away the pieces that are embedding themselves into my feet, but when Karmine shouts something about backup, I decide to suck it the fuck up and keep going.

Hans ran after me with a bullet hole in his leg. I can walk with some broken pottery in my feet.

I slip on the final step, my soles now slick with blood, but I keep my balance and peer around the edge of the wall.

A gross, prickling feeling covers my body.

This level isn't like the other ones. Instead of marble and chandeliers, the floors and walls are smooth cement, and the ceiling has recessed lighting, giving off a dim glow. And instead of one long hallway, this one breaks off in three directions. Left, right, or straight. And after a few yards, the halls turn. Like they were designed to be a jagged maze.

This just went from action movie to horror film.

I have to fight against the urge to curl up in the corner and wait for Hans.

He knows I'm here. Karmine knows where I went. Once again, I just need to keep myself intact until Hans can find me.

"Fuck you!" Karmine's shout echoes down the stairs, and I *rock paper scissors* in my mind and take off to the left.

I try to shift my weight off the balls of my feet, but pretty much my entire body is sore, so I end up hobbling.

Bracing my left hand on the wall, I hold the gun out ahead of me as I go.

My feet are tracking bloody footprints, so it's not like it would be hard for someone to follow me, but I want to keep moving. It feels safer.

I try to listen for anyone approaching but can't hear anything.

I hit the turn in the hallway, and I slowly creep around it.

Still empty.

But I spot a door.

A door with a giant deadbolt on the outside.

Bile rises in my throat, but I push forward through my trepidation.

Nothing good locks from the outside.

Sorrow and rage crash into me.

I know what these men do. I know who Gabriel Marcoux is to Hans.

He's the man responsible for Freya's disappearance.

He's the man responsible for her torture and death.

He's the man who crushed the soul of a teenage Hans.

He's the type of man who would keep human beings locked in a basement.

I hurry my steps until I stop in front of the door.

My body starts to tremble, so I press my left hand to my chest. *Just breathe.*

I want to yell through the door. Let whoever's inside know I don't mean them harm. But I can't be sure there isn't a bad guy on the other side.

Admitting to myself that I have no idea what the fuck I'm doing, but that I'm going to do it anyway, I decide to mimic every police reenactment I've ever seen in my true crime documentaries. *Quick and low.*

Steadying the gun, I use my left hand to flip the dead bolt and shove the door open. Then I rush into the room, crouching low and stepping to the side so my back is against the wall.

When I'm not immediately filled with bullets, I tell myself to take a breath.

The room has the same dim lighting as the hall, but it's enough.

Enough to see the small table and chairs, the pair of bunk beds, the kitchenette in the corner.

But I can't look at any of that. Because staring back at me, from the other side of the room, are three women.

CHAPTER 119
Hans

KARMINE'S SHOUT FOR BACKUP PULLS MY ATTENTION away from the man Nero just shot through the heart.

She's supposed to be getting Cassandra to safety.

There's another burst of gunfire from the direction of her shout, then it quiets.

A man sprawled on the floor stretches his arm out to the side, reaching for the pistol that lies just out of his grip.

Walking past, I twirl the sword in my hand and slice through his upper arm, severing tendons and his brachial artery.

I haven't seen Gabriel yet. But I know he's close. I can fucking taste it.

When I turn the corner into the main hall, I see Karmine and three of her fighters, the backup she needed.

"Where is she?" I bark while I slide my katana back into its sheath.

Karmine points down the stairs to the basement.

CHAPTER 120

MY HEART IS CRAWLING UP MY THROAT.

I knew—I knew what I might find in here. But the devastation of seeing them, of having them be so real...

My eyes fill with tears, and I lower the gun to my side.

Freya would have been in a room like this.

"We—" I have to swallow. "We're here to help."

The women—closer to Freya's age than my own—all look at me, then glance past me to the empty hallway.

"There are more of us," I promise. "I'm not—I'm sorry."

I fight down a sob. They don't need my sympathy.

They need me to keep my shit together.

"Come with—"

Before I can finish, a door I hadn't noticed on the far side of the room opens, and Gabriel Marcoux steps through.

I swing my gun up, shakily aiming at him, and steady it with my left hand.

"Isn't this sweet." He takes a menacing step forward.

"Stop!" My voice is hoarse, but I yell it as loud as I can and move farther into the room, putting myself between Gabriel and the women.

I can't do much. But I can do this.

"What?" he laughs. "You're going to kill me, an unarmed man, in cold blood?" He shakes his head. "You're not like the *women* upstairs. Quit pretending to be." He takes another step forward and points to the women behind me. "This isn't about you."

I think of the way Hans holds me like he's afraid to lose me.

I think of those three lonely graves somewhere in this desert.

I think of all the women whose voices are never heard.

And I think about how much better the world will be without this piece of shit man in it.

"No, it's not about me." I take a breath. "But this fight belongs to all of us."

I pull the trigger.

CHAPTER 121

Hans

A GUNSHOT RINGS OUT THROUGH THE BASEMENT, AND I race after the blood smeared across the floor.

Cassandra.

I want to shout her name. I want to scream.

But my chest is so tight I can't make a sound.

She's already bleeding.

She's already hurt.

My feet fly beneath me as I round the corner.

There's an open door just ahead, and I swear I'll give my life for hers if she can just be okay.

The gun in my hand is shaking. For the first time in twenty years, I'm shaking.

She has to be okay.

I brace myself as I reach the doorway.

But I'm not prepared.

Standing in the center of the awful room, between the man I've been chasing for two decades and three more of his victims, is Cassandra.

Her arms are stretched out in front of her. And she's gripping a gun that's pointed at Gabriel.

And there's blood blossoming across his chest.

Cassandra lifts her aim, just a bit. "This one is for Freya."
She fires.

For Freya.

A lifetime of guilt and torment unlatches from my soul as I watch the bullet penetrate Gabriel Marcoux's forehead and blow out the back of his skull.

Blood and gray matter spray through the open door behind him.

It's done.

The world shifts around me.

It's truly done.

My beautiful Butterfly ended it.

She took my burden and made it her own.

My sister's radiant smile flashes before my eyes.

Images of my family, my parents and Freya, sitting around the breakfast table flicker in my mind.

Memories of a time when we were all happy slip back into existence.

Reminders of who they were before...

A vision of me bringing my children to visit their grandparents' graves presses me to the doorframe.

I haven't visited them.

I couldn't bear to face them, not until I put this to rest.

The dead body of Gabriel Marcoux falls to the floor.

It is over.

My family can finally rest.

And so can I.

Because of her.

CHAPTER 122
Cassie

"Butterfly."

At the sound of Hans's whisper, I drop the gun and turn.

I don't even make it a step before he's there. Before his strong arms wrap around me, and he lifts me against his body.

I circle my arms around his neck and hitch my legs around his hips.

My Hans.

He's here. Right here.

Behind Hans, Karmine and several of her soldiers enter the room. Two of them step over Gabriel's corpse to check the room he came from, while Karmine and the others go to the three women who are still standing along the wall.

"Thank you," Hans murmurs into my neck, holding me tightly. "Thank you, Cassandra. My Girl. My Butterfly."

Over and over, he thanks me, and all I can do is cling to him while I cry against his shoulder.

Tears of relief.

Tears from the fear I felt.

Tears for all of the women who have been through too much.

I hug Hans tighter.

I don't know how he's dealt with so much on his own. But

never again. Never again.

"I love you." I choke out the words.

He squeezes me to him until it's hard to breathe. "I love you so fucking much."

A small laugh bubbles up in response to him cursing while telling me he loves me.

I lift my head so I can look at him.

Blood is spattered across his face and in his hair. His eyes are rimmed red. And I swear I can feel his heart pounding through the thick vest he's wearing.

"Don't ever fucking scare me like that again," Hans growls, then presses his lips to mine. "Thank you." He presses a softer kiss to my mouth. "I-I hate that you had to do that." His eyes are so bright, so alive. "But..." He gives his head the smallest shake. "Thank you, Cassandra. What you've given me..."

I unhook one arm from around his neck and press it to his cheek. "I'd do anything for you."

He nuzzles his stubbled cheek into my palm and exhales. "You thought I was obsessed before."

I snicker, imagining a Hans even more obsessed.

He leans in like he's going to kiss me again, then he stops, his brows furrowing. "I saw blood. Where are you hurt?" He starts to lower me as he asks it.

"My feet!" I tighten my legs around his hips so he can't put me down.

Hans instantly rights himself and boosts me higher. "Your feet?"

He cranes his neck to try and look at my feet behind his back.

"While I was knocked out on the plane, that big asshole took my boots off," I explain. "And the stupid marble floors were too slippery with my socks on, so I took them off. But then I stepped on—it doesn't matter. It's just my feet."

He shifts so one hand is under my butt, and then he uses his other to gently brush the backs of his fingers against my cheek. "It's not just your feet."

My chin wobbles as I think about all the parts of me that hurt, including my butt, but I don't mind that right now.

Hans wraps his arm back around me. "You're going to tell me about every single bruise. Okay, Butterfly?"

I nod. "Okay."

"If it helps"—he gives me a soft smile—"I cut the big asshole's hands off after I shot him. Twice."

I sniff and nod my head. "That helps."

Hans turns his head to where Karmine is talking with the women. "You good?"

Karmine says one last thing to the women, then turns to Hans. "We're gonna need to check the garages for a vehicle. I want us"—she tips her head to the three new bodies who will be joining our exodus—"to have our own ride."

"Take the one we rode over in, and I'll find out if Nero can fly a chopper."

My eyes widen at that.

"Sounds good." Karmine nods, even though it does not *sound good*. "We'll triple check every room, but it won't take us long."

"Copy that." Hans starts to turn, then stops. "I heard over the radio that someone found a store of gasoline in the garage, which is handy. All things considered, it'll probably take about ten minutes to rig the place."

Hans's reply is so casual. And it's a reminder that even though this was absolutely the worst day of my life, they're used to this. It's what they do.

He gives Karmine a nod, then turns and strides toward the door, me still in his arms.

I lift my gaze over his shoulder and lock eyes with one of the women.

I hate the reasons why Hans and Karmine are so used to this violence. But I am glad they're so good at it.

The woman gives me the smallest smile. And I give her one back before Hans carries me out of view.

CHAPTER 123

Hans

With Cassandra plastered to my body, we step out of the stairwell and onto the main floor.

"I'd tell you to keep your eyes closed, but I'm certain you wouldn't listen." I rub my cheek against hers. "So just be prepared for the bodies."

I don't need to explain more. One glance toward the floor, in either direction, and she'll see a dead man.

The place is a wreck, and over the scents of death and gunpowder, the distinct smell of gasoline is starting to permeate the air.

On the flight over from Dallas, we made the plan to level the estate to the ground after rescuing Cassandra and anyone else we found.

From the looks of it, it's only those three women in the house. King was ripping fingernails off a man earlier, extracting information, and three was the number he gave too.

It's three too many, but Karmine will take them out of here, and she'll give them the same options she gives everyone else. She can pay to get them home. She can provide them with new IDs and money if they don't want to go home or don't have a home. Or they can join her crew. It's not a perfect system, but they're the best options outside of involving the legal system. And, of course, if the women want to press charges against the men responsible, they're welcome to. The only problem is that those men are always dead.

"Found a live one!" Dom calls out from the corner of the massive living room.

Nero enters the room at the same time we do.

He nods to me. "You good?"

I nod back as Cassandra tries to twist around.

I squeeze her tighter. "Quit squirming."

"Bring him here," Nero tells Dom.

Dom grips the sniveling man by the back of the neck and forces him to walk.

Nero looks at the man. "What the fuck? There's not a drop of blood on him."

Dom snorts. "He was hiding behind the curtains."

We all turn and look at the massive *broken* window and the heavy velvet drapes bunched up on either side.

Nero glares at the man. "Seriously?"

"You wanna kill him?" Dom asks Nero. "If my calculations are correct, I'm still two up on you."

Nero rolls his eyes. "Your calculations are never correct. And I want to kill him just for hiding like a bitch in a cartoon." Dom snorts, and Nero looks at me. "Can I borrow that sword?"

I narrow my eyes. "You gonna give it back?"

Nero lets out the most dramatic sigh ever, causing Cassandra to snicker against my chest. "Yes, I'll give it back."

Keeping my eyes narrowed, I draw the katana and twist my wrist so I hand it to Nero handle first.

The man in Dom's grip starts to struggle, but a pair of Alliance guys step over to help hold him still.

Nero gives the sword a few lazy figure eights. "Hans, mind opening his shirt for me? I don't want to fuck it up and accidentally gut him." He turns his attention to the man and whispers like he's sharing a secret, "I'm still learning."

The man suddenly holds deathly still.

No idea where this is going, but willing to play along, I shift Cassandra's weight onto one arm and withdraw the straight blade at my hip.

"Can you pull his shirt tight?" I direct my question to the guys holding the man, but Cassandra is the one to reach out and grab the bottom of the man's shirt, pulling it taut.

"I didn't mean you," I grumble.

But I don't bother asking her to let go. I just slice my knife up the center of the man's shirt, splitting it open.

When I step back, Nero steps forward.

Nero presses the tip of the sword to the man's sternum. "We're letting you live so you can pass on a message to anyone who will listen."

The man nods frantically.

"Hans is with The Alliance now." Nero presses the blade just a little bit harder, and blood starts to seep down the man's chest. "You come for Hans. You come for us."

The man's nod turns into a scream as Nero slashes the blade down once, then twice, with a third and final swipe left to right, carving a giant A into the man's chest.

Blood oozes from the cuts, but Nero's control was solid. None of the slices will be fatal.

Nero steps back. "Now start running."

The man stumbles away from us, and I wonder if he'll manage to get away with his message or if he'll get caught up by whatever authorities are bound to show up soon.

"So... I'm part of The Alliance, huh?"

"You've practically been begging to join," Nero lies as he reluctantly hands my sword back.

"Uh-huh." *The Alliance. Who'd have thought?* I sheath the katana and start walking with Nero out of the room. "Any chance you know how to fly a helicopter?"

His mouth pulls into a devious smile. "Thought you'd never ask."

CHAPTER 124
King

THE NOISE OF THE ROTOR BLADE WHIRLING ABOVE US IS louder than I expected.

"You sure you know how to fly this thing?" I shout to Nero.

He looks over his shoulder at me from the pilot's seat. "Pretty sure."

Dom, in the copilot position, tightens his seat belt. "How about we don't tell the wives this part?"

Nero grins. "Pussy."

Dom gives his seat belt another tug. "Get Payton pregnant and then see how reasonable she is."

I glance over at Hans and Cassie.

He refused to set her down until they were inside the chopper, and only when he realized he couldn't get her buckled in if she was on his lap. So he's got her tucked into the corner of the rear bench seat, with her feet propped up on a duffel bag full of cash that's been strapped to the floor. And he's plastered to her side. Never taking his hands off her.

I get it.

Memories of my woman at the fingertips of a madman are still too fresh.

They'll always be too fresh.

I take a deep inhale, the helicopter's open side door letting in the dry Arizona air.

The rest of the money we found in Gabriel's house left with Karmine—it's for a good cause, and I wasn't about to argue with the terrifying woman. But we all agreed we should use some of the found money to pay off Cain for all the weaponry. Especially since most of it is staying behind to be torched.

"Hold on to your butts," Nero calls out, then we start to lift from the ground.

We were the last people out of the compound. As we rise, I'm able to see the final group of SUVs as they drive away.

The properties out here are massive, and people this rich—people like us—tend to mind their own business. But there was *a lot* of gunfire, and I can already see the flickering lights of emergency response vehicles in the distance.

Meaning it's time to light this bitch up.

"Go time," I call to Hans.

He slides away from Cassandra to open the door on the opposite side of the cabin, the one in front of me still open from before takeoff.

"You sure this is a good idea?" Dom shouts over the wind.

I grin and repeat Nero's response from a moment ago. "Pretty sure."

Dom shakes his head, saying something about *fucking assholes* as he shakes out a fireproof blanket and tucks it between his seat and Nero's, creating a flimsy excuse for a wall.

Hans already has his blanket pulled up over himself and Cassie, so there's no more delaying.

I don't have a blanket. But I don't need one. Backblast isn't a problem for the operator. And with both doors open, it shouldn't be a problem at all. We're just playing it safe.

Safe.

My laugh gets lost in the wind as I pick up the item that first caught my eye in the back of Cain's van.

With a big stupid grin, I hoist the rocket launcher onto my shoulder.

"Fire in the hole!" I shout. Then I pull the trigger.

A burst of flames shoots out behind me, getting sucked out the open door before anything inside the cabin can catch fire.

In my periphery, I see Dom rip his blanket down so he can watch through the open door.

We're moving. And I'm not exactly professionally trained to handle rocket launchers. But it's a big fucking target.

And when it hits, it hits.

The first explosion is immediate. And then the entire structure vibrates as smaller explosions are ignited.

When the gas lines blow, they set off the pile of grenades that Hans left in the kitchen, and I have to close my eyes against the brightness.

But it doesn't stop my smile.

CHAPTER 125
Cassie

"Hans," I sigh, but he just carries me into the airplane hangar, refusing to set me down.

We took the chopper to an empty patch of desert, where Nero landed it fairly well. Then we were met by some guy driving a catering van, which wasn't actually a catering van.

Not much was said as we all lounged against the walls, sitting on the floor in the back of the van, but just now, when we got out, I noticed they left that big bag full of money behind.

"Baby, I'm okay." I try to reason with Hans.

"You're not okay," he grits out next to my ear.

I made the mistake of gingerly touching my head a few minutes ago, causing Hans to ask what was wrong. So I told him about Dead Andre pulling me by my hair, and he said something along the lines of *I should've kept his hands for you*. And Hans has been boiling with rage ever since.

So, while everyone else is working to ready the plane we'll take back to Minnesota, I continue to cling to Hans like a koala.

I expect him to set me on one of the benches along the wall, but he veers off and takes us into one of the unused offices.

It's just a plain square room with one door, a set of windows that look into the hangar, and a round table with four folding chairs.

Hans lowers me onto a chair. "Stay right here."

"Hans, seriously, I—"

He holds up one finger. "Cassandra, we have at least three hours in that plane and then another hour before I tuck you into bed at Nero's house."

"Nero's house?"

He holds up a second finger, and my body reacts as though it heard him say *that's two*. "I am not going to let you sit around for the next four hours with pieces of glass, or whatever it is, in your fucking feet."

I'm hardly even listening to him. But he's right. I don't want my feet to throb for the next however many hours. But his little scolding has my body responding, and I also don't want to wait the same number of hours until we're back at *Nero's house* to do something about it.

Leaving me where I am, Hans stomps out of the office, and I assume he's off to find a first aid kit.

I shift on the seat, but the hard metal chair is uncomfortable against the bruises that are definitely forming on my ass.

Gingerly, I climb onto the floor.

If Hans wants access to my feet, he can have it.

CHAPTER 126
Hans

AFTER REPRESSING EVERY FEELING, ASIDE FROM RAGE, for the past twenty years, I feel like I'm vibrating with emotions.

Relief and sadness over my past battle with fear and pride over my woman.

Cassandra.

I force my heart to slow.

What she did.

What she did for me.

I can't decide if I want to spank her ass for doing anything other than sitting meekly while waiting for me to rescue her, or if I want to shower her with affection for being exactly what I need.

She's my everything.

I'd pulled the office door shut as I left, so I shift the first aid kit and bottles of water into one arm and open the door.

And then lust slams past all my other emotions because Cassandra is there, on her knees and elbows, with her lush ass in the air.

I slam the door shut behind me and depress the flimsy lock button on the handle.

"What the fuck are you doing?" My words come out choked.

She turns her head to look back at me over her shoulder. "That chair was hurting my butt."

My mouth opens and closes as I look between her face, her perfect ass hugged in black tactical pants, and the soles of her feet that are facing the ceiling and smeared with blood.

I stomp to the windows and lower the cheap blinds as quickly as I can. If anyone inside the hangar saw her like this...

"Cassandra Lynn," I growl.

"Hans..." Her face scrunches up. "What's your middle name?"

"Tomas." I don't want to humor her in this, but there's nothing about myself I won't tell her.

"Hans Tomas, my butt is sore from sliding down the stairs. My hands are sore from holding that gun. My feet hurt"—she wiggles her toes—"so on my knees and elbows is the most comfortable way for me to be right now."

I shove away my desire to reach out and rip her pants down her hips and focus on the fact that my Butterfly is hurting.

Then she smiles at me. "And if being like this makes you want to fuck me, well, I bet that would make me feel better too."

She shifts her weight on her elbow and holds up three fingers.

I drop the first aid kit and sink to my knees behind her, the wound in my leg protests at the movement, but I'm beyond noticing.

Cassandra sighs and relaxes into the pose, arching her back and lifting her ass.

I shuffle closer to her, my pants catching on the rough carpet. But then I remember her bloody feet.

"Butterfly." I lightly drag a finger down the outside of her foot. "You're hurting."

"Hans, I'm aching." Her hips shift.

And I decide I can multitask.

CHAPTER 127

Cassie

HANS REACHES AROUND MY WAIST AND STARTS TO undo my pants.

"You're going to have to hold still and stay quiet." He tugs the zipper down. "If you can't do that, I won't let you finish."

I nod my head, agreeing to whatever he wants, as he works my pants and underwear down my hips, stopping with the material bunched just below the juncture of my thighs.

Hans clicks his tongue. "Little Girl, what have you done to yourself?"

I feel his breath a moment before he presses a soft kiss to the center of my butt cheek.

A tickling sensation dances up my spine at the tender touch, but I stay still.

I can hear him shift behind me, but I've dropped my head forward so I can't see what he's doing.

A fingertip traces a pattern across my skin, then it ghosts down my crack, toward my entrance, without applying any pressure.

My legs are pressed together, but with the way I'm presenting myself to him, he can see my core. So I'm sure he can see how ready I am.

"Remember," Hans whispers. "Stay still. And stay quiet."

Even covered with blinds, the thin window does nothing to dampen the sound of the men on the other side.

I nod my head.

"Hand over your mouth, Butterfly."

The bratty part of me wants to argue that I can stay quiet on my own. But the needy part of me wants to do whatever it will take for him to hurry up and put his dick in me.

I put my hand over my mouth, and Hans rubs his finger against my slit just as he pours water over the sole of my foot.

It's cold. And I jerk at the shock, my body shifting forward, but at the same time, Hans shoves two fingers inside me.

Involuntarily, I make a sound between a moan and a cry, and I press my hand harder against my mouth.

Water splashes over my other foot, but the fingers inside of me stay put.

I squeeze my eyes shut. The mixture of arousal and discomfort swirls, making me even hotter.

"My poor girl," Hans murmurs behind me, sliding his fingers in and out of me.

There's a click, and I assume he's opening the first aid kit.

"You're doing so good." His fingers push deeper. "Just keep holding still."

There's a sharp zing of pain in the heel of my foot, and I wince.

"Shh." Hans leans forward and presses another kiss to my skin.

His fingers keep working, and my mind is fogging over so I hardly feel the next few pieces being pulled from my feet.

"Just one more, Butterfly." He sinks his fingers in until I can feel his knuckles pressed against me. Then he pushes another finger, his thumb, between my folds and rubs against my clit.

I bite down on my palm as a moan rolls out of me, and Hans pulls the piece from my foot. Something drops to the floor, and I imagine it was some sort of tweezers.

"Good girl. That's my good girl." He splashes water on my feet again, and this time, I clench around him. "One more bad part left, then I'll make it all better. I promise."

I squeeze my eyes shut even tighter.

I don't know much about first aid, but I'm certain some sort of painful antiseptic is next.

"Hold still, remember?"

I nod again, beyond words.

The thumb against my clit pulls away, and I feel Hans's fingers twist inside me.

Then his thumb is on the other side of my entrance, pushing my wetness up between my cheeks until he's pressing against my rear entrance.

He rubs his thumb in a little circle. "Wish there was some lube in this first aid kit." He applies more pressure. "When you're feeling better, I'm going to claim this ass." I moan louder than before. And I hear Hans unbuckling his belt. "When I do, you'll take all of me." I arch my back and push against him. "You'll take every inch of my cock in this ass, and you'll like it."

I remember how good it felt the first time we were together. How good it felt to have his finger there.

"Take a deep breath for me."

I do.

And as I'm inhaling, more liquid is splashed over my feet. It stings so badly tears form in the corners of my closed eyes, and I want to whimper. But then he pushes his thumb into me and jiggles his fingers inside me, and I can no longer feel the pain, only the pleasure.

"Such a good girl." I feel his knees on the outside of my own as he gets closer. "My perfect Butterfly."

The fingers inside my pussy spread, stretching me, and then something else, something bigger and blunter, pushes between them.

Hans pulls his fingers free from my channel as he pushes his hips forward, inch by inch, until his entire cock is inside me.

411

He groans, low and deep, and my pussy starts to throb.

"Fuck." He slides out, his thumb mimicking his motion.

He slides back in.

"Hans." I can't stop myself from crying his name.

He brings his free hand around the front of my body until his fingers brush against my clit.

"We're gonna practice for that baby now, okay, Cassandra?"

"Yes. Please," I whisper into the floor.

"Your pussy is gonna suck the cum right out of me."

Another slow pull out, but when he presses back in, he thrusts his hips hard.

My body bounces with the motion, but the arm hooked around my hips, the one with the fingers rubbing against my clit, holds me in place.

"You're gonna sit on my lap, leaking my release out of your pretty little slit the whole plane ride home." The finger in my ass pushes deeper, and I know he can feel his dick through the thin barrier as he thrusts in again. "And when we get home, I'm going to learn how to take that birth control out of your arm myself."

He increases the pressure on my clit, and I start to tremble.

"And I'm going to remove it while I'm buried inside you." His voice is so rough I know he's just as close as I am. "We're not going to waste another drop."

His words are so filthy.

And I'm so close.

"Tell me you understand."

I nod again, but I can't form words anymore. All that comes out is a cry.

"Come for me, Butterfly. Flutter that pussy around my cock and pull me with you."

He rolls my clit between his fingers, and I drag him over the edge with me, just like he told me to.

CHAPTER 128
Hans

WRUNG DRY AND FEELING HAPPIER THAN I CAN EVER remember feeling, I tighten my arms around Cassandra, my Butterfly, my pretty little neighbor, and board the plane for home.

She tries to take her own seat, but I pull her into my lap, and by the time the aircraft leaves the ground, she's fast asleep, her head lolling against my shoulder.

I watch the darkness grow outside the window and stroke my hand up and down Cassandra's thigh.

I need to find the realtor who sold Cassandra 1304 Holly Court and give her a million dollars. Maybe four.

Nero and King are in the two seats across from me, so I kick my foot out toward the aisle, getting Nero's attention.

He slowly turns to face me. "Yes?"

I nod past him to King, knowing he's the digital guy. "Can you find someone for me and set up an anonymous transfer?"

King lifts a brow. "Can you not?"

I roll my eyes. "I don't exactly have a computer these days." Then I think about it. "I'll need to scope out another hotel."

Nero waves me off. "We already talked about it, you're staying at my place tonight."

"Savannah's still there too," King adds. "So we'll crash in our usual room."

Nero shrugs. "Whatever. Just don't wake me up at five a.m."

"That happened once. Get over it." King shakes his head, then looks at me. "Who do you need me to find?"

"The realtor that sold Cassandra her old house. Kinda feel like I owe her."

"Because you blew it up?" Nero jokes.

I give him the middle finger but admit, "I will need to find a realtor, but yeah, don't really want to try and explain the circumstances to anyone who already knows Cassandra."

Nero tips his head. "What sort of place are you looking for?"

I hug Cassandra to me as I answer. "Something big, lots of space for kids. And a big yard. Obviously fenced in and rigged for security." I think about it. "Pool would be nice. I grew up with one and I miss it."

Nero nods slowly. "Sounds like my neighbor's place."

"They selling?" I joke.

"I'm sure I can convince them to."

"What? No. Nero, that's—" I was going to say crazy, but crazy is kind of his brand.

He leans back against the seat and closes his eyes. "Tomorrow."

CHAPTER 129
Hans
THREE DAYS LATER

"Baby, you need to calm down." Cassandra pats my chest, and I trap her hand against my body. "They're going to love this place."

I blow out a breath and look around the grand entryway with the double staircase and multicolored blown glass chandelier.

"I don't doubt that they'll think it's fine—"

"Fine?" Cassandra scoffs. "This is a ten-thousand-square-foot mansion with a pool, a seven-burner stove, and a greenhouse. It's more than fine. We're gonna have to kick them out when we want them to leave."

I tug her against my body with my free hand. "Yeah, but the reason you don't have your old house anymore is probably going to bother them."

My girl knows her touch helps my nerves, so she slides her hand up the front of my T-shirt, resting her palm against my skin and giving me her warmth.

True to his word, the day after we landed, Nero walked over to his neighbor's house—neighbor being a relative term since the lots are several acres—and told them I'd pay double the market value for them to leave the furniture—minus any heirlooms or things of sentimental value—and be out in twenty-four hours.

They did. I paid. And now this home belongs to us. Which is great. But her parents are on their way over for dinner, and I feel like I'm going to throw up.

Cassandra's phone rings.

She pulls it out of her pocket and puts it on speaker, her mom's name on the screen.

"You lost?" Cassandra asks.

"I think we must be." She says something to Mr. Cantrell. "That address you sent, was it correct?"

"Yes, Mom."

"This is Hans's new house?" Mrs. Cantrell's tone is understandably skeptical.

"Just tell Dad to pull up to the gate. They'll let you in."

In order to get them here, we told them it was just my house.

Plus, I have an important question I need to ask her dad before we tell them Cassandra lives here too.

Cassandra knows I'm asking. And she's already told me she'll say yes. But I've never had a chance to do any of the traditional dating things, so I want to do this.

When we can hear them talking to the property guards, Cassandra hangs up.

Sliding her phone back in her pocket, she lifts her hands to hold my face. "I love you, Hans. They will too." She pulls me down and presses her lips to mine. "And they'll forgive the rest."

I swallow and kiss her once more, then pull the front door open.

Mr. Cantrell drives his Buick up the driveway and around the fountain in front of the house. He slows on the far side, near the garages, but I can see Mrs. Cantrell waving her hands around inside the car, and eventually, Mr. Cantrell circles the fountain again, stopping directly at the bottom of the stairs leading up to the gigantic house.

I keep my hand on Cassandra's lower back as we walk down the steps to meet them.

Mrs. Cantrell climbs out of the car first and holds her hands up toward the house. "Holy shit!"

Cassandra cracks up next to me. "Mom!"

"Well, seriously, Cassandra." She drops her hands to her hips. "You cannot just go from that cute little cul-de-sac to this and expect me to pretend that's normal."

I wince a little when she calls our old street cute.

Casandra has been taking their calls and texts the last few days like nothing was amiss. Her mom was extra attentive, making sure Cassandra was still okay after everything that happened in Mexico, so I'm sure she'll insist on moving in for the next month when she finds out what else has happened.

We talked about it and agreed to tell them everything. Or at least the broad strokes. And if they ask us a question, we won't lie. Cassandra is certain they won't try to turn me in to the authorities, and I trust my Butterfly, so I'll trust them.

Mrs. Cantrell turns to me after she hugs Cassandra. "The house is beautiful. And absurd."

"Mom!"

Some of my anxiousness fades. "It is both of those things." I start to hold out my hand to Cassandra's mom, but she just pushes it away and grabs me for a hug.

"I don't know why you lived in that sad little house when you could afford this." She pulls back and smiles at me. "But I'm glad you did."

"Mom, you can't go from calling it cute to sad."

We both ignore Cassandra.

"I'm glad I did too." My words feel so inadequate for how true they are.

Mrs. Cantrell hooks her arm in Cassandra's. "Show me inside." As they pass me and head up the steps, I hear Mrs. Cantrell say, "*Your* house is cute. His was sad."

Both houses are equally destroyed now, but it's still a fair description.

Mr. Cantrell stops before me, making no attempt to follow the ladies.

I'm significantly larger than he is, but I suddenly feel like I'm back in my teenaged body. Trying to stand straighter. Trying to prove I'm worthy.

I take a breath.

I've battled against so many odds.

I've fought for my life and survived.

I can do this too.

"I love your daughter," I tell him. "Cassandra is... She's my everything. And I'd like to ask you for her hand."

Mr. Cantrell looks past me to the mansion at my back. "I wasn't in communications in the army. I wasn't even in the army." He pauses, and my nerves spike. "I was with something else."

I swallow. "Three-letter agency?"

He doesn't confirm.

"I saw a lot of shit. Most of it had nothing to do with wars, but I saw a lot of dangerous men." His eyes move back to meet mine. "They're easy to recognize when you know what to look for."

I fight my body's instinct to move back and hold his gaze.

He dips his head like he's making a decision. "I knew what you were the first time we met."

His words feel like ice across my skin. "If you try to stop me—"

I cut myself off because I don't know how to finish that sentence. I won't ever give her up, but I'd never do anything to hurt the man who raised her.

"I still know some people. And that night when Cassie was stuck in Mexico, after her bus got hijacked and then miraculously saved... I had some images sent my way."

I brace myself. Ready for the questions. Dreading his rejection of me.

But then he takes a step closer and reaches up to grip my shoulder.

"Thank you." He fights to keep his composure. "I owe you my life. She—" He nods toward the house. "She is my life."

Tightness grips my throat.

His love for her is what my parents had for Freya. And I watched it destroy them.

But his girl is still here. And he's one of the parents that understands just how precious that is.

"I would do anything for her." My voice cracks on the truth.

"I wouldn't accept anything less." The hand on my shoulder squeezes. "That girl is a handful. She needs someone dangerous to protect her. So yeah, son, you have my blessing. And that makes you family. Meaning you have my wife too. However you need us."

Son.

I nod.

Then I nod again.

Because fuck, it feels good to have a family.

Epilogue

Payton

My heart squeezes as I watch Hans walk Mrs. Cantrell up the aisle.

She's openly crying, clinging to his arm, and it's clear to see that she's never been happier.

Cassandra's parents know all about our little band of heathens. And they love us.

I squeeze my hands together against my chest.

Mr. and Mrs. Cantrell have become parents to all of us, and their acceptance is more than I ever could have hoped for. Nero is more than enough, but this... I look around at the people gathered... This is family.

I take a deep breath.

The aisle is short, just a few rows of chairs set up in King's backyard. So after a few more steps, Hans stops with Mrs. Cantrell at the first row, bending to let her kiss his cheek.

In contrast to his adorable soon-to-be mother-in-law, Hans looks like a warrior, with his hair flowing in the late October breeze and his jaw clenched tight.

She says something to him, and when he pulls her into a hug, I lift the tissue clutched in my hand to the corner of my eye.

He really is the perfect match for Cassandra, my newest best friend.

Mrs. Cantrell pats him on the back as she pulls away, then waves to all of us with a watery apology.

Val is in the row behind her, sitting with Dom, and she puts her hand on Mrs. Cantrell's shoulder.

I wish my husband was at my side. I would love to lean against him right now. But he's not next to me because he's standing before us all, next to Hans.

It was his idea to officiate this wedding. He argued that since he was already ordained, there was no reason to use anyone else. But we all know it's because he and Hans have become nearly inseparable.

Nero claims it's just because Hans is our neighbor, so it's convenient to see him, but really, those two are a pair of peas in an unhinged pod.

It was also Nero's idea to order that ridiculous black robe to wear over his suit. It's truly absurd. And when he stepped into the backyard wearing it, I figured Hans would tell him to take it off. But instead, Hans grinned and presented Nero with a red-handled katana as a thank-you for marrying them.

So now the two men stand together, under an arch of beautiful flowers, with Hans in his three-piece dark gray suit with black shirt and tie, and Nero in his black robe with a sword strapped to his back.

It's ridiculous. And wonderful.

And then I watch Hans's expression change, and I know she's here.

Hans

I DON'T DESERVE HER.

Cassandra smiles at me, her arm tucked into her dad's, as she walks toward me.

Her black curls are twisted with silver threads and pulled back into a loose braid down her back, letting me see all of her glowing face, her cheeks pink from joy and the chill in the air.

Each step she takes has her dress fluttering around her. The silver gauzy material is absolutely stunning on her and just a few shades lighter than my suit.

I would have married her in her jean shorts, but she wanted a dress. And her parents wanted to help plan. So we waited these few long months. And it was worth it.

She's so fucking worth it.

She wouldn't let me see the dress, and as much as I love it, I can't stop looking at her smile.

I haven't seen her since this morning. And it's been too long.

I step away from Nero and meet them at the front row.

Mr. Cantrell kisses both of Cassandra's cheeks, then holds his hand out to me. "Take care of her, yeah?"

I shake his hand, then turn to the woman I'm about to make my wife. "Until my last breath."

Cassie

"I HAVE SOMETHING FOR YOU," I WHISPER UP AT MY new husband.

Hans looks down at me. "What more could you possibly give me?"

The ceremony ended a few minutes ago, and now everyone is mingling in the garden while we get ready to take photos.

I drag him over to one of the planters along the side of the house, where I stashed the surprise.

"Close your eyes," I tell him, and he listens.

Grabbing his hand, I turn it upward and set the gift in his palm.

Hans opens his eyes. And then he breathes deep, tracing a finger across the lettering.

It's just a stack of yellow Post-it notes. With the same words as before.

"Thank you," he whispers.

And just like I knew he would, he lifts each piece of paper to make sure they're all there.

I did them in the opposite order from the way he'd saved them before, with the newest at the bottom.

When he reaches the last one, he pauses at the words.

And when he looks up at me, I lift the little plastic bag with two Skittles sugar cookies in it.

Without saying a word, Hans takes the bag, removes the cookies, then shoves both of them into his mouth.

Savannah

Mr. Cantrell spins me around in my art studio turned dance floor one last time, then laughs and presses a hand to his chest. "If I don't go sit down, someone is going to have to call the paramedics to get me off the floor."

He hugs me, then makes a show of staggering off toward the chairs in the courtyard.

"Mind if I cut in?" King rumbles from beside me.

I turn to my husband and lean into his chest.

He wraps his arms around me, and we rock slowly together while the fast-paced music thuds around us.

I loved our vow renewal and have no regrets about our unconventional ceremony, but this might be the best wedding I've ever been to. It's so full of love.

King settles his hand on the back of my neck. "I'm pretty sure Cassie's parents would adopt us all if they could."

"They really would." I smile against him. "I have to admit, I wouldn't say no."

King hums his agreement.

Dom is the only one out of all of us with a parent worth speaking of. And we all love Bibi, but she doesn't like to leave

Chicago, so we only get to see her when we visit. Which we should do more.

Aspen, my sister-in-law, dances into view with her boyfriend, Rob, and I can feel King's sigh.

He pretends to disapprove, but Rob is a good guy. And as Dom's second in command of the Chicago mafia, he's perfectly suited for Aspen's intensity.

Aspen shuffles over, cookie in her hand. "Is this the one you made?"

I look at the sugar cookie with the yellow bits in it and smile. "It is."

"They're good." She grins and pops the last bite in her mouth.

Rob lifts Aspen's hand to his mouth and licks the crumbs off her fingers.

"Oh, fuck off," King grumbles, then turns us the other way.

I can't help my laugh. They do such a good job of needling him.

Then I realize a cookie sounds like a good idea, so I drag King toward the dessert table.

Each of us girls picked a cookie from Cassie's food blog and made them as our wedding present to her. Even the men made some, with Nero choosing Cassie's twist on Rice Krispies bars that are made out of popcorn instead of cereal.

As soon as we showed her the desserts, Cassie broke into big, noisy tears, making the three batches of corn cookies that I had to throw away after burning them totally worth it.

Val

"I've always wanted to do this." Cassie grins, then turns her back to us, ready to toss her bouquet into the air.

While Payton does the countdown, I look across the room to where my husband is standing. He's talking to King, and his big, tattooed hands are gently cradling Danielle, our infant daughter, to his chest.

I'll never get tired of the sight.

He's a wonderful father. But that's no surprise. And as soon as I'm done breastfeeding, I'm going to have Dom give me another tattoo. It will be a different name this time, but I don't think he'll mind.

"One!" Payton yells, and Cassie throws her bouquet.

I stretch my arms up.

I'm already married, but those flowers are pretty, and I want them.

But before anyone catches them, a man leaps up and snags the bouquet out of the air.

Rob is grinning ear to ear as he holds them above his head. And I don't care how much Dom complains about me saying it, Rob is hot.

"Put those down!" King shouts, stomping toward the man dating our sister.

Rob skips backward, away from King, and finds Aspen in the small crowd.

Then he drops down onto one knee in front of her.

King's "Oh, hell no!" is drowned out by all the women gasping.

"Aspen, my love." Rob looks up at his woman. "Will you do me the honor of telling your terrifying brother that we're already married?"

My mouth drops open, and I whip my head over to look at Dom.

My husband is smiling at the pair, and when his gaze moves to find mine, he winks.

That bastard already knew.

King stomps over to Aspen. "Is this true?"

Aspen, not at all intimidated by his attitude, slips her hand into her dress pocket and pulls out a big, shiny ring.

"We did it last week." She slides the ring onto her finger, then uses her left hand to pat King's chest. "You can stop worrying about me now. I promise I'm happy."

King heaves out a loud exhale, then pulls her into a hug.

Rob is grinning when he stands, and he holds his arms out for a hug next.

King rolls his eyes, then embraces the other man, but when he lets go, he punches Rob in the shoulder. Hard. "Don't fuck this up."

Cassie

The music has ended, and the couples of The Alliance are all lounged around King's living room, and I feel like I could carry the whole world if I wanted to.

Hans is standing across the room from me, talking with Nero. And I can't help but be drawn to the silver band on his left hand. He looks so good marked as mine.

I look down at the matching band on my hand.

Hans wanted to get me diamonds, but I wanted us to match. And we both know that Hans will always give me what I want.

God, I love him so much.

I'm about to cross to him, needing to be closer, ready to give him his final wedding gift, when Val addresses the room.

"So I know this is a little bit of short notice, but everyone is invited—"

"Expected," Dom interrupts.

Val shakes her head. "We would like you all to come to Chicago for Christmas. It's Danielle's first Christmas." She strokes her hand over her daughter's head. "And we want her to spend it surrounded by her loved ones."

I watch Hans, my heart swelling even more with my love for him.

For half of his life, he's had no one to share holidays with. And now we have *this*.

"We'll be there," Hans answers first.

When his eyes move to meet mine, I can see it all in his face. The affection. The peace.

My fingers reach up to touch the spot on my arm, next to my tracker, where the other implant used to be.

And I can't wait any longer.

I have to tell him.

Tears fill my eyes as I mouth, "I'm pregnant."

Hans opens his mouth, then slams it closed.

His throat works, and his eyes lower to my wedding-dress-covered stomach.

Then his eyes move back up to meet mine, and he mouths, "That's one."

Epilogue 2 - Hans
FIVE MONTHS LATER

"I'm SORRY I DIDN'T DO THIS SOONER," I TELL THE three graves in front of me as emotion chokes my voice.

I close my eyes as the Arizona sun beats down on me.

"A part of me will always be buried here with you." A tear tracks down my cheek. For them. For me. For everything I've done. "I'm not the same man you knew."

I'm not the same.

But I became who I had to be.

"It's still hard for me to believe it's over. That this battle is done. But it is." I bow my head. "It is."

A gentle gust of wind passes over me. And it feels like the world is taking a breath with me.

Lifting my head, I look over at Cassandra standing near our car, stomach round with twins, a boy and a girl. And I picture the smile my mother would give her. I picture the way she'd hug my children and shower them with love. I think of Freya as an aunt. How she would spoil the kids. How she would love to tell embarrassing stories about me to Cassandra.

A little more lightness fills my chest.

"I think you'd like my wife," I tell my family. "She's... She's my second chance. My new beginning."

I step forward to Freya's headstone and press the Post-it to the top.

This one is in my handwriting.

This isn't goodbye.

Author's Note

This is the first series I wrote start to finish, and the characters all mean so much to me. Each man, each woman... they'll be a part of me forever.

So thank you, to each and every reader who has made this series into more than I could have dreamed.

The Alliance might be complete, but it's never really goodbye in Tilly World. Because you never know who you'll bump into. And you never know who might have a story to tell.

Like Cain.

xoxo

Acknowledgments

As is habit, the first thank you goes to my mother, Karen. I appreciate all of your encouragement and feedback and edits and suggestions—even when I argue over them. The Alliance was a new path, and I'm glad you happily skipped down it with me.

Kerissa, you are the absolute fucking best. I don't know how you put up with me as a friend or a colleague, but I'm glad that you do. My life is better with you in it.

To my editors Jeanine and Beth, thank you both for working so hard to make me look smarter than I am.

To Lori, my cover designer, thank you for knowing exactly what these books need. They wouldn't be the same without your stunning covers.

To Nikki, here is your spot to preen over The Alliance Bros until the end of time. You earned it.

Gabby, (G. Marie—author of Snowed in Fling) thank you for all the dark romance chats.

To my sprint group, thank you for helping to keep me on track and thank you for putting up with all of my dictator-like moods. I appreciate you.

Ashley, thank you for the amazing designs.

Thank you to all of the friends who I have met through this book world. There are too many of you to name now, and that makes me feel like the luckiest fucking person alive.

To my ARC readers, I owe you so much. Your support and excitement mean so damn much to me.

Thank you, Valentine PR, for all the help.

Thank you to my husband, Mr. Tilly, for feeding me while I live in my writing cave and for not judging me for still being awake when you're getting up in the morning.

Thank you to my family and friends who constantly support me.

And to all the members of my BeanBag Book Club (my reader Facebook group). I love all the posts and comments and interactions with you. As my world gets bigger, it's so important to have that safe space with you.

Finally, thank you to my parents for banging decades ago. Between nature and nurture, you formed my brain into a pile of mush capable of creating worlds. I'll be forever grateful for this talent that has somehow crawled out of my brain and put itself on paper. The fictional world is so much more fun that working in sales.

Xoxoxo

About the Author

Like all her books, S. J. Tilly resides in the glorious state of Minnesota, where she was born and raised. To avoid the freezing cold winters, S. J. enjoys burying her head in books, whether to read them or write them or listen to them.

When she's not busy writing her contemporary smut, she can be found lounging with her husband and their herd of rescue boxers. And when the weather permits, she loves putting her compost to use in the garden, pretending to know what she's doing. The neighbors may not like the flowery mayhem of her yard, but the bees sure do. And really, that's more important.

To stay up to date on all things Tilly, make sure to follow her on her socials, join her newsletter, and interact whenever you feel like it! Links to everything on her website www.sjtilly.com

Books By This Author

Love Letter Series

Contemporary Romance

(Coming soon)

-

Alliance Series

Dark Mafia Romance

NERO

Payton

Running away from home at seventeen wasn't easy. Let's face it, though, nothing before, or in the ten years since, has ever been easy for me.

And I'm doing okay. Sorta. I just need to keep scraping by, living under the radar. Staying out of people's way, off people's minds.

So when a man walks through my open patio door, stepping boldly into my home and my life, I should be scared. Frightened. Terrified.

But I must be more broken than I realized because I'm none of those things.

I'm intrigued.

And I'm wondering if the way to take control of my life is by giving in to him.

Nero

The first time I took a man's life, I knew there'd be no going back. No normal existence in the cards for me.

So instead of walking away, I climbed a mountain of bodies and created my own destiny. By forming The Alliance.

And I was fine with that. Content enough to carry on.

Until I stepped through those open doors and into her life.

I should've walked away. Should've gone right back out the door I came through. But I didn't.

And now her life is in danger.

But that's the thing about being a bad man. I'll happily paint the streets red to protect what's mine.

And Payton is mine. Whether she knows it or not.

KING

Okay, so, my bad for assuming the guy I was going on a date with *wasn't* married. And my bad for taking him to a friend's house for dinner, only to find out my friend is also friends with *his* wife. Because, in fact, he *is* married. And she happens to be at my friend's house because her husband was *busy working*.

Confused? So am I.

Unsurprisingly, my date's wife is super angry about finding out that her husband is a cheating asshole.

Girl, I get it.

Then, to make matters more convoluted, there is the man sitting next to my date's wife. A man named King, who is apparently her brother and who lives up to his name.

And since my *date* is a two-timing prick, I'm not going to feel bad about drooling over King,

especially since I'll never see him again.

Or at least I don't plan to.

I plan to take an Uber to the cheater's apartment to get my car keys.

I plan for it to be quick.

And if I had to list a thousand possible outcomes... witnessing my date's murder, being kidnapped by his killer, and then being forced to marry the super attractive but clearly

deranged crime lord would not have been on my Bingo card.

But alas, here I am.

DOM

VAL

When I was nine, I went to my first funeral. Along with accepting my father's death, I had to accept new and awful truths I wasn't prepared for.

When I was nineteen, I went to my mother's funeral. We weren't close, but with her gone, I became more alone than ever before.

Sure, I have a half brother who runs The Alliance. And yeah, he's given me his protection—in the form of a bodyguard and chauffeur. But I don't have anyone that really knows me. No one to really love me.

Until I meet him. The man in the airport.

And when one chance meeting turns into something hotter, something more serious, I let myself believe that maybe he's the one. Maybe this man is the one who will finally save me from my loneliness. The one to give me the family I've always craved.

DOM

The Mafia is in my blood. It's what I do.

So when that blood is spilled and one funeral turns into three, drastic measures need to be taken.

And when this battle turns into a war, I'm going to need more men. More power.

I'm going to need The Alliance.

And I'll become a member. By any means necessary.

HANS

Cassie

How to make the handsome, brooding man across the street notice me.

Step one: Deliver baked goods to his front porch, even though he never answers his door and always returns the containers when I'm not home.

Step two: Slowly lose my mind as a whole year passes without ever running into him, no matter how hard I try.

Step three: Have my boudoir photos accidentally delivered to his mailbox instead of mine. Have him open the package. Then have him storm into my home for the most panty-melting scolding of my life.

Step four: Still figuring out step four.

Hans

I'm a dangerous man.

A man who has spent the last two decades removing so many souls from this earth that it's a miracle my hands aren't permanently stained red.

I'm a man who belongs in the shadows.

I certainly don't belong in my pretty little neighbor's bedroom when she's not home, touching her things and inhaling her scent.

I shouldn't follow her. Shouldn't watch her. Because no number of cookies on my doorstep will change the fact that love isn't an option for me.

The only option left for me is violence.

Sin Series

Romantic Suspense

Mr. Sin

I should have run the other way. Paid my tab and gone back to my room. But he was there. And he was... everything. I figured, what's the harm in letting passion rule my decisions for one night? So what if he looks like the Devil in a suit? I'd be leaving in the morning. Flying home, back to my pleasant but predictable life. I'd never see him again.

Except I do. In the last place I expected. And now everything I've worked so hard for is in jeopardy.

We can't stop what we've started, but this is bigger than the two of us.

And when his past comes back to haunt him, love might not be enough to save me.

Sin Too

Beth

It started with tragedy.

And secrets.

Hidden truths that refused to stay buried have come out to chase me. Now I'm on the run, living under a blanket of constant fear, pretending to be someone I'm not. And if I'm not really me, how am I supposed to know what's real?

Angelo

Watch the girl.

It was supposed to be a simple assignment. But like everything else in this family, there's nothing simple about it. Not my task. Not her fake name. And not my feelings for her.

But Beth is mine now.

So when the monsters from her past come out to play, they'll have to get through me first.

Miss Sin

I'm so sick of watching the world spin by. Of letting people think I'm plain and boring, too afraid to just be myself.

Then I see *him*.

John.

He's strength and fury and unapologetic.

He's everything I want. And everything I wish I was.

He won't want me, but that doesn't matter. The sight of him is all the inspiration I need to finally shatter this glass house I've built around myself.

Only he does want me. And when our worlds collide, details we can't see become tangled, twisting together, ensnaring us in an invisible trap.

When it all goes wrong, I don't know if I'll be able to break free of the chains binding us or if I'll suffocate in the process.

Sleet Series

Hockey Romantic Comedy

Sleet Kitten

There are a few things that life doesn't prepare you for. Like what to do when a super-hot guy catches you sneaking around in his basement. Or what to do when a mysterious package shows up with tickets to a hockey game, because apparently, he's a professional athlete. Or how to handle it when you get to the game and realize he's freaking famous since half of the 20,000 people in the stands are wearing his jersey.

I thought I was a well-adjusted adult, reasonably prepared for life. But one date with Jackson Wilder, a viral video, and a "I didn't know she was your mom" incident, and I'm suddenly questioning everything I thought I knew.

But he's fun. And great. And I think I might be falling for him. But I don't know if he's falling for me too, or if he's as much of a player off the ice as on.

Sleet Sugar

My friends have convinced me. No more hockey players.

With a dad who is the head coach for the Minnesota Sleet, it seemed like an easy decision.

My friends have also convinced me that the best way to boost my fragile self-esteem is through a one-night stand.

A dating app. A hotel bar. A sexy-as-hell man, who's sweet and funny, and did I mention, sexy as hell... I fortified my courage and invited myself up to his room.

Assumptions. There's a rule about them.

I assumed he was passing through town. I assumed he was a businessman or maybe an investor or accountant or literally anything other than a professional hockey player. I assumed I'd never see him again.

I assumed wrong.

Sleet Banshee

Mother-freaking hockey players. My friends found their happily ever afters with a couple of sweet, doting, over-the-top, in-love athletes. They got nicknames like *Kitten* and *Sugar*. But me? I got stuck with a dickhead who riles me up on purpose and calls me *Banshee*. Yeah, he might have a voice made specifically for wet dreams. And he might have a body and face carved by the gods. And he might have a level of Alpha-hole that gets me all hot and bothered.

But when he presses my buttons, he presses ALL of my buttons. And I'm not the type of girl who takes things sitting down. And I only got caught on my knees that one time. In the museum.

But when one of my decisions gets one of my friends hurt... I can't stop blaming myself. And him.

Except he can't take a hint. And I can't keep my panties on.

Darling Series

Contemporary Small Town Romance

Smoky Darling

Elouise

I fell in love with Beckett when I was seven.

He broke my heart when I was fifteen.

When I was eighteen, I promised myself I'd forget about him.

And I did. For a dozen years.

But now he's back home. Here. In Darling Lake. And I don't know if I should give in to the temptation swirling between us or run the other way.

Beckett

She had a crush on me when she was a kid. But she was my brother's best friend's little sister. I didn't see her like that. And even if I had, she was too young. Our age difference was too great.

But now I'm back home. And she's here. And she's all the way grown up.

It wouldn't have worked back then. But I'll be damned if I won't get a taste of her now.

Latte Darling

I have a nice life—living in my hometown, owning the coffee shop I've worked at since I was sixteen.

It's comfortable.

On paper.

But I'm tired of doing everything by myself. Tired of being in charge of every decision in my life.

I want someone to lean on. Someone to spend time with. Sit with. Hug.

And I really don't want to go to my best friend's wedding alone.

So, I signed up for a dating app and agreed to meet with the first guy who messaged me.

And now here I am, at the bar.

Only it's not my date that just sat down in the chair across from me. It's his dad.

And holy hell, he's the definition of silver fox. If a silver fox can be thick as a house, have piercing blue eyes and tattoos from his neck down to his fingertips.

He's giving me *big bad wolf* vibes. Only instead of running, I'm blushing. And he looks like he might just want to eat me whole.

Tilly World Holiday Novellas

Second Bite

When a holiday baking competition goes incredibly wrong. Or right...

Michael

I'm starting to think I've been doing this for too long. The screaming fans. The constant media attention. The fat paychecks. None of it brings me the happiness I yearn for.

Yet here I am. Another year. Another holiday special. Another Christmas spent alone in a hotel room.

But then the lights go up. And I see *her*.

Alice

It's an honor to be a contestant, I know that. But right now, it feels a little like punishment. Because any second, Chef Michael Kesso, the man I've been in love with for years, the man who doesn't even know I exist, is going to walk onto the set, and it will be a miracle if I don't pass out at the sight of him.

But the time for doubts is over. Because *Second Bite* is about to start "in three... two... one..."

Made in the USA
Coppell, TX
22 February 2024

29325011R00251